Vampire Doll
Guilt-na-Zan

VOLUME 2

CREATED BY
ERIKA KARI

TOKYOPOP®

HAMBURG // LONDON // LOS ANGELES // TOKYO

Vampire Doll Guilt-Na-Zan Vol. 2
Created By Erika Kari

Translation - Yoohae Yang
English Adaptation - Patricia Duffield
Retouch and Lettering - Nancy Star
Production Artist - Courtney Geter
Graphic Designer - Fawn Lau

Editor - Alexis Kirsch
Digital Imaging Manager - Chris Buford
Pre-Production Supervisor - Erika Terriquez
Art Director - Anne Marie Horne
Production Manager - Elisabeth Brizzi
VP of Production - Ron Klamert
Editor-in-Chief - Rob Tokar
Publisher - Mike Kiley
President and C.O.O. - John Parker
C.E.O. and Chief Creative Officer - Stuart Levy

A  Manga

TOKYOPOP Inc.
Wilshire Blvd. Suite 2000
os Angeles, CA 90036

ail: info@TOKYOPOP.com
s online at www.TOKYOPOP.com

ISBN: 978-1-59816-520-3

First TOKYOPOP printing: January 2007
10 9 8 7 6 5
Printed in the USA

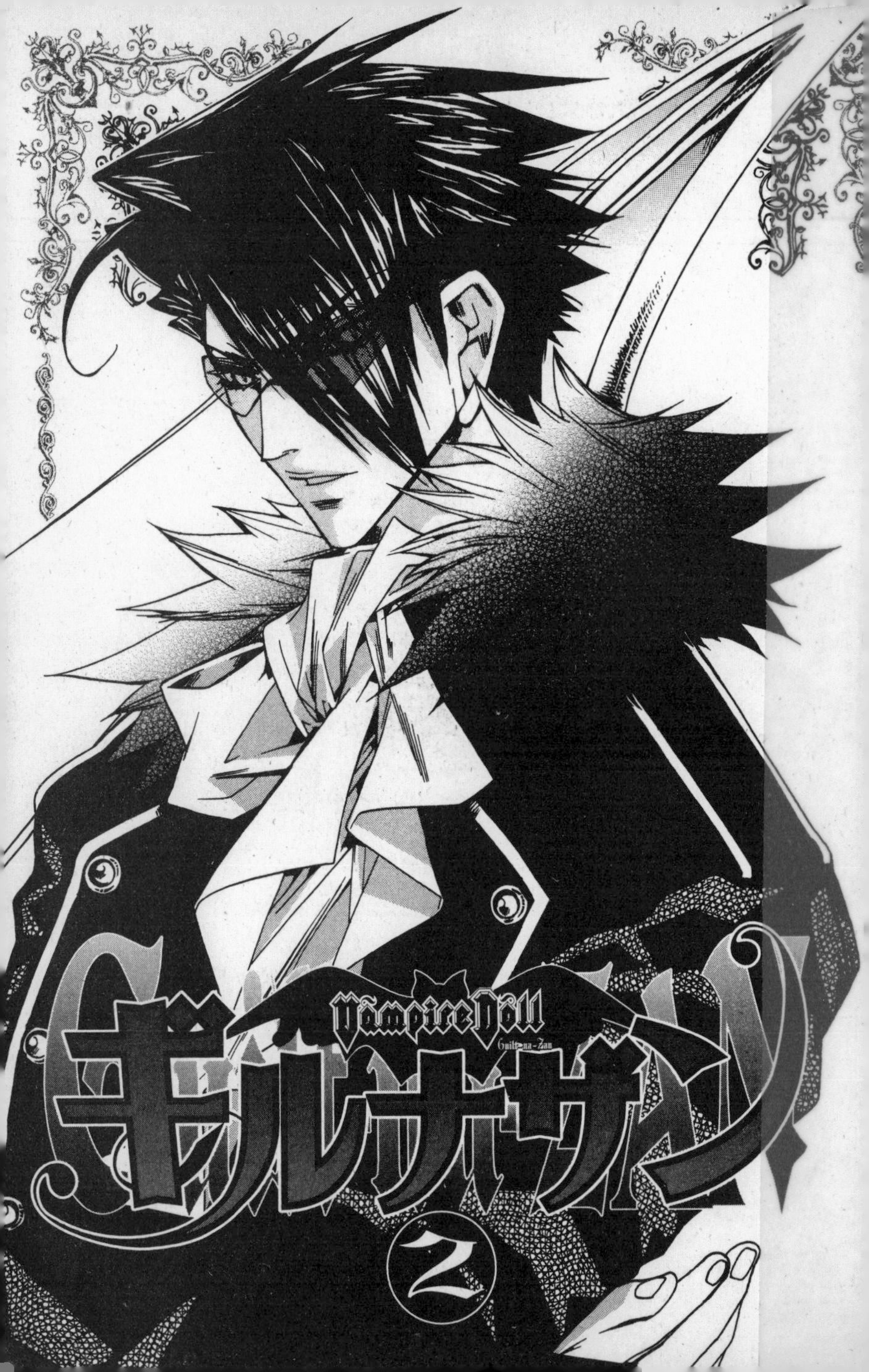
Vampire Doll
ギルナザン
Guilt-na-Zan
2

Main Characters

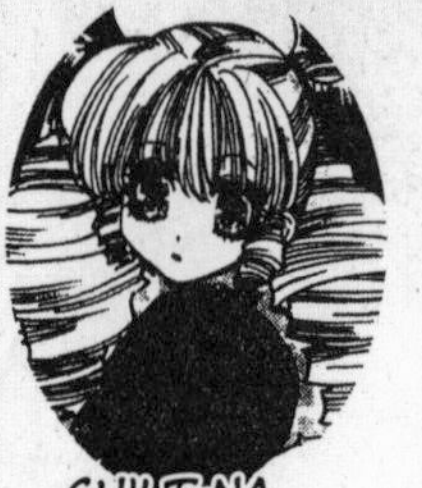

GUILT-NA

LONG AGO, HE WAS KNOWN AS THE LORD OF VAMPIRES, THE MOST FEARED OF ALL HIS KIND. KYOJI RESURRECTED HIM INTO THE FIGURE OF A WAX DOLL. NOW HE MUST OBEY KYOJI.

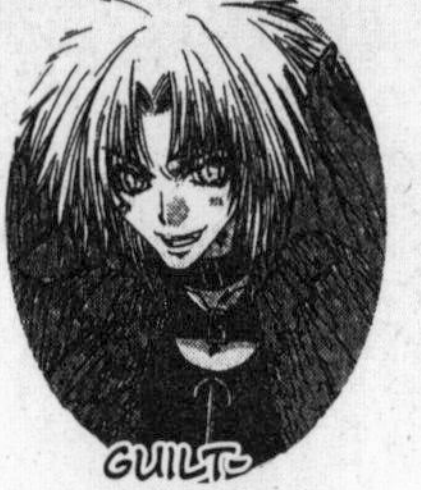

GUILT-NA-ZAN

THIS IS WHAT GUILT-NA ORIGINALLY LOOKED LIKE. BY SUCKING 1CC OF TONAE'S BLOOD, HE CAN TRANSFORM INTO HIMSELF--BUT ONLY FOR TEN MINUTES!

KYOJI

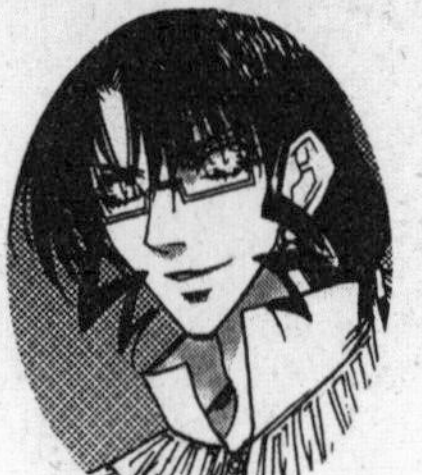

A VERY SKILLED BUT LAZY EXORCIST, HE SPENDS MOST OF HIS TIME MAKING FUN OF GUILT-NA.

TONAE

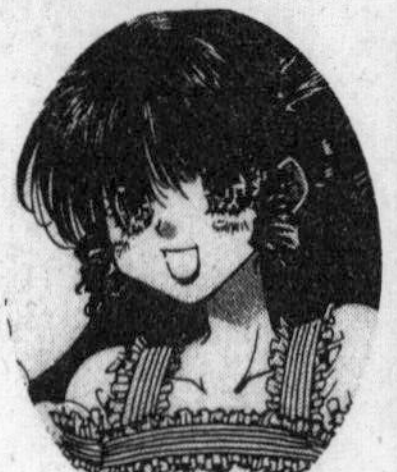

SHE IS THE PURE AND SPACEY YOUNGER SISTER OF KYOJI. SHE AND VINCENT GOOF OFF TOGETHER

バンパイアドール・ギルナサン

Story so far…

In Europe, Guilt-na-Zan once ruled the night as the most feared of vampires. Sealed into a cross by a powerful exorcist, he slept for a century, but that exorcist's descendent, Kyoji, has revived him–into the body of a female doll! Now, he lives as a maid for the Yotobari family and aids Kyoji in hunting monsters. The hardships of Guilt-na-Zan continue…

KYOICHI

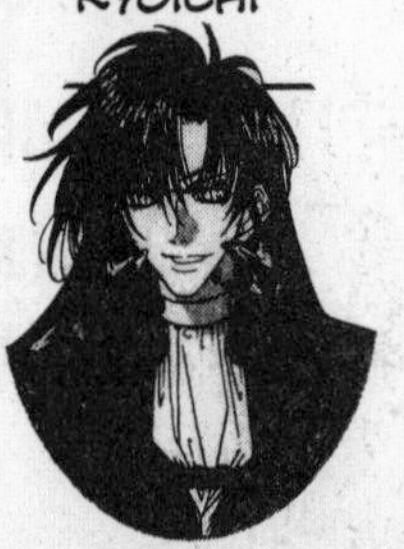

THIS IS KYOJI'S OLDER TWIN. ALTHOUGH HE IS THE BIGGEST IDIOT IN THE ENTIRE WORLD, HE HAS A GREAT POWER

DUNE

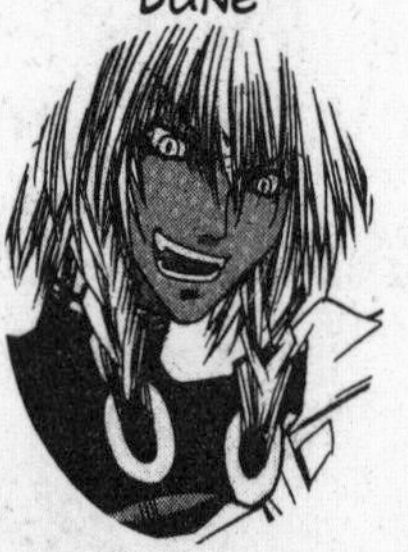

HE FEEDS BY ABSORBING NEGATIVE ENERGY FROM HUMANS AND IS CURRENTLY LIVING AND WORKING AT MITSUHACHI ACADEMY.

VINCENT

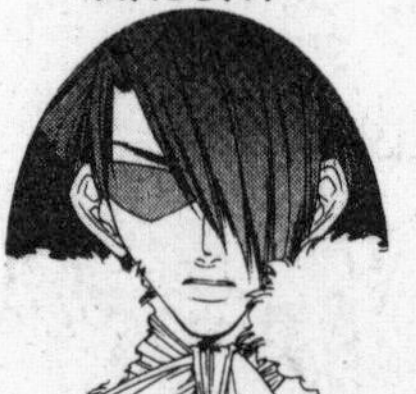

ORIGINALLY A BAT, VINCENT IS A SERVANT OF GUILT-NA-ZAN. HE'S TOO NICE TO BE CALLED A MONSTER

SHIZUKA

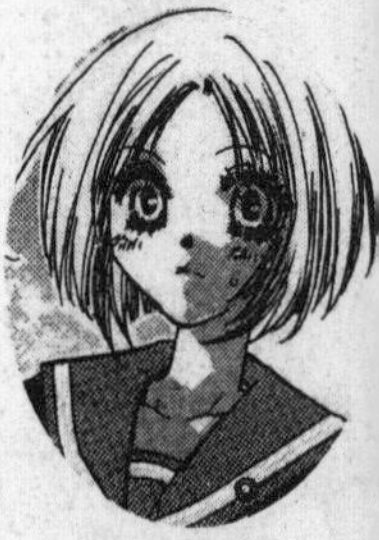

ONE OF TONAE'S CLASSMATES AND THE STUDENT PRESIDENT, SHE'S RESPONSIBLE AND CUTE.

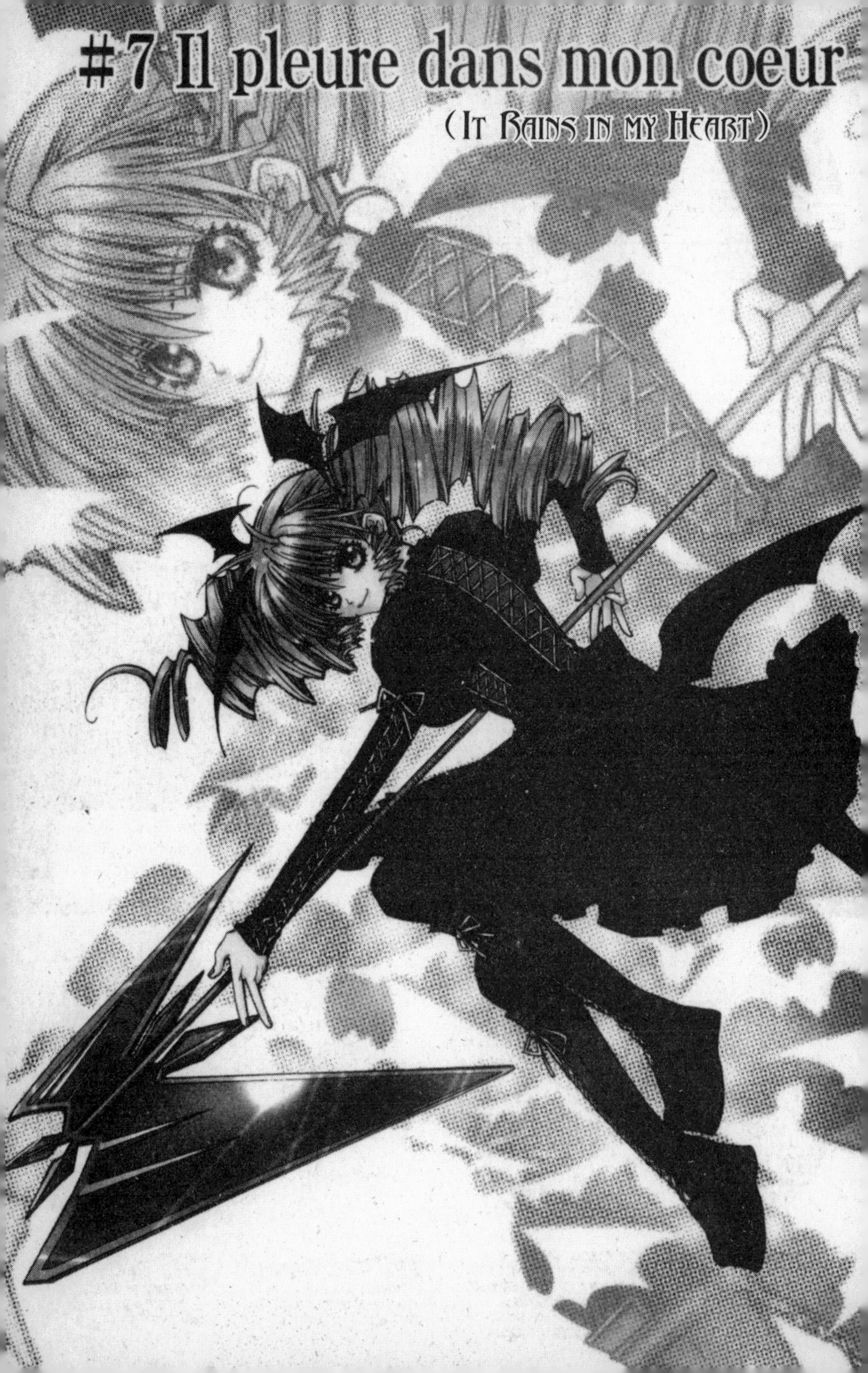
#7 Il pleure dans mon coeur
(It Rains in my Heart)

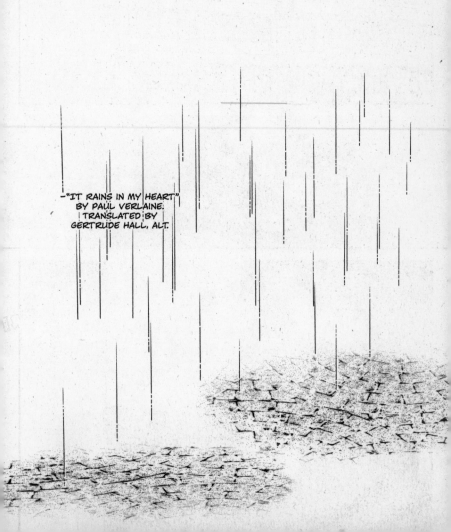

IT RAINS IN
MY HEART
AS IT RAINS ON
THE TOWN.
WHAT IS THIS
DULL SMART
POSSESSING
MY HEART?

SOFT SOUND
OF THE RAIN
ON THE GROUND
AND THE ROOFS!
TO A HEART
IN PAIN,
O THE SONG
OF THE RAIN!

IT WEEPS
WITHOUT CAUSE
IN MY HEART-
SICK HEART.
IN HER FAITH,
WHAT? NO
FLAWS?
THIS GRIEF HAS
NO CAUSE.

'TIS SURE THE
WORST WOE
TO KNOW NOT
WHEREFORE
MY HEART
SUFFERS SO
WITHOUT JOY
OR WOE.

—"IT RAINS IN MY HEART"
BY PAUL VERLAINE.
TRANSLATED BY
GERTRUDE HALL, ALT.

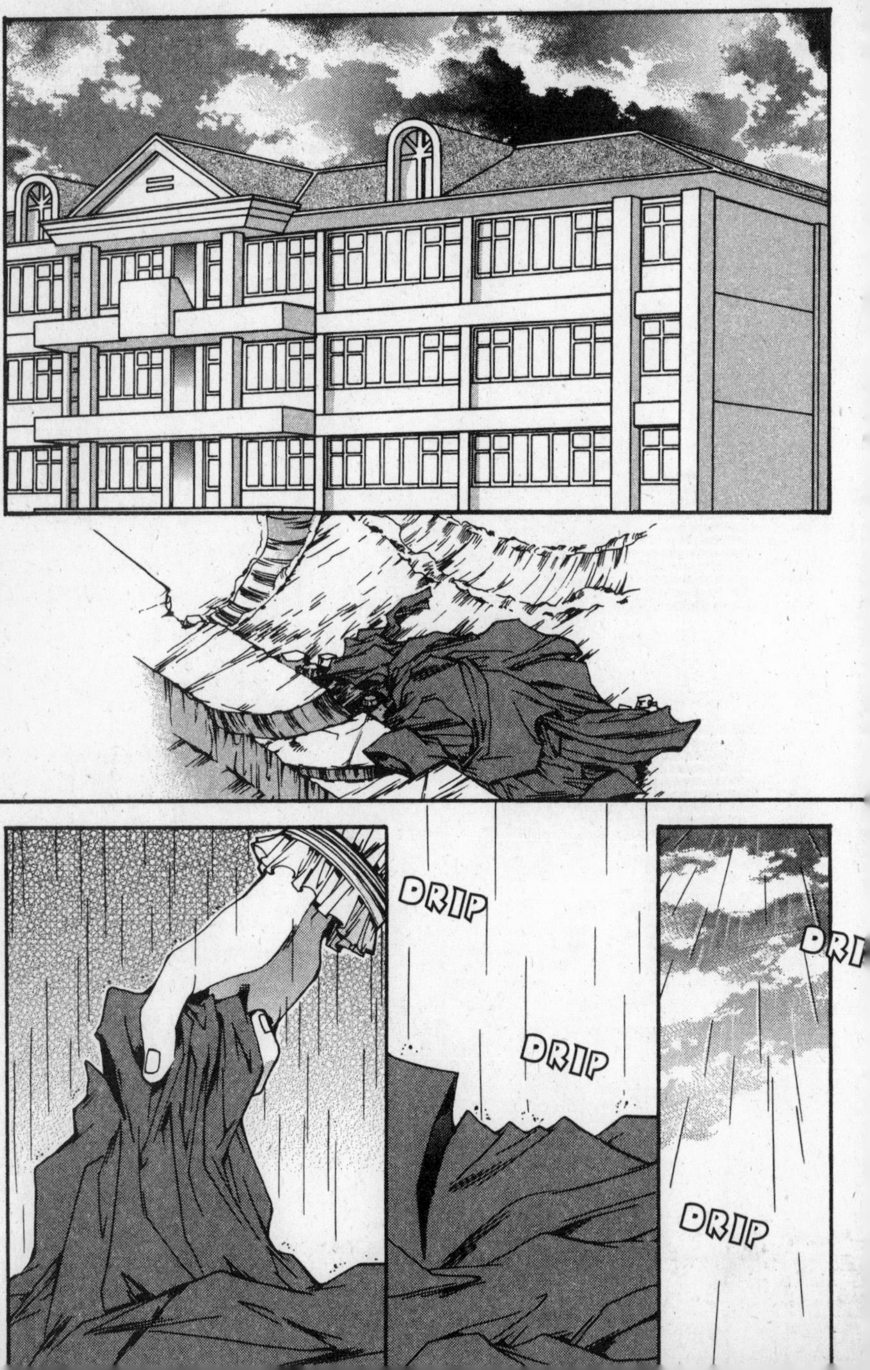
DRI
DRIP
DRIP
DRIP

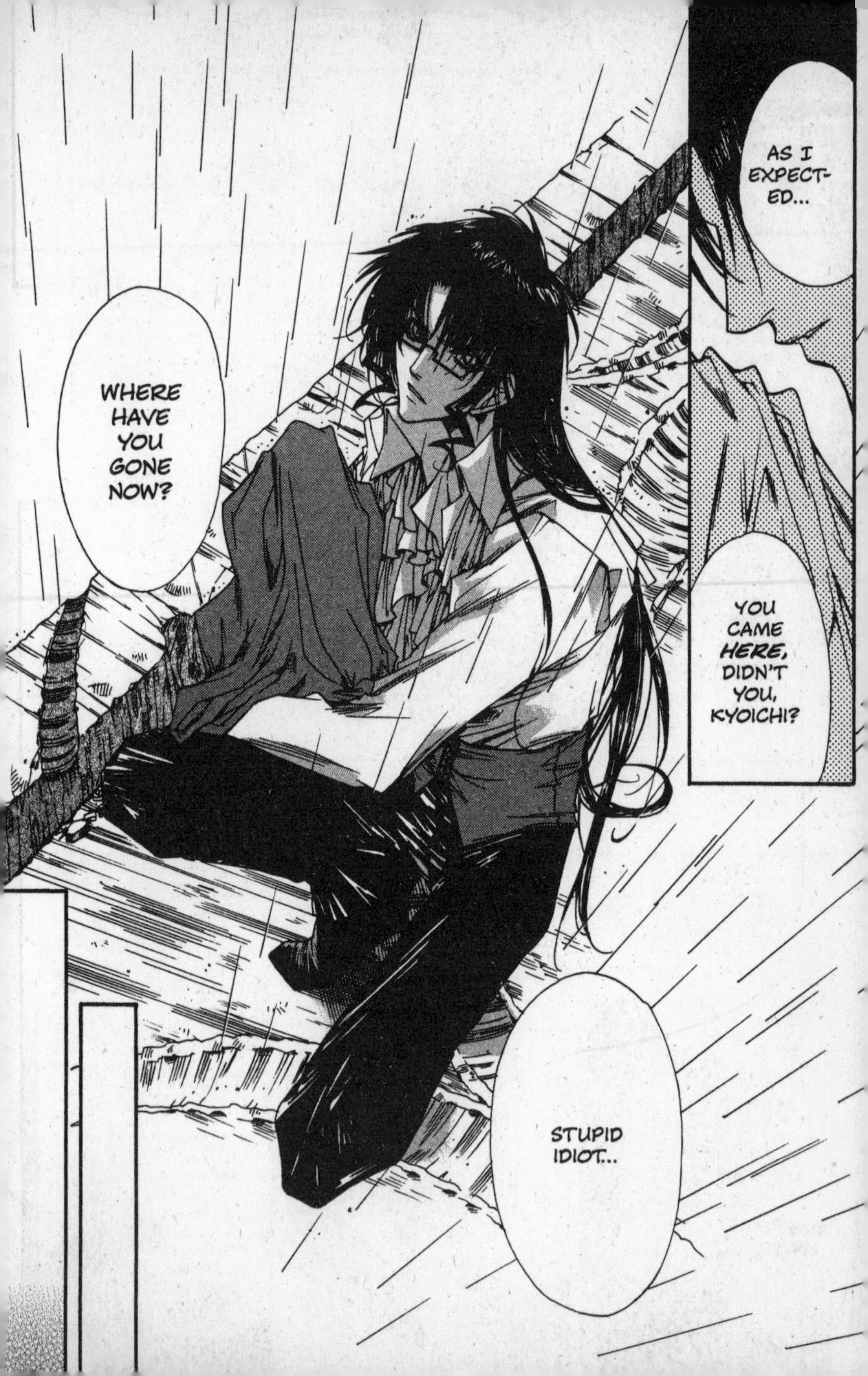
AS I EXPECTED...
YOU CAME HERE, DIDN'T YOU, KYOICHI?
WHERE HAVE YOU GONE NOW?
STUPID IDIOT...

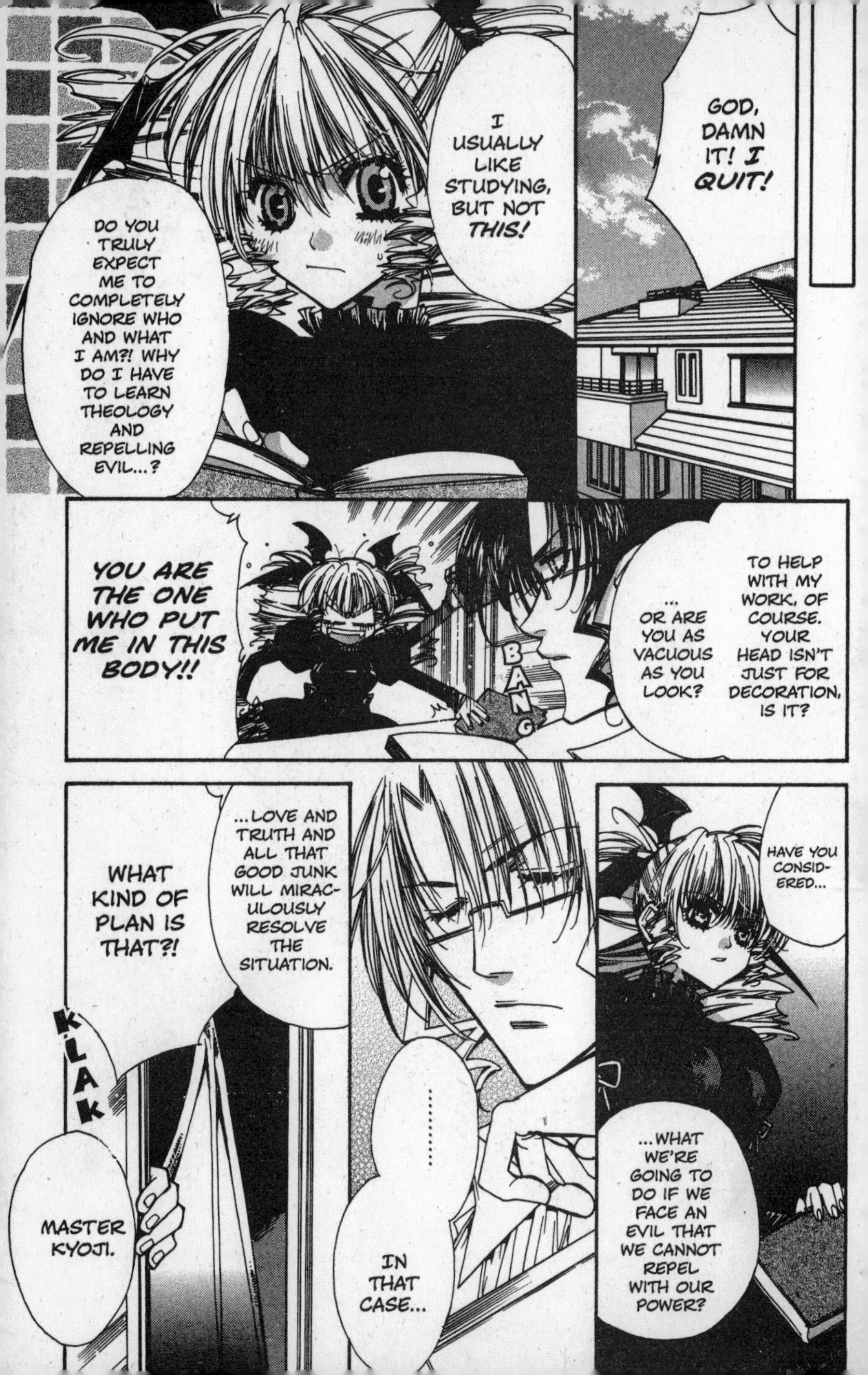
GOD, DAMN IT! I QUIT!
I USUALLY LIKE STUDYING, BUT NOT THIS!
DO YOU TRULY EXPECT ME TO COMPLETELY IGNORE WHO AND WHAT I AM?! WHY DO I HAVE TO LEARN THEOLOGY AND REPELLING EVIL...?
TO HELP WITH MY WORK, OF COURSE. YOUR HEAD ISN'T JUST FOR DECORATION, IS IT?
... OR ARE YOU AS VACUOUS AS YOU LOOK?
BANG
YOU ARE THE ONE WHO PUT ME IN THIS BODY!!
HAVE YOU CONSIDERED...
...WHAT WE'RE GOING TO DO IF WE FACE AN EVIL THAT WE CANNOT REPEL WITH OUR POWER?
......
IN THAT CASE...
...LOVE AND TRUTH AND ALL THAT GOOD JUNK WILL MIRACULOUSLY RESOLVE THE SITUATION.
WHAT KIND OF PLAN IS THAT?!
KLAK
MASTER KYOJI.

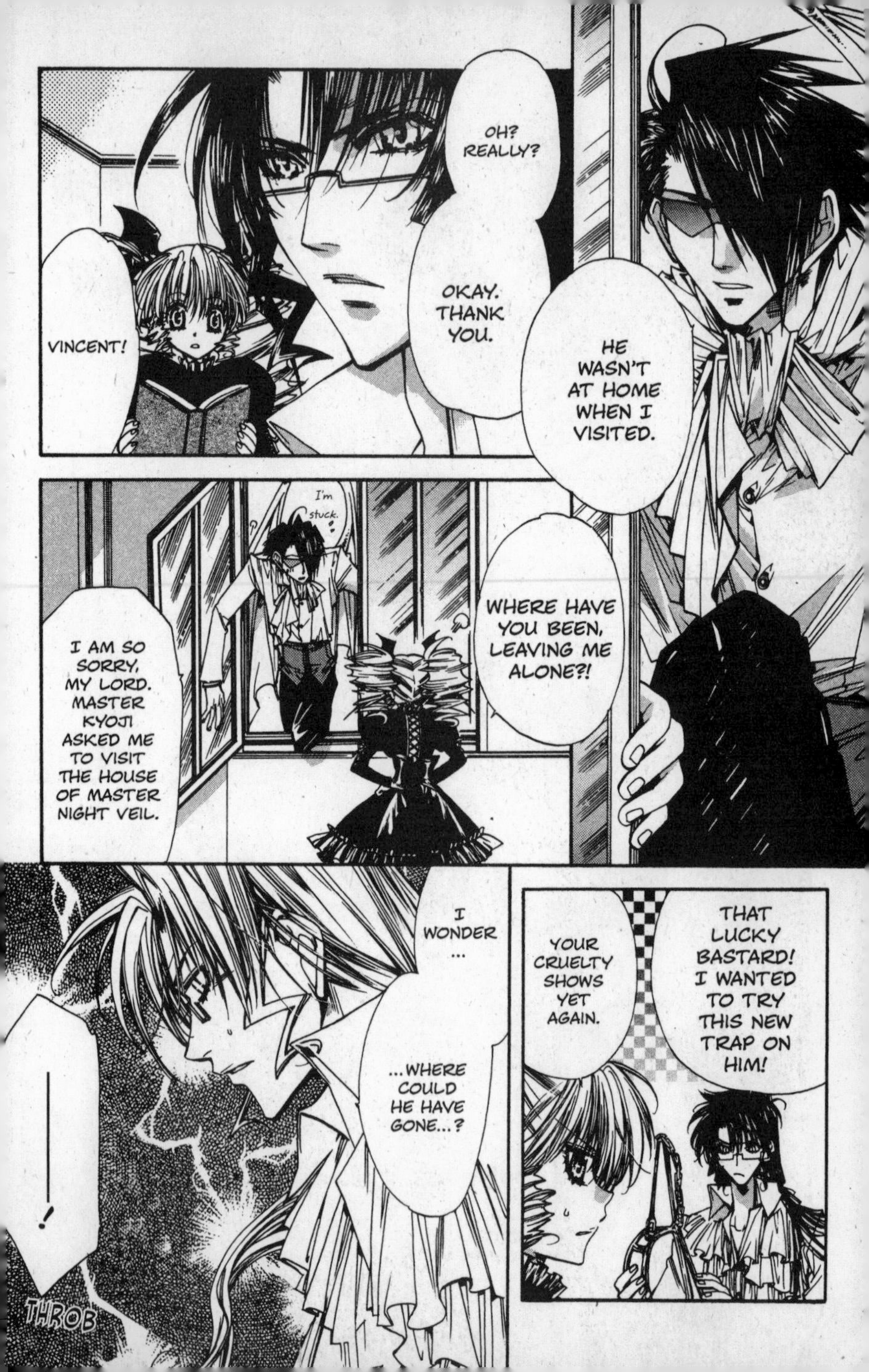
HE WASN'T AT HOME WHEN I VISITED.
OH? REALLY?
OKAY. THANK YOU.
VINCENT!
I'm stuck.
WHERE HAVE YOU BEEN, LEAVING ME ALONE?!
I AM SO SORRY, MY LORD. MASTER KYOJI ASKED ME TO VISIT THE HOUSE OF MASTER NIGHT VEIL.
THAT LUCKY BASTARD! I WANTED TO TRY THIS NEW TRAP ON HIM!
YOUR CRUELTY SHOWS YET AGAIN.
I WONDER ...
...WHERE COULD HE HAVE GONE...?
—!
THROB

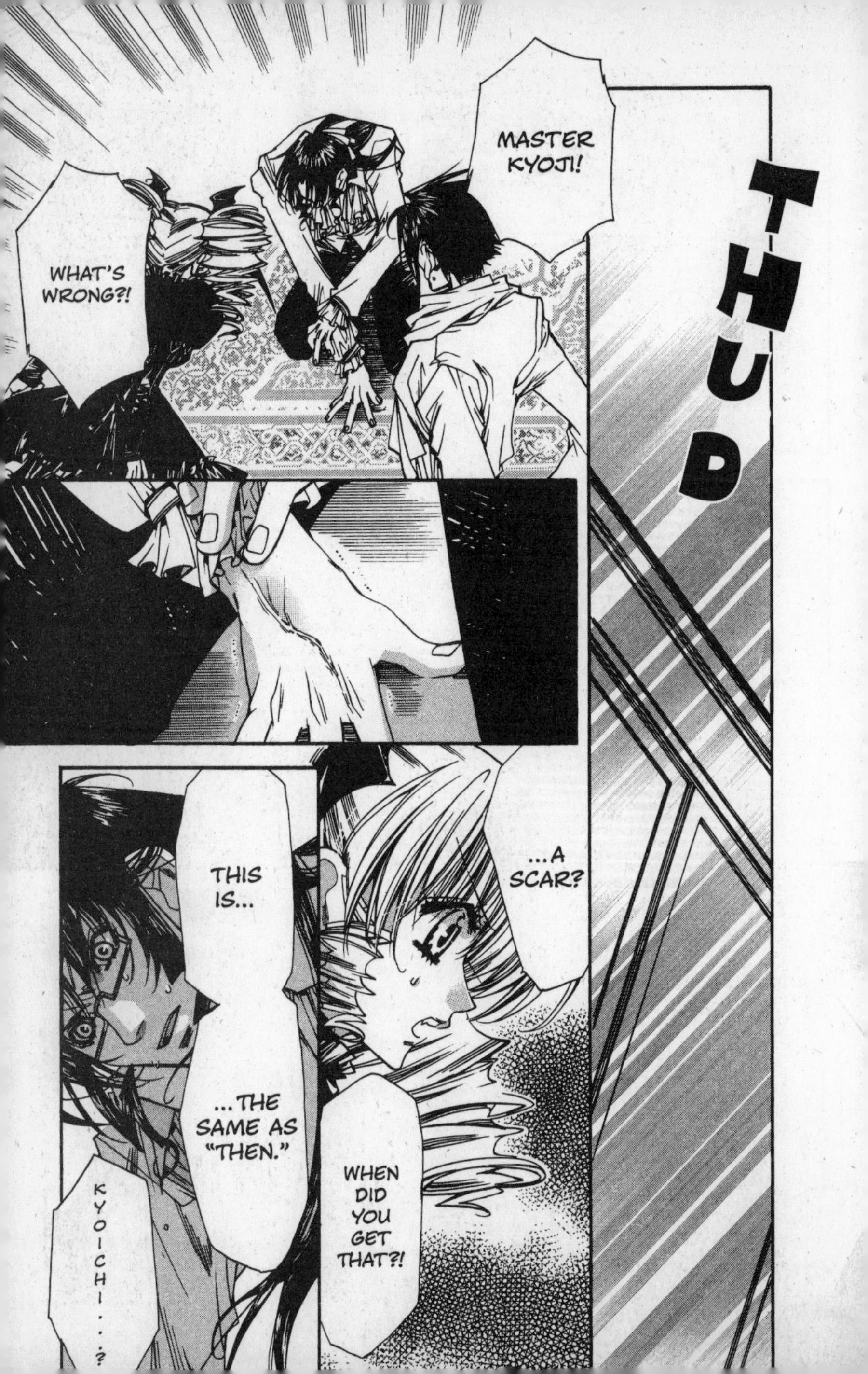
THUD
MASTER KYOJI!
WHAT'S WRONG?!
...A SCAR?
THIS IS...
...THE SAME AS "THEN."
WHEN DID YOU GET THAT?!
KYOICHI...?

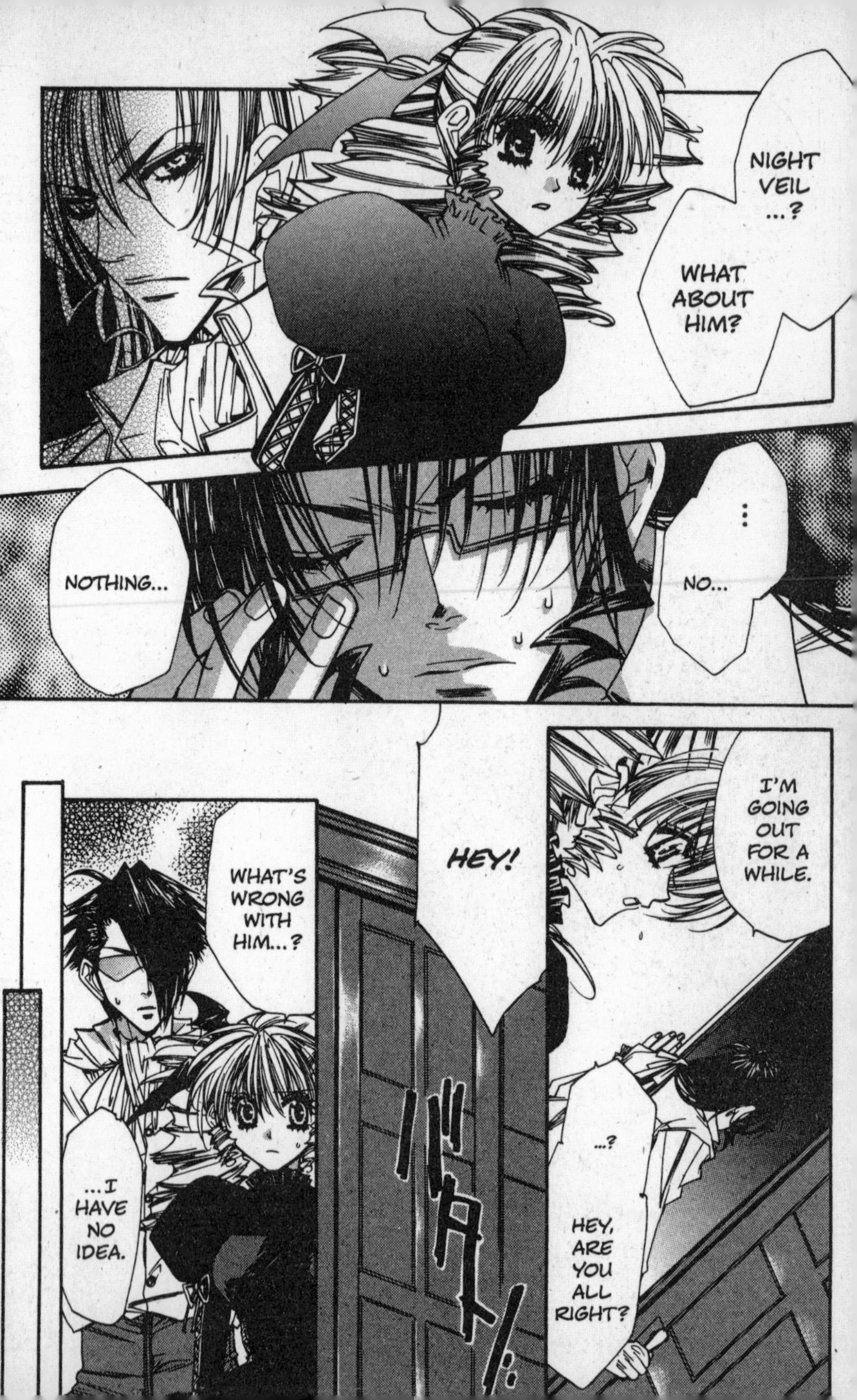
NIGHT VEIL ...?
WHAT ABOUT HIM?
...
NO...
NOTHING...
I'M GOING OUT FOR A WHILE.
HEY!
...?
HEY, ARE YOU ALL RIGHT?
バタン!
WHAT'S WRONG WITH HIM...?
...I HAVE NO IDEA.

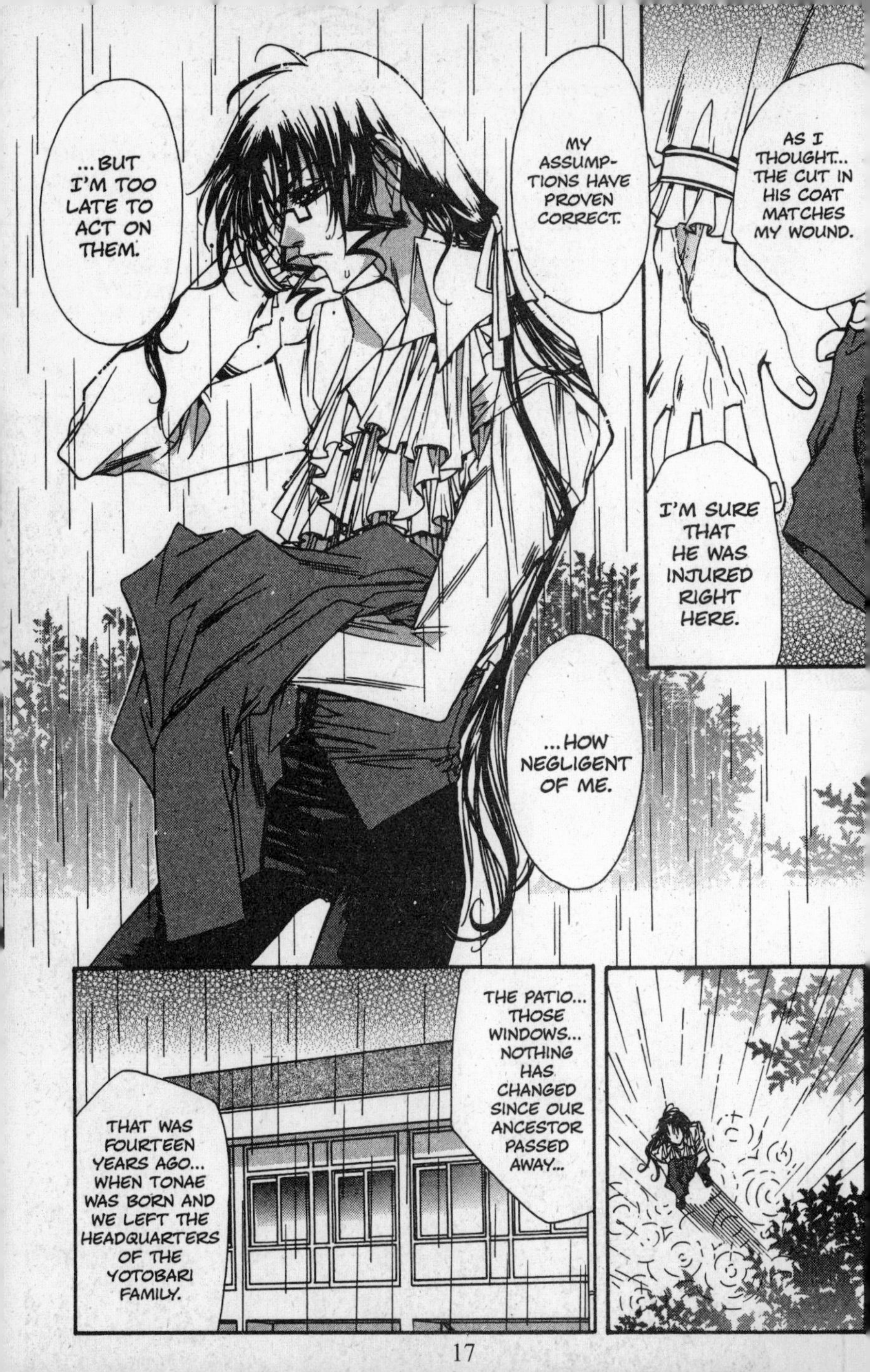
AS I THOUGHT... THE CUT IN HIS COAT MATCHES MY WOUND.
I'M SURE THAT HE WAS INJURED RIGHT HERE.
MY ASSUMPTIONS HAVE PROVEN CORRECT.
...BUT I'M TOO LATE TO ACT ON THEM.
...HOW NEGLIGENT OF ME.
THE PATIO... THOSE WINDOWS... NOTHING HAS CHANGED SINCE OUR ANCESTOR PASSED AWAY...
THAT WAS FOURTEEN YEARS AGO... WHEN TONAE WAS BORN AND WE LEFT THE HEADQUARTERS OF THE YOTOBARI FAMILY.

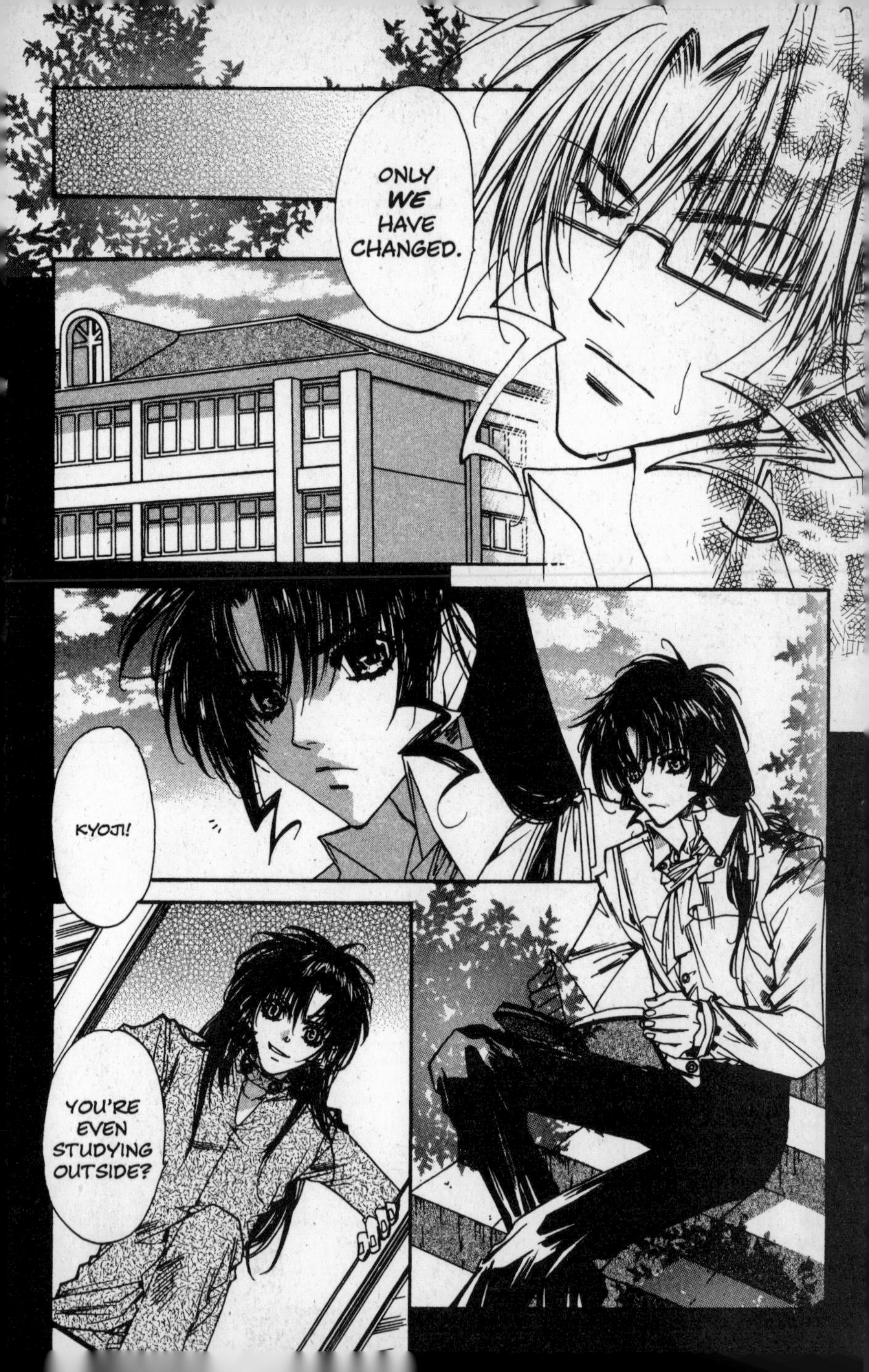
ONLY WE HAVE CHANGED.
KYOJI!
YOU'RE EVEN STUDYING OUTSIDE?

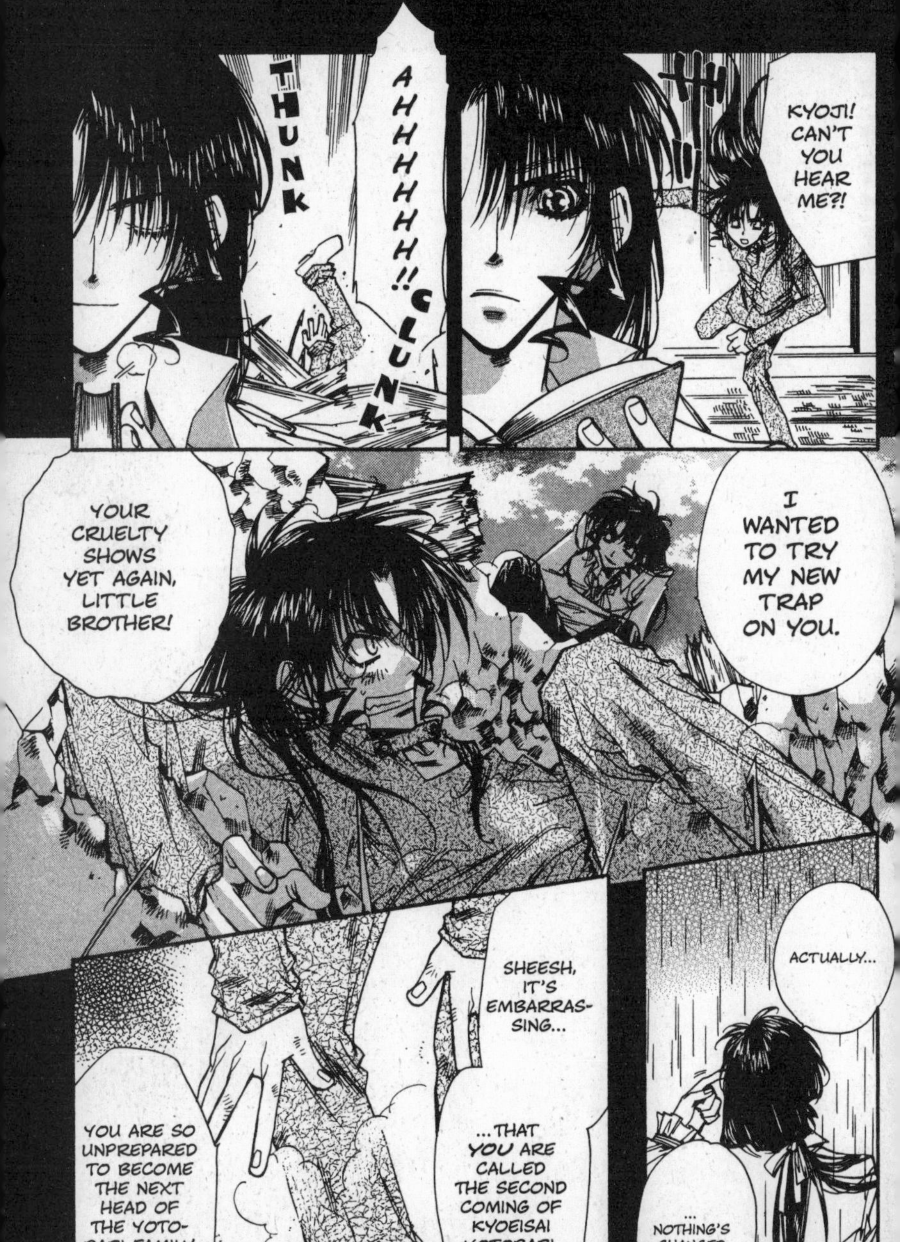
KYOJI! CAN'T YOU HEAR ME?!
AHHHHHH!!
THUNK
CLUNK
I WANTED TO TRY MY NEW TRAP ON YOU.
YOUR CRUELTY SHOWS YET AGAIN, LITTLE BROTHER!
ACTUALLY...
...NOTHING'S CHANGED MUCH.
SHEESH, IT'S EMBARRAS-SING...
...THAT YOU ARE CALLED THE SECOND COMING OF KYOEISAI YOTOBARI.
YOU ARE SO UNPREPARED TO BECOME THE NEXT HEAD OF THE YOTO-BARI FAMILY.

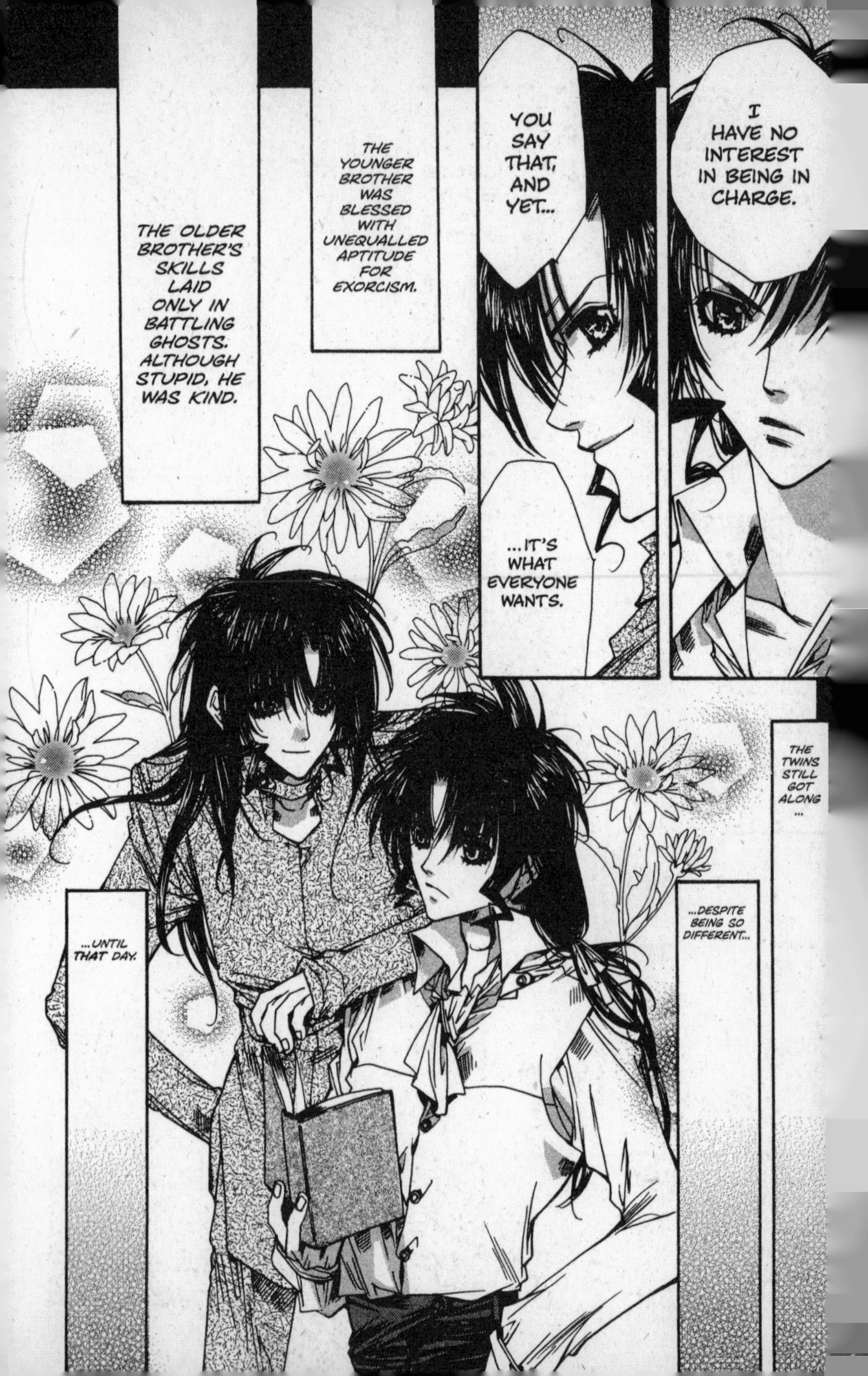
I HAVE NO INTEREST IN BEING IN CHARGE.
YOU SAY THAT, AND YET...
...IT'S WHAT EVERYONE WANTS.
THE YOUNGER BROTHER WAS BLESSED WITH UNEQUALLED APTITUDE FOR EXORCISM.
THE OLDER BROTHER'S SKILLS LAID ONLY IN BATTLING GHOSTS. ALTHOUGH STUPID, HE WAS KIND.
THE TWINS STILL GOT ALONG ...
...DESPITE BEING SO DIFFERENT...
...UNTIL THAT DAY.

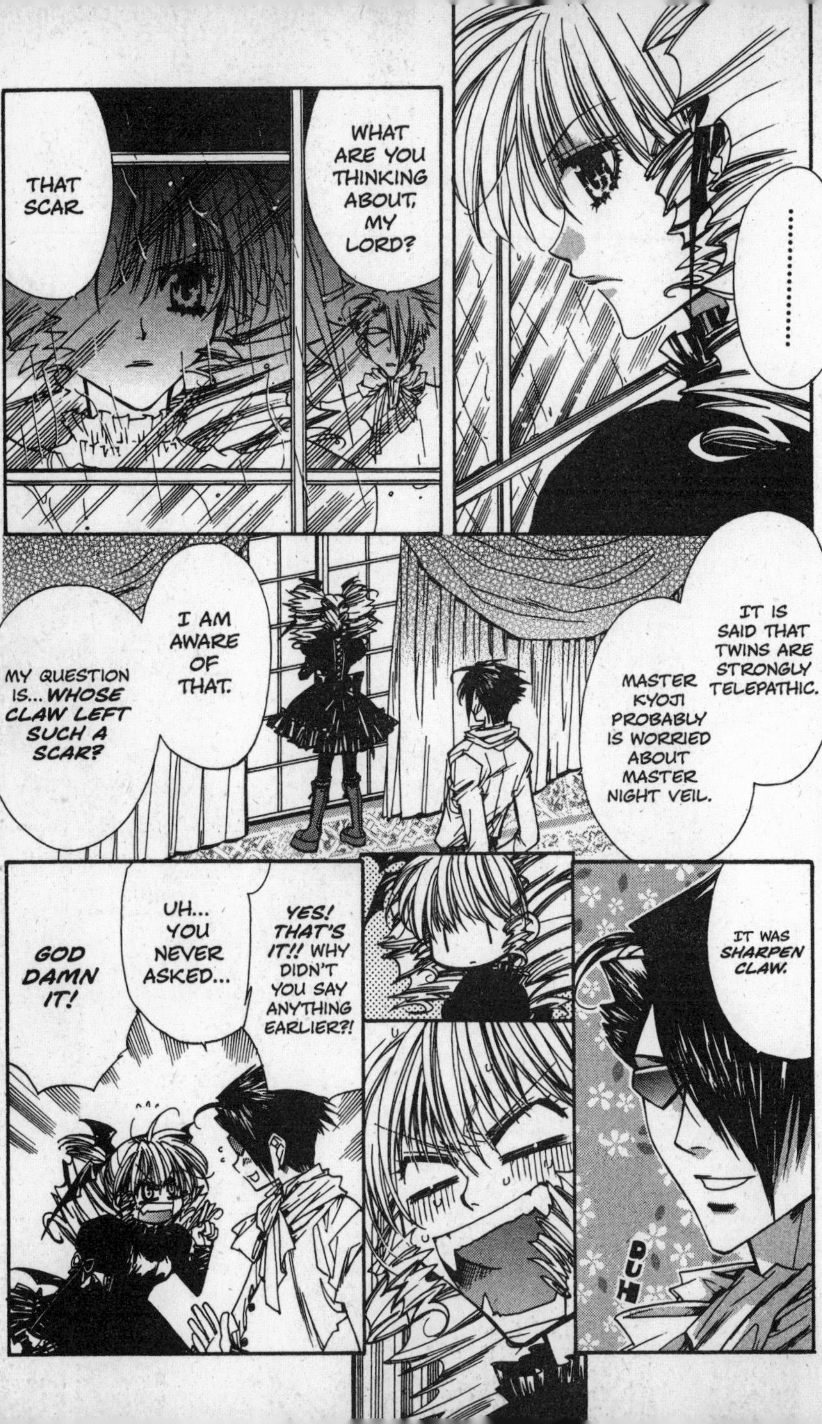
……
WHAT ARE YOU THINKING ABOUT, MY LORD?
THAT SCAR.
IT IS SAID THAT TWINS ARE STRONGLY TELEPATHIC.
MASTER KYOJI PROBABLY IS WORRIED ABOUT MASTER NIGHT VEIL.
I AM AWARE OF THAT.
MY QUESTION IS...WHOSE CLAW LEFT SUCH A SCAR?
IT WAS SHARPEN CLAW.
DUH
YES! THAT'S IT!! WHY DIDN'T YOU SAY ANYTHING EARLIER?!
UH... YOU NEVER ASKED...
GOD DAMN IT!

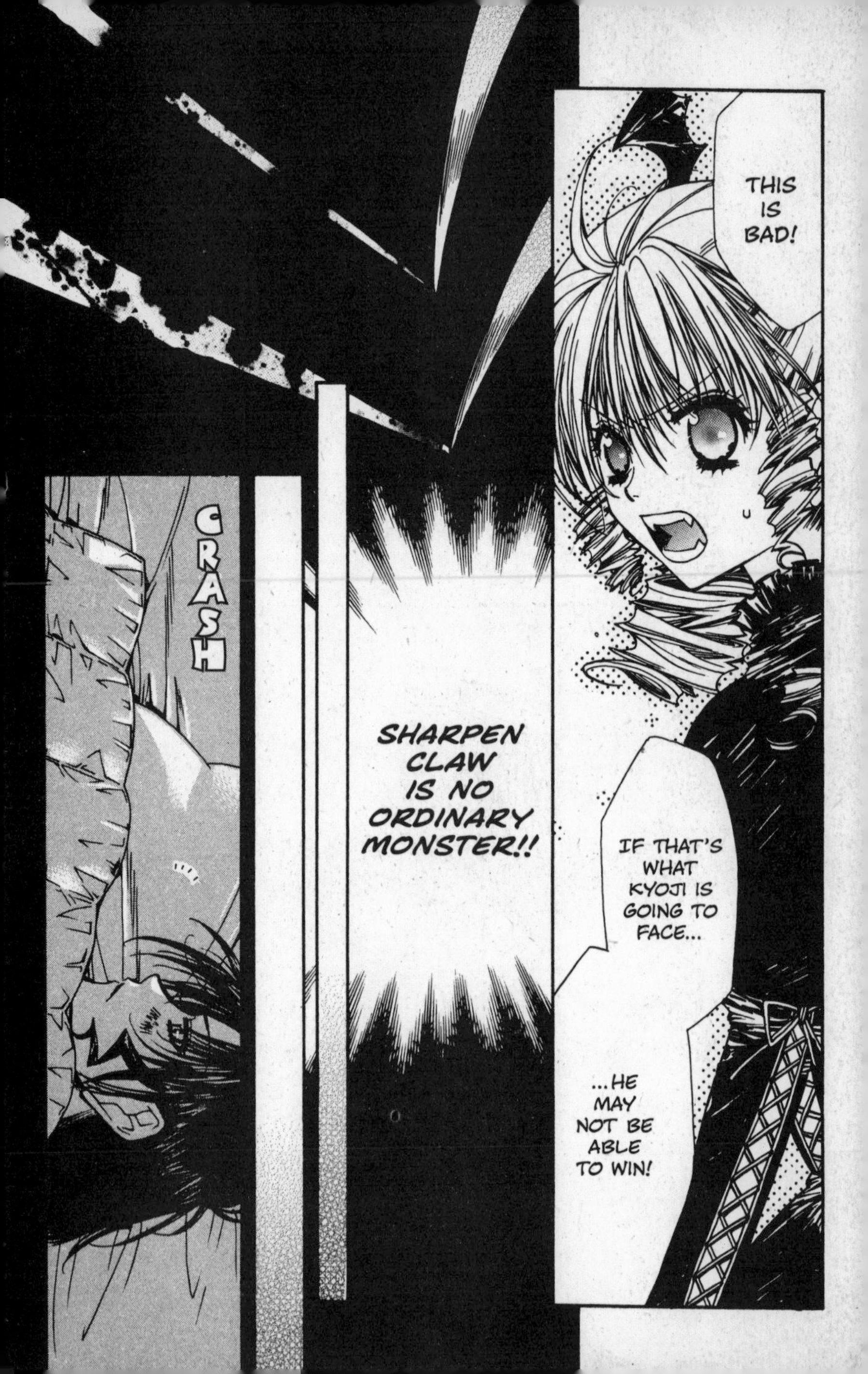
THIS IS BAD!
IF THAT'S WHAT KYOJI IS GOING TO FACE...
...HE MAY NOT BE ABLE TO WIN!
SHARPEN CLAW IS NO ORDINARY MONSTER!!
CRASH

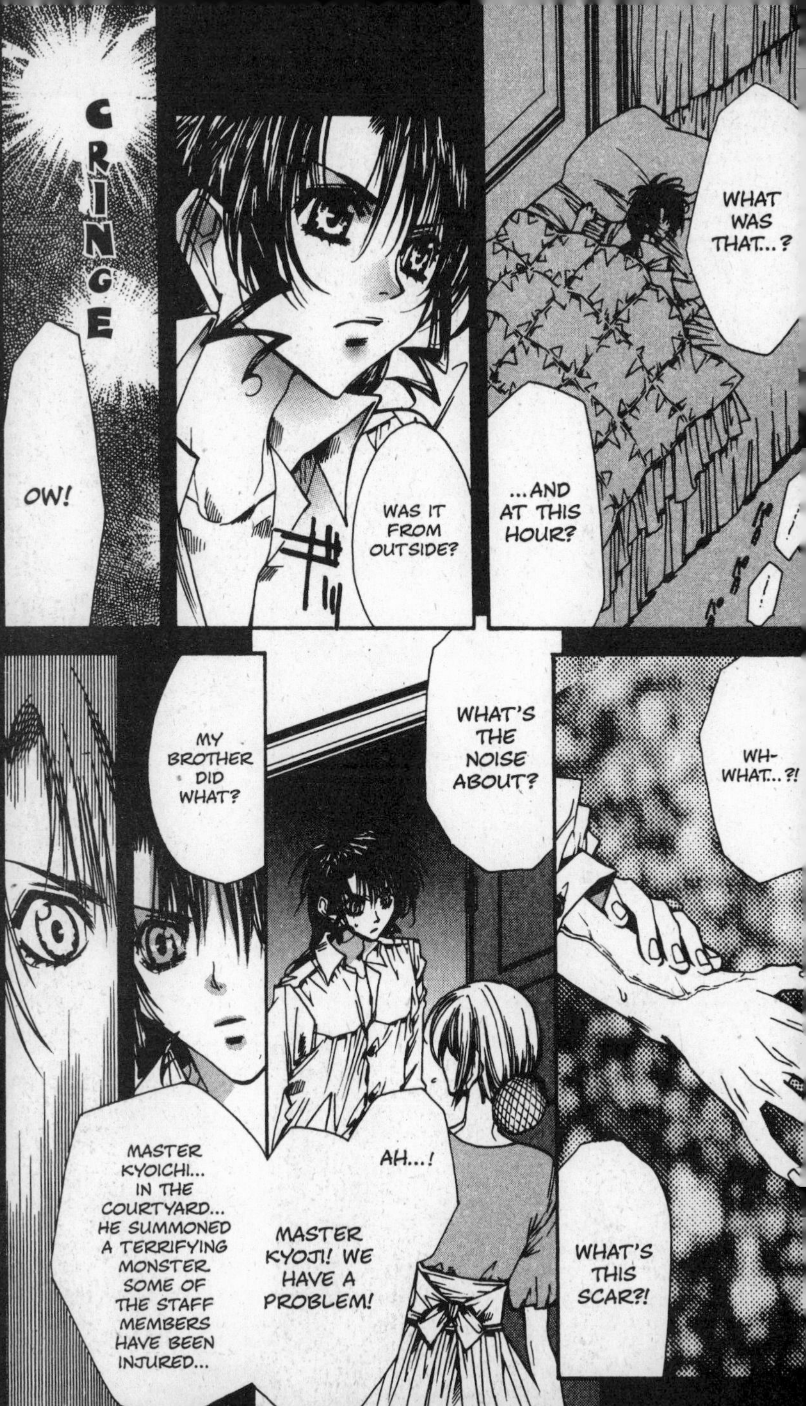
WHAT WAS THAT...?
!
!
...AND AT THIS HOUR?
WAS IT FROM OUTSIDE?
CRINGE
OW!
WH- WHAT...?!
WHAT'S THIS SCAR?!
WHAT'S THE NOISE ABOUT?
AH...!
MASTER KYOJI! WE HAVE A PROBLEM!
MASTER KYOICHI... IN THE COURTYARD... HE SUMMONED A TERRIFYING MONSTER SOME OF THE STAFF MEMBERS HAVE BEEN INJURED...
MY BROTHER DID WHAT?

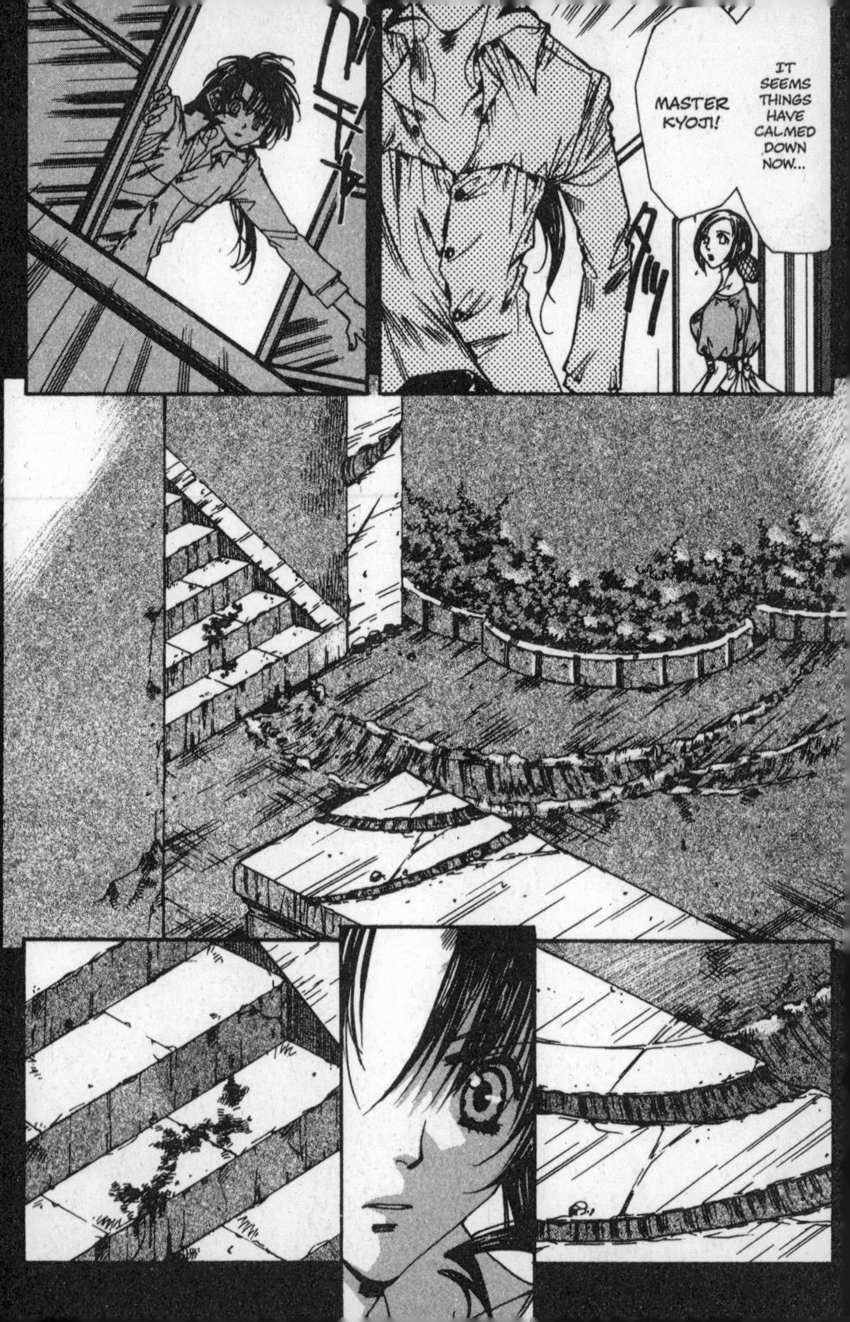
IT SEEMS THINGS HAVE CALMED DOWN NOW...
MASTER KYOJI!

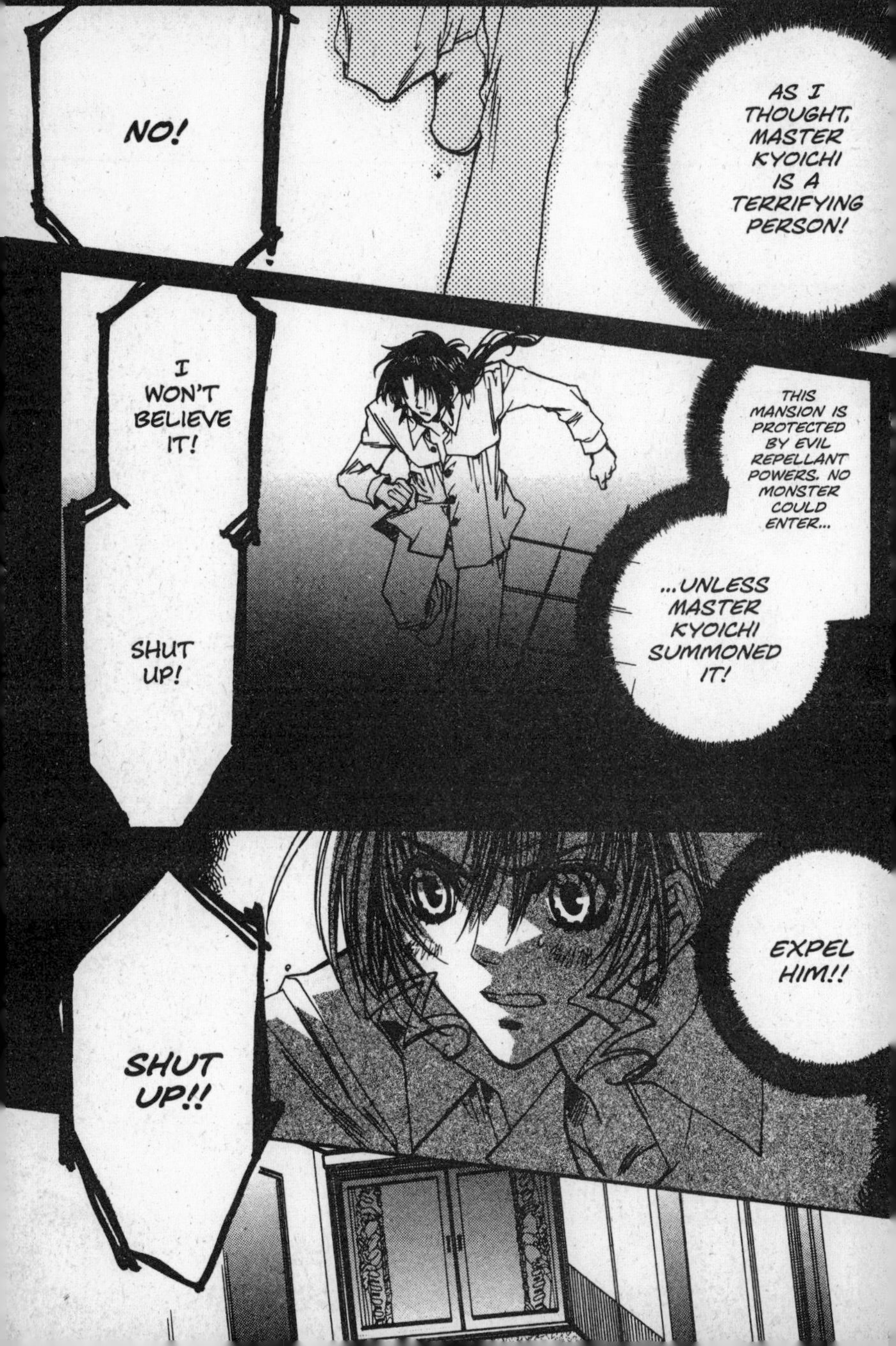
AS I THOUGHT, MASTER KYOICHI IS A TERRIFYING PERSON!
NO!
THIS MANSION IS PROTECTED BY EVIL REPELLANT POWERS. NO MONSTER COULD ENTER...
...UNLESS MASTER KYOICHI SUMMONED IT!
I WON'T BELIEVE IT!
SHUT UP!
EXPEL HIM!!
SHUT UP!!

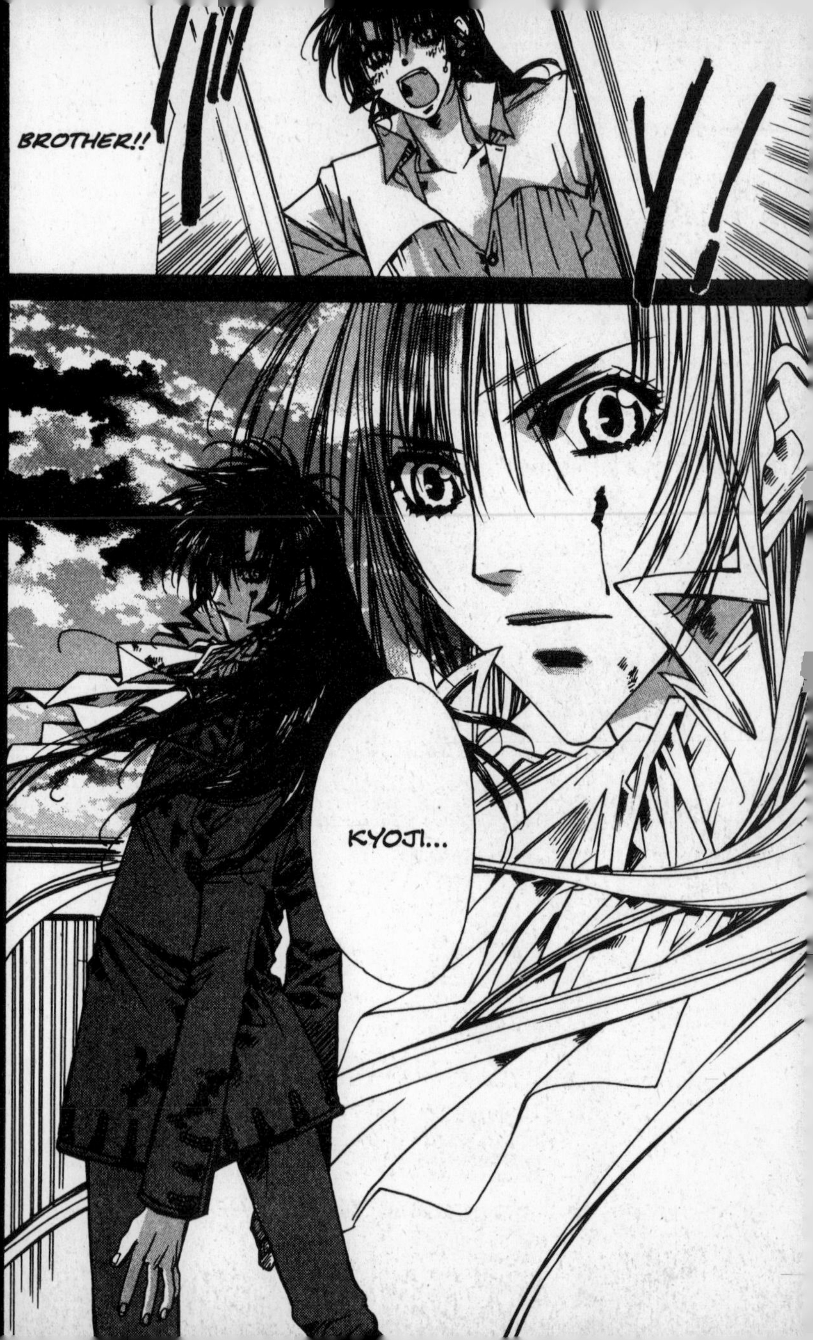
BROTHER!!
KYOJI...

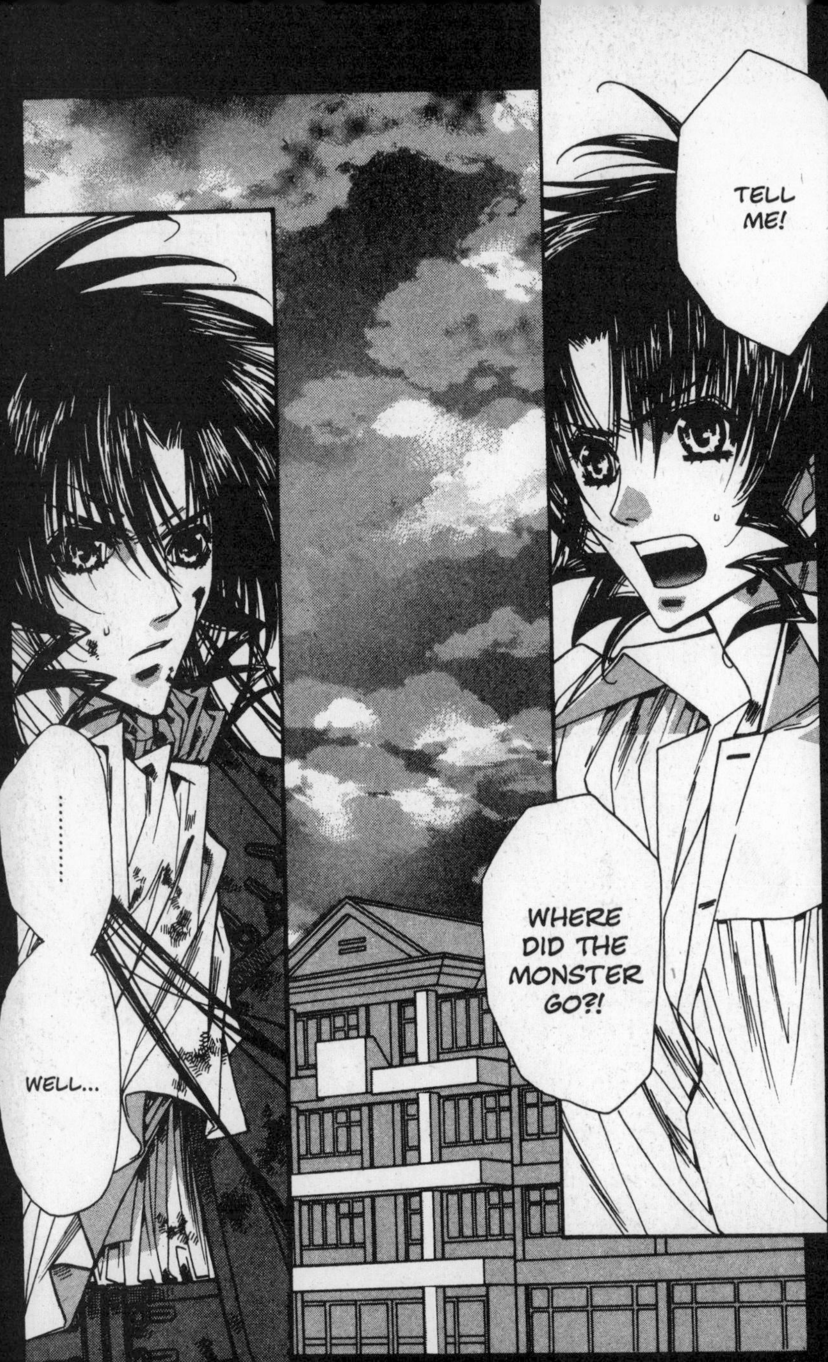
TELL ME!
WHERE DID THE MONSTER GO?!
......
WELL...

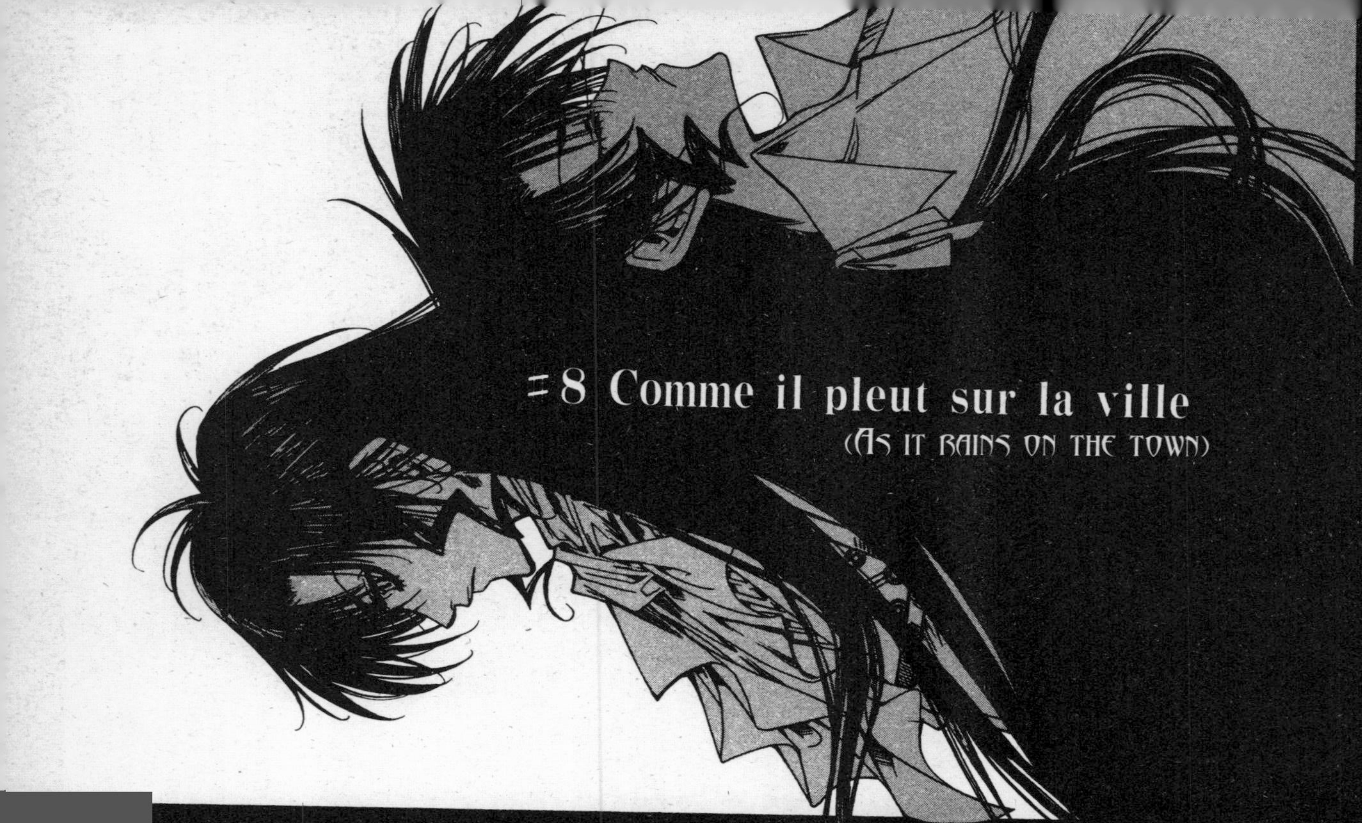
#8 Comme il pleut sur la ville
(As it rains on the town)

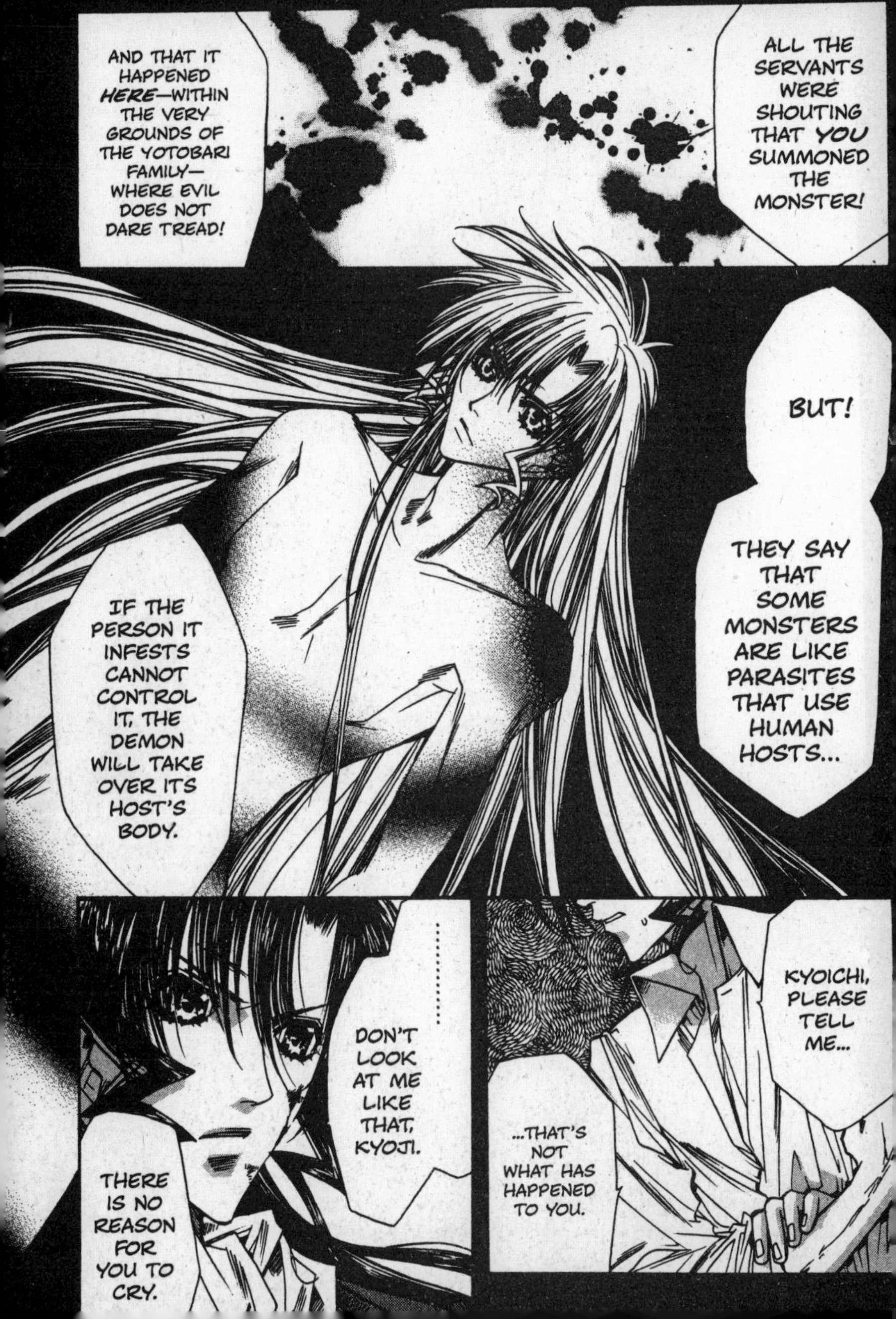
ALL THE SERVANTS WERE SHOUTING THAT YOU SUMMONED THE MONSTER!
AND THAT IT HAPPENED HERE—WITHIN THE VERY GROUNDS OF THE YOTOBARI FAMILY—WHERE EVIL DOES NOT DARE TREAD!
BUT!
THEY SAY THAT SOME MONSTERS ARE LIKE PARASITES THAT USE HUMAN HOSTS...
IF THE PERSON IT INFESTS CANNOT CONTROL IT, THE DEMON WILL TAKE OVER ITS HOST'S BODY.
KYOICHI, PLEASE TELL ME...
...THAT'S NOT WHAT HAS HAPPENED TO YOU.
......
DON'T LOOK AT ME LIKE THAT, KYOJI.
THERE IS NO REASON FOR YOU TO CRY.

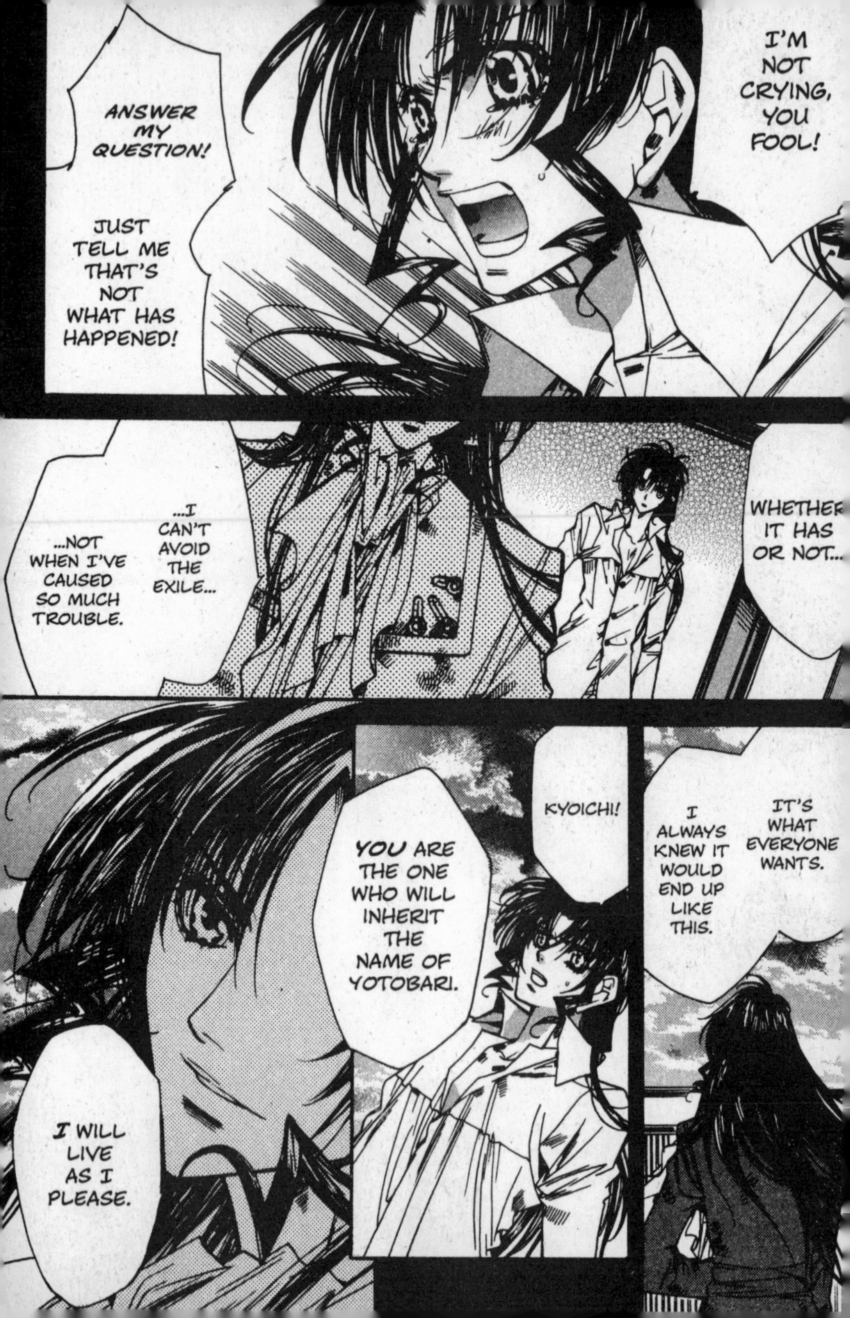
I'M NOT CRYING, YOU FOOL!
ANSWER MY QUESTION!
JUST TELL ME THAT'S NOT WHAT HAS HAPPENED!
WHETHER IT HAS OR NOT...
...I CAN'T AVOID THE EXILE...
...NOT WHEN I'VE CAUSED SO MUCH TROUBLE.
IT'S WHAT EVERYONE WANTS.
I ALWAYS KNEW IT WOULD END UP LIKE THIS.
KYOICHI!
YOU ARE THE ONE WHO WILL INHERIT THE NAME OF YOTOBARI.
I WILL LIVE AS I PLEASE.

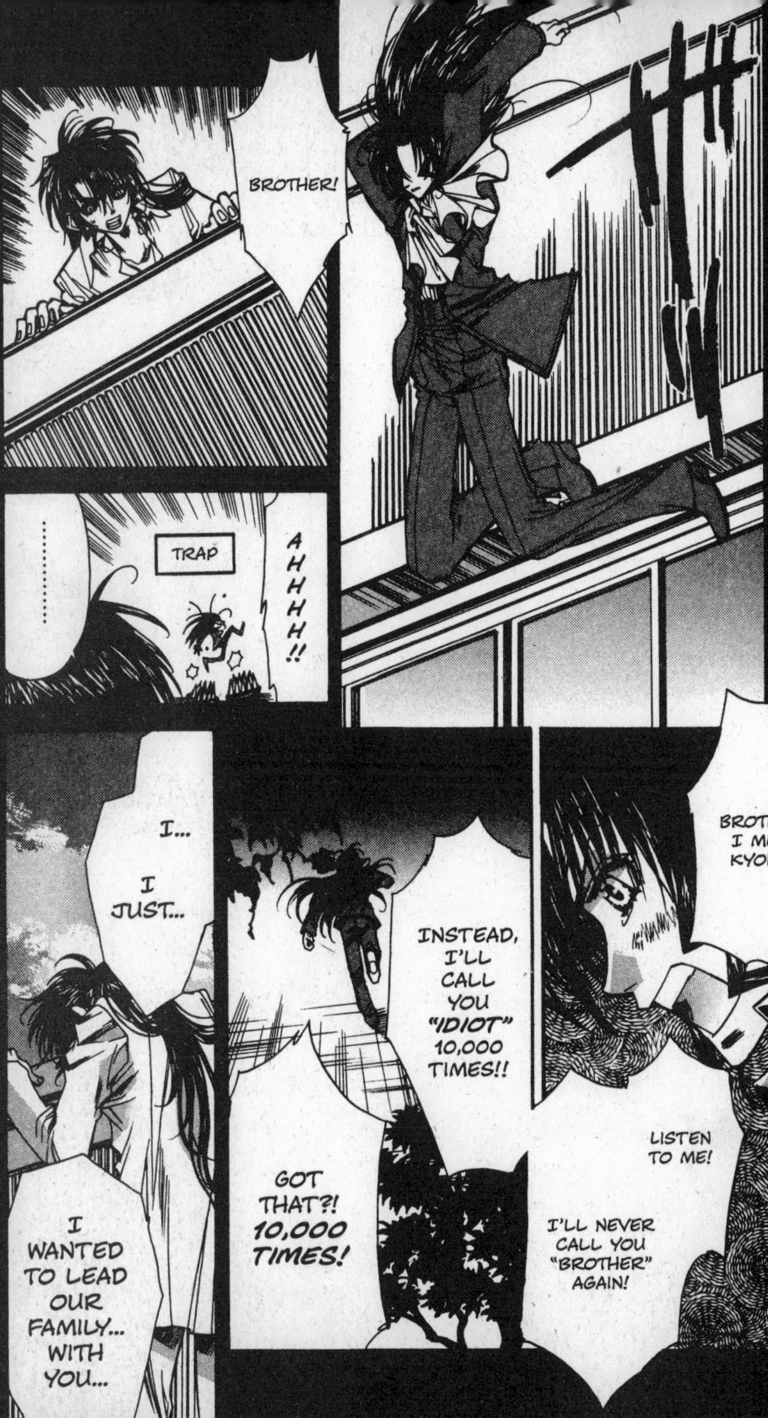
BROTHER!
AHHHH!!
TRAP
......
BROTHER... I MEAN, KYOICHI!
LISTEN TO ME!
I'LL NEVER CALL YOU "BROTHER" AGAIN!
INSTEAD, I'LL CALL YOU "IDIOT" 10,000 TIMES!!
GOT THAT?! 10,000 TIMES!
I...
I JUST...
I WANTED TO LEAD OUR FAMILY... WITH YOU...

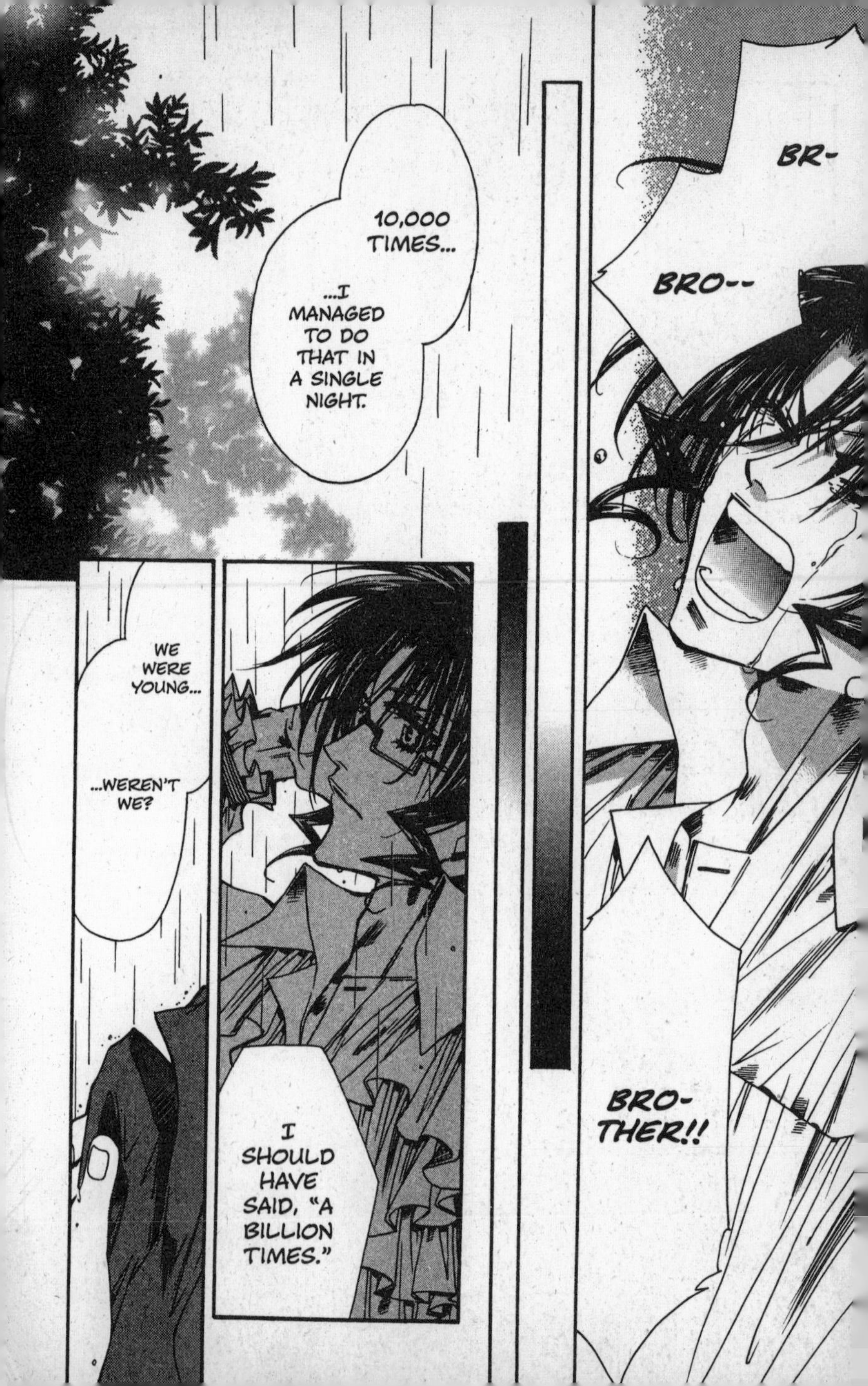
BR-
BRO--
BRO-THER!!
10,000 TIMES...
...I MANAGED TO DO THAT IN A SINGLE NIGHT.
I SHOULD HAVE SAID, "A BILLION TIMES."
WE WERE YOUNG...
...WEREN'T WE?

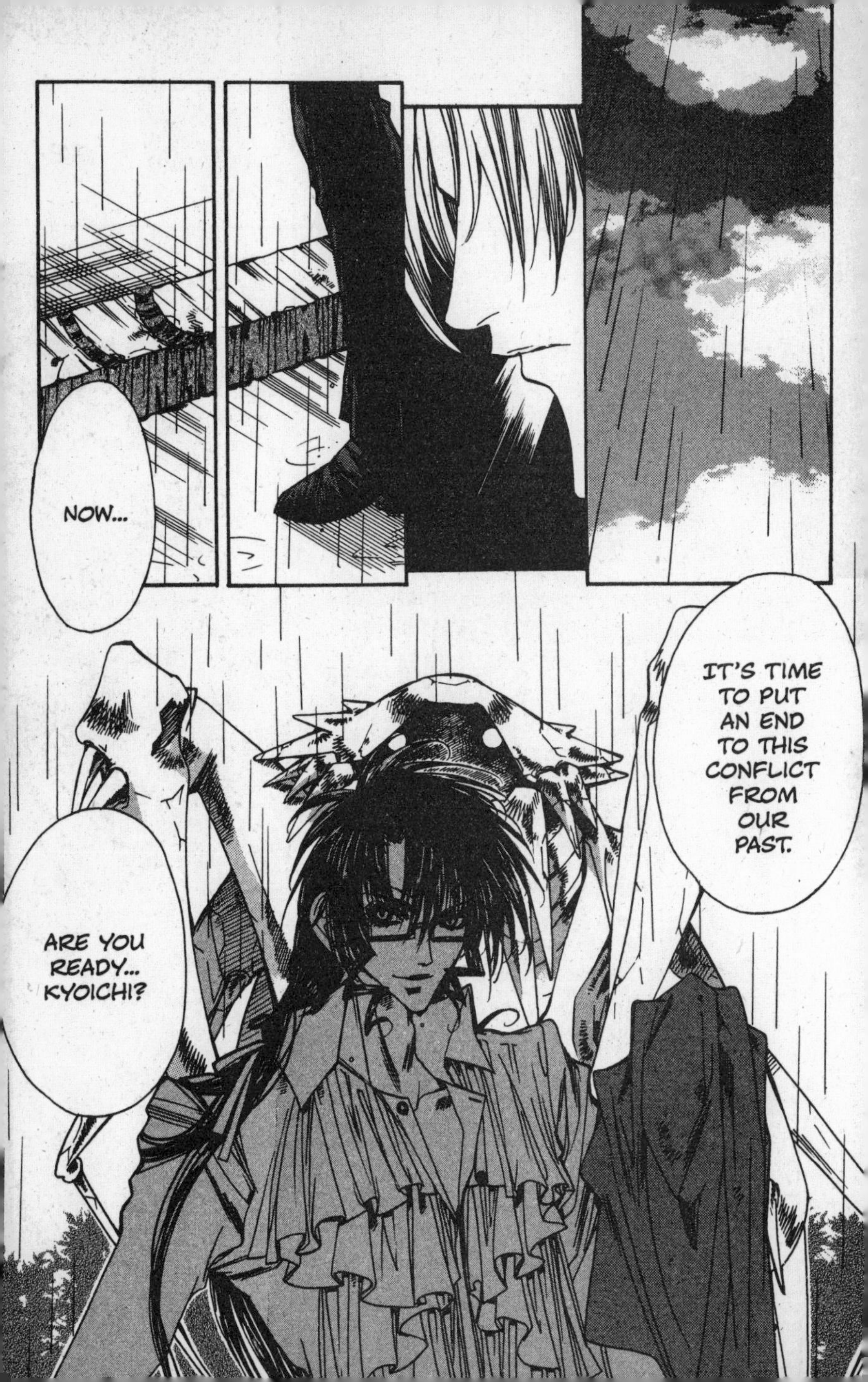
NOW...
IT'S TIME TO PUT AN END TO THIS CONFLICT FROM OUR PAST.
ARE YOU READY... KYOICHI?

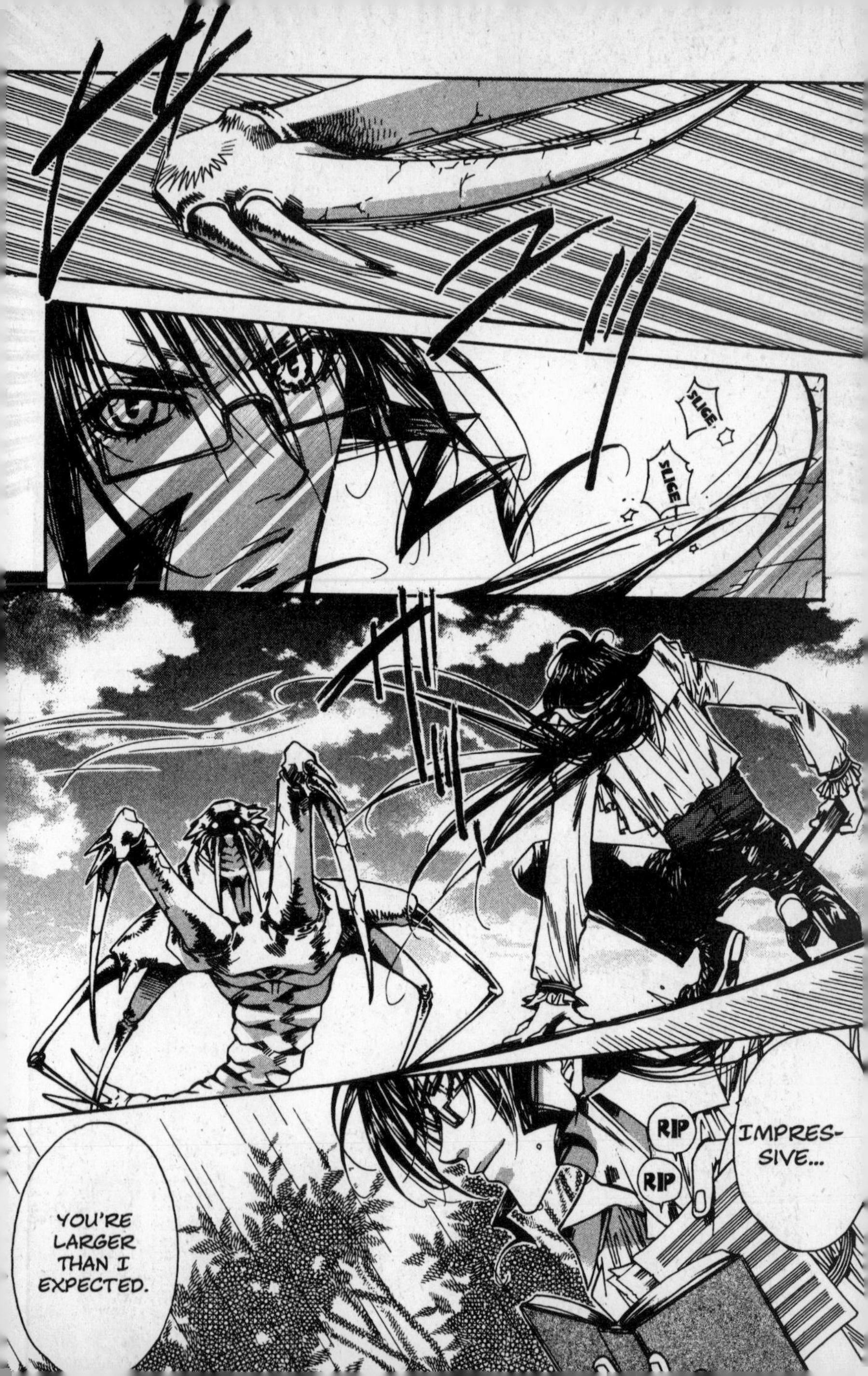
SLICE
SLICE
IMPRES-SIVE...
RIP
RIP
YOU'RE LARGER THAN I EXPECTED.

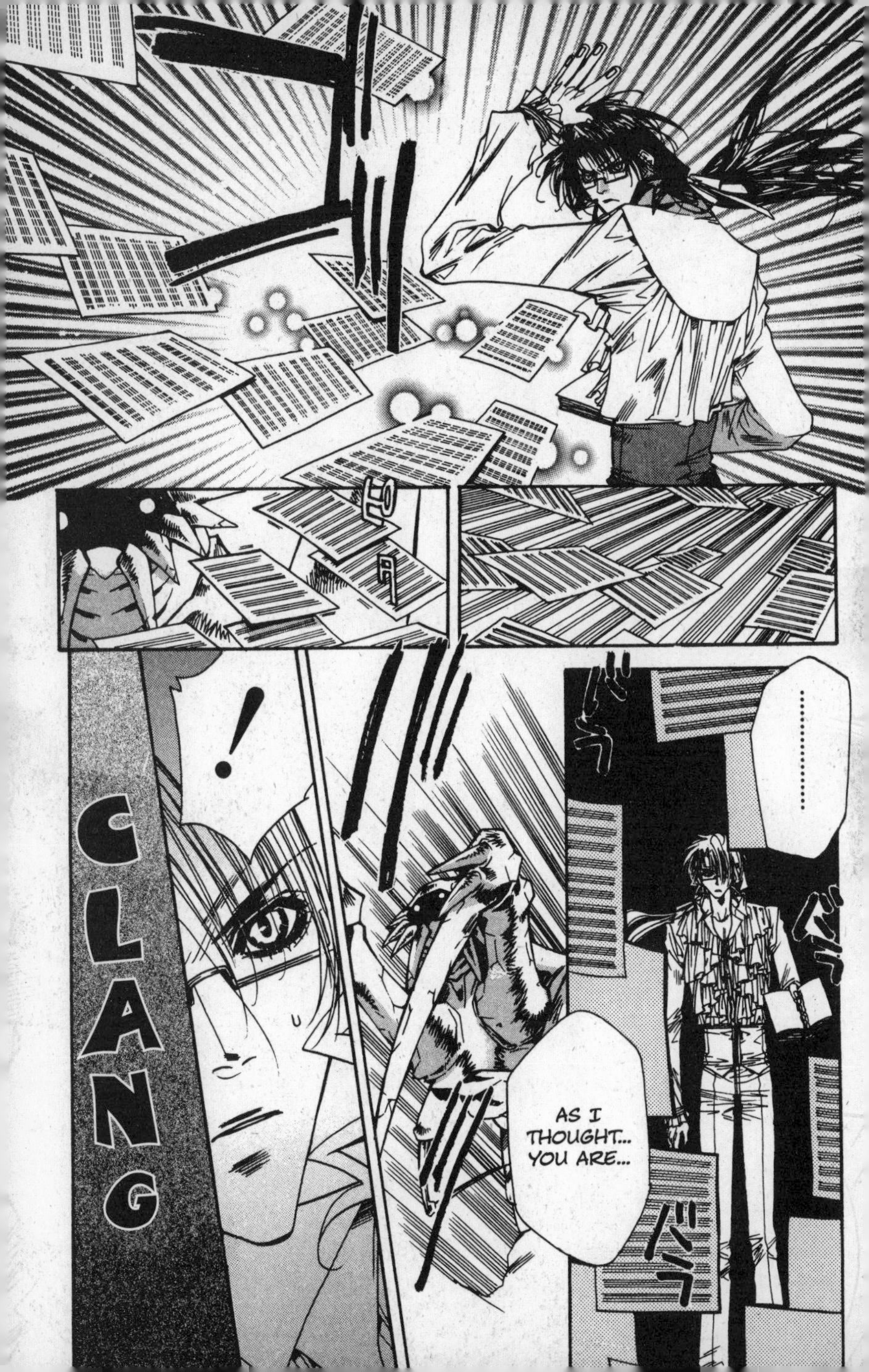
......
AS I THOUGHT... YOU ARE...
!
CLANG

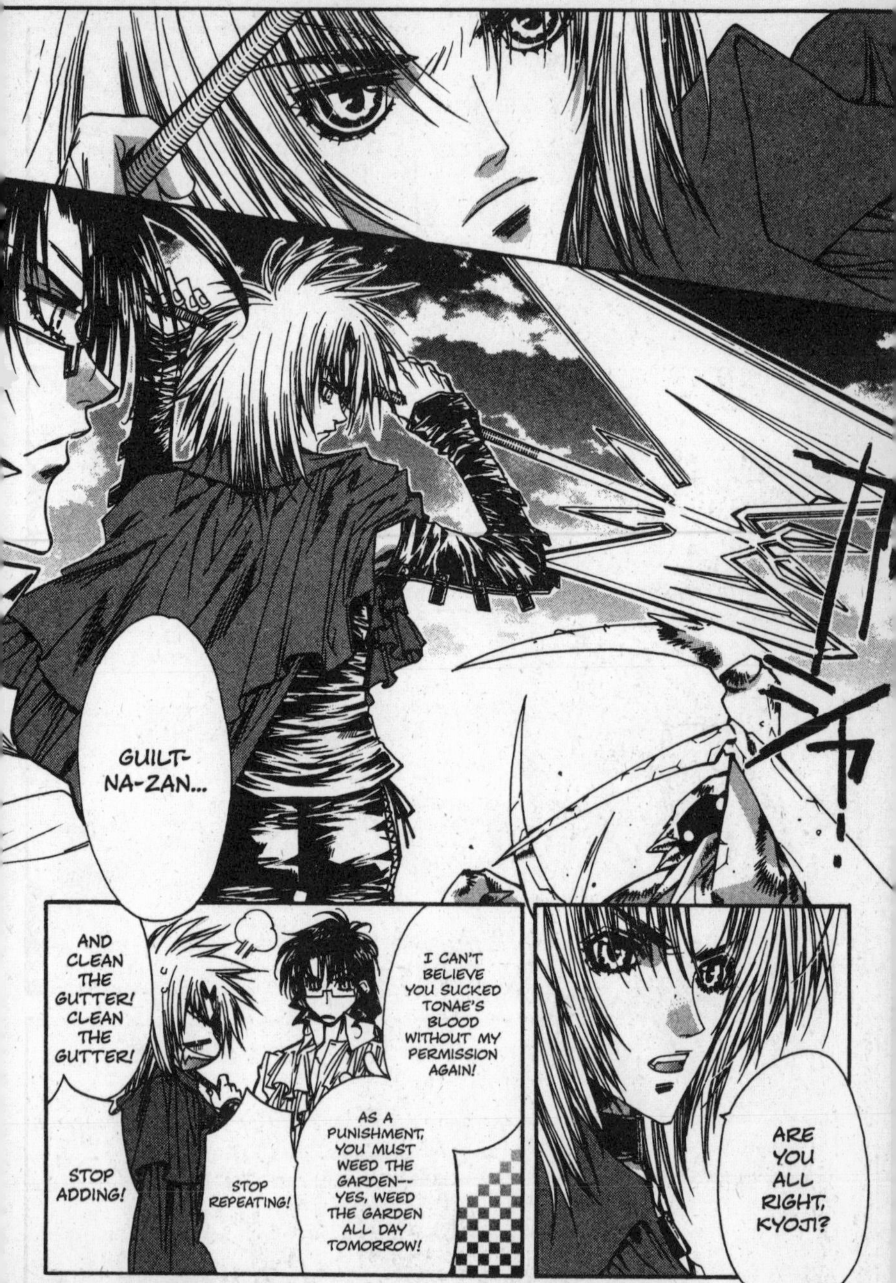
GUILT-NA-ZAN...
ARE YOU ALL RIGHT, KYOJI?
I CAN'T BELIEVE YOU SUCKED TONAE'S BLOOD WITHOUT MY PERMISSION AGAIN!
AS A PUNISHMENT, YOU MUST WEED THE GARDEN--YES, WEED THE GARDEN ALL DAY TOMORROW!
AND CLEAN THE GUTTER! CLEAN THE GUTTER!
STOP REPEATING!
STOP ADDING!

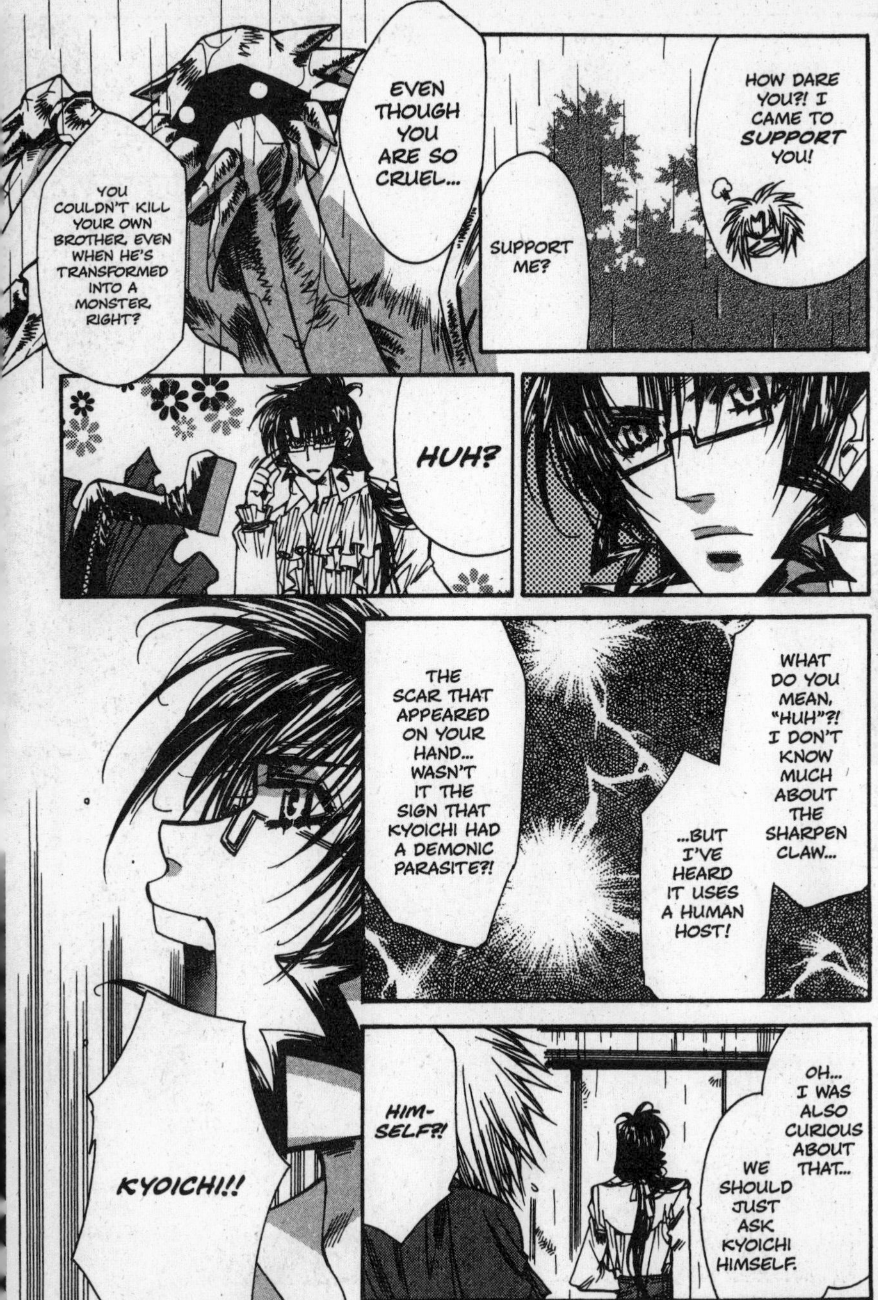
HOW DARE YOU?! I CAME TO SUPPORT YOU!
SUPPORT ME?
EVEN THOUGH YOU ARE SO CRUEL...
YOU COULDN'T KILL YOUR OWN BROTHER, EVEN WHEN HE'S TRANSFORMED INTO A MONSTER, RIGHT?
HUH?
WHAT DO YOU MEAN, "HUH"?! I DON'T KNOW MUCH ABOUT THE SHARPEN CLAW...
...BUT I'VE HEARD IT USES A HUMAN HOST!
THE SCAR THAT APPEARED ON YOUR HAND... WASN'T IT THE SIGN THAT KYOICHI HAD A DEMONIC PARASITE?!
OH... I WAS ALSO CURIOUS ABOUT THAT...
WE SHOULD JUST ASK KYOICHI HIMSELF.
HIM-SELF?!
KYOICHI!!

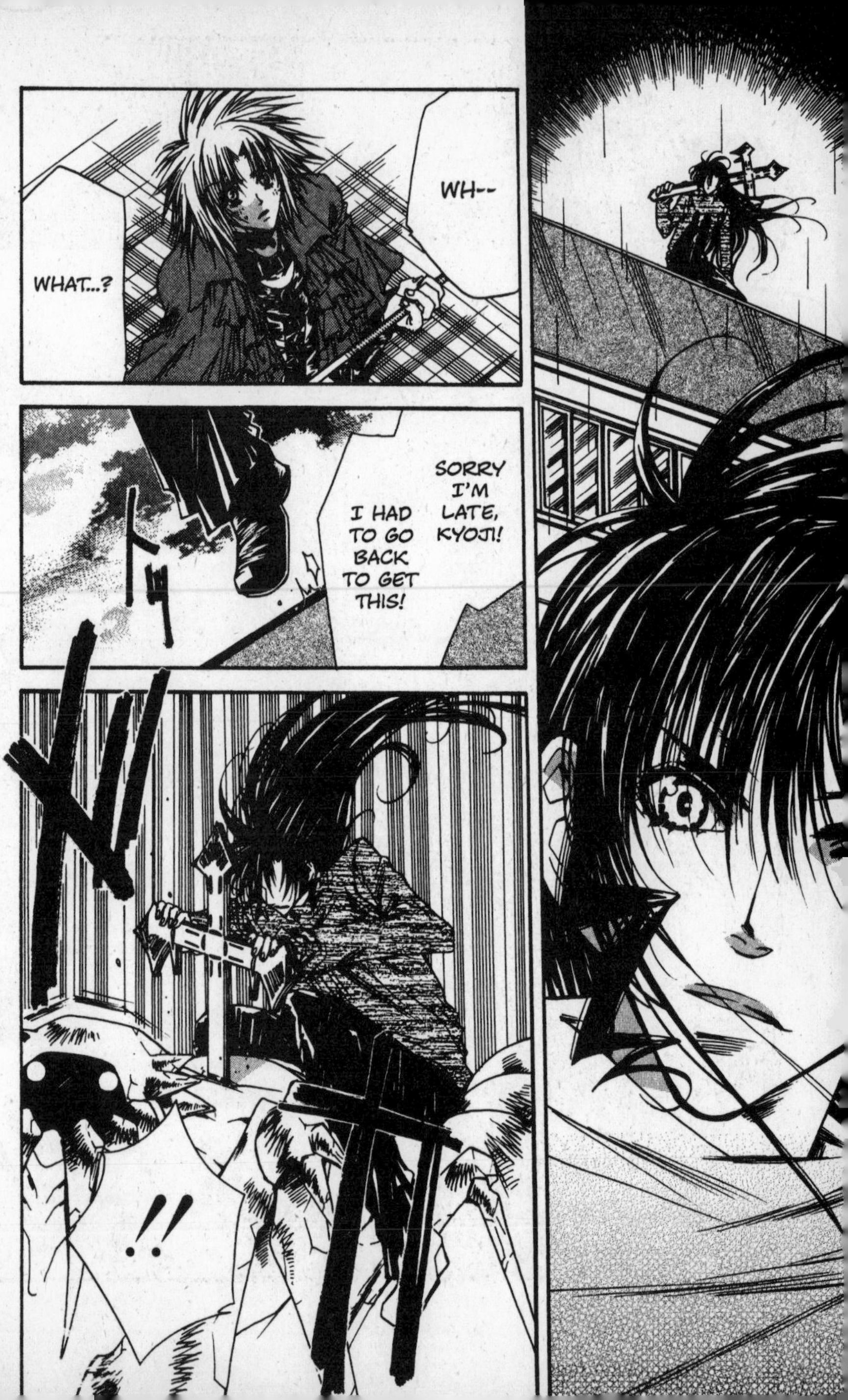
WH--
WHAT...?
SORRY I'M LATE, KYOJI!
I HAD TO GO BACK TO GET THIS!
!!

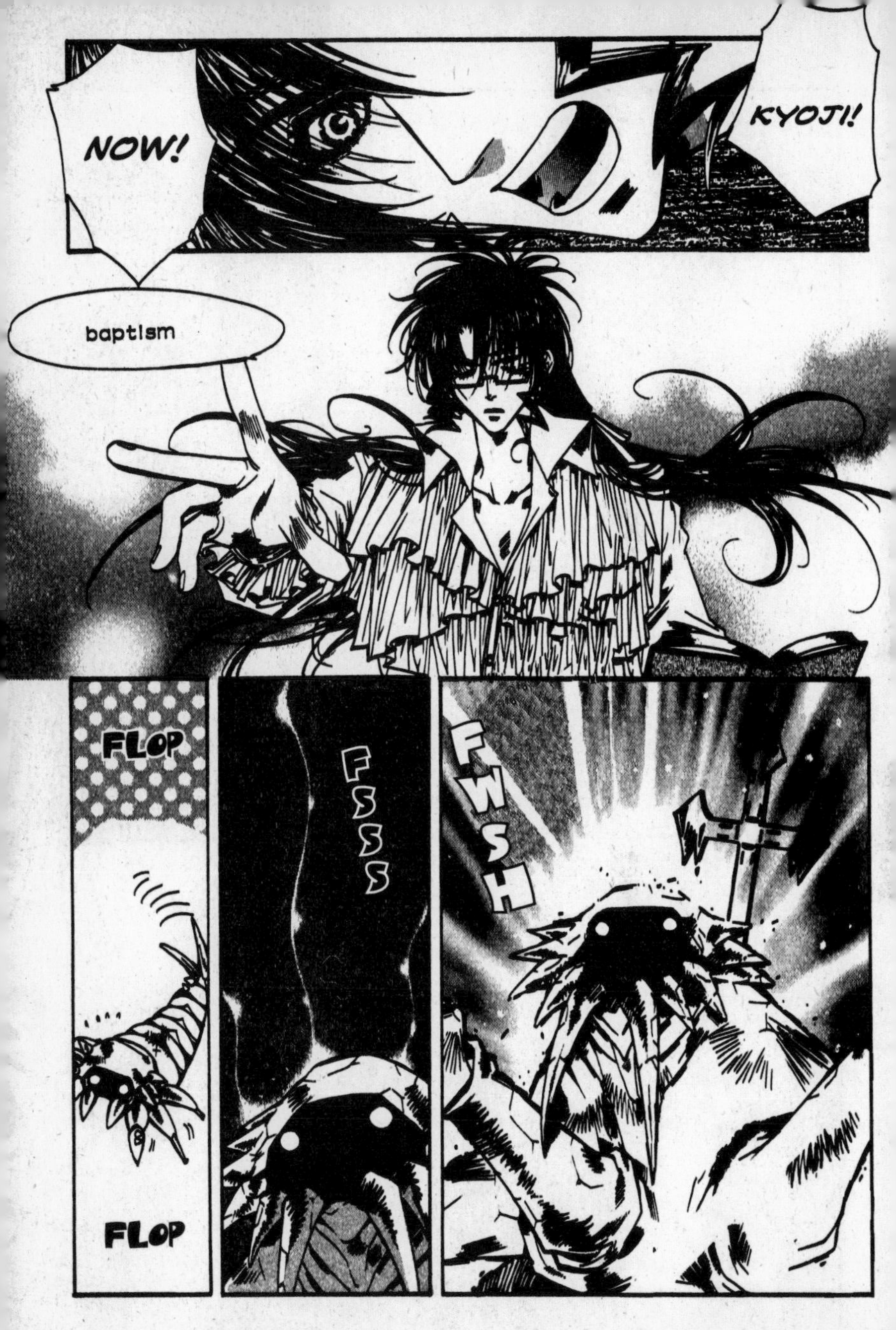
KYOJI!
NOW!
baptism
FWSH
FSSS
FLOP
FLOP

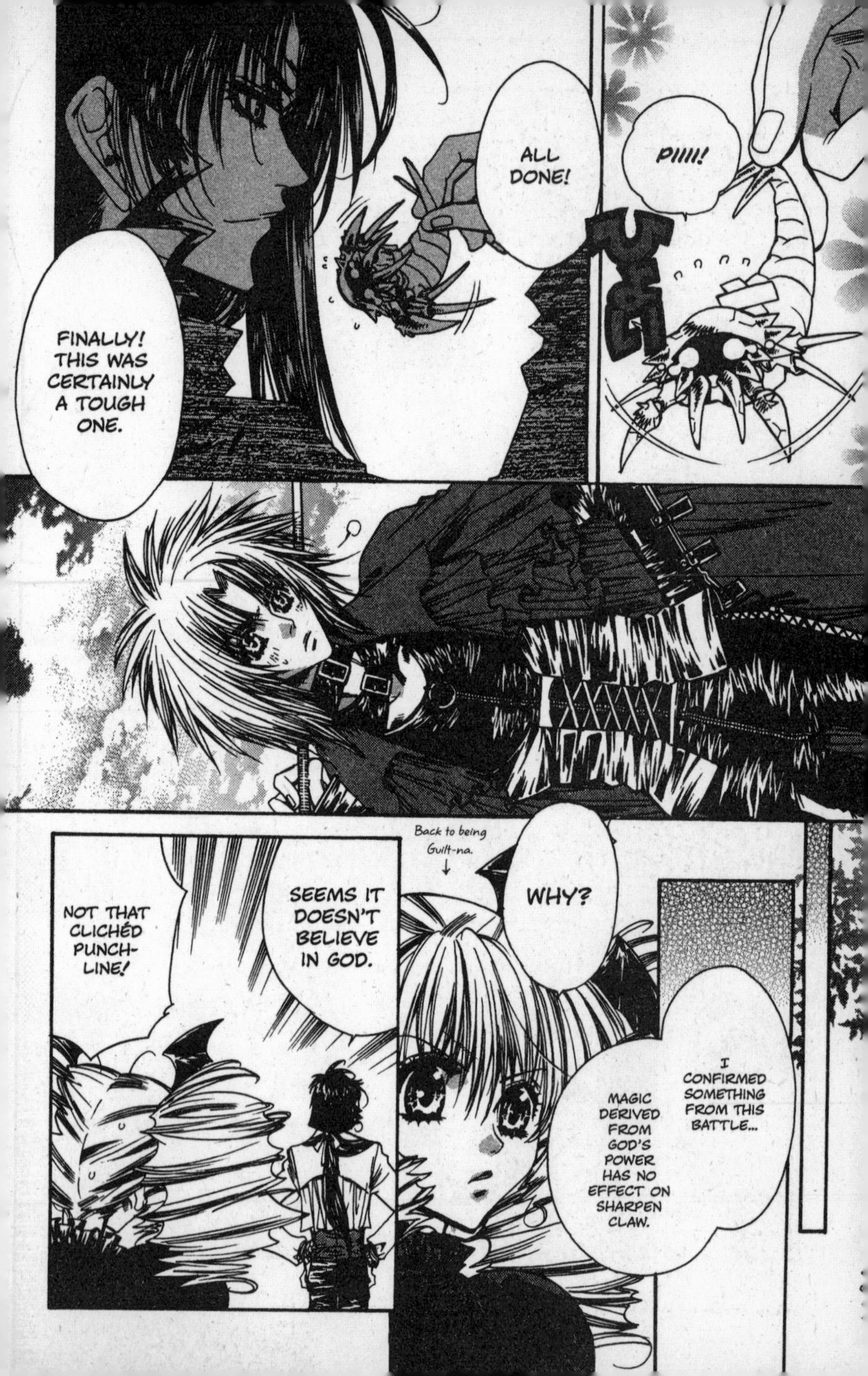
PIIII!
ALL DONE!
FINALLY! THIS WAS CERTAINLY A TOUGH ONE.
WHY?
Back to being Guilt-na.
I CONFIRMED SOMETHING FROM THIS BATTLE...
MAGIC DERIVED FROM GOD'S POWER HAS NO EFFECT ON SHARPEN CLAW.
SEEMS IT DOESN'T BELIEVE IN GOD.
NOT THAT CLICHÉD PUNCH-LINE!

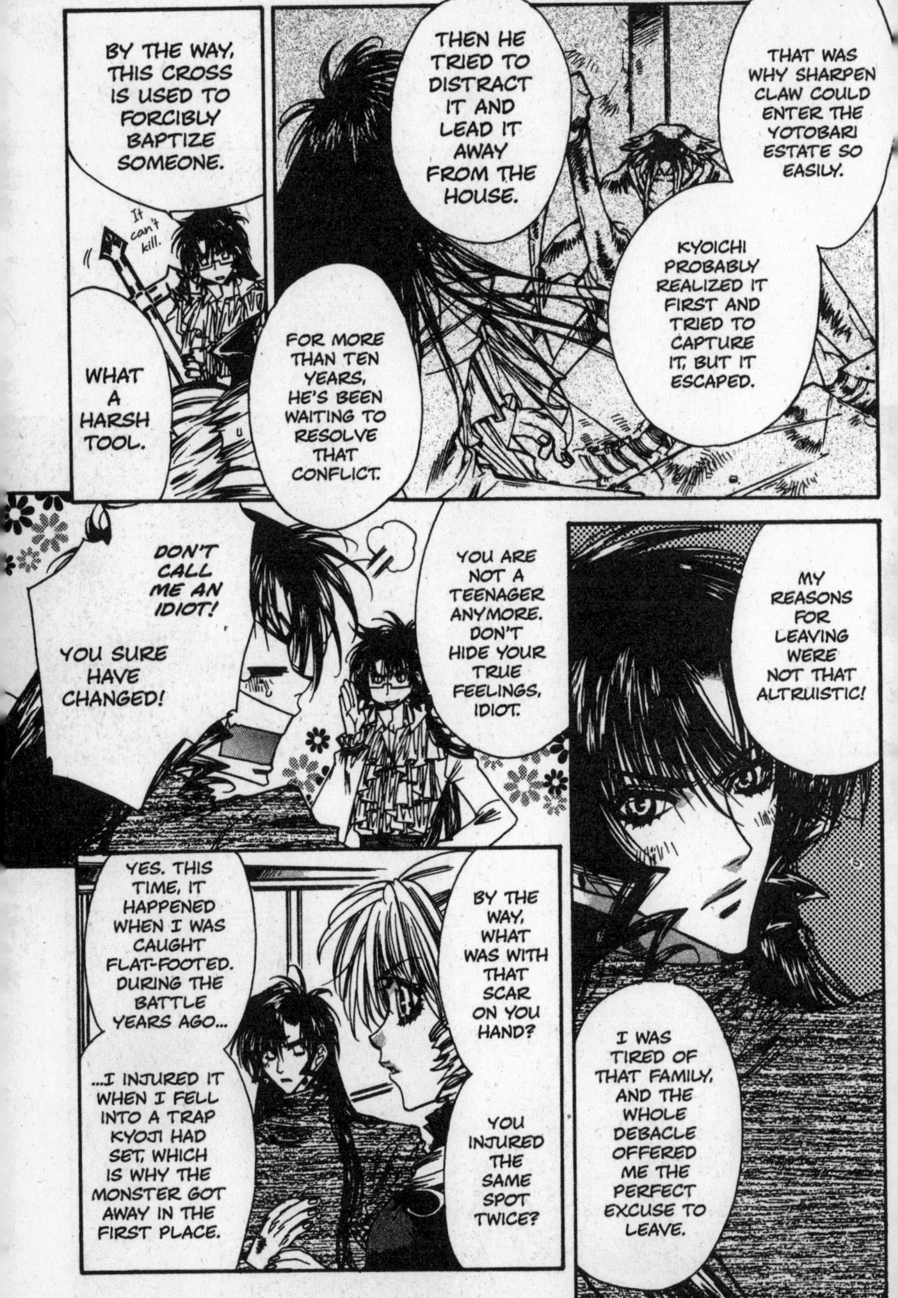
THAT WAS WHY SHARPEN CLAW COULD ENTER THE YOTOBARI ESTATE SO EASILY.
KYOICHI PROBABLY REALIZED IT FIRST AND TRIED TO CAPTURE IT, BUT IT ESCAPED.
THEN HE TRIED TO DISTRACT IT AND LEAD IT AWAY FROM THE HOUSE.
FOR MORE THAN TEN YEARS, HE'S BEEN WAITING TO RESOLVE THAT CONFLICT.
BY THE WAY, THIS CROSS IS USED TO FORCIBLY BAPTIZE SOMEONE.
It can't kill.
WHAT A HARSH TOOL.
MY REASONS FOR LEAVING WERE NOT THAT ALTRUISTIC!
I WAS TIRED OF THAT FAMILY, AND THE WHOLE DEBACLE OFFERED ME THE PERFECT EXCUSE TO LEAVE.
YOU ARE NOT A TEENAGER ANYMORE. DON'T HIDE YOUR TRUE FEELINGS, IDIOT.
DON'T CALL ME AN IDIOT!
YOU SURE HAVE CHANGED!
BY THE WAY, WHAT WAS WITH THAT SCAR ON YOU HAND?
YOU INJURED THE SAME SPOT TWICE?
YES. THIS TIME, IT HAPPENED WHEN I WAS CAUGHT FLAT-FOOTED. DURING THE BATTLE YEARS AGO...
...I INJURED IT WHEN I FELL INTO A TRAP KYOJI HAD SET, WHICH IS WHY THE MONSTER GOT AWAY IN THE FIRST PLACE.

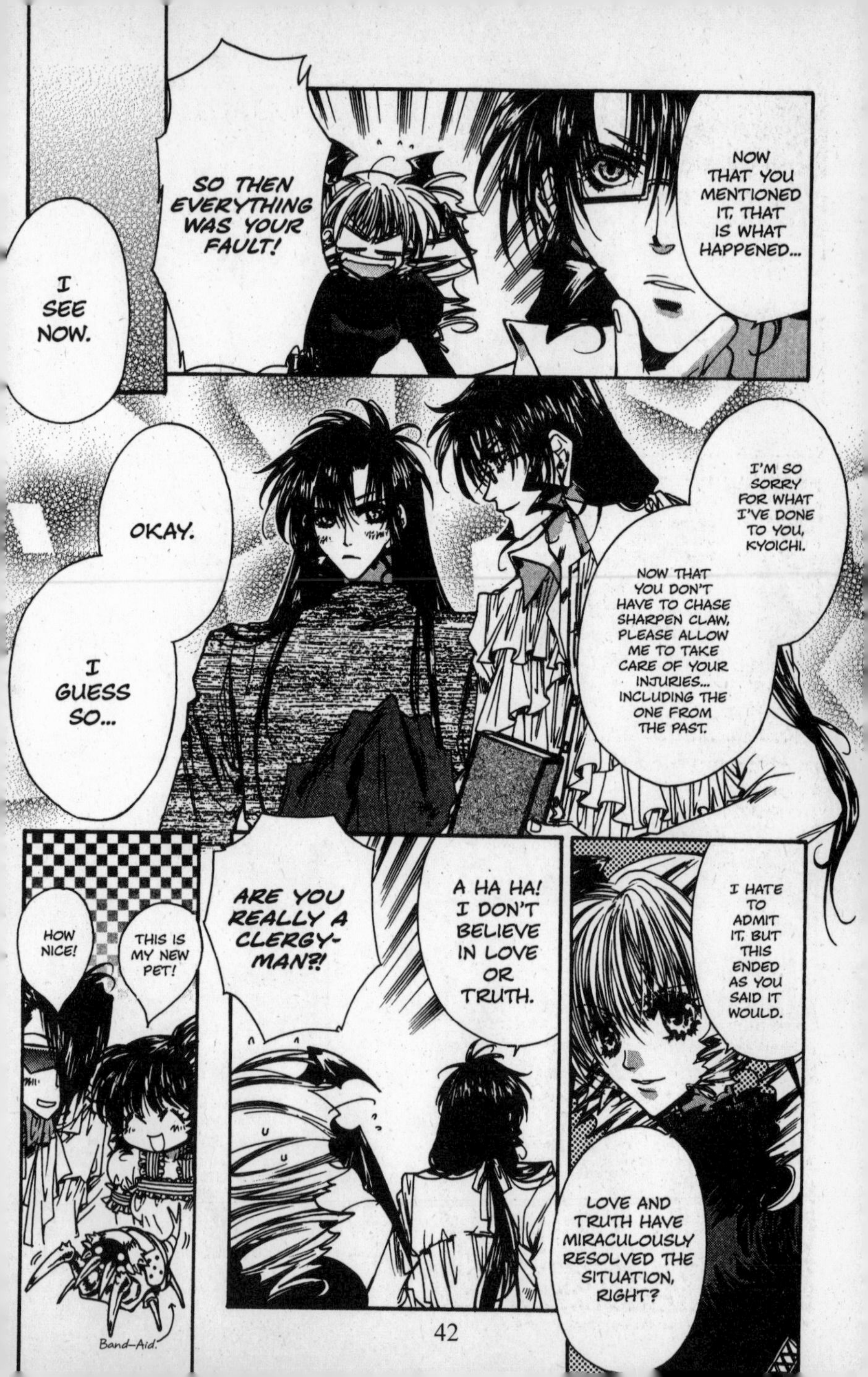
NOW THAT YOU MENTIONED IT, THAT IS WHAT HAPPENED...
SO THEN EVERYTHING WAS YOUR FAULT!
I SEE NOW.
I'M SO SORRY FOR WHAT I'VE DONE TO YOU, KYOICHI.
NOW THAT YOU DON'T HAVE TO CHASE SHARPEN CLAW, PLEASE ALLOW ME TO TAKE CARE OF YOUR INJURIES... INCLUDING THE ONE FROM THE PAST.
OKAY.
I GUESS SO...
I HATE TO ADMIT IT, BUT THIS ENDED AS YOU SAID IT WOULD.
LOVE AND TRUTH HAVE MIRACULOUSLY RESOLVED THE SITUATION, RIGHT?
A HA HA! I DON'T BELIEVE IN LOVE OR TRUTH.
ARE YOU REALLY A CLERGYMAN?!
THIS IS MY NEW PET!
HOW NICE!
Band-Aid.

Bonus Comic Strip

Vampire Doll Reflections

IT RAINS IN MY HEART AS IT RAINS ON THE TOWN

QUESTION: WHAT KIND OF MONSTER IS SHARPEN CLAW?
CLICK CLICK CLICK
SKRSH SKRSH
Hello.
SHARP PENCIL...
...CLAW!
I SEE!!
YOUR NEMESIS WAS A MECHANICAL PENCIL?

*"SHA-PEN" IS A TERM USED FOR "MECHANICAL PENCIL" IN JAPANESE.

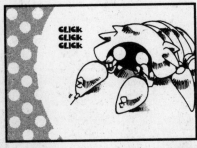

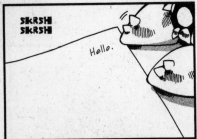

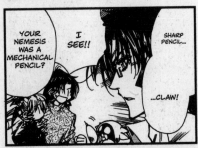

夜帳響壱

Kyoichi Yotobari
male
tribe: human
attribute: evil
job: evil magician
height: 184
eyes: ash gray
hair: black

The Yotobari brothers attack!
What do you do?

夜帳響司

Kyoji Yotobari
male
tribe: human
attribute: neutral
job: holy orders
height: 184
eyes: silver gray
hair: black

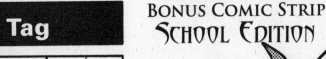

BONUS COMIC STRIP
SCHOOL EDITION

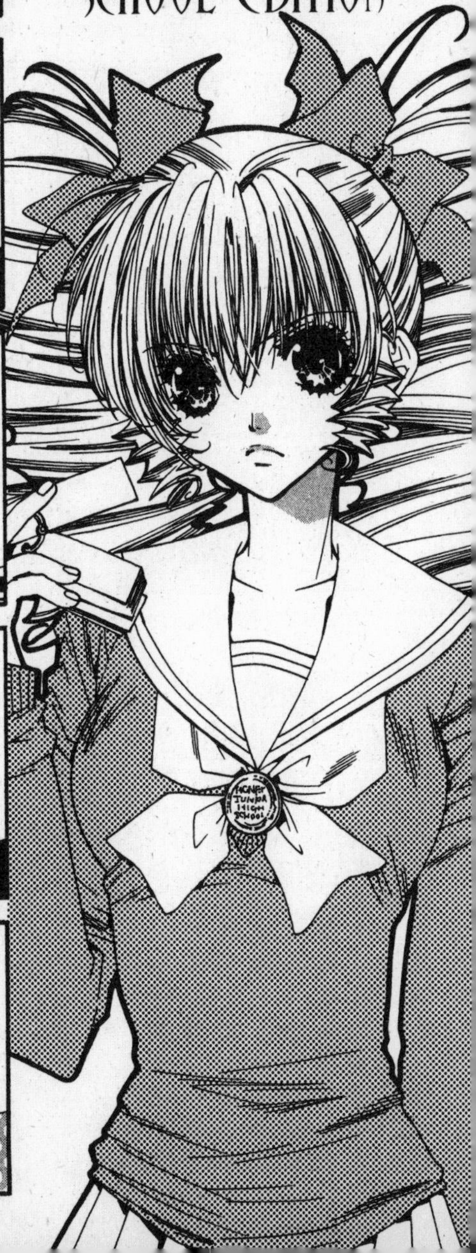

Tag

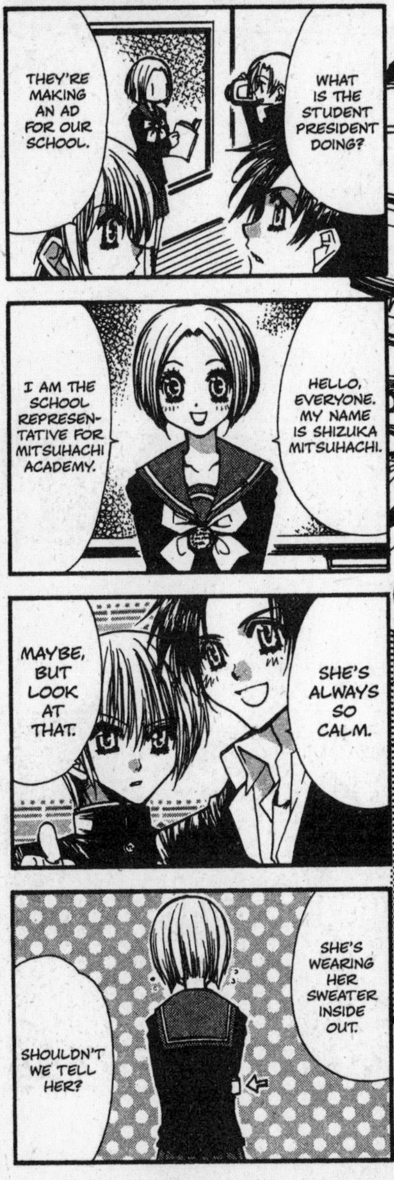
WHAT IS THE STUDENT PRESIDENT DOING?
THEY'RE MAKING AN AD FOR OUR SCHOOL.
HELLO, EVERYONE. MY NAME IS SHIZUKA MITSUHACHI.
I AM THE SCHOOL REPRESENTATIVE FOR MITSUHACHI ACADEMY.
SHE'S ALWAYS SO CALM.
MAYBE, BUT LOOK AT THAT.
SHE'S WEARING HER SWEATER INSIDE OUT.
SHOULDN'T WE TELL HER?

Tension

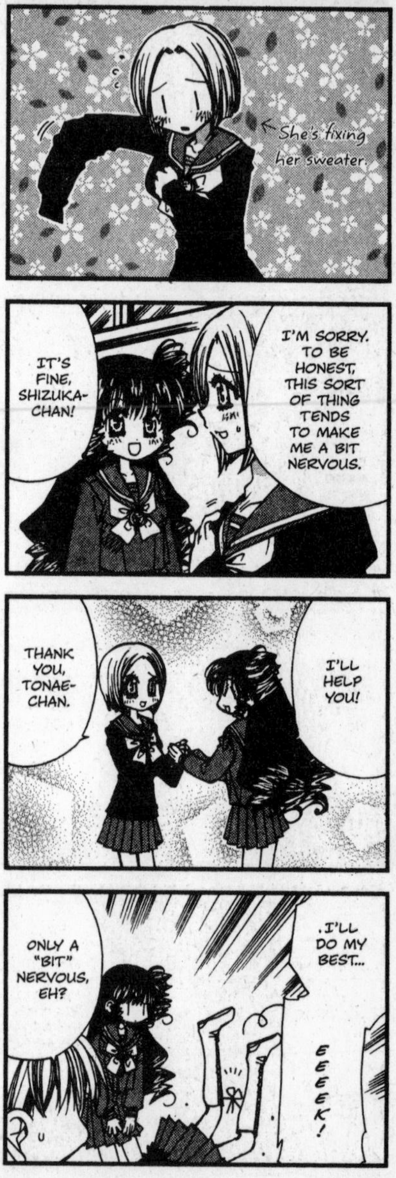
She's fixing her sweater.
I'M SORRY. TO BE HONEST, THIS SORT OF THING TENDS TO MAKE ME A BIT NERVOUS.
IT'S FINE, SHIZUKA-CHAN!
I'LL HELP YOU!
THANK YOU, TONAE-CHAN.
.I'LL DO MY BEST...
EEEEK!
ONLY A "BIT" NERVOUS, EH?

R

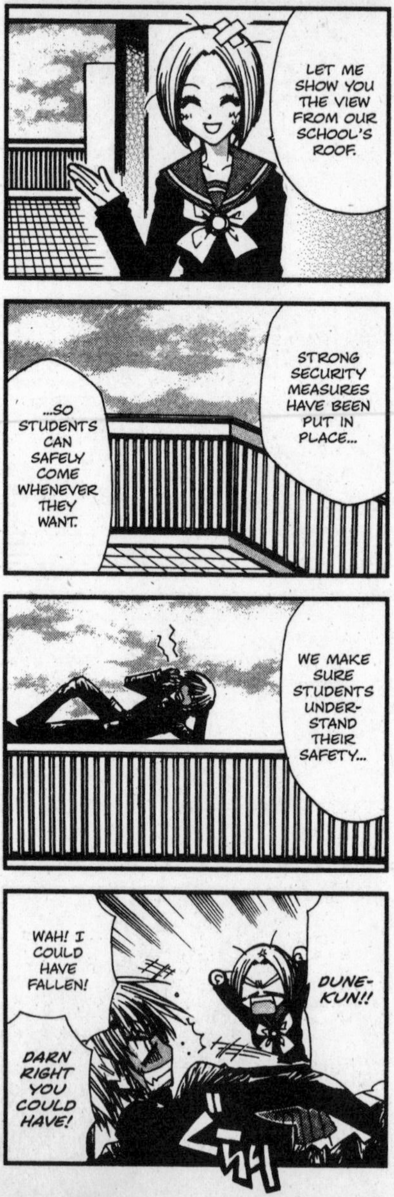
LET ME SHOW YOU THE VIEW FROM OUR SCHOOL'S ROOF.
STRONG SECURITY MEASURES HAVE BEEN PUT IN PLACE...
...SO STUDENTS CAN SAFELY COME WHENEVER THEY WANT.
WE MAKE SURE STUDENTS UNDER-STAND THEIR SAFETY...
DUNE-KUN!!
WAH! I COULD HAVE FALLEN!
DARN RIGHT YOU COULD HAVE!

Maze

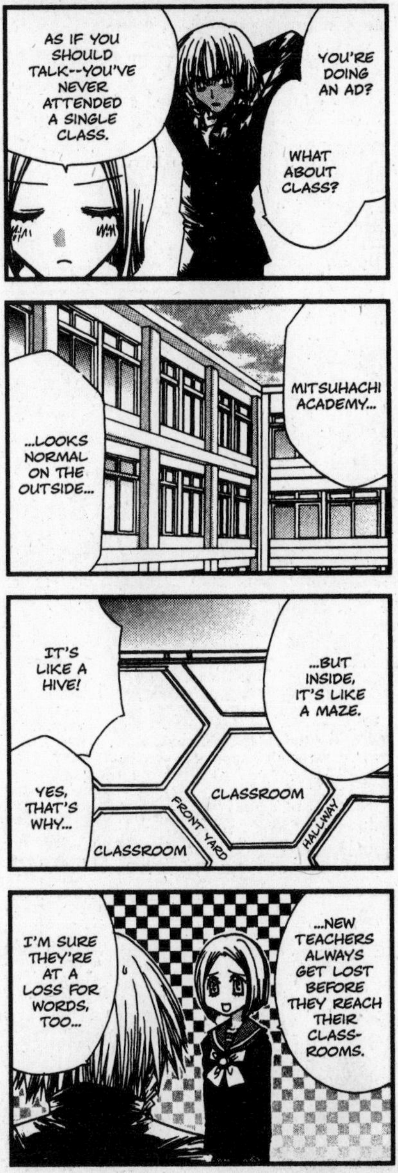
YOU'RE DOING AN AD?
WHAT ABOUT CLASS?
AS IF YOU SHOULD TALK--YOU'VE NEVER ATTENDED A SINGLE CLASS.
MITSUHACHI ACADEMY...
...LOOKS NORMAL ON THE OUTSIDE...
...BUT INSIDE, IT'S LIKE A MAZE.
IT'S LIKE A HIVE!
CLASSROOM
HALLWAY
FRONT YARD
YES, THAT'S WHY...
CLASSROOM
...NEW TEACHERS ALWAYS GET LOST BEFORE THEY REACH THEIR CLASS-ROOMS.
I'M SURE THEY'RE AT A LOSS FOR WORDS, TOO...

Yotobari Brand

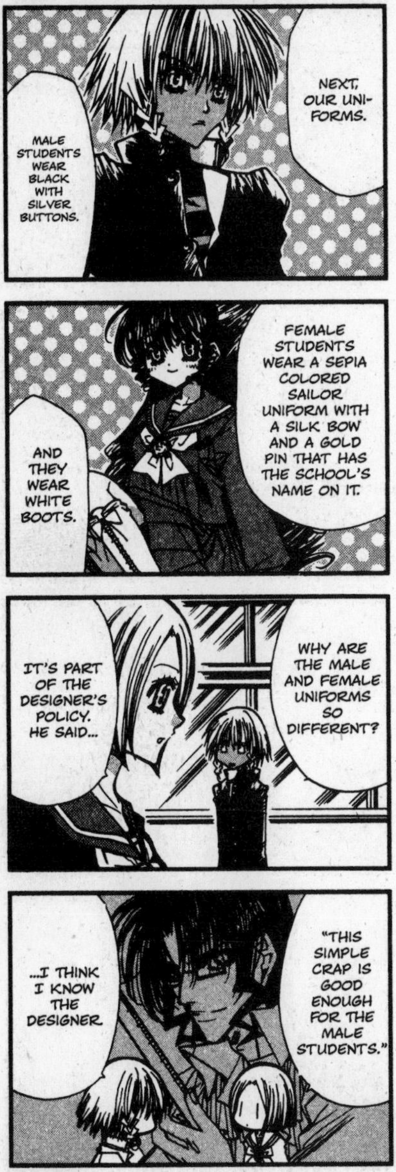
NEXT, OUR UNI-FORMS.
MALE STUDENTS WEAR BLACK WITH SILVER BUTTONS.
FEMALE STUDENTS WEAR A SEPIA COLORED SAILOR UNIFORM WITH A SILK BOW AND A GOLD PIN THAT HAS THE SCHOOL'S NAME ON IT.
AND THEY WEAR WHITE BOOTS.
WHY ARE THE MALE AND FEMALE UNIFORMS SO DIFFERENT?
IT'S PART OF THE DESIGNER'S POLICY. HE SAID...
"THIS SIMPLE CRAP IS GOOD ENOUGH FOR THE MALE STUDENTS."
...I THINK I KNOW THE DESIGNER.

Again

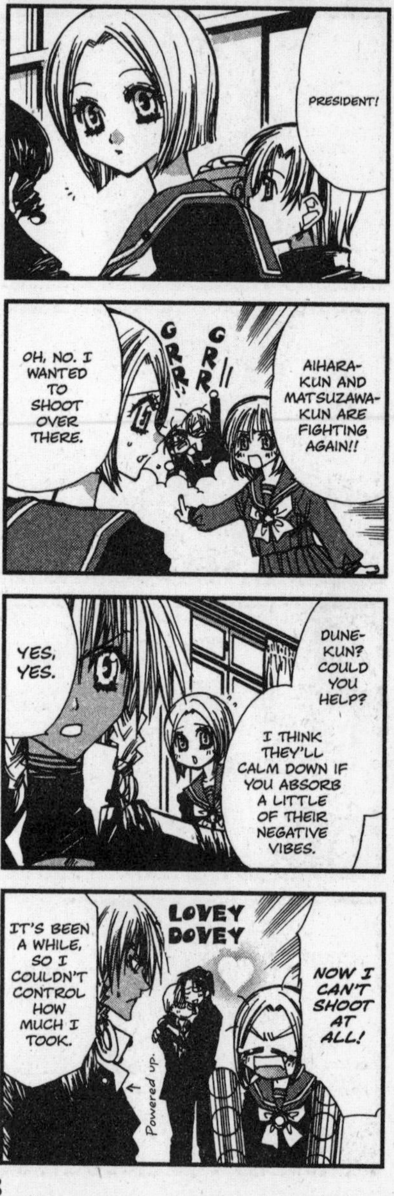
PRESIDENT!
AIHARA-KUN AND MATSUZAWA-KUN ARE FIGHTING AGAIN!!
GRR
GRR
OH, NO. I WANTED TO SHOOT OVER THERE.
DUNE-KUN? COULD YOU HELP?
I THINK THEY'LL CALM DOWN IF YOU ABSORB A LITTLE OF THEIR NEGATIVE VIBES.
YES, YES.
NOW I CAN'T SHOOT AT ALL!
LOVEY DOVEY
IT'S BEEN A WHILE, SO I COULDN'T CONTROL HOW MUCH I TOOK.
Powered up.

Opportunity

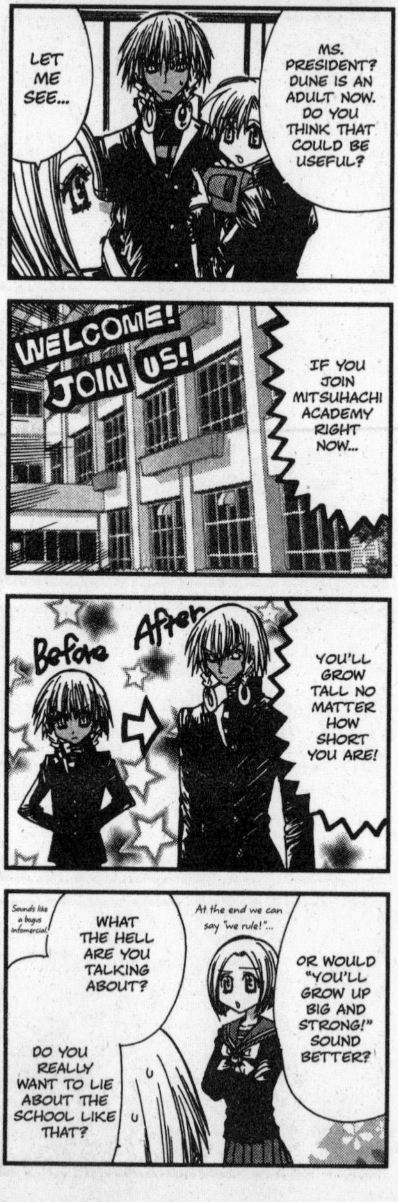
MS. PRESIDENT? DUNE IS AN ADULT NOW. DO YOU THINK THAT COULD BE USEFUL?
LET ME SEE...
IF YOU JOIN MITSUHACHI ACADEMY RIGHT NOW...
WELCOME! JOIN US!
YOU'LL GROW TALL NO MATTER HOW SHORT YOU ARE!
After
Before
OR WOULD "YOU'LL GROW UP BIG AND STRONG!" SOUND BETTER?
At the end we can say "we rule!"...
WHAT THE HELL ARE YOU TALKING ABOUT?
Sounds like a bogus infomercial!
DO YOU REALLY WANT TO LIE ABOUT THE SCHOOL LIKE THAT?

Restoration

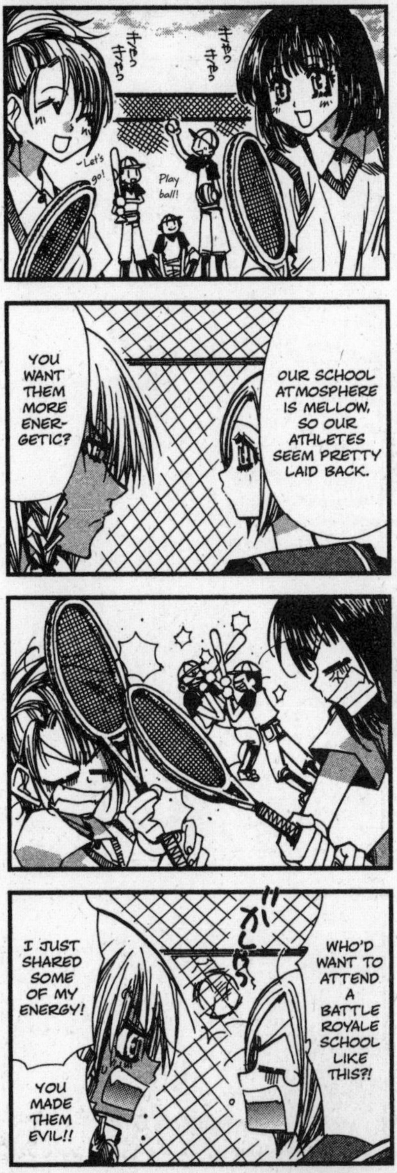

きゃっ きゃっ
きゃっ きゃっ
Play ball!
Let's go!
OUR SCHOOL ATMOSPHERE IS MELLOW, SO OUR ATHLETES SEEM PRETTY LAID BACK.
YOU WANT THEM MORE ENER-GETIC?
WHO'D WANT TO ATTEND A BATTLE ROYALE SCHOOL LIKE THIS?!
がしゃ
I JUST SHARED SOME OF MY ENERGY!
YOU MADE THEM EVIL!!

Arriving at the Holy Land

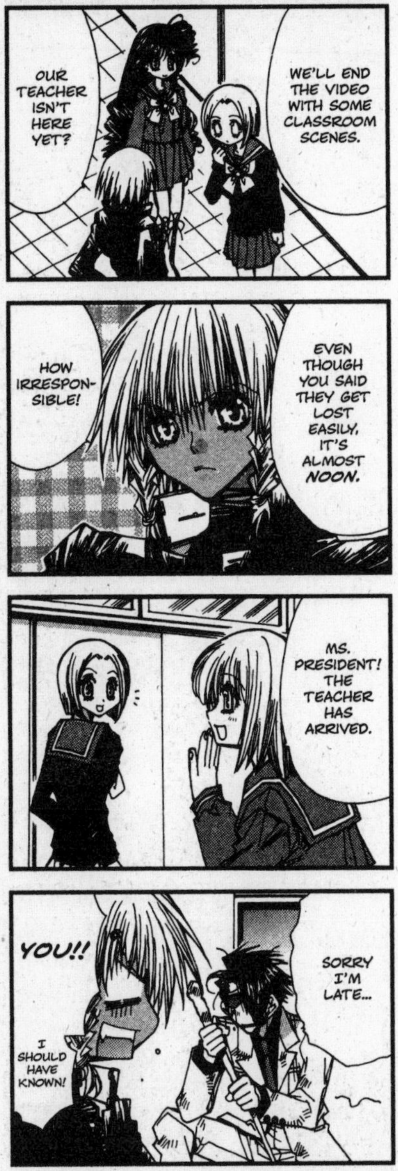

WE'LL END THE VIDEO WITH SOME CLASSROOM SCENES.
OUR TEACHER ISN'T HERE YET?
EVEN THOUGH YOU SAID THEY GET LOST EASILY, IT'S ALMOST *NOON*.
HOW IRRESPON-SIBLE!
MS. PRESIDENT! THE TEACHER HAS ARRIVED.
SORRY I'M LATE...
YOU!!
I SHOULD HAVE KNOWN!

Only One Page Left

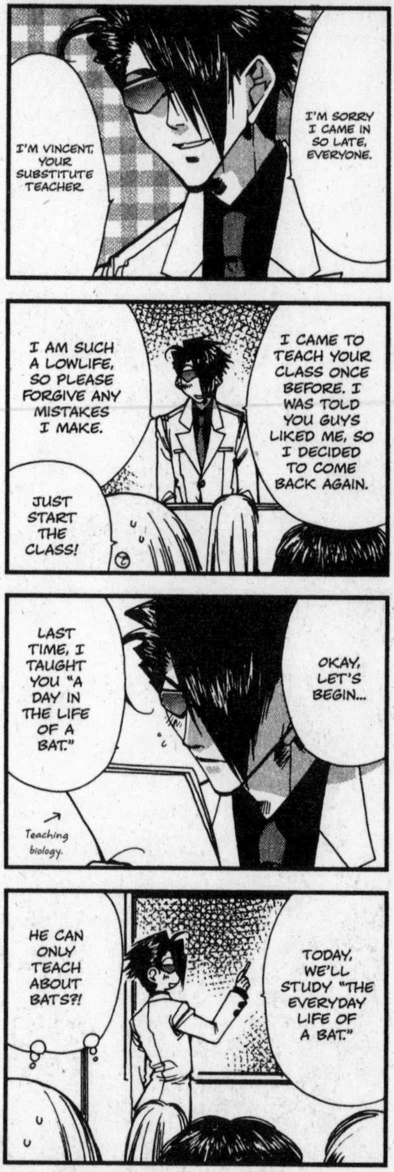
I'M SORRY I CAME IN SO LATE, EVERYONE.
I'M VINCENT, YOUR SUBSTITUTE TEACHER
I CAME TO TEACH YOUR CLASS ONCE BEFORE. I WAS TOLD YOU GUYS LIKED ME, SO I DECIDED TO COME BACK AGAIN.
I AM SUCH A LOWLIFE, SO PLEASE FORGIVE ANY MISTAKES I MAKE.
JUST START THE CLASS!
OKAY, LET'S BEGIN...
LAST TIME, I TAUGHT YOU "A DAY IN THE LIFE OF A BAT."
Teaching biology.
TODAY, WE'LL STUDY "THE EVERYDAY LIFE OF A BAT."
HE CAN ONLY TEACH ABOUT BATS?!

Only Half A Page Left

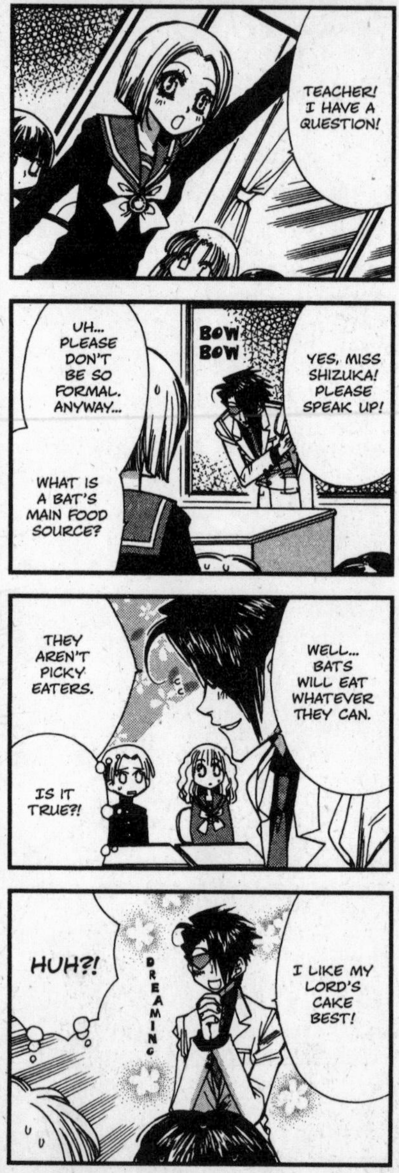
TEACHER! I HAVE A QUESTION!
YES, MISS SHIZUKA! PLEASE SPEAK UP!
BOW BOW
UH... PLEASE DON'T BE SO FORMAL. ANYWAY...
WHAT IS A BAT'S MAIN FOOD SOURCE?
WELL... BATS WILL EAT WHATEVER THEY CAN.
THEY AREN'T PICKY EATERS.
IS IT TRUE?!
I LIKE MY LORD'S CAKE BEST!
DREAMING
HUH?!

♯9 DOLCE

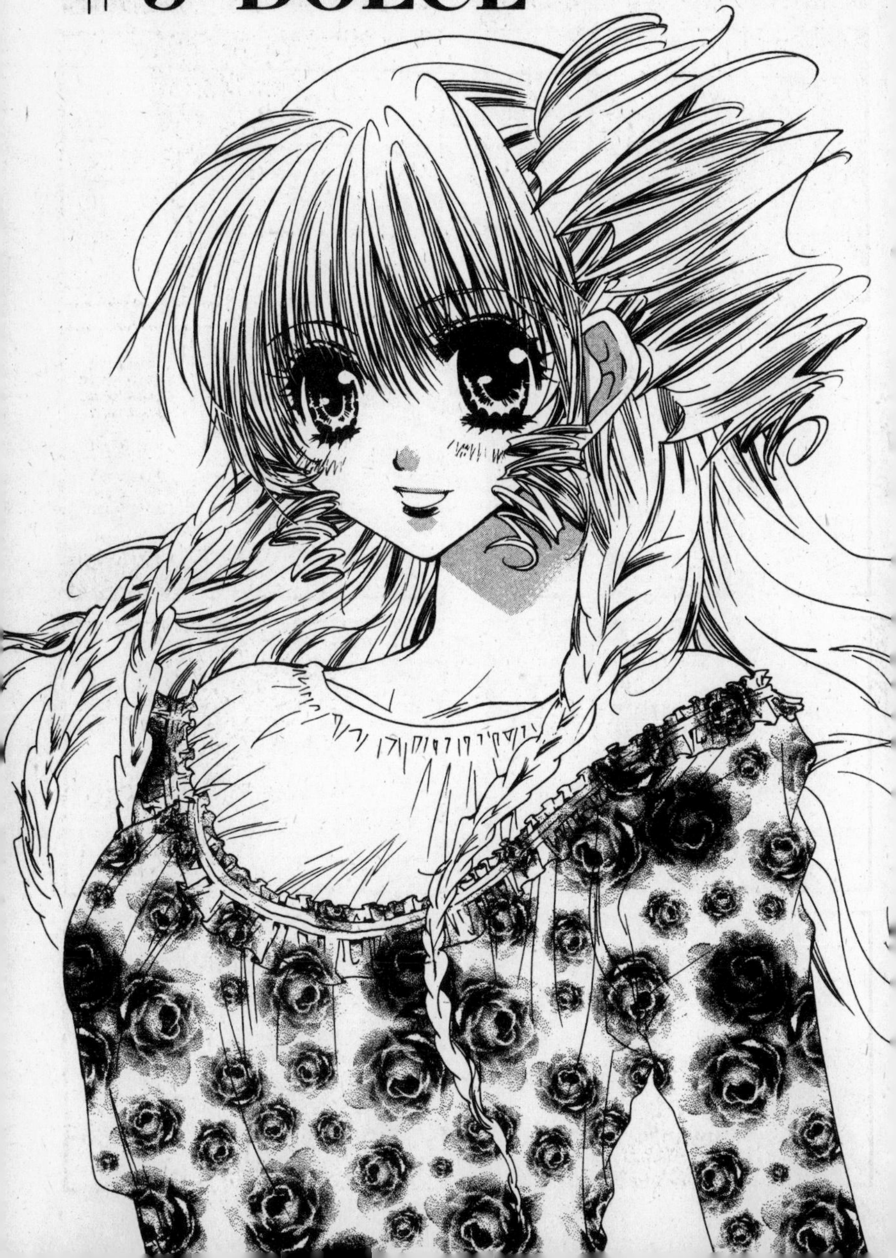

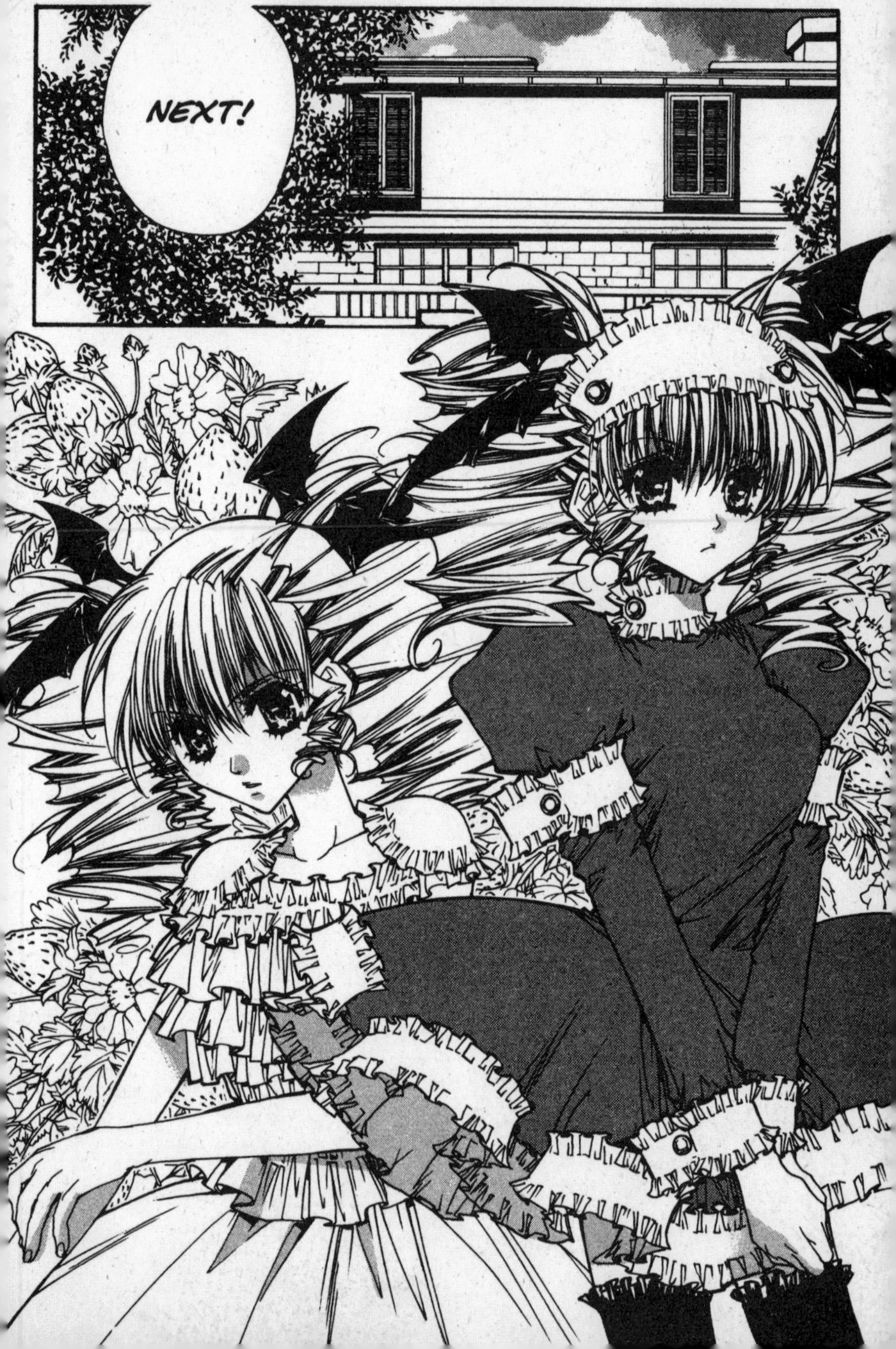
NEXT!

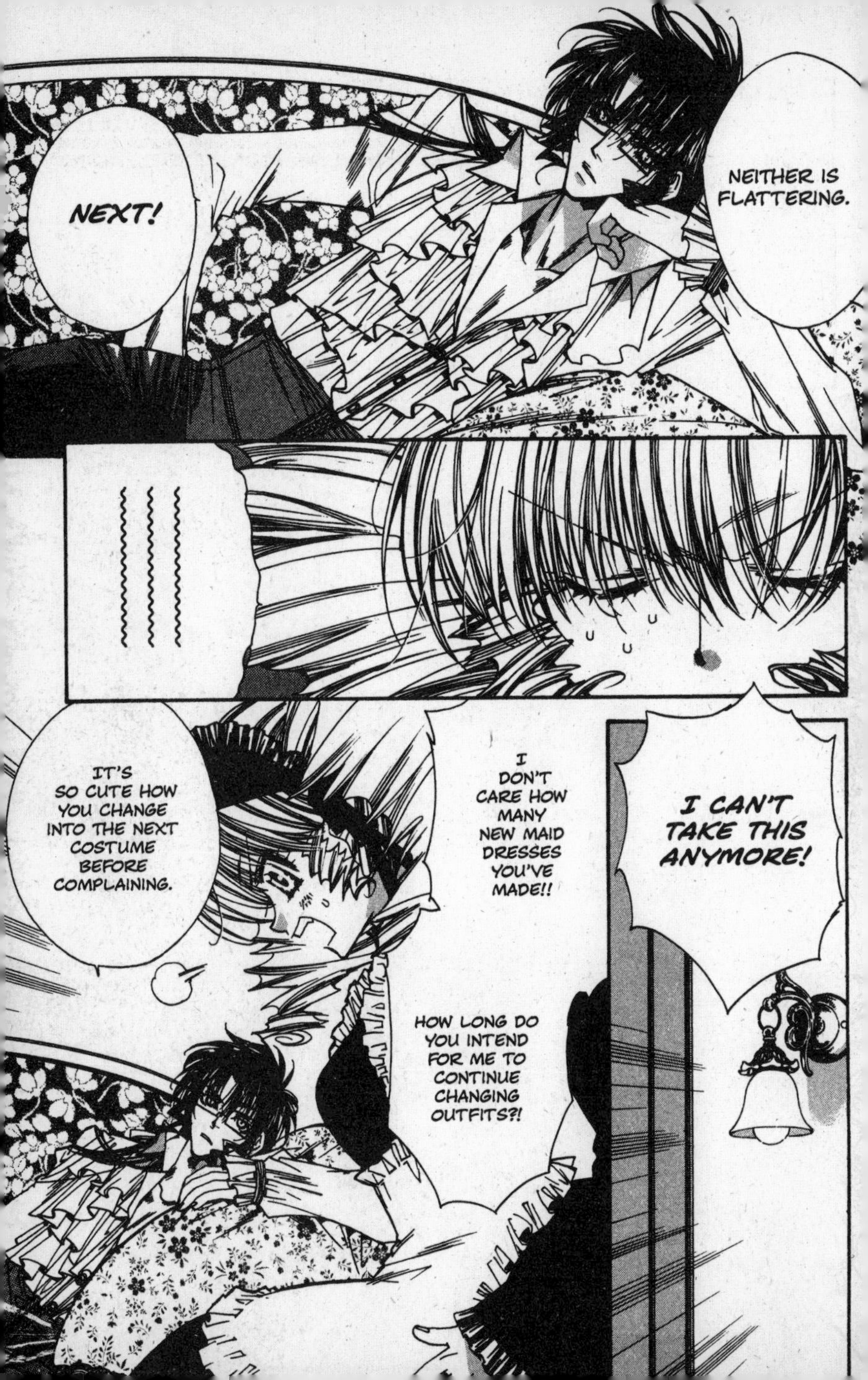
NEITHER IS FLATTERING.
NEXT!
I CAN'T TAKE THIS ANYMORE!
I DON'T CARE HOW MANY NEW MAID DRESSES YOU'VE MADE!!
HOW LONG DO YOU INTEND FOR ME TO CONTINUE CHANGING OUTFITS?!
IT'S SO CUTE HOW YOU CHANGE INTO THE NEXT COSTUME BEFORE COMPLAINING.

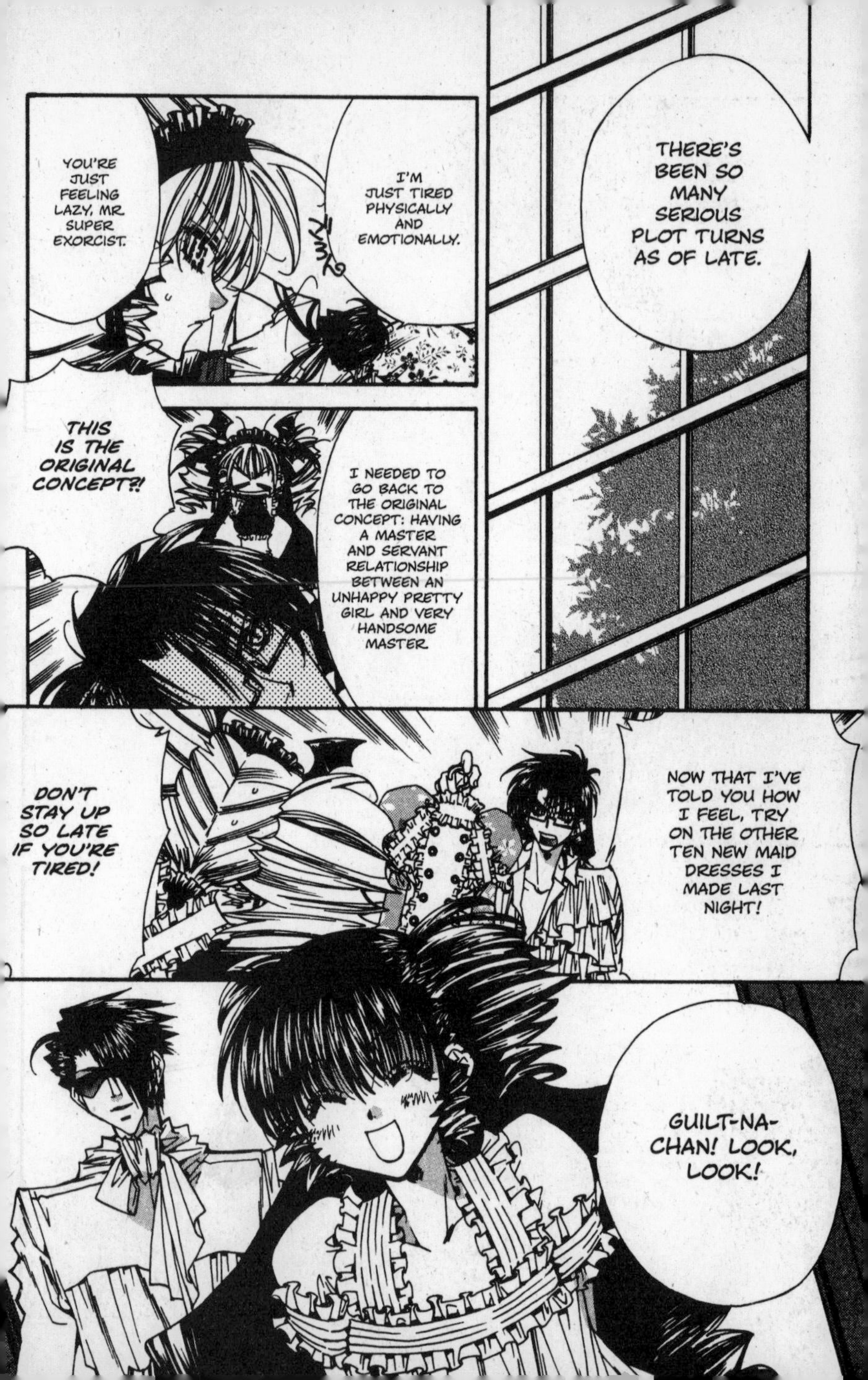
THERE'S BEEN SO MANY SERIOUS PLOT TURNS AS OF LATE.
I'M JUST TIRED PHYSICALLY AND EMOTIONALLY.
YOU'RE JUST FEELING LAZY, MR SUPER EXORCIST.
I NEEDED TO GO BACK TO THE ORIGINAL CONCEPT: HAVING A MASTER AND SERVANT RELATIONSHIP BETWEEN AN UNHAPPY PRETTY GIRL AND VERY HANDSOME MASTER
THIS IS THE ORIGINAL CONCEPT?!
NOW THAT I'VE TOLD YOU HOW I FEEL, TRY ON THE OTHER TEN NEW MAID DRESSES I MADE LAST NIGHT!
DON'T STAY UP SO LATE IF YOU'RE TIRED!
GUILT-NA-CHAN! LOOK, LOOK!

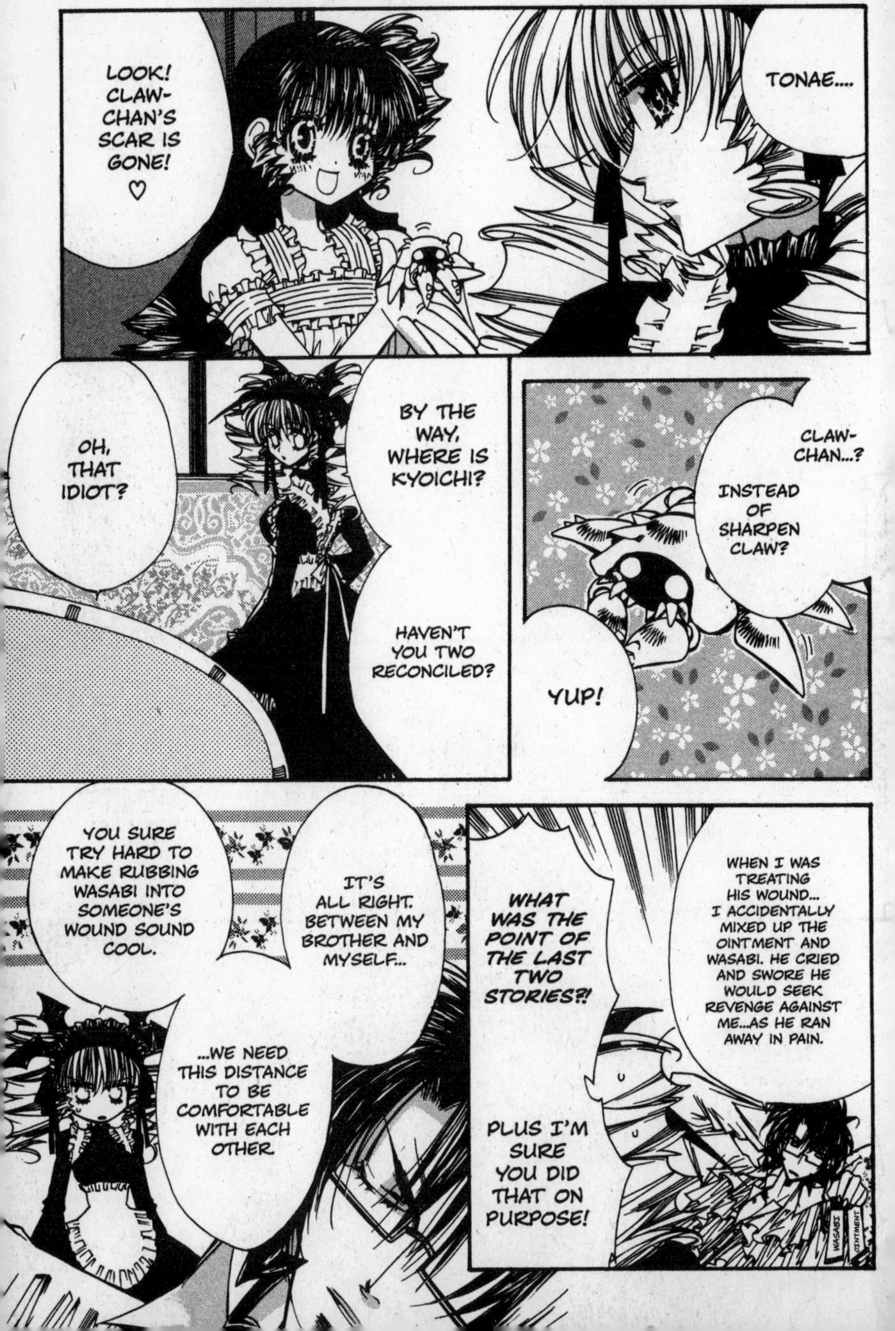
TONAE....
LOOK! CLAW-CHAN'S SCAR IS GONE! ♡
BY THE WAY, WHERE IS KYOICHI?
OH, THAT IDIOT?
HAVEN'T YOU TWO RECONCILED?
CLAW-CHAN...?
INSTEAD OF SHARPEN CLAW?
YUP!
WHEN I WAS TREATING HIS WOUND... I ACCIDENTALLY MIXED UP THE OINTMENT AND WASABI. HE CRIED AND SWORE HE WOULD SEEK REVENGE AGAINST ME...AS HE RAN AWAY IN PAIN.
WHAT WAS THE POINT OF THE LAST TWO STORIES?!
PLUS I'M SURE YOU DID THAT ON PURPOSE!
WASABI
OINTMENT
IT'S ALL RIGHT. BETWEEN MY BROTHER AND MYSELF...
...WE NEED THIS DISTANCE TO BE COMFORTABLE WITH EACH OTHER
YOU SURE TRY HARD TO MAKE RUBBING WASABI INTO SOMEONE'S WOUND SOUND COOL.

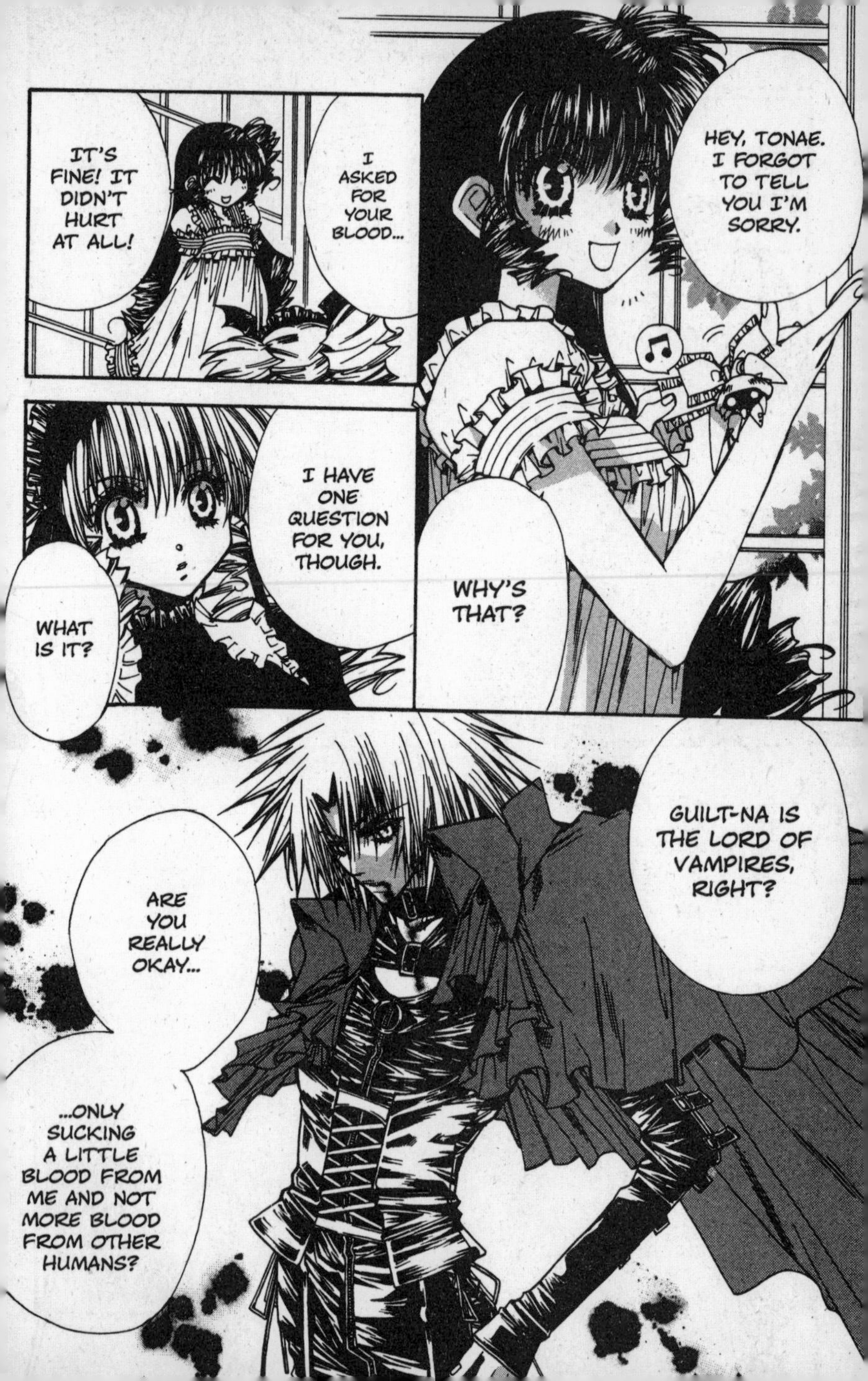
HEY, TONAE. I FORGOT TO TELL YOU I'M SORRY.
WHY'S THAT?
I ASKED FOR YOUR BLOOD...
IT'S FINE! IT DIDN'T HURT AT ALL!
I HAVE ONE QUESTION FOR YOU, THOUGH.
WHAT IS IT?
GUILT-NA IS THE LORD OF VAMPIRES, RIGHT?
ARE YOU REALLY OKAY...
...ONLY SUCKING A LITTLE BLOOD FROM ME AND NOT MORE BLOOD FROM OTHER HUMANS?

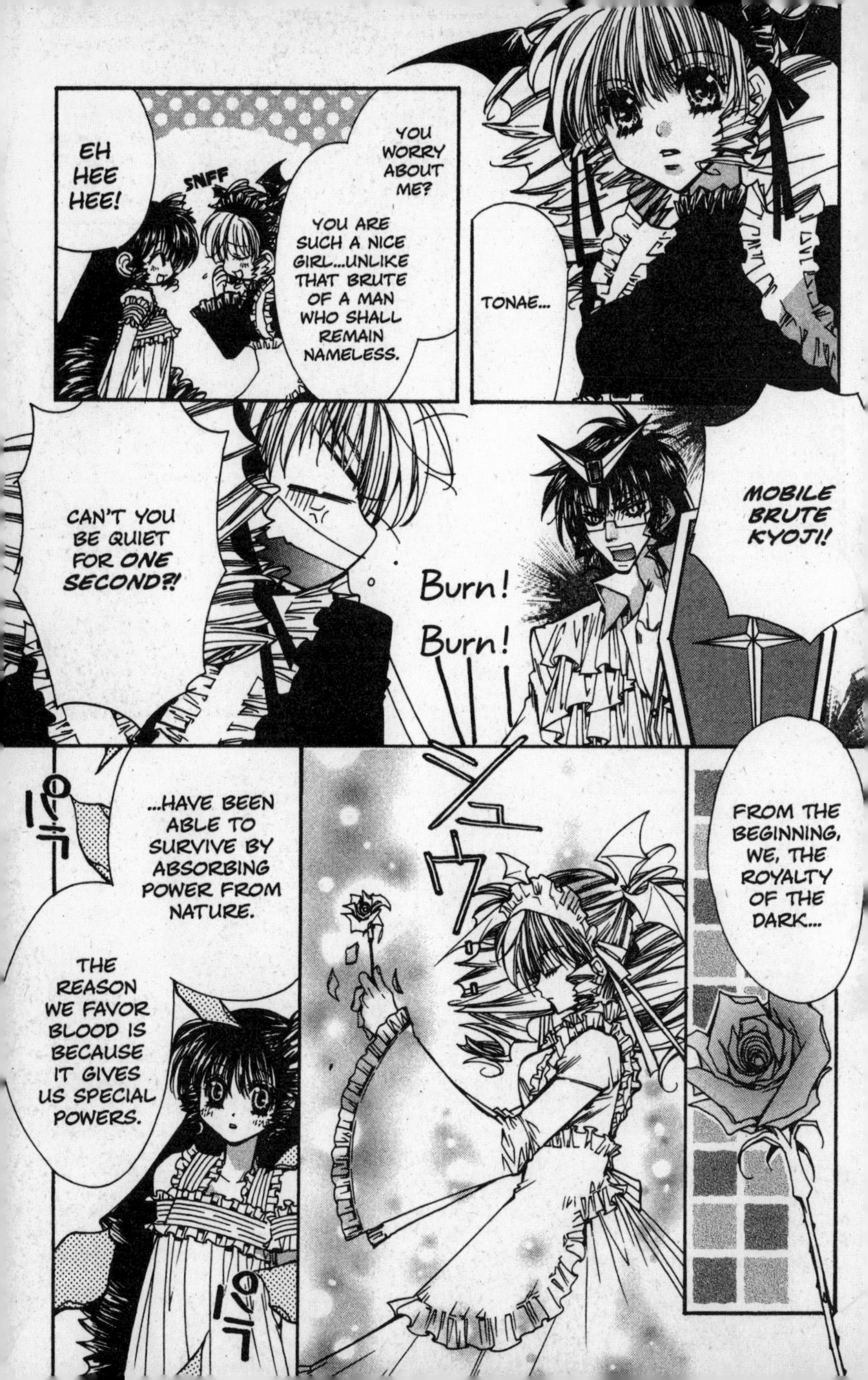
TONAE...
YOU WORRY ABOUT ME?
YOU ARE SUCH A NICE GIRL...UNLIKE THAT BRUTE OF A MAN WHO SHALL REMAIN NAMELESS.
SNFF
EH HEE HEE!
MOBILE BRUTE KYOJI!
Burn! Burn!
CAN'T YOU BE QUIET FOR ONE SECOND?!
FROM THE BEGINNING, WE, THE ROYALTY OF THE DARK...
...HAVE BEEN ABLE TO SURVIVE BY ABSORBING POWER FROM NATURE.
THE REASON WE FAVOR BLOOD IS BECAUSE IT GIVES US SPECIAL POWERS.

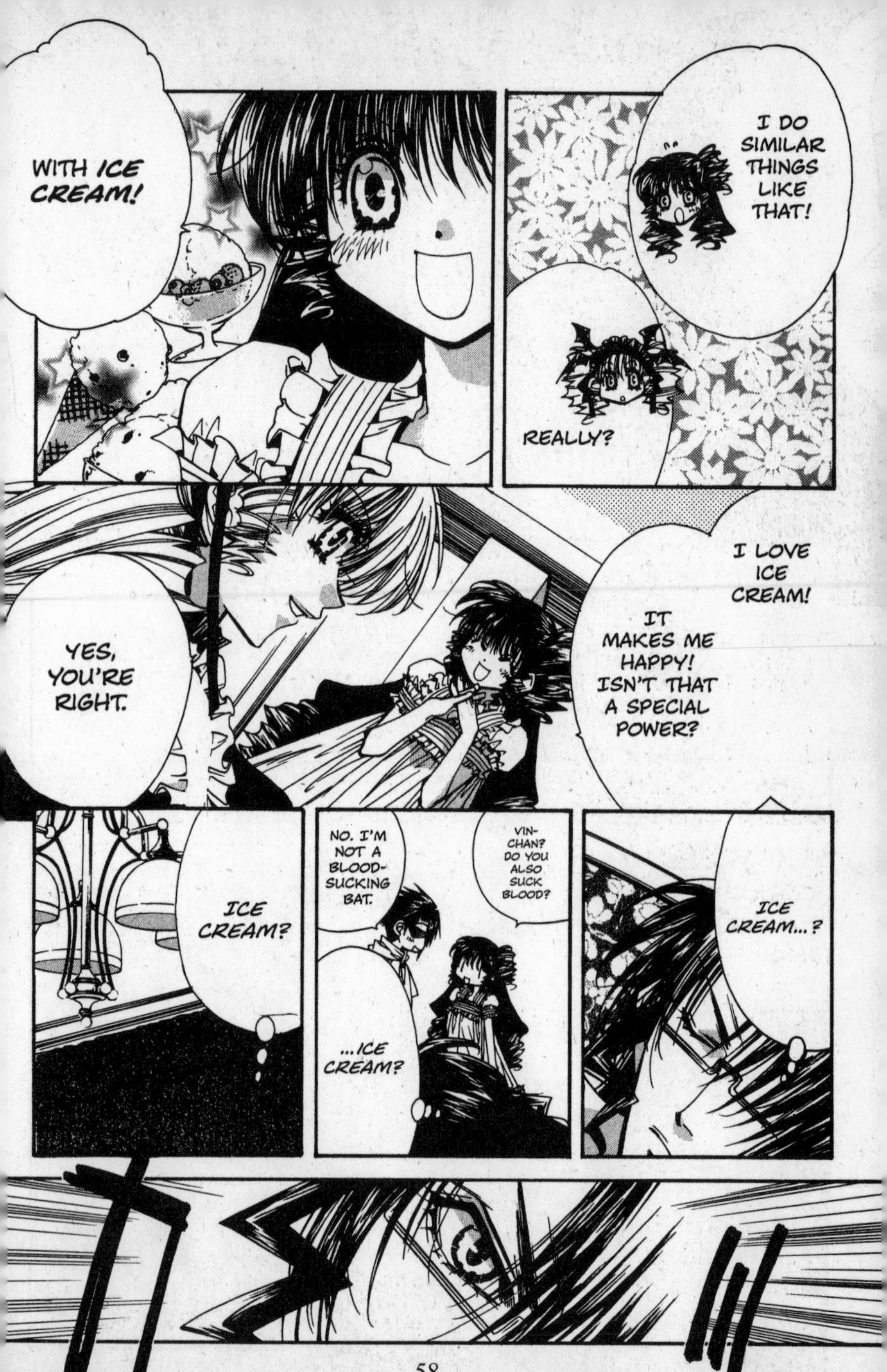
I DO SIMILAR THINGS LIKE THAT!
REALLY?
WITH ICE CREAM!
I LOVE ICE CREAM!
IT MAKES ME HAPPY! ISN'T THAT A SPECIAL POWER?
YES, YOU'RE RIGHT.
ICE CREAM...?
VIN-CHAN? DO YOU ALSO SUCK BLOOD?
NO. I'M NOT A BLOOD-SUCKING BAT.
...ICE CREAM?
ICE CREAM?

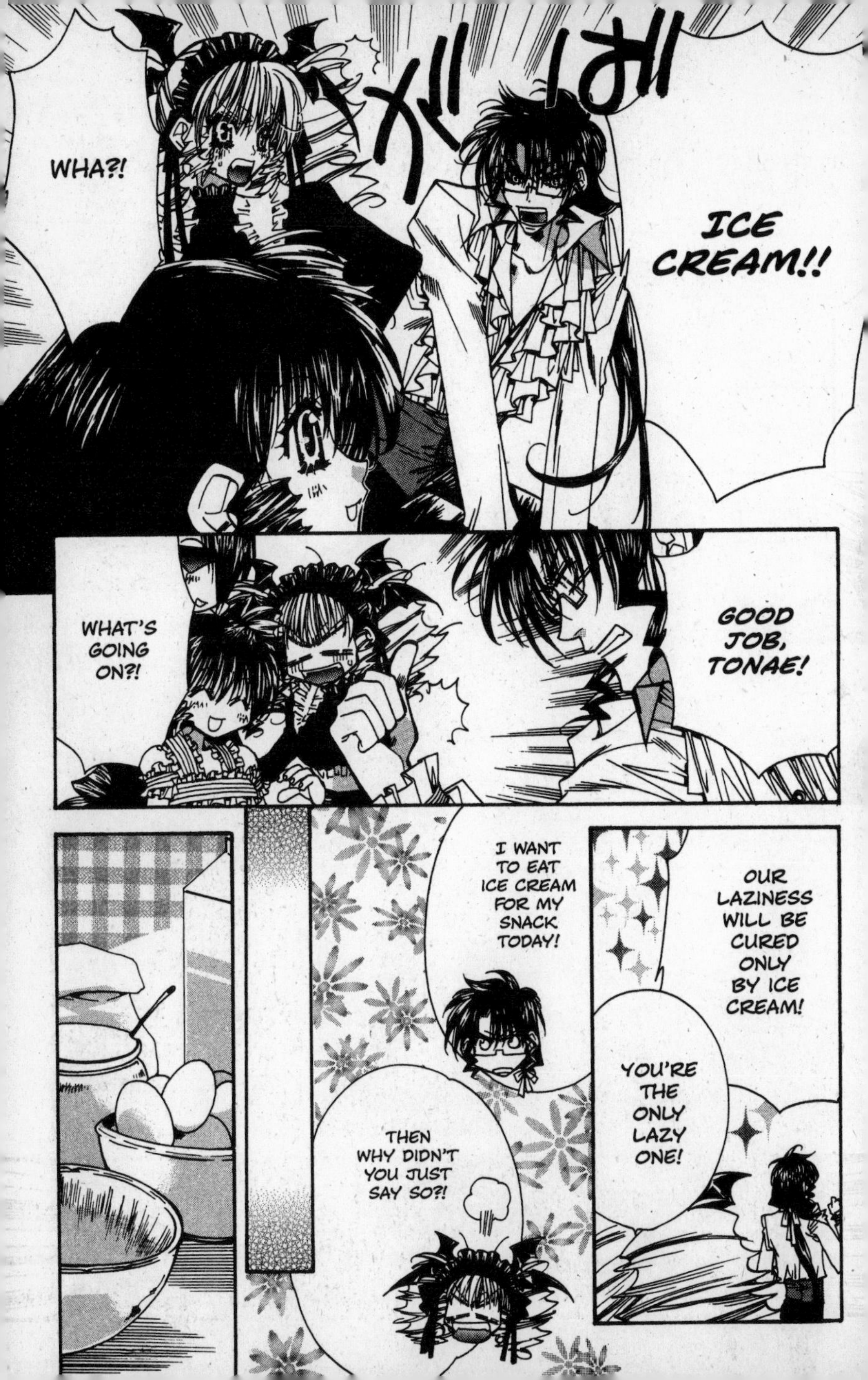
ICE CREAM!!
WHA?!
GOOD JOB, TONAE!
WHAT'S GOING ON?!
OUR LAZINESS WILL BE CURED ONLY BY ICE CREAM!
YOU'RE THE ONLY LAZY ONE!
I WANT TO EAT ICE CREAM FOR MY SNACK TODAY!
THEN WHY DIDN'T YOU JUST SAY SO?!

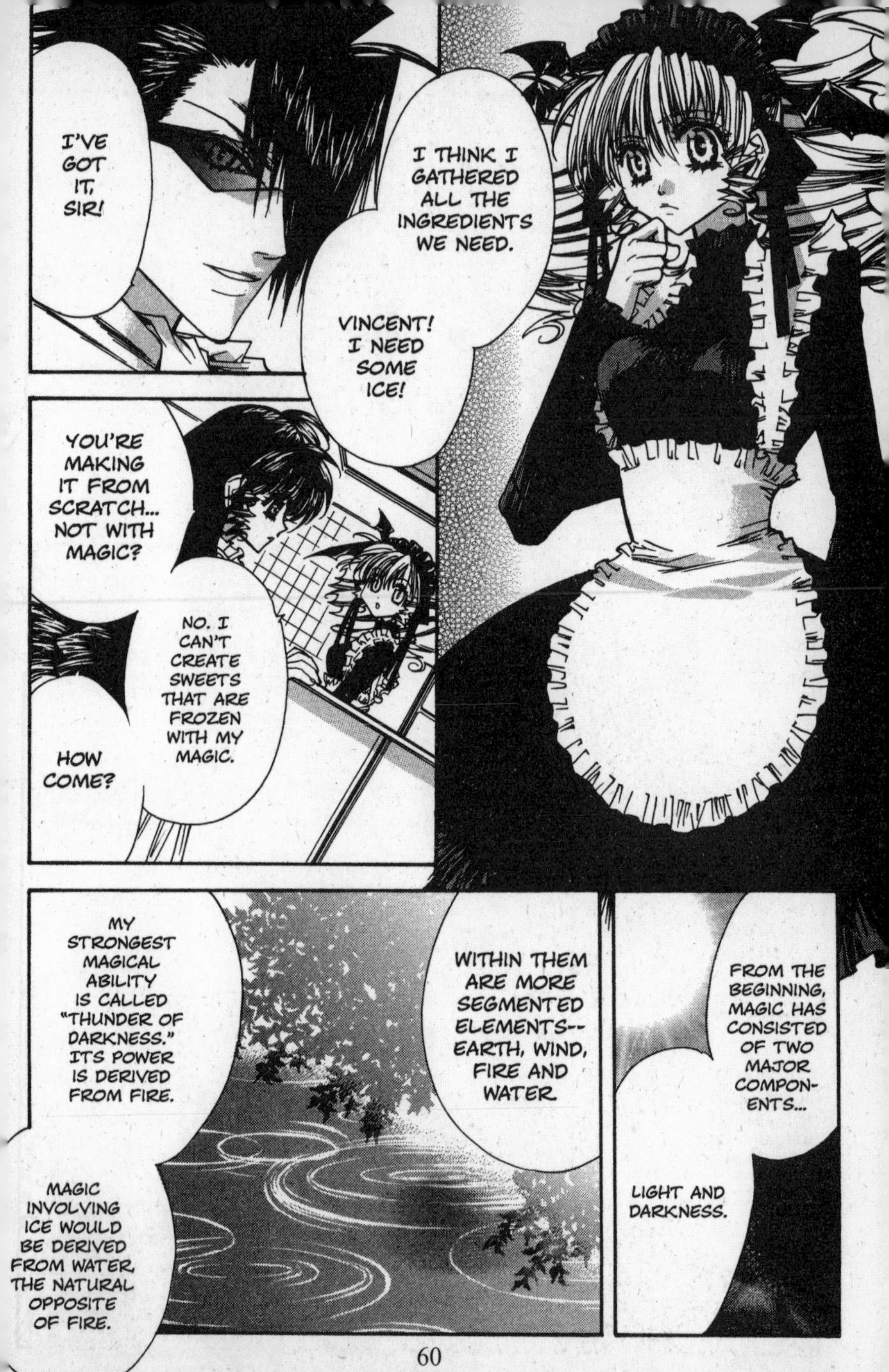
I THINK I GATHERED ALL THE INGREDIENTS WE NEED.
VINCENT! I NEED SOME ICE!
I'VE GOT IT, SIR!
YOU'RE MAKING IT FROM SCRATCH... NOT WITH MAGIC?
NO. I CAN'T CREATE SWEETS THAT ARE FROZEN WITH MY MAGIC.
HOW COME?
FROM THE BEGINNING, MAGIC HAS CONSISTED OF TWO MAJOR COMPON-ENTS...
LIGHT AND DARKNESS.
WITHIN THEM ARE MORE SEGMENTED ELEMENTS--EARTH, WIND, FIRE AND WATER
MY STRONGEST MAGICAL ABILITY IS CALLED "THUNDER OF DARKNESS." ITS POWER IS DERIVED FROM FIRE.
MAGIC INVOLVING ICE WOULD BE DERIVED FROM WATER, THE NATURAL OPPOSITE OF FIRE.

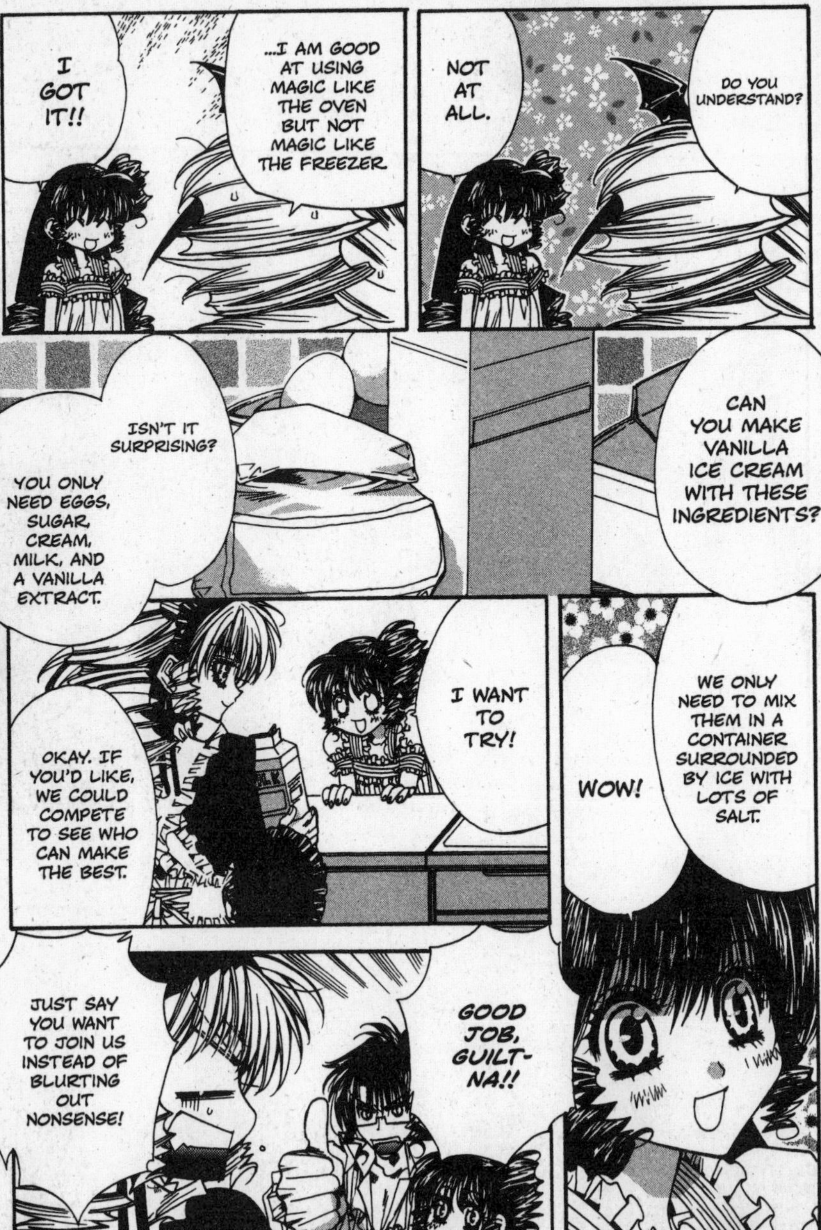

DO YOU UNDERSTAND?
NOT AT ALL.
...I AM GOOD AT USING MAGIC LIKE THE OVEN BUT NOT MAGIC LIKE THE FREEZER
I GOT IT!!
CAN YOU MAKE VANILLA ICE CREAM WITH THESE INGREDIENTS?
ISN'T IT SURPRISING?
YOU ONLY NEED EGGS, SUGAR, CREAM, MILK, AND A VANILLA EXTRACT.
WE ONLY NEED TO MIX THEM IN A CONTAINER SURROUNDED BY ICE WITH LOTS OF SALT.
WOW!
I WANT TO TRY!
OKAY. IF YOU'D LIKE, WE COULD COMPETE TO SEE WHO CAN MAKE THE BEST.
GOOD JOB, GUILT-NA!!
JUST SAY YOU WANT TO JOIN US INSTEAD OF BLURTING OUT NONSENSE!

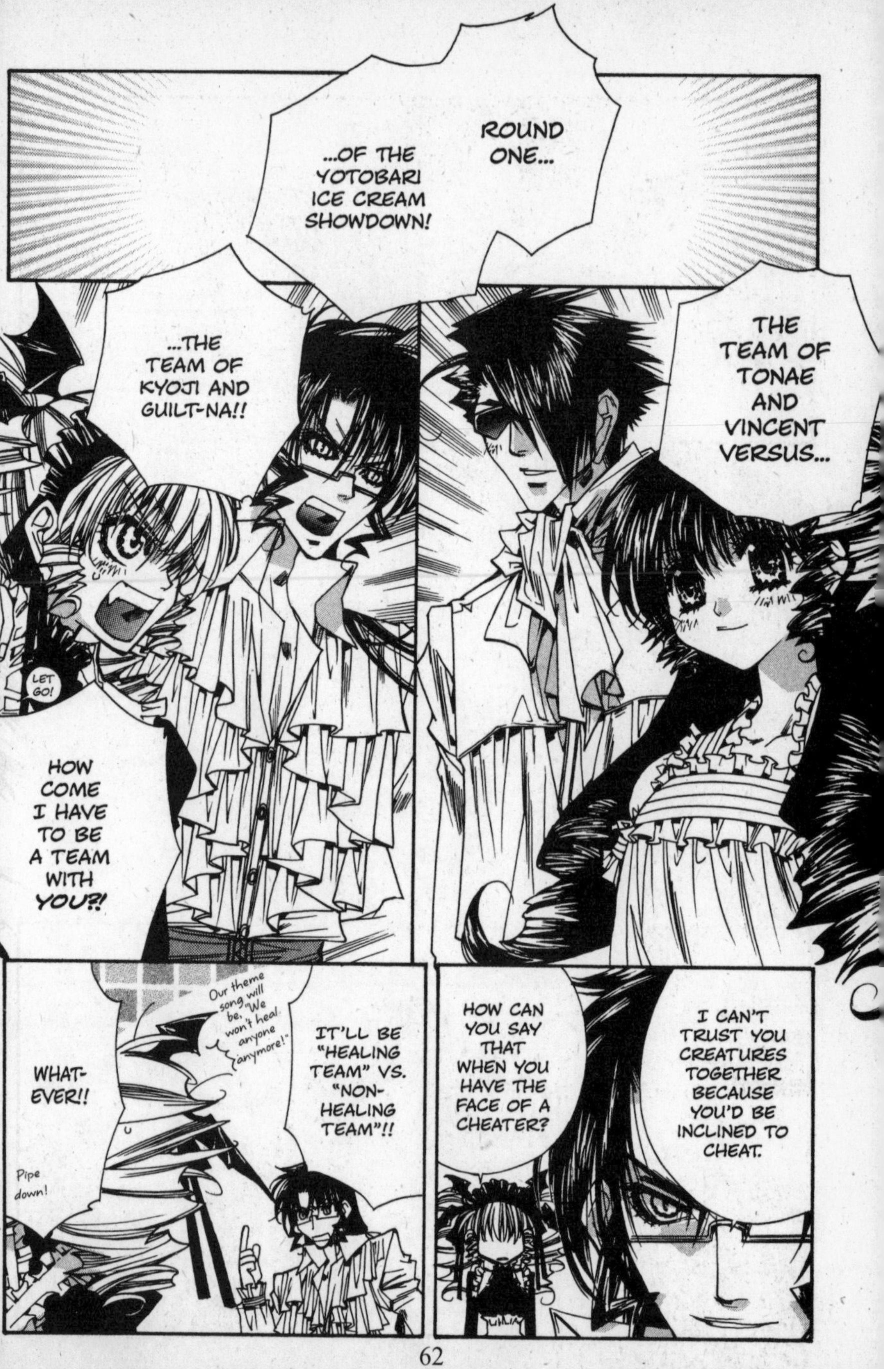
ROUND ONE...
...OF THE YOTOBARI ICE CREAM SHOWDOWN!
THE TEAM OF TONAE AND VINCENT VERSUS...
...THE TEAM OF KYOJI AND GUILT-NA!!
LET GO!
HOW COME I HAVE TO BE A TEAM WITH YOU?!
I CAN'T TRUST YOU CREATURES TOGETHER BECAUSE YOU'D BE INCLINED TO CHEAT.
HOW CAN YOU SAY THAT WHEN YOU HAVE THE FACE OF A CHEATER?
IT'LL BE "HEALING TEAM" VS. "NON-HEALING TEAM"!!
Our theme song will be, "We won't heal anyone anymore!"
WHAT-EVER!!
Pipe down!

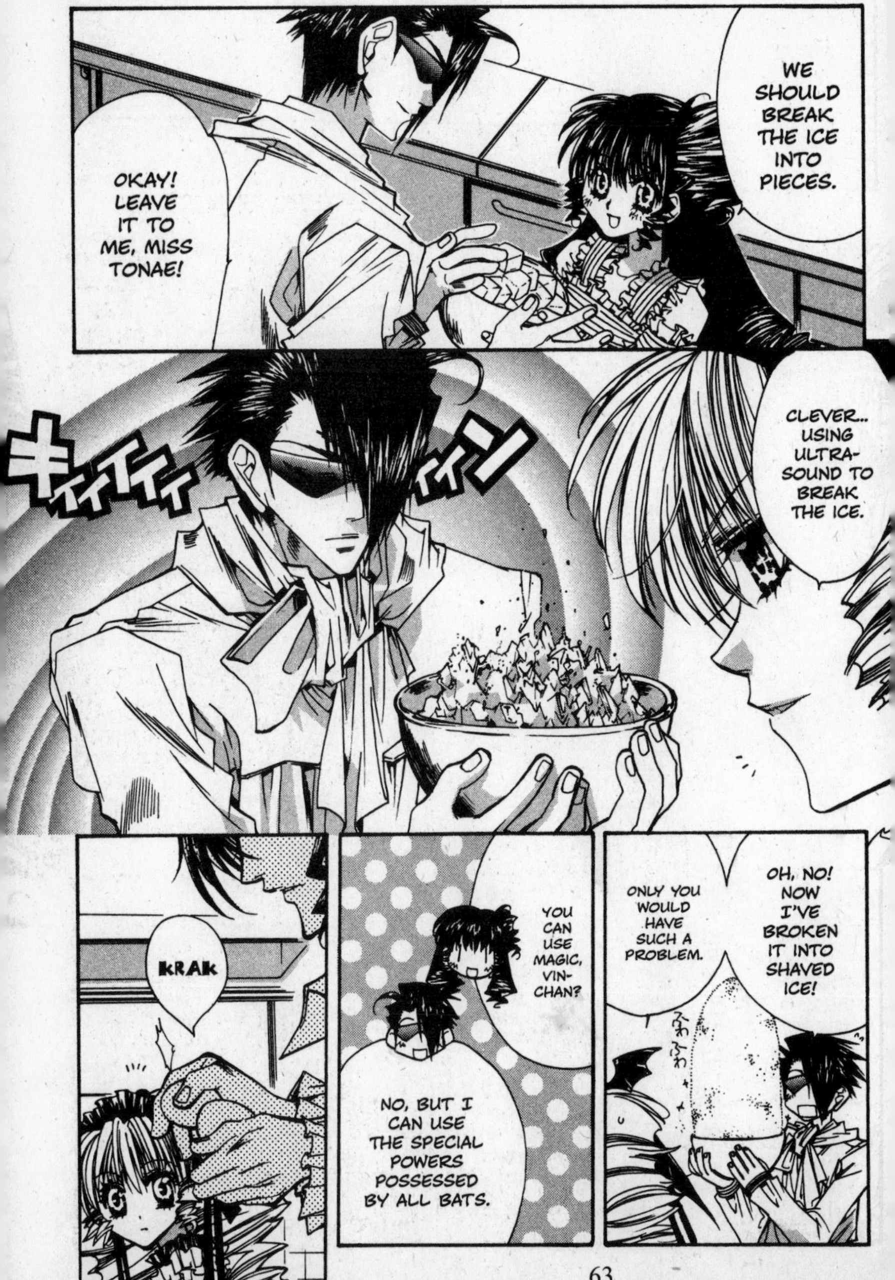
WE SHOULD BREAK THE ICE INTO PIECES.
OKAY! LEAVE IT TO ME, MISS TONAE!
CLEVER... USING ULTRA-SOUND TO BREAK THE ICE.
キィイイイ
イイン
OH, NO! NOW I'VE BROKEN IT INTO SHAVED ICE!
ONLY YOU WOULD HAVE SUCH A PROBLEM.
ふわふわ
YOU CAN USE MAGIC, VIN-CHAN?
NO, BUT I CAN USE THE SPECIAL POWERS POSSESSED BY ALL BATS.
KRAK

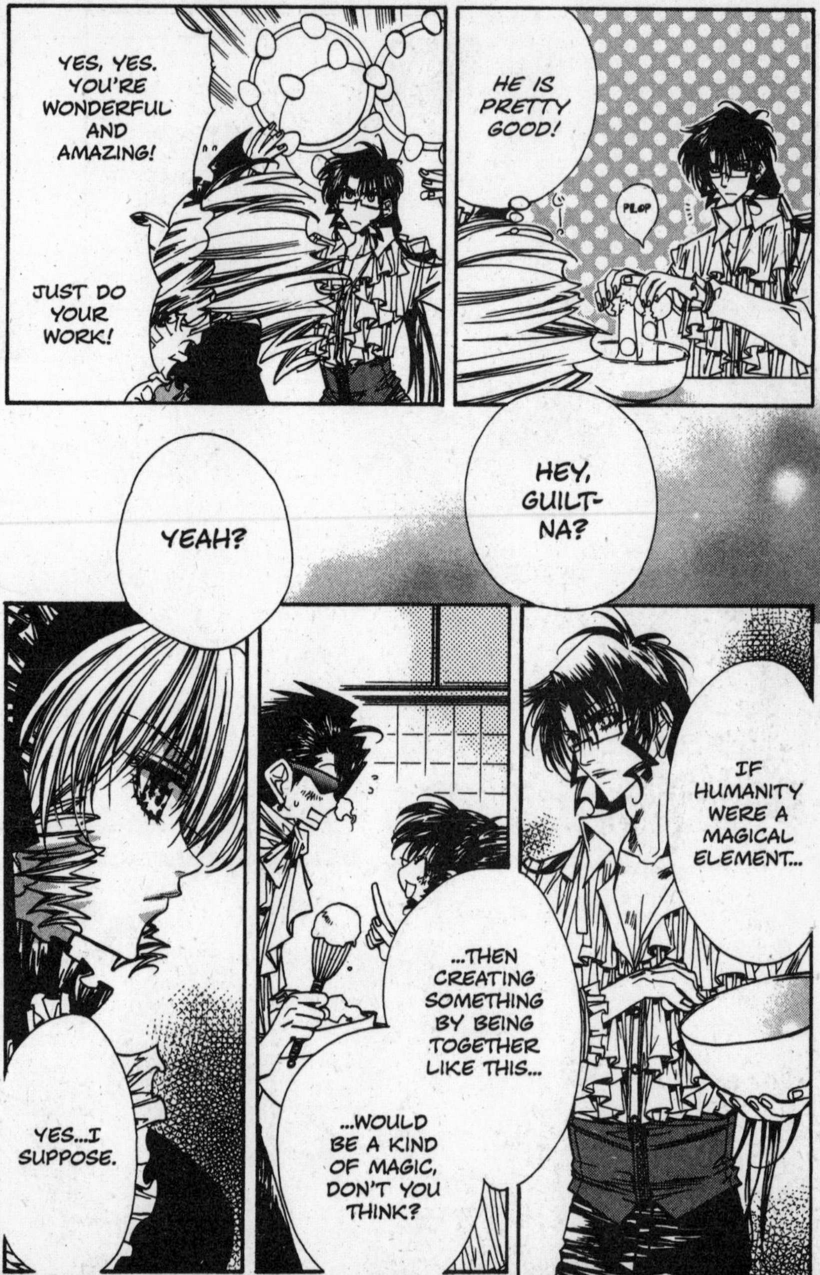
HE IS PRETTY GOOD!
PLOP
YES, YES. YOU'RE WONDERFUL AND AMAZING!
JUST DO YOUR WORK!
HEY, GUILT-NA?
YEAH?
IF HUMANITY WERE A MAGICAL ELEMENT...
...THEN CREATING SOMETHING BY BEING TOGETHER LIKE THIS...
...WOULD BE A KIND OF MAGIC, DON'T YOU THINK?
YES...I SUPPOSE.

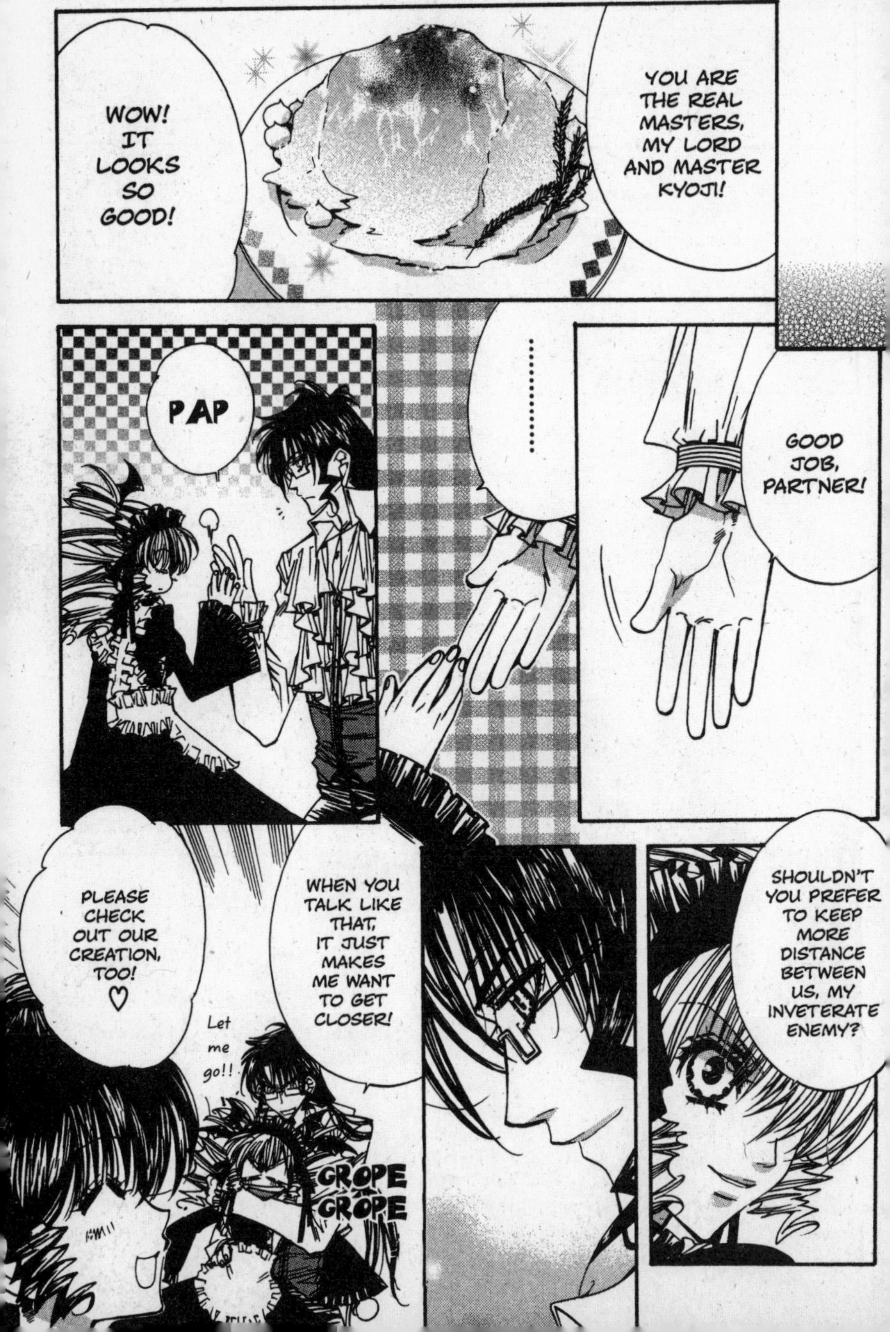
YOU ARE THE REAL MASTERS, MY LORD AND MASTER KYOJI!
WOW! IT LOOKS SO GOOD!
GOOD JOB, PARTNER!
......
PAP
SHOULDN'T YOU PREFER TO KEEP MORE DISTANCE BETWEEN US, MY INVETERATE ENEMY?
WHEN YOU TALK LIKE THAT, IT JUST MAKES ME WANT TO GET CLOSER!
Let me go!!
GROPE GROPE
PLEASE CHECK OUT OUR CREATION, TOO! ♡

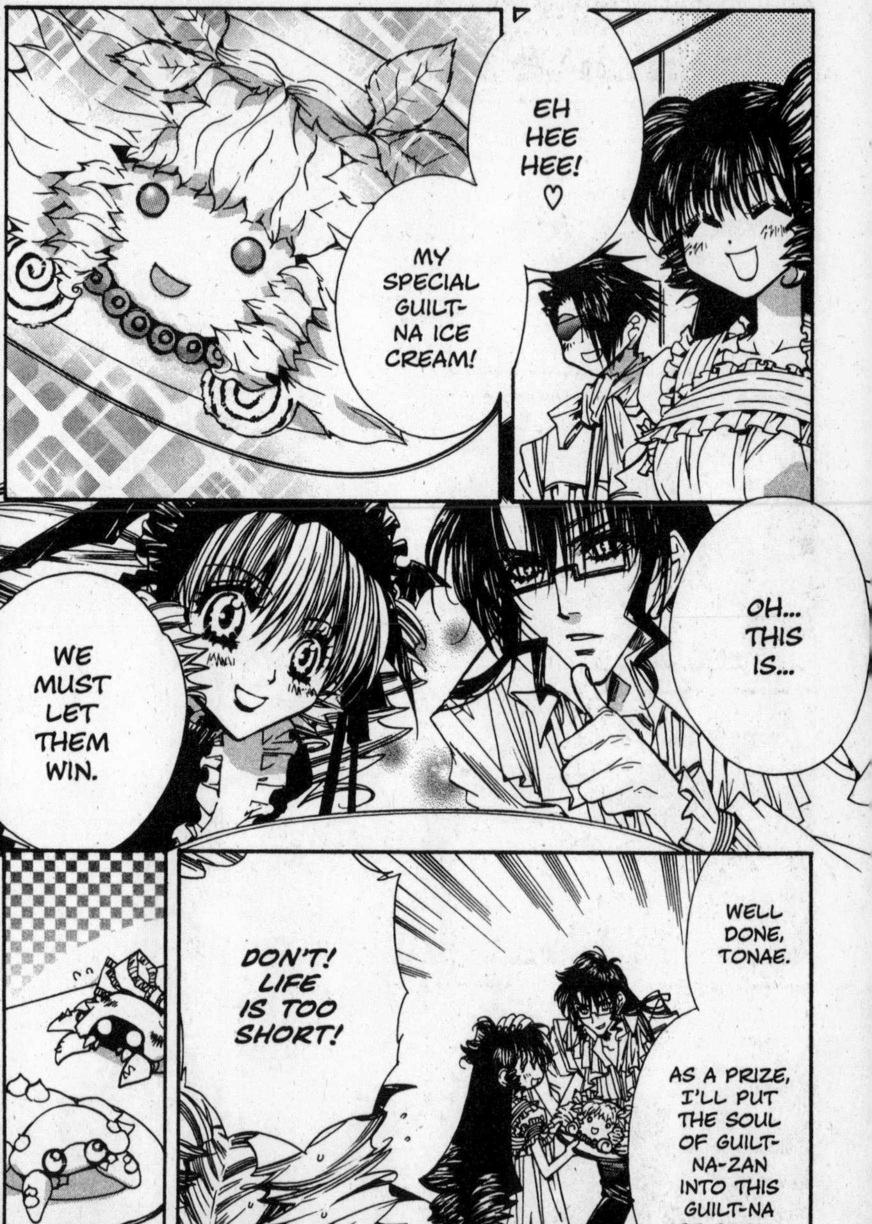

EH HEE HEE! ♡
MY SPECIAL GUILT-NA ICE CREAM!
OH... THIS IS...
WE MUST LET THEM WIN.
WELL DONE, TONAE.
AS A PRIZE, I'LL PUT THE SOUL OF GUILT-NA-ZAN INTO THIS GUILT-NA ICE CREAM.
DON'T! LIFE IS TOO SHORT!
↑ Bonus.

Bonus Comic Strip

Vampire Doll Reflections

Dolce

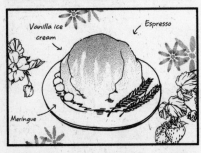

QUESTION: WHAT KIND OF ICE CREAM DESSERTS DID THEY MAKE?
Espresso
Vanilla ice cream
Meringue
Mint leaves
Whipped cream
Blueberries
Cookies
THEY'RE KINDA PURPLE, BUT I USED BLUEBERRIES FOR YOUR EYES.
SHOULD I HAVE USED MARBLES INSTEAD?
WE'D CHIP OUR TEETH...

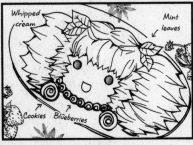

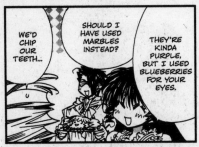

ギルナ

Guiltna
female
tribe: vampire doll
attribute: evil
job: maid
height: 153
eyes: corn flower sapphire
hair: honey gold

An angel and a little devil
appear! What do you do?

夜帳唱

Tonae Yotobari
female
tribe: human
attribute: good
job: holy girl
height: 153
eyes: chocolate brown
hair: cocoa brown

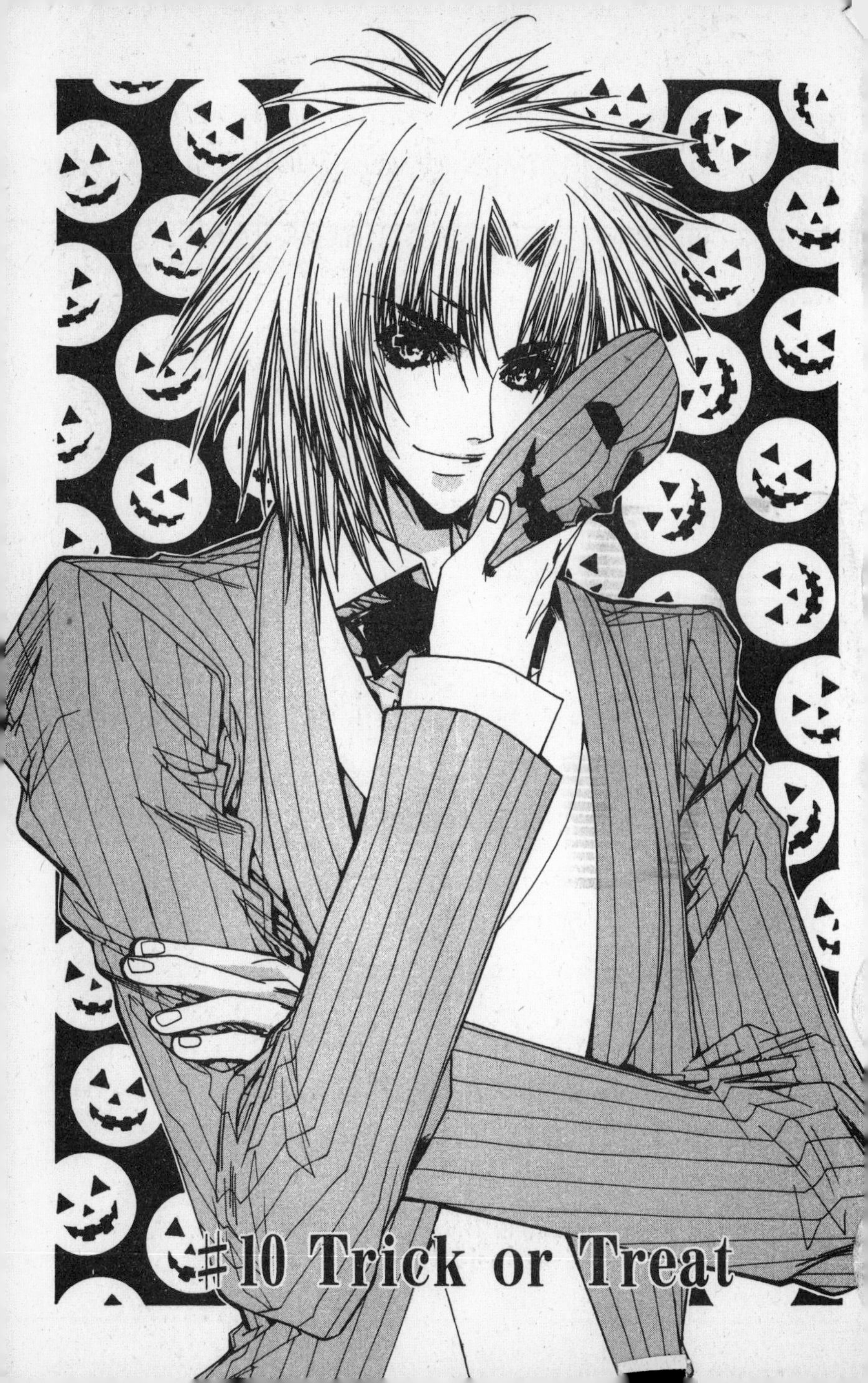
#10 Trick or Treat

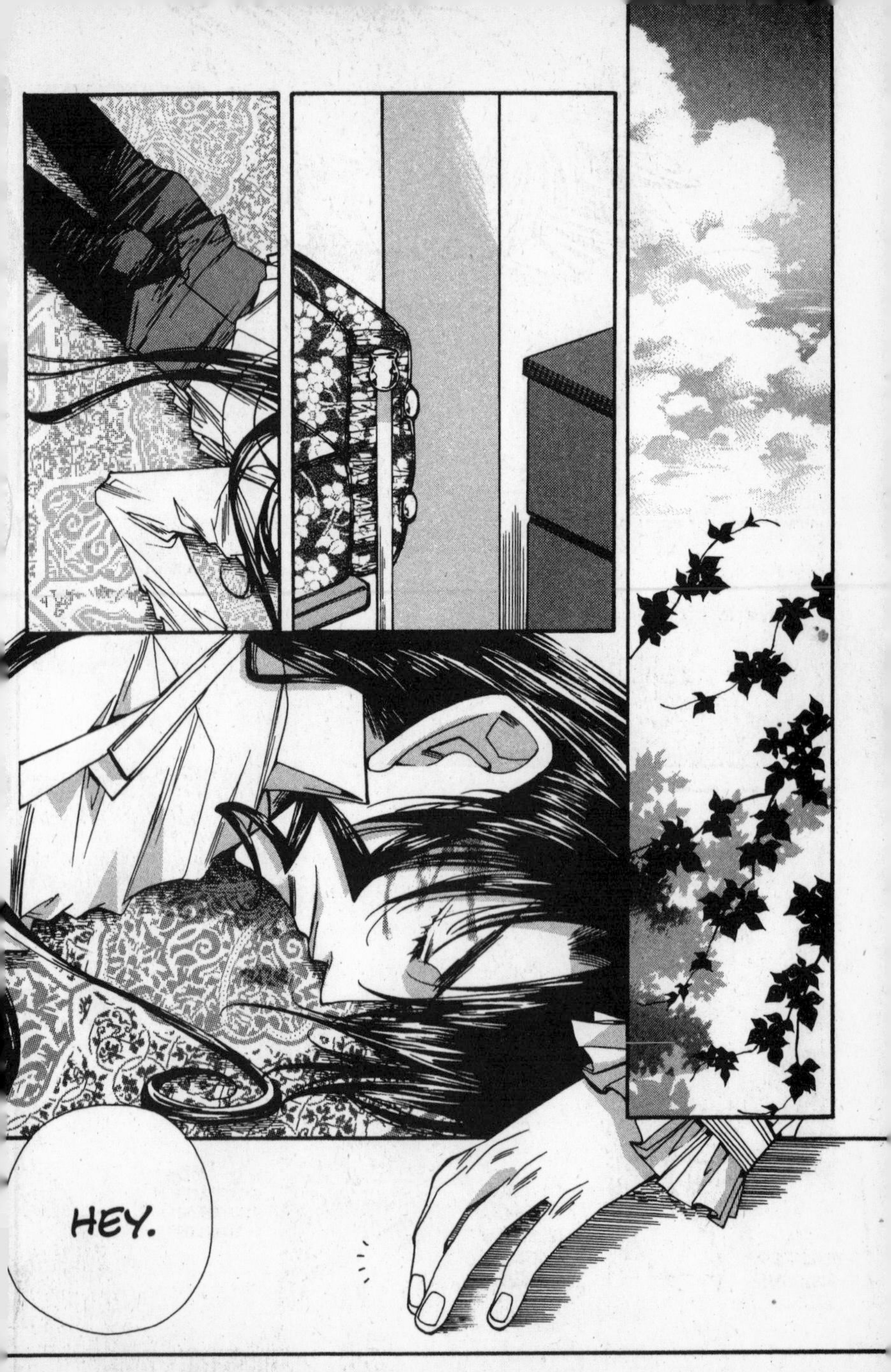
HEY.

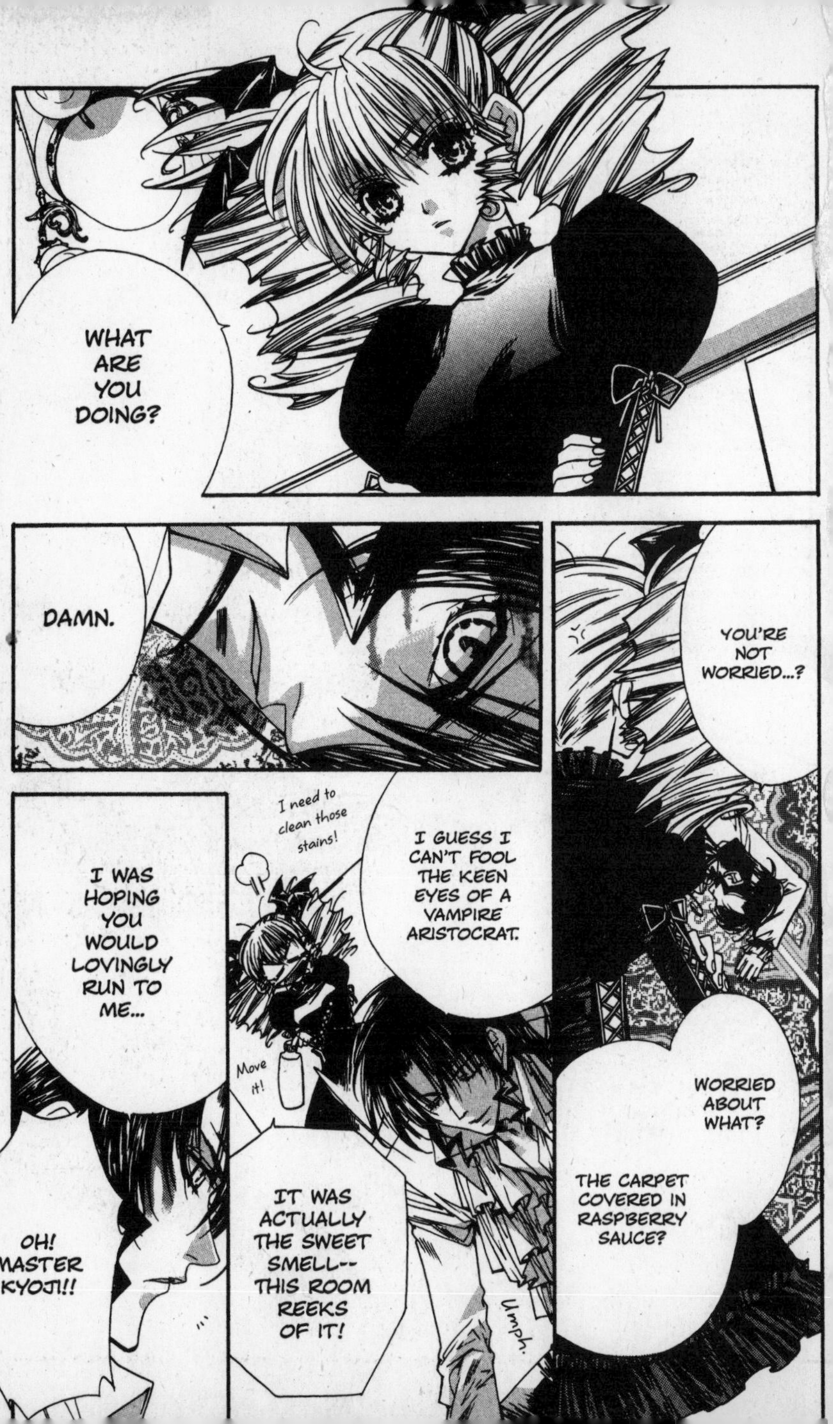
WHAT ARE YOU DOING?
YOU'RE NOT WORRIED...?
WORRIED ABOUT WHAT?
THE CARPET COVERED IN RASPBERRY SAUCE?
DAMN.
I GUESS I CAN'T FOOL THE KEEN EYES OF A VAMPIRE ARISTOCRAT.
I need to clean those stains!
I WAS HOPING YOU WOULD LOVINGLY RUN TO ME...
Move it!
Umph.
IT WAS ACTUALLY THE SWEET SMELL-- THIS ROOM REEKS OF IT!
OH! MASTER KYOJI!!

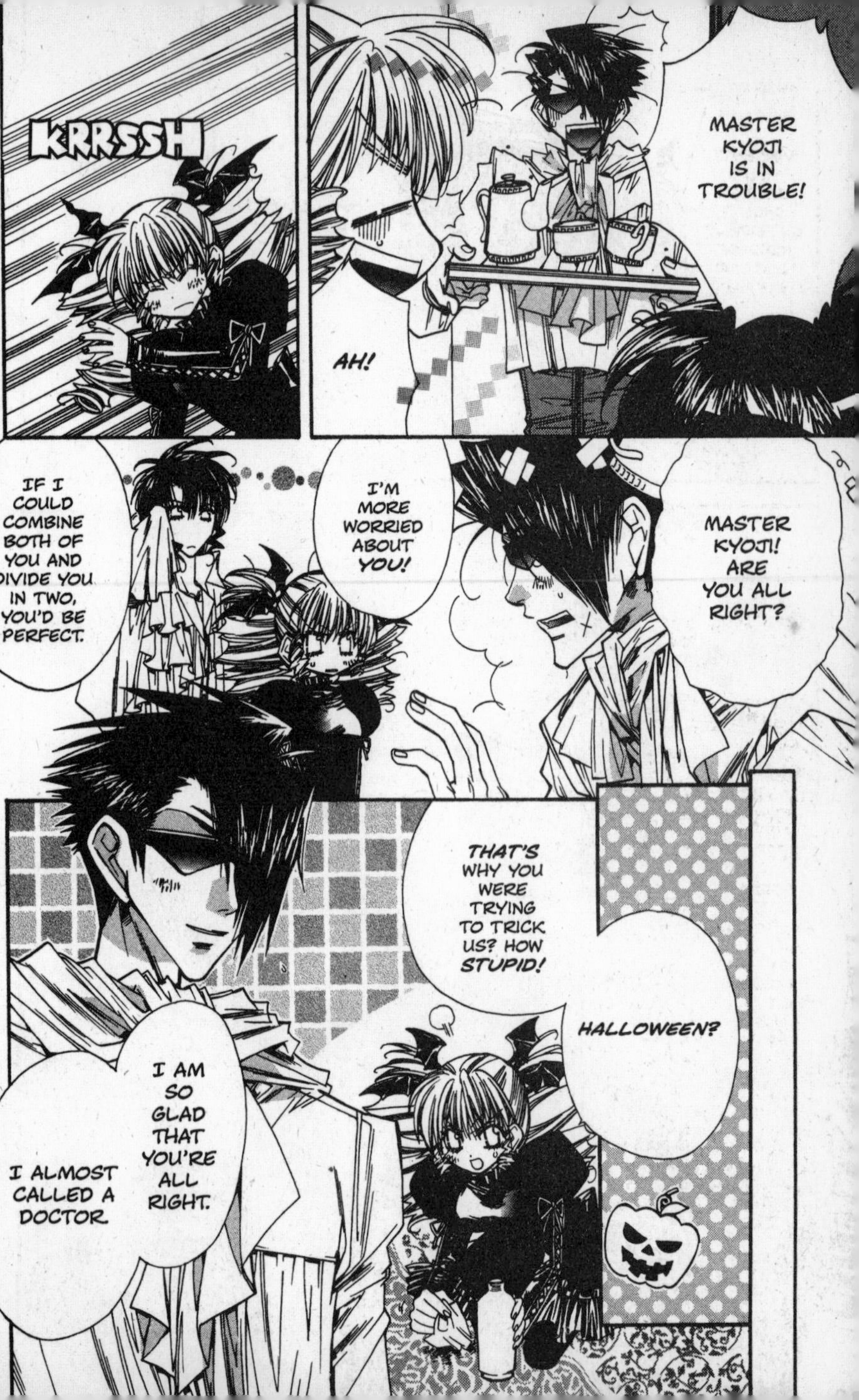
MASTER KYOJI IS IN TROUBLE!
AH!
KRRSSH
MASTER KYOJI! ARE YOU ALL RIGHT?
I'M MORE WORRIED ABOUT YOU!
IF I COULD COMBINE BOTH OF YOU AND DIVIDE YOU IN TWO, YOU'D BE PERFECT.
THAT'S WHY YOU WERE TRYING TO TRICK US? HOW STUPID!
HALLOWEEN?
I AM SO GLAD THAT YOU'RE ALL RIGHT.
I ALMOST CALLED A DOCTOR.

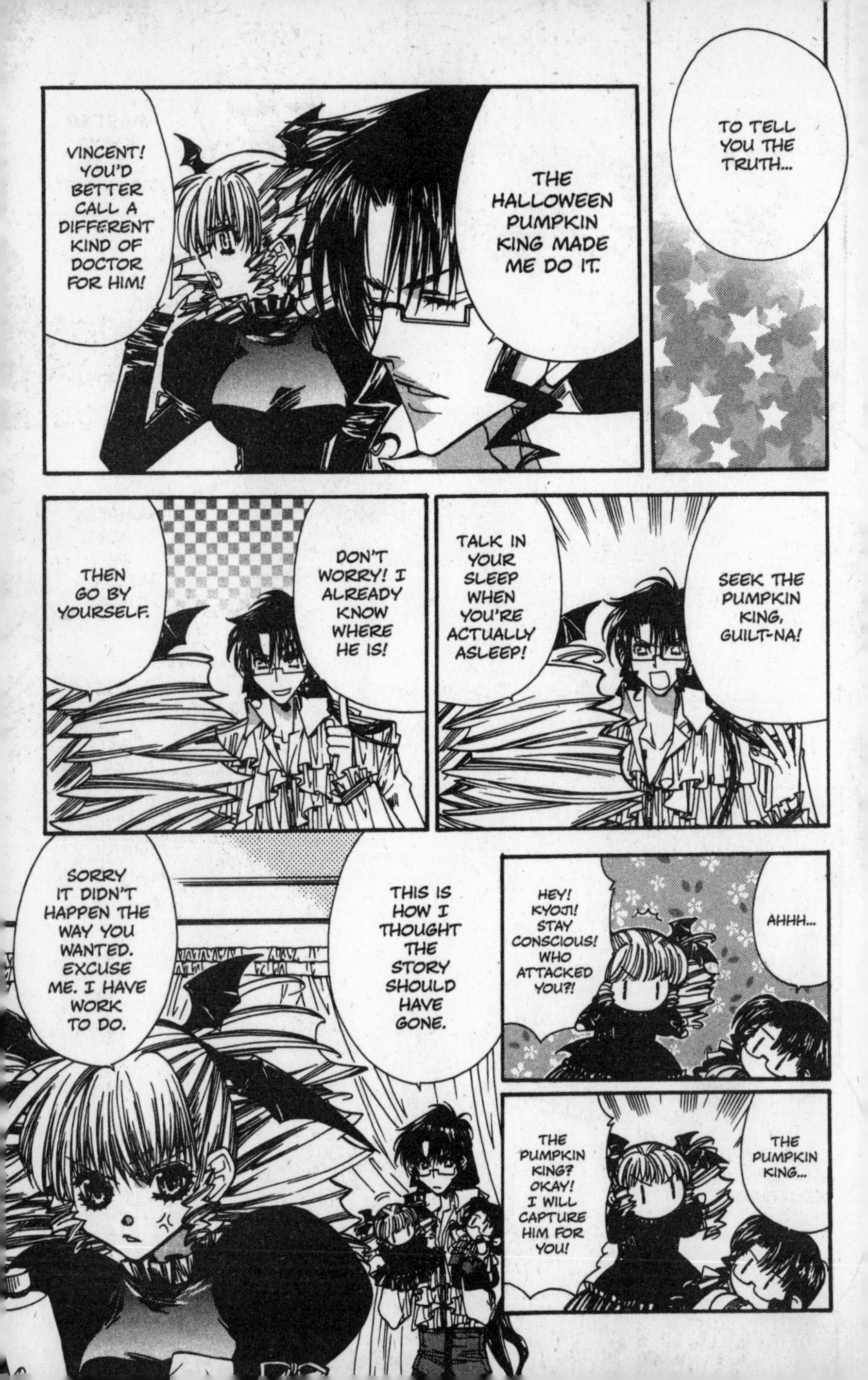
TO TELL YOU THE TRUTH...
THE HALLOWEEN PUMPKIN KING MADE ME DO IT.
VINCENT! YOU'D BETTER CALL A DIFFERENT KIND OF DOCTOR FOR HIM!
SEEK THE PUMPKIN KING, GUILT-NA!
TALK IN YOUR SLEEP WHEN YOU'RE ACTUALLY ASLEEP!
DON'T WORRY! I ALREADY KNOW WHERE HE IS!
THEN GO BY YOURSELF.
AHHH...
HEY! KYOJI! STAY CONSCIOUS! WHO ATTACKED YOU?!
THE PUMPKIN KING...
THE PUMPKIN KING? OKAY! I WILL CAPTURE HIM FOR YOU!
THIS IS HOW I THOUGHT THE STORY SHOULD HAVE GONE.
SORRY IT DIDN'T HAPPEN THE WAY YOU WANTED. EXCUSE ME. I HAVE WORK TO DO.

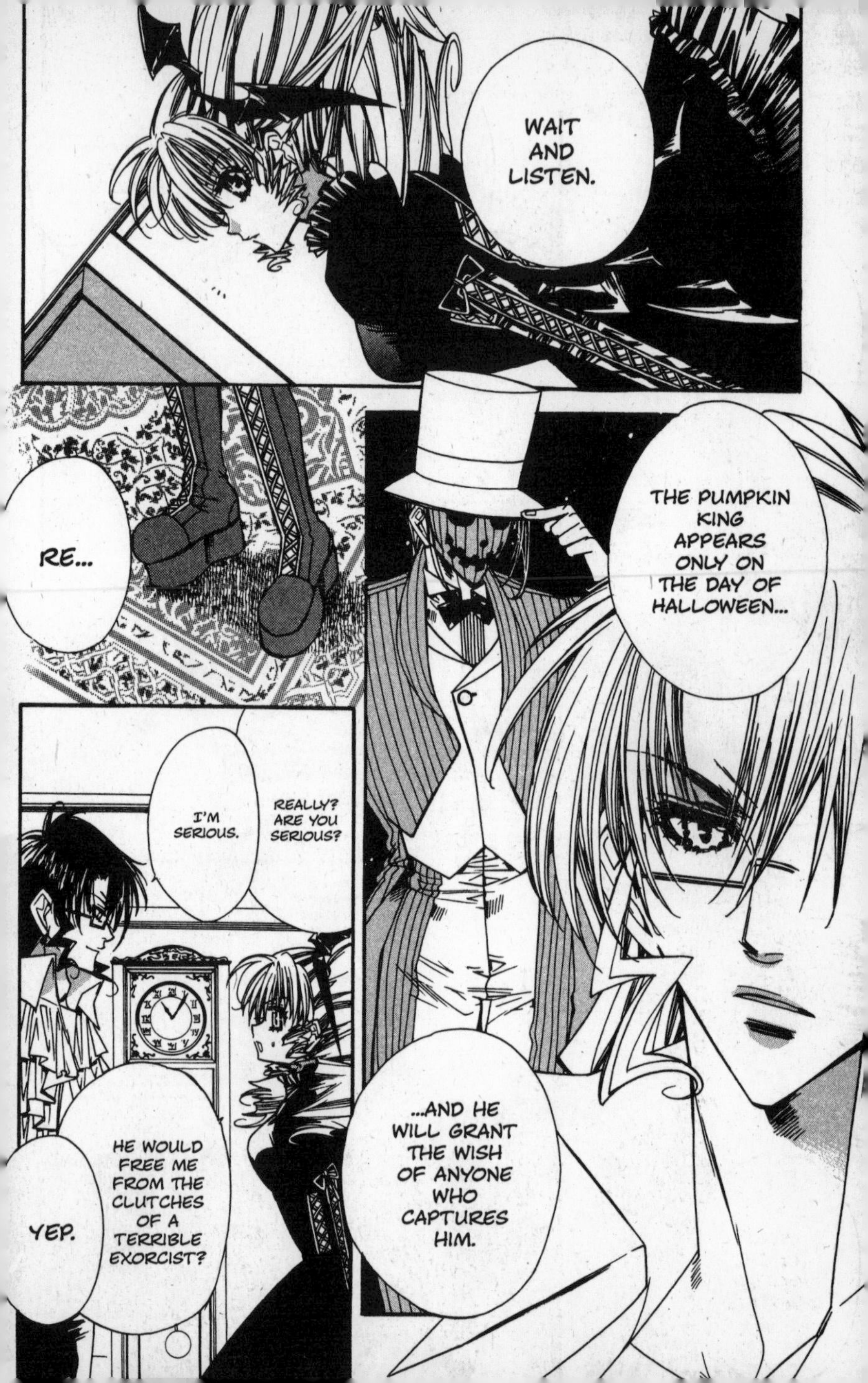
WAIT AND LISTEN.
THE PUMPKIN KING APPEARS ONLY ON THE DAY OF HALLOWEEN...
...AND HE WILL GRANT THE WISH OF ANYONE WHO CAPTURES HIM.
RE...
REALLY? ARE YOU SERIOUS?
I'M SERIOUS.
HE WOULD FREE ME FROM THE CLUTCHES OF A TERRIBLE EXORCIST?
YEP.

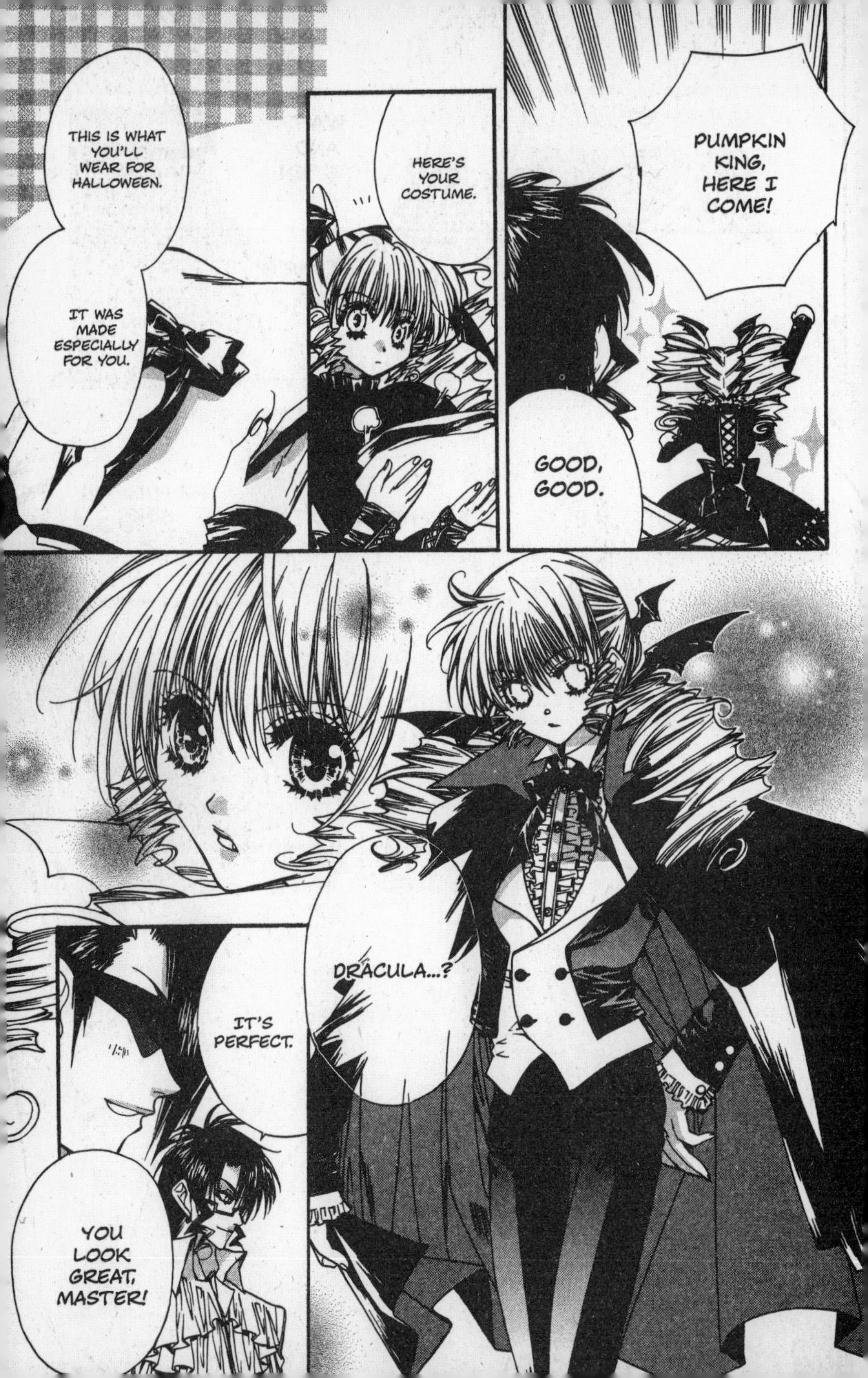
PUMPKIN KING, HERE I COME!
GOOD, GOOD.
HERE'S YOUR COSTUME.
THIS IS WHAT YOU'LL WEAR FOR HALLOWEEN.
IT WAS MADE ESPECIALLY FOR YOU.
DRACULA...?
IT'S PERFECT.
YOU LOOK GREAT, MASTER!

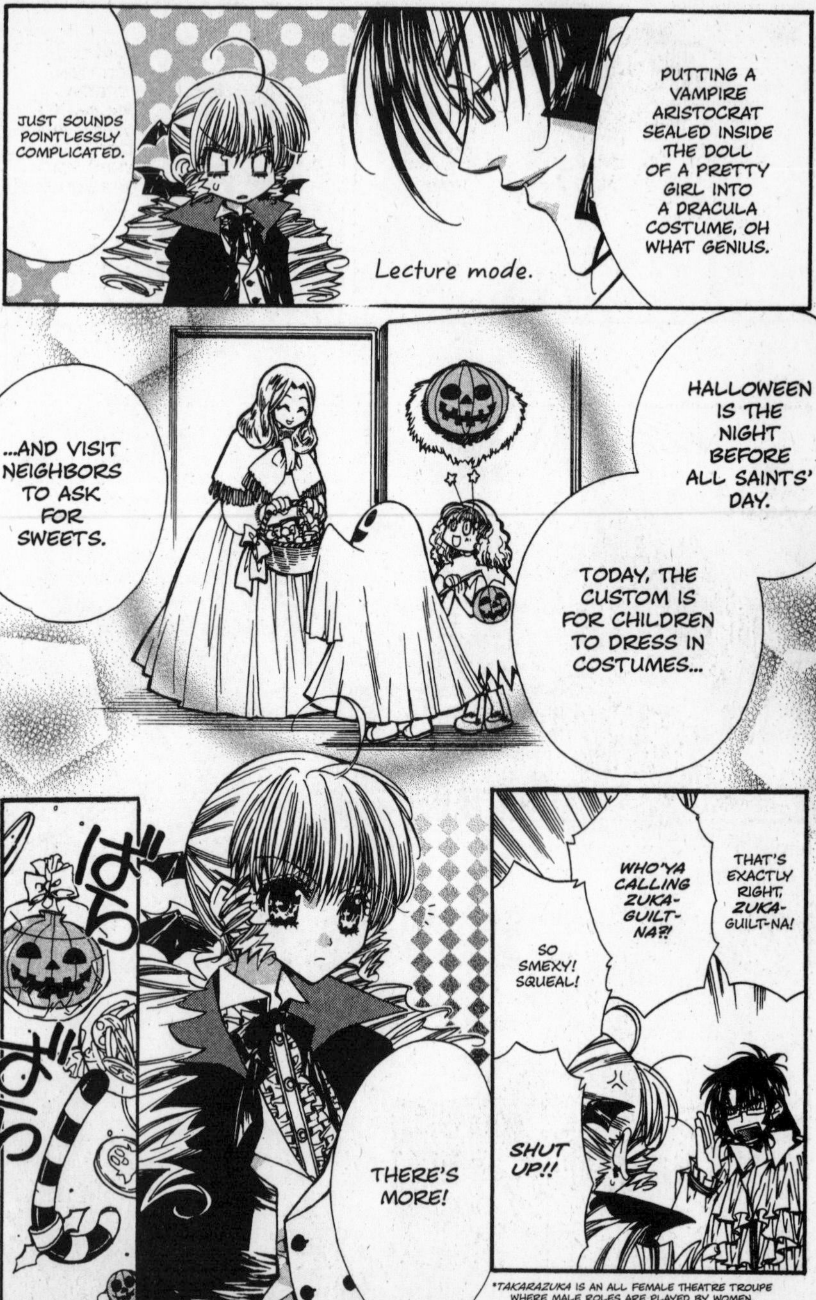
PUTTING A VAMPIRE ARISTOCRAT SEALED INSIDE THE DOLL OF A PRETTY GIRL INTO A DRACULA COSTUME, OH WHAT GENIUS.
Lecture mode.
JUST SOUNDS POINTLESSLY COMPLICATED.
HALLOWEEN IS THE NIGHT BEFORE ALL SAINTS' DAY.
TODAY, THE CUSTOM IS FOR CHILDREN TO DRESS IN COSTUMES...
...AND VISIT NEIGHBORS TO ASK FOR SWEETS.
THAT'S EXACTLY RIGHT, ZUKA-GUILT-NA!
WHO'YA CALLING ZUKA-GUILT-NA?!
SO SMEXY! SQUEAL!
SHUT UP!!
ばら
ばら
THERE'S MORE!

*TAKARAZUKA IS AN ALL FEMALE THEATRE TROUPE WHERE MALE ROLES ARE PLAYED BY WOMEN.

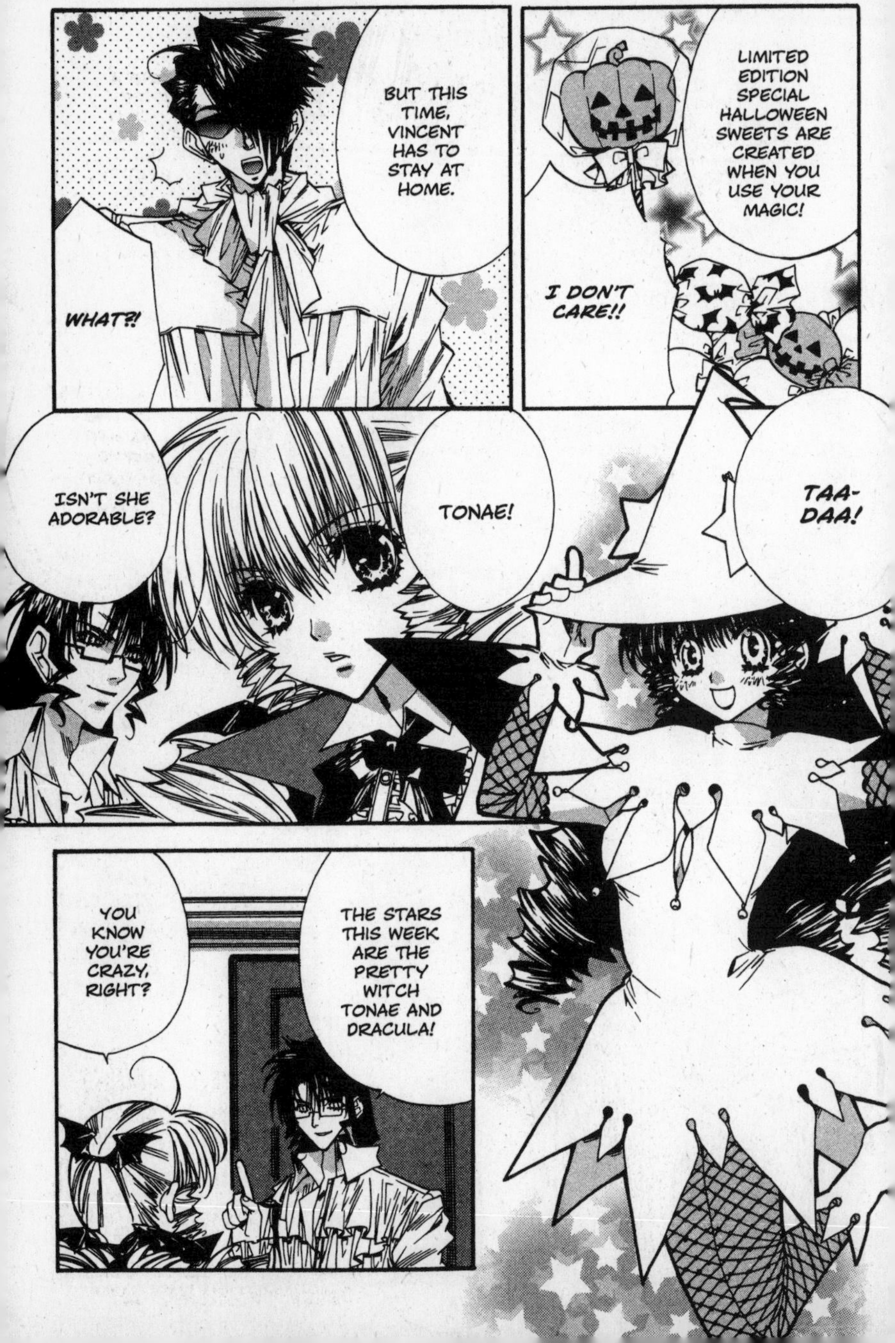
LIMITED EDITION SPECIAL HALLOWEEN SWEETS ARE CREATED WHEN YOU USE YOUR MAGIC!
I DON'T CARE!!
BUT THIS TIME, VINCENT HAS TO STAY AT HOME.
WHAT?!
TAA-DAA!
TONAE!
ISN'T SHE ADORABLE?
THE STARS THIS WEEK ARE THE PRETTY WITCH TONAE AND DRACULA!
YOU KNOW YOU'RE CRAZY, RIGHT?

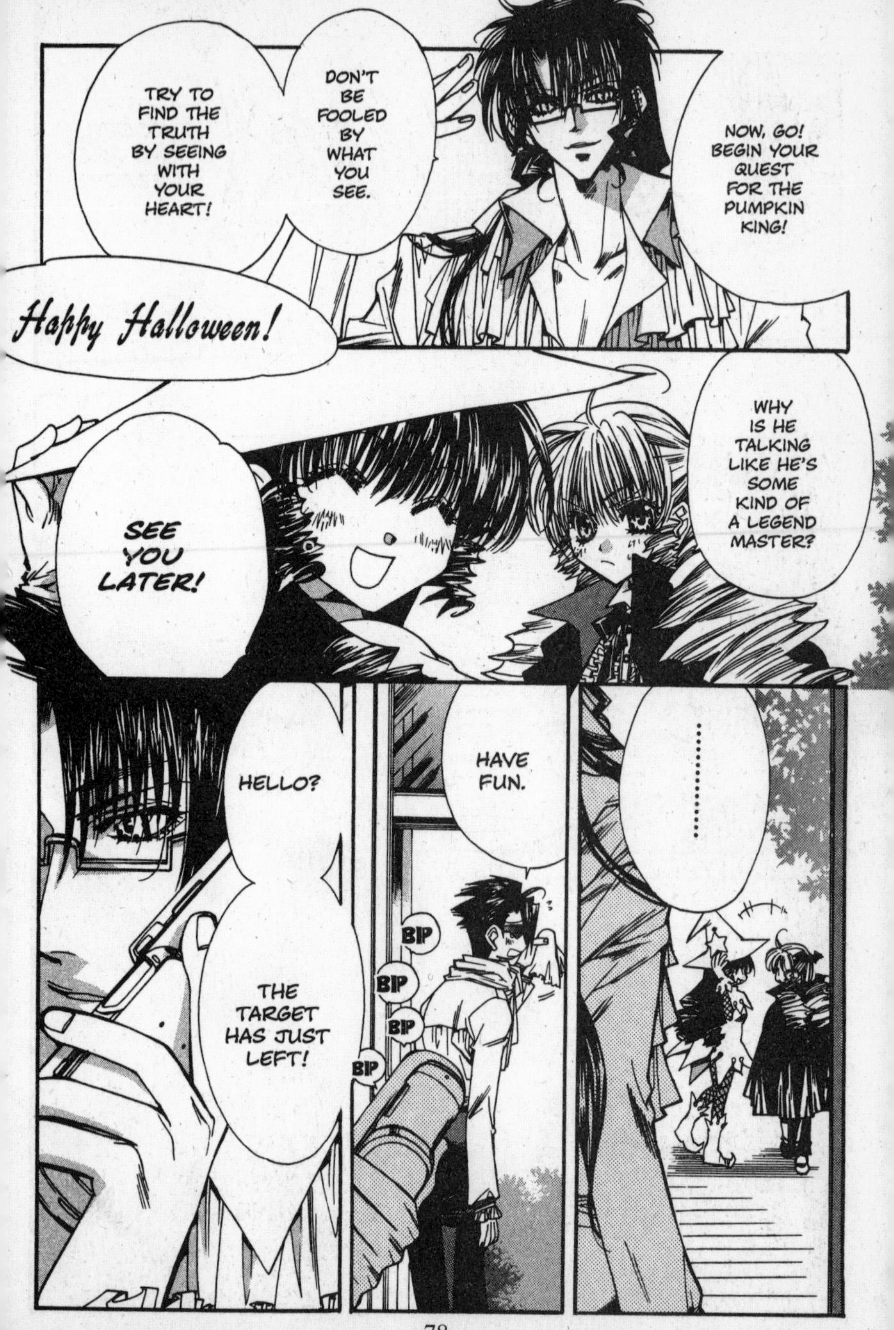
NOW, GO! BEGIN YOUR QUEST FOR THE PUMPKIN KING!
DON'T BE FOOLED BY WHAT YOU SEE.
TRY TO FIND THE TRUTH BY SEEING WITH YOUR HEART!
Happy Halloween!
WHY IS HE TALKING LIKE HE'S SOME KIND OF A LEGEND MASTER?
SEE YOU LATER!
....
HAVE FUN.
BIP
BIP
BIP
BIP
HELLO?
THE TARGET HAS JUST LEFT!

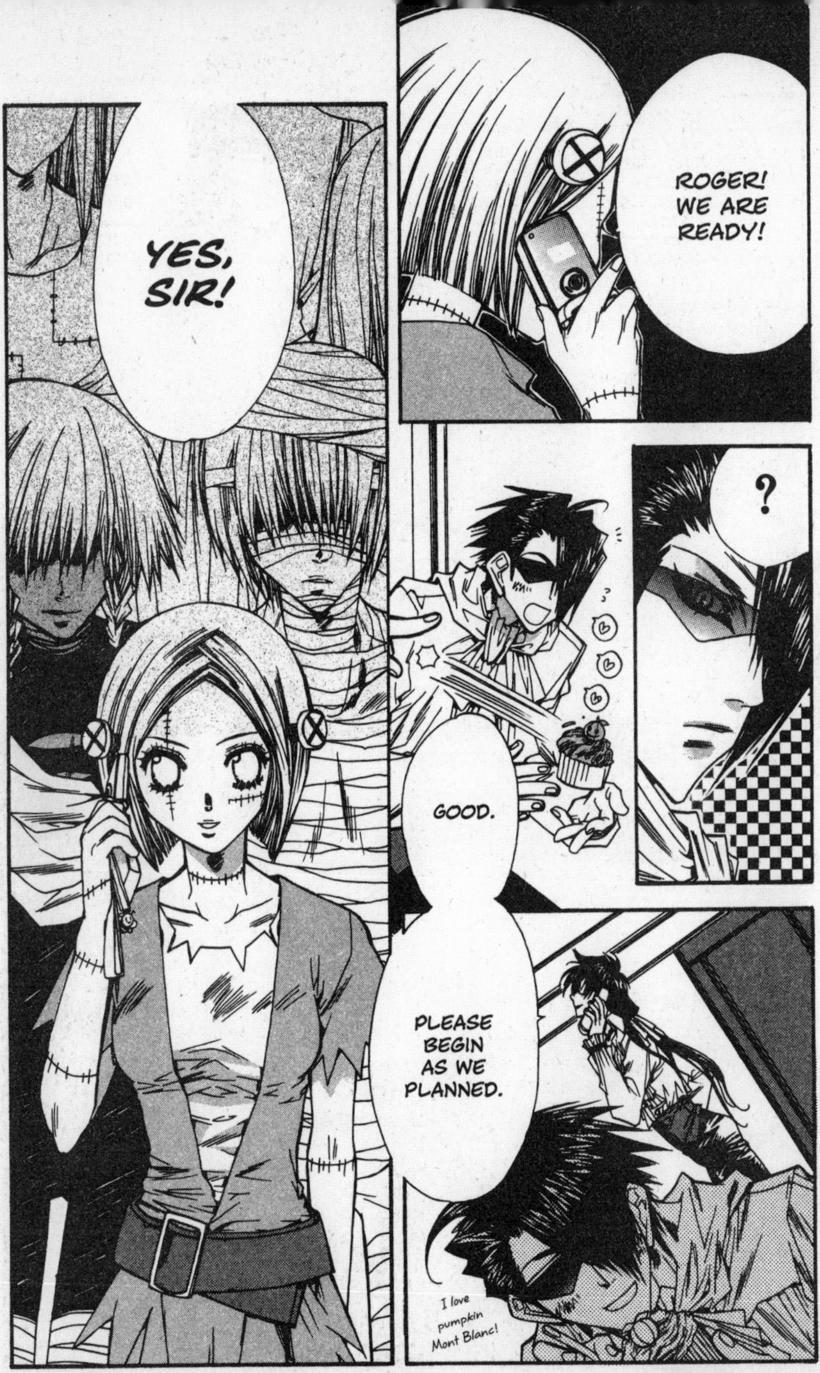
ROGER! WE ARE READY!
?
GOOD.
PLEASE BEGIN AS WE PLANNED.
I love pumpkin Mont Blanc!
YES, SIR!

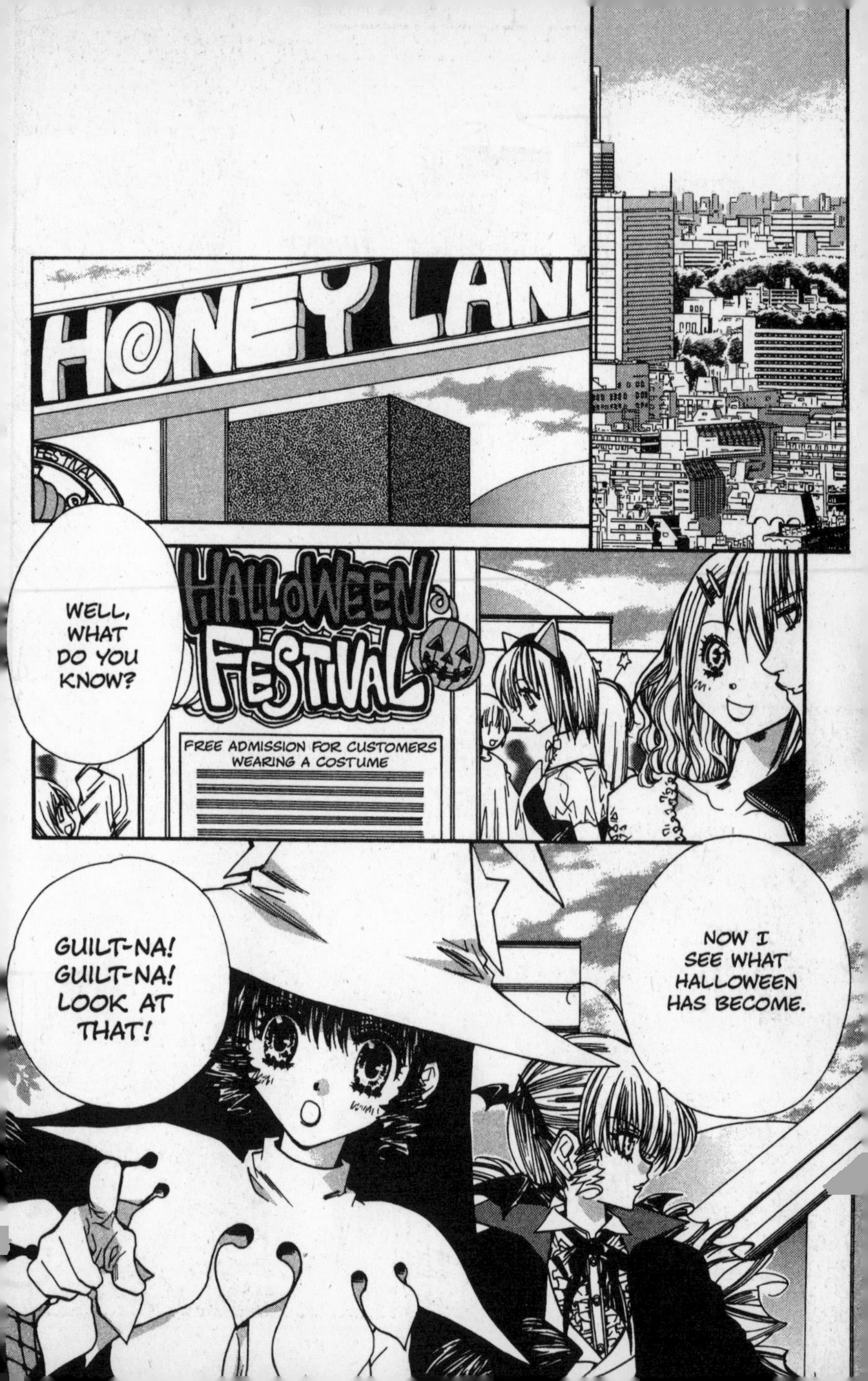

HONEYLAN
HALLOWEEN FESTIVAL
FREE ADMISSION FOR CUSTOMERS WEARING A COSTUME
WELL, WHAT DO YOU KNOW?
NOW I SEE WHAT HALLOWEEN HAS BECOME.
GUILT-NA! GUILT-NA! LOOK AT THAT!

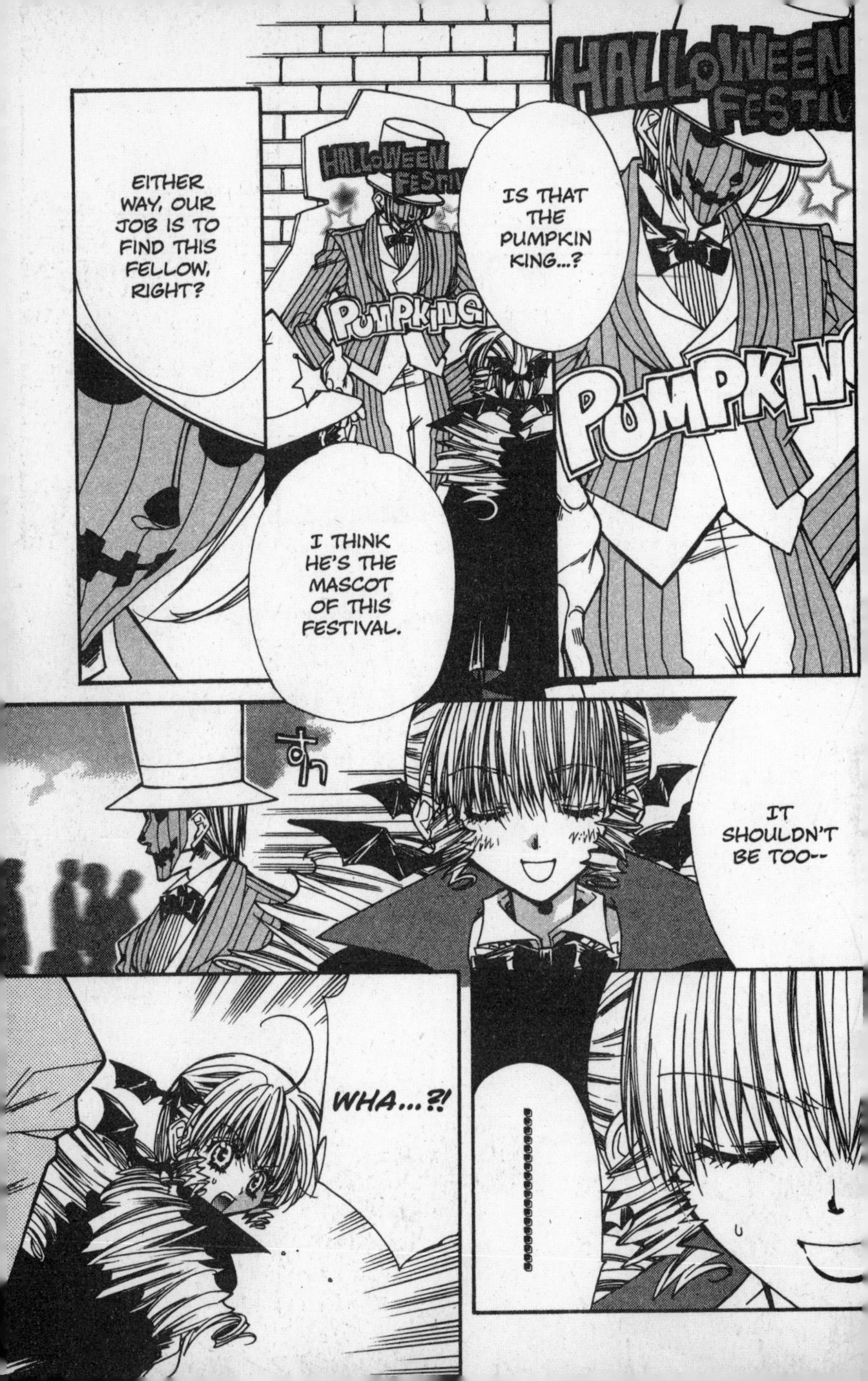
HALLOWEEN FESTIV
PUMPKING
IS THAT THE PUMPKIN KING...?
I THINK HE'S THE MASCOT OF THIS FESTIVAL.
HALLOWEEN FESTIV
PUMPKING
EITHER WAY, OUR JOB IS TO FIND THIS FELLOW, RIGHT?
IT SHOULDN'T BE TOO--
....
WHA...?!

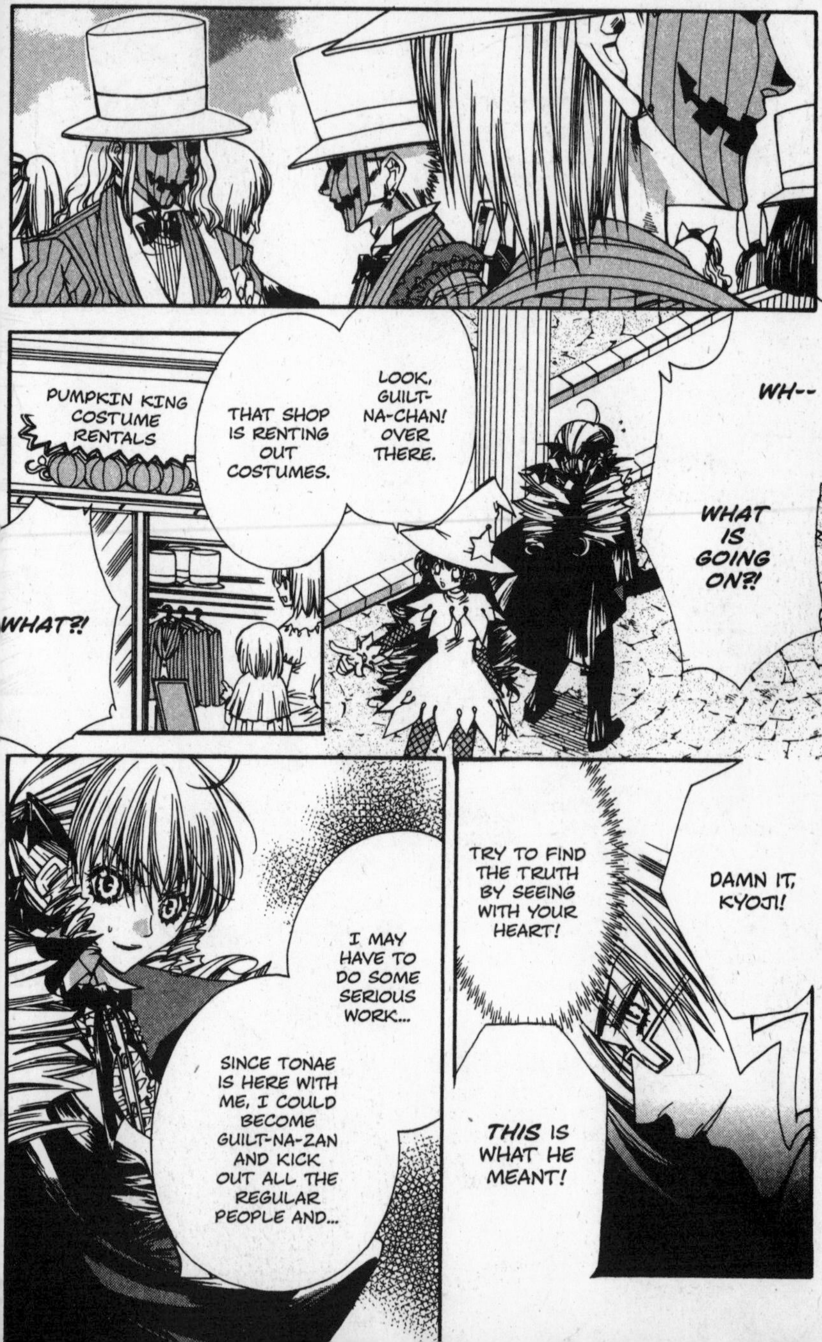
WH-- WHAT IS GOING ON?!
LOOK, GUILT-NA-CHAN! OVER THERE.
THAT SHOP IS RENTING OUT COSTUMES.
PUMPKIN KING COSTUME RENTALS
WHAT?!
DAMN IT, KYOJI!
TRY TO FIND THE TRUTH BY SEEING WITH YOUR HEART!
THIS IS WHAT HE MEANT!
I MAY HAVE TO DO SOME SERIOUS WORK...
SINCE TONAE IS HERE WITH ME, I COULD BECOME GUILT-NA-ZAN AND KICK OUT ALL THE REGULAR PEOPLE AND...

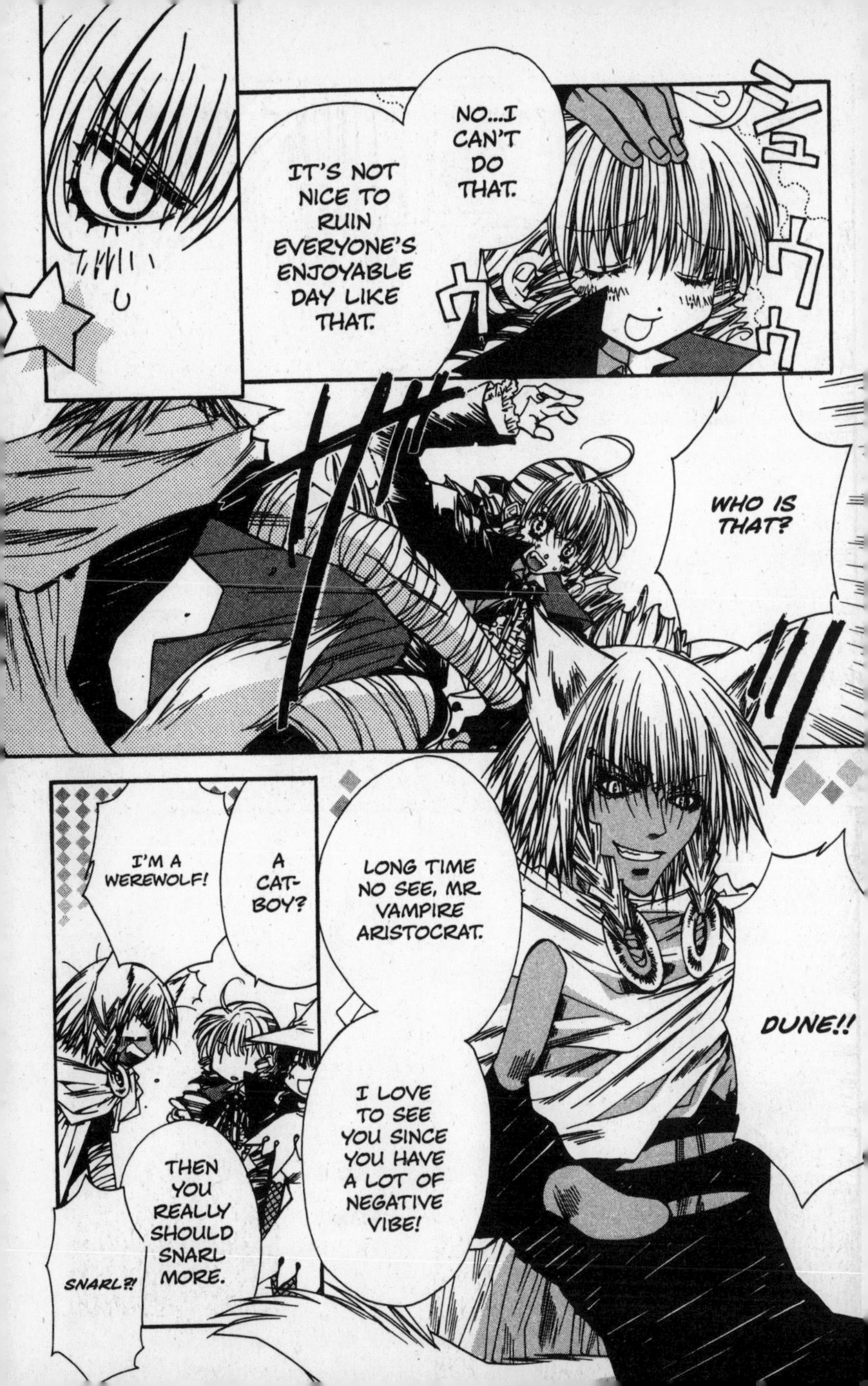
NO...I CAN'T DO THAT.
IT'S NOT NICE TO RUIN EVERYONE'S ENJOYABLE DAY LIKE THAT.
WHO IS THAT?
DUNE!!
LONG TIME NO SEE, MR VAMPIRE ARISTOCRAT.
I LOVE TO SEE YOU SINCE YOU HAVE A LOT OF NEGATIVE VIBE!
A CAT-BOY?
I'M A WEREWOLF!
THEN YOU REALLY SHOULD SNARL MORE.
SNARL?!

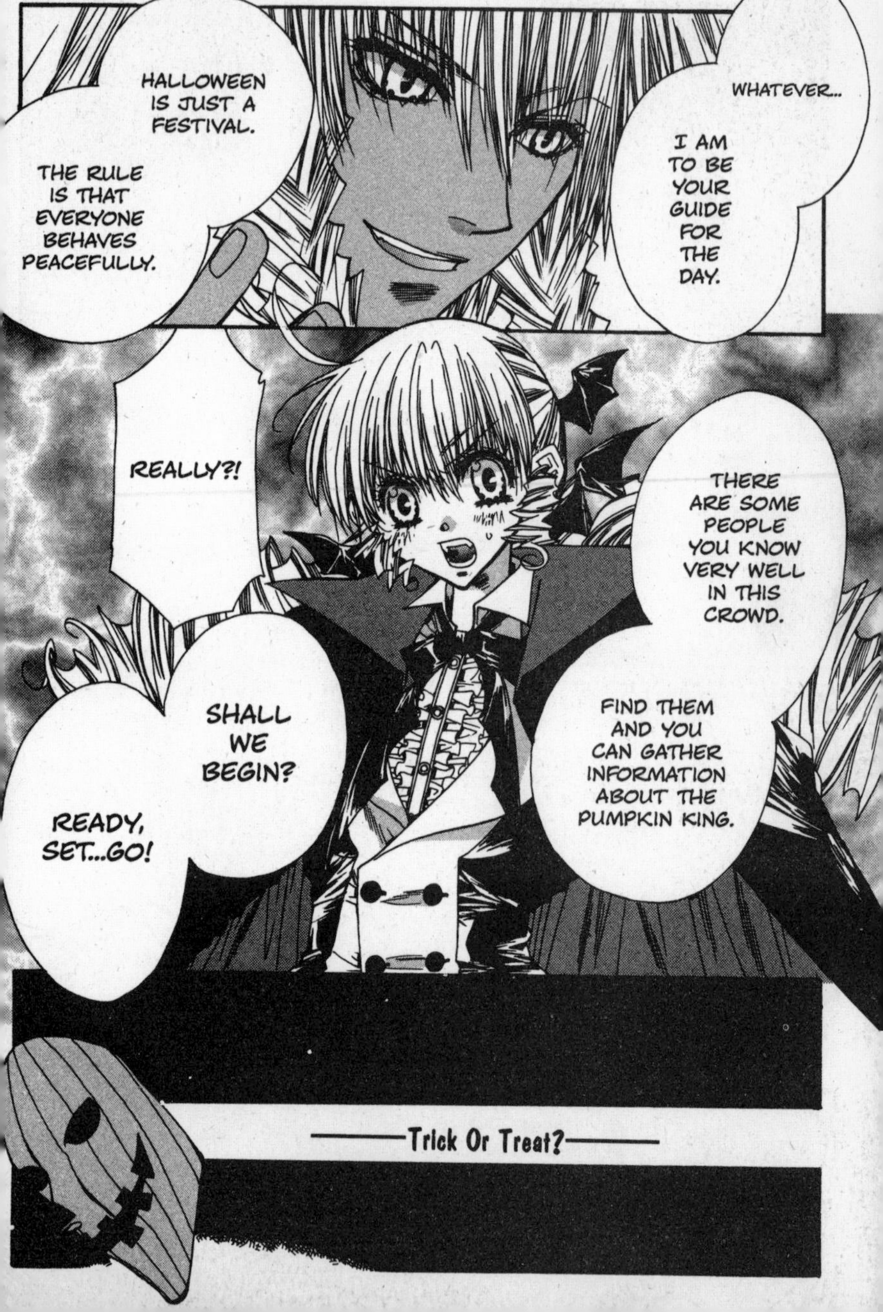
WHATEVER...
I AM TO BE YOUR GUIDE FOR THE DAY.
HALLOWEEN IS JUST A FESTIVAL.
THE RULE IS THAT EVERYONE BEHAVES PEACEFULLY.
THERE ARE SOME PEOPLE YOU KNOW VERY WELL IN THIS CROWD.
REALLY?!
FIND THEM AND YOU CAN GATHER INFORMATION ABOUT THE PUMPKIN KING.
SHALL WE BEGIN?
READY, SET...GO!
——Trick Or Treat?——

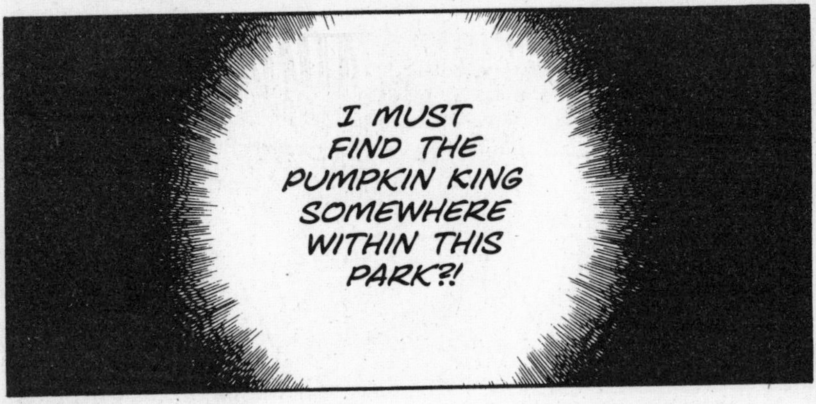
I MUST FIND THE PUMPKIN KING SOMEWHERE WITHIN THIS PARK?!

#11 Trick or Treat②

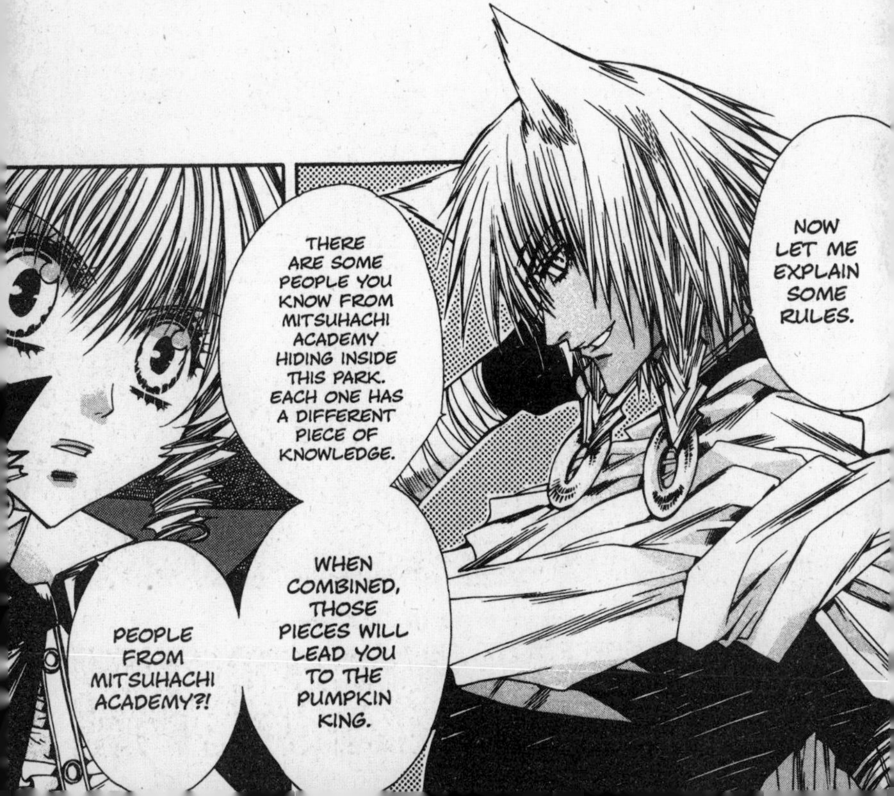
NOW LET ME EXPLAIN SOME RULES.
THERE ARE SOME PEOPLE YOU KNOW FROM MITSUHACHI ACADEMY HIDING INSIDE THIS PARK. EACH ONE HAS A DIFFERENT PIECE OF KNOWLEDGE.
WHEN COMBINED, THOSE PIECES WILL LEAD YOU TO THE PUMPKIN KING.
PEOPLE FROM MITSUHACHI ACADEMY?!

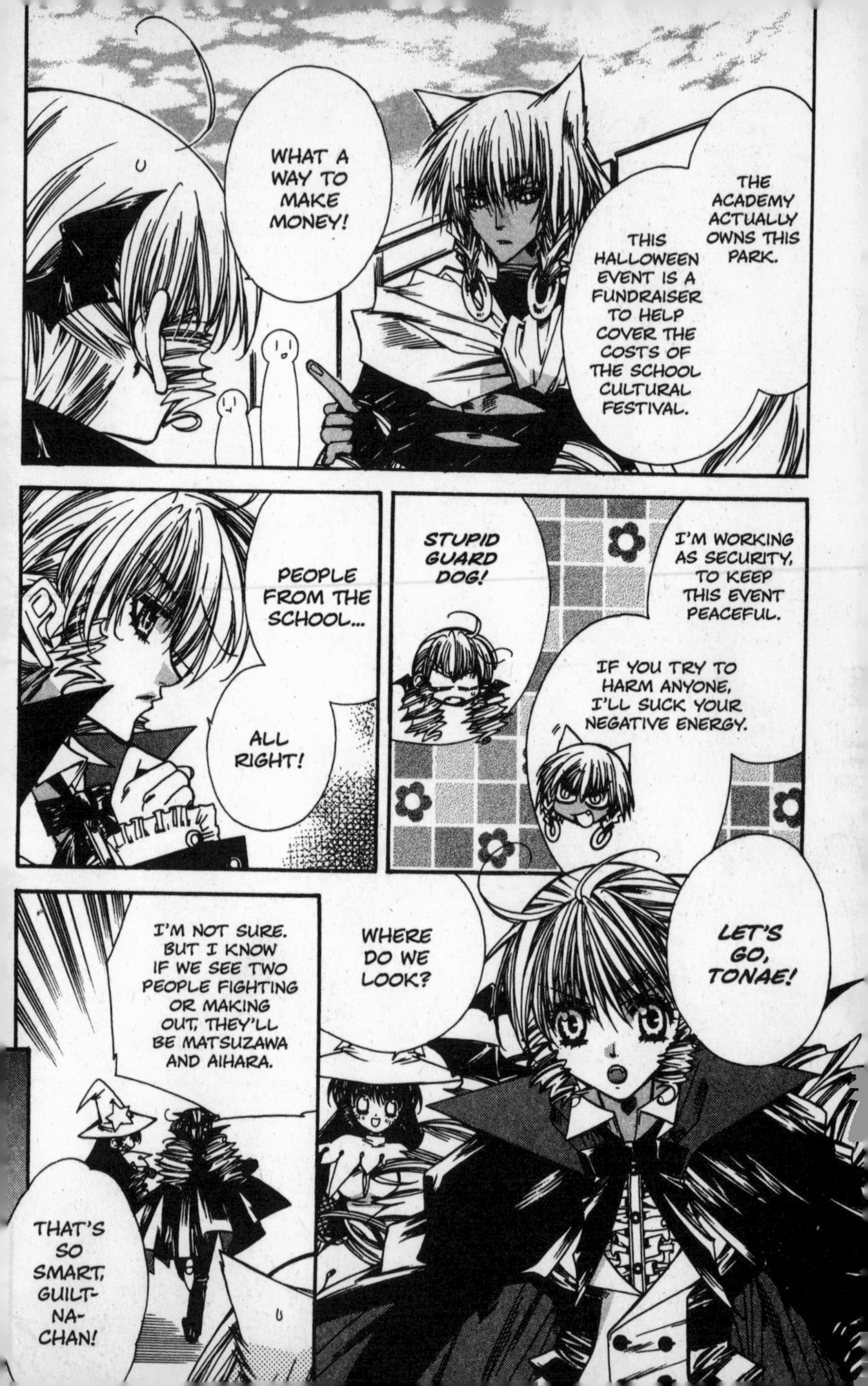
THE ACADEMY ACTUALLY OWNS THIS PARK.
THIS HALLOWEEN EVENT IS A FUNDRAISER TO HELP COVER THE COSTS OF THE SCHOOL CULTURAL FESTIVAL.
WHAT A WAY TO MAKE MONEY!
I'M WORKING AS SECURITY, TO KEEP THIS EVENT PEACEFUL.
STUPID GUARD DOG!
IF YOU TRY TO HARM ANYONE, I'LL SUCK YOUR NEGATIVE ENERGY.
PEOPLE FROM THE SCHOOL...
ALL RIGHT!
LET'S GO, TONAE!
WHERE DO WE LOOK?
I'M NOT SURE. BUT I KNOW IF WE SEE TWO PEOPLE FIGHTING OR MAKING OUT, THEY'LL BE MATSUZAWA AND AIHARA.
THAT'S SO SMART, GUILT-NA-CHAN!

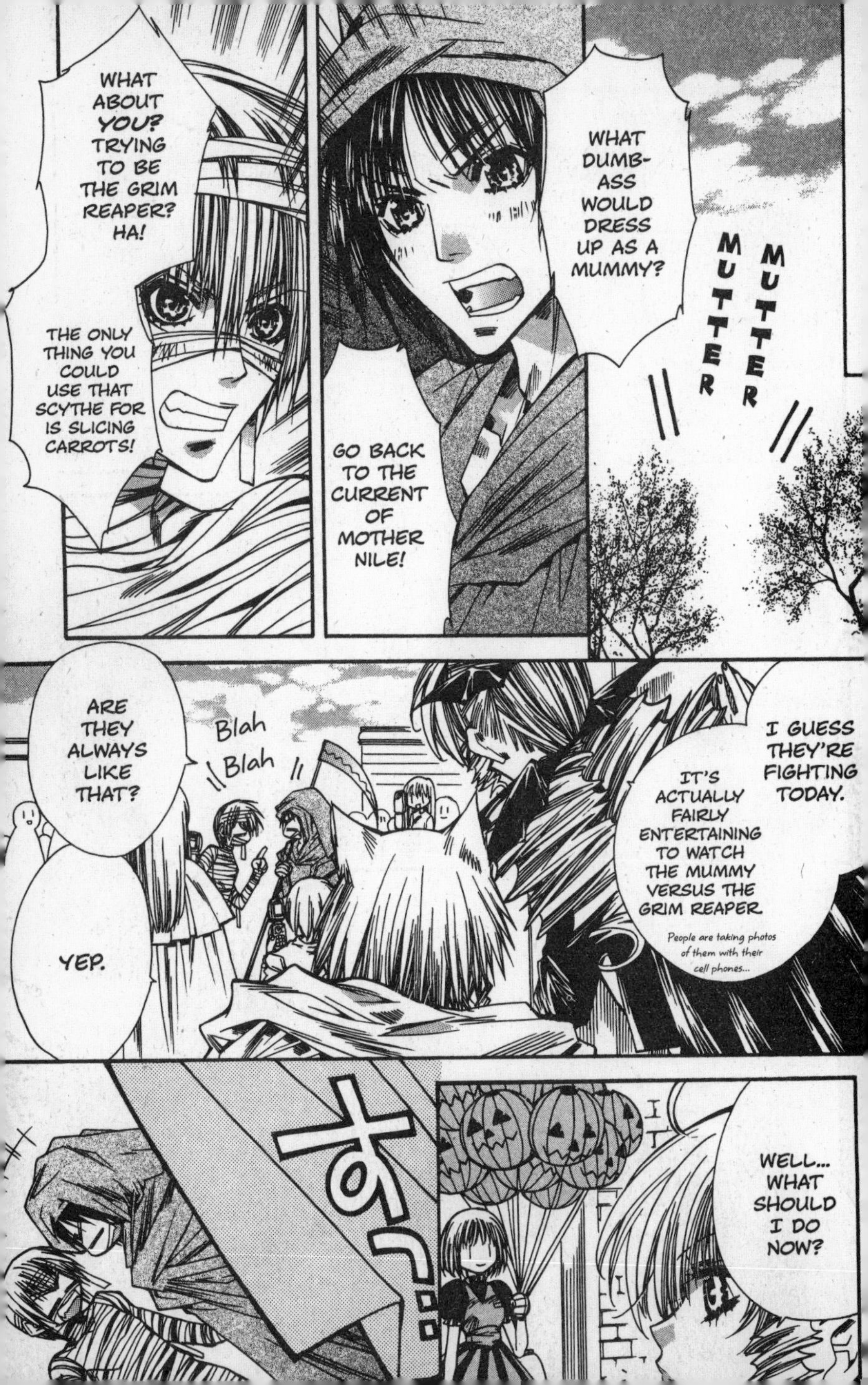
WHAT DUMB-ASS WOULD DRESS UP AS A MUMMY?
MUTTER MUTTER
GO BACK TO THE CURRENT OF MOTHER NILE!
WHAT ABOUT YOU? TRYING TO BE THE GRIM REAPER? HA!
THE ONLY THING YOU COULD USE THAT SCYTHE FOR IS SLICING CARROTS!
I GUESS THEY'RE FIGHTING TODAY.
IT'S ACTUALLY FAIRLY ENTERTAINING TO WATCH THE MUMMY VERSUS THE GRIM REAPER.
People are taking photos of them with their cell phones...
ARE THEY ALWAYS LIKE THAT?
Blah Blah
YEP.
WELL... WHAT SHOULD I DO NOW?
すっ

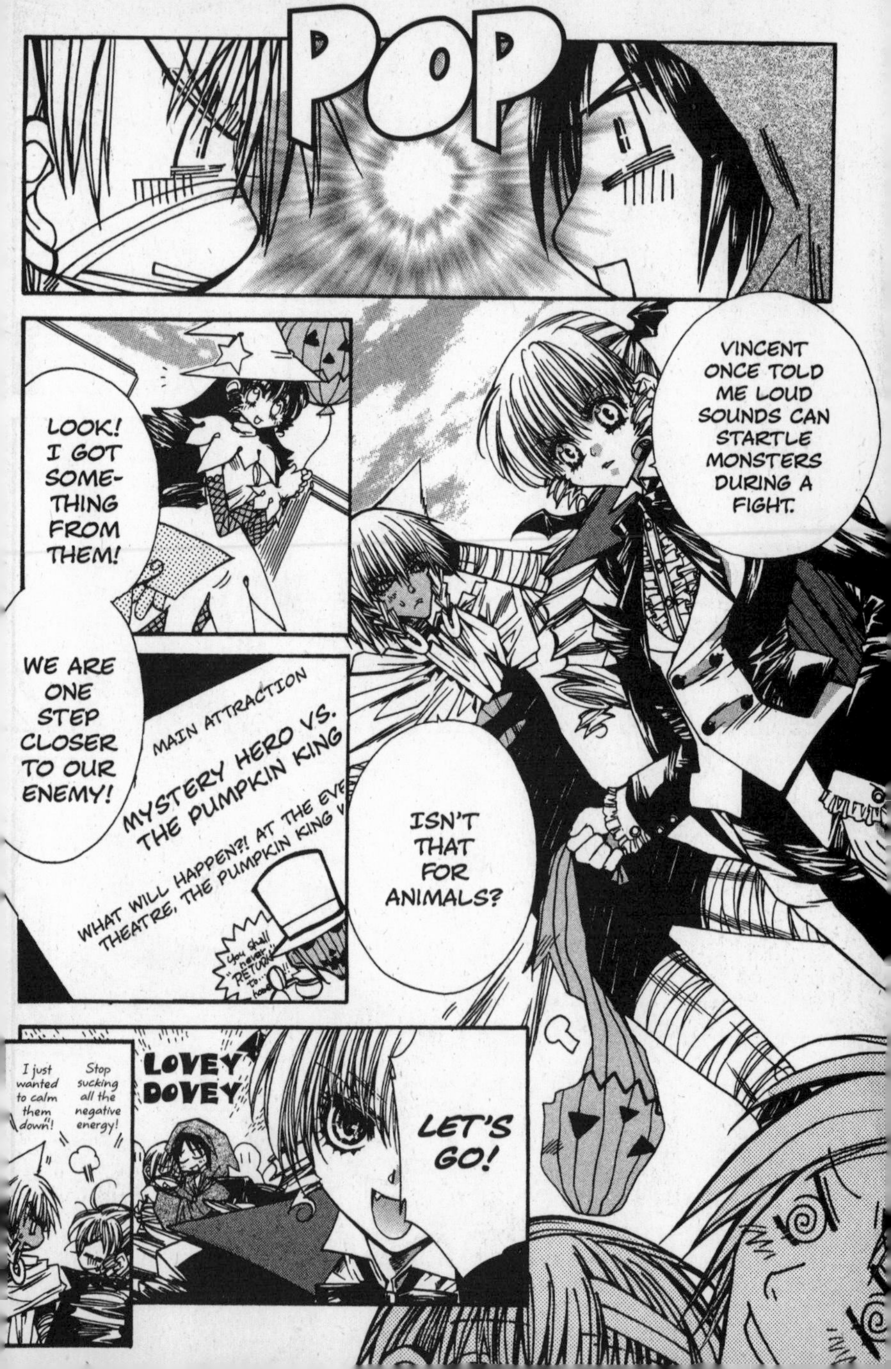
POP
VINCENT ONCE TOLD ME LOUD SOUNDS CAN STARTLE MONSTERS DURING A FIGHT.
ISN'T THAT FOR ANIMALS?
LOOK! I GOT SOME-THING FROM THEM!
WE ARE ONE STEP CLOSER TO OUR ENEMY!
MAIN ATTRACTION
MYSTERY HERO V.S. THE PUMPKIN KING
WHAT WILL HAPPEN?! AT THE EVE
THEATRE, THE PUMPKIN KING W
You shall never "RETURN" to...
LET'S GO!
LOVEY DOVEY
Stop sucking all the negative energy!
I just wanted to calm them down!

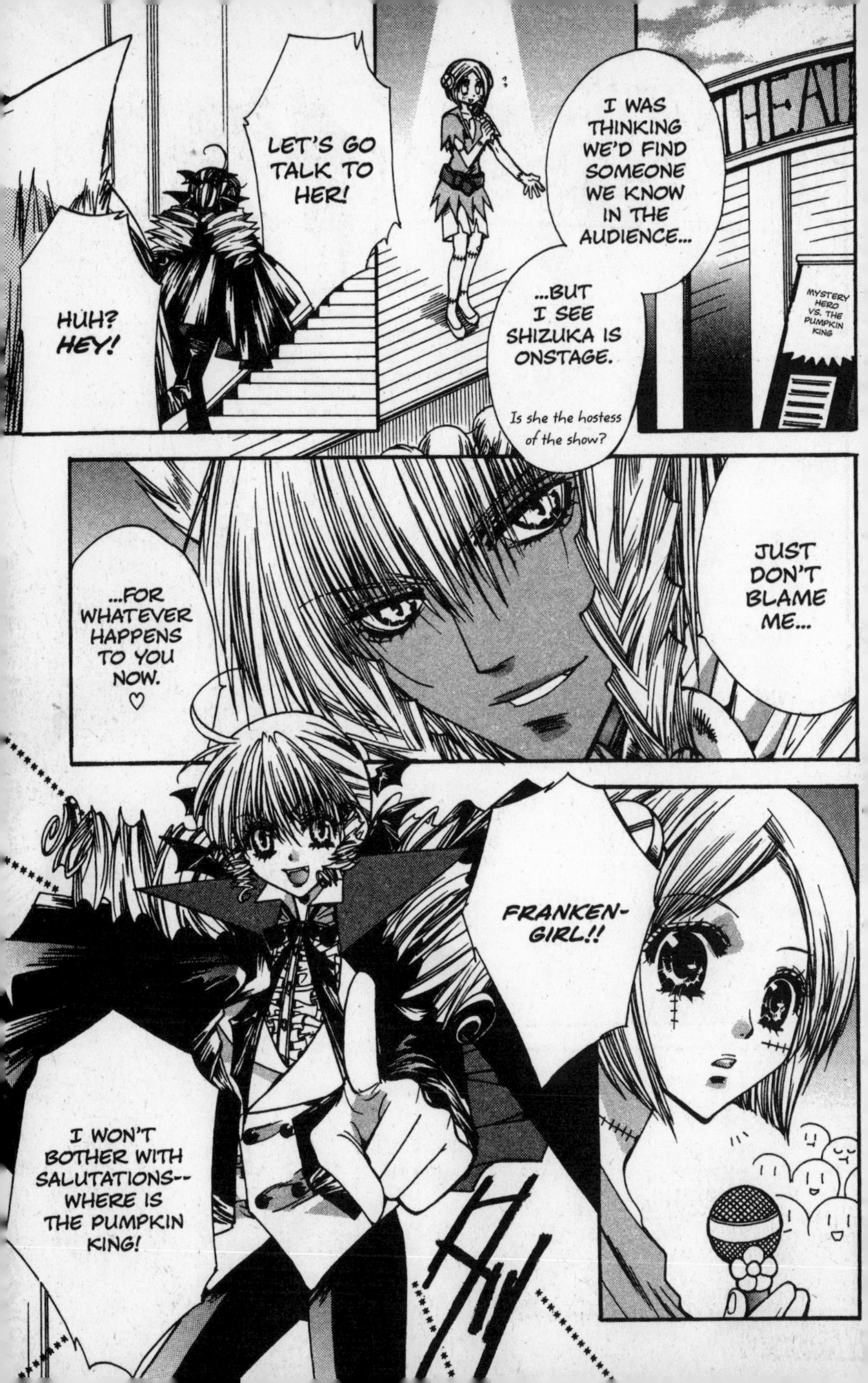
I WAS THINKING WE'D FIND SOMEONE WE KNOW IN THE AUDIENCE...
...BUT I SEE SHIZUKA IS ONSTAGE.
Is she the hostess of the show?
MYSTERY HERO VS. THE PUMPKIN KING
LET'S GO TALK TO HER!
HUH? HEY!
JUST DON'T BLAME ME...
...FOR WHATEVER HAPPENS TO YOU NOW. ♡
FRANKEN-GIRL!!
I WON'T BOTHER WITH SALUTATIONS--WHERE IS THE PUMPKIN KING!

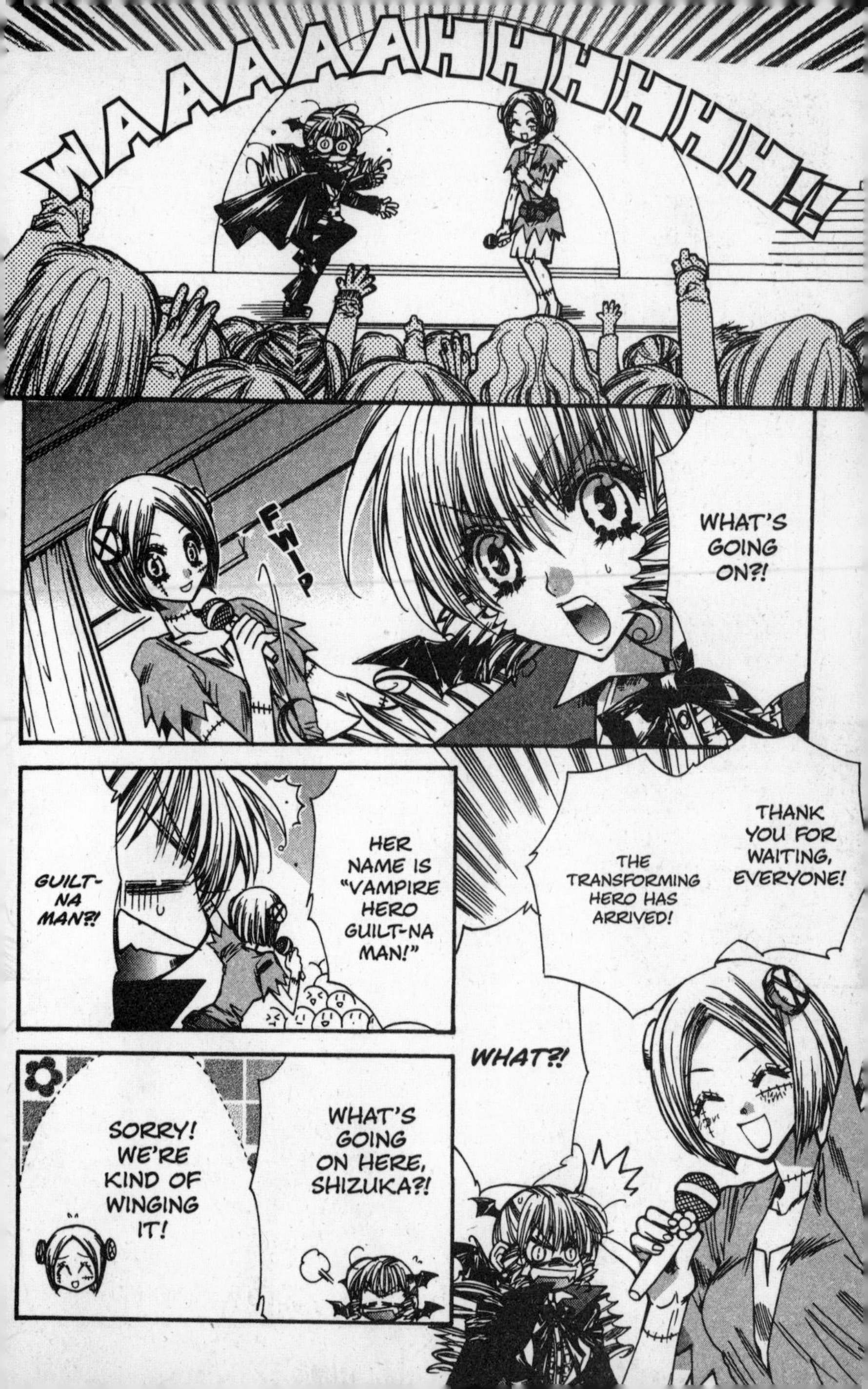

WAAAAAHHHHHHH!!
WHAT'S GOING ON?!
FWIP
THANK YOU FOR WAITING, EVERYONE!
THE TRANSFORMING HERO HAS ARRIVED!
WHAT?!
HER NAME IS "VAMPIRE HERO GUILT-NA MAN!"
GUILT-NA MAN?!
WHAT'S GOING ON HERE, SHIZUKA?!
SORRY! WE'RE KIND OF WINGING IT!

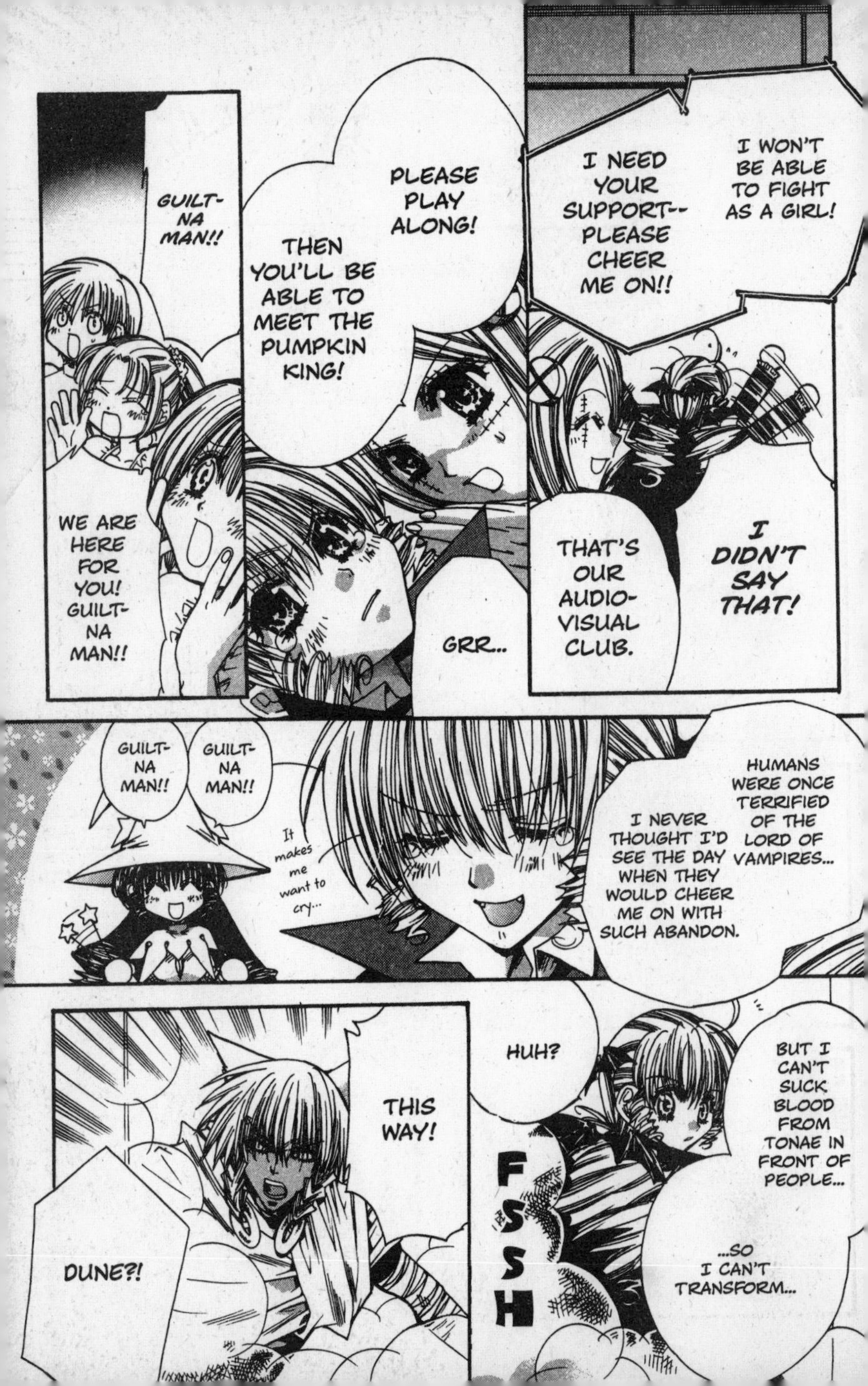
I WON'T BE ABLE TO FIGHT AS A GIRL!
I NEED YOUR SUPPORT-- PLEASE CHEER ME ON!!
I DIDN'T SAY THAT!
THAT'S OUR AUDIO-VISUAL CLUB.
PLEASE PLAY ALONG!
THEN YOU'LL BE ABLE TO MEET THE PUMPKIN KING!
GRR...
GUILT-NA MAN!!
WE ARE HERE FOR YOU! GUILT-NA MAN!!
HUMANS WERE ONCE TERRIFIED OF THE LORD OF VAMPIRES...
I NEVER THOUGHT I'D SEE THE DAY WHEN THEY WOULD CHEER ME ON WITH SUCH ABANDON.
It makes me want to cry...
GUILT-NA MAN!!
GUILT-NA MAN!!
BUT I CAN'T SUCK BLOOD FROM TONAE IN FRONT OF PEOPLE...
...SO I CAN'T TRANSFORM...
HUH?
FSSH
THIS WAY!
DUNE?!

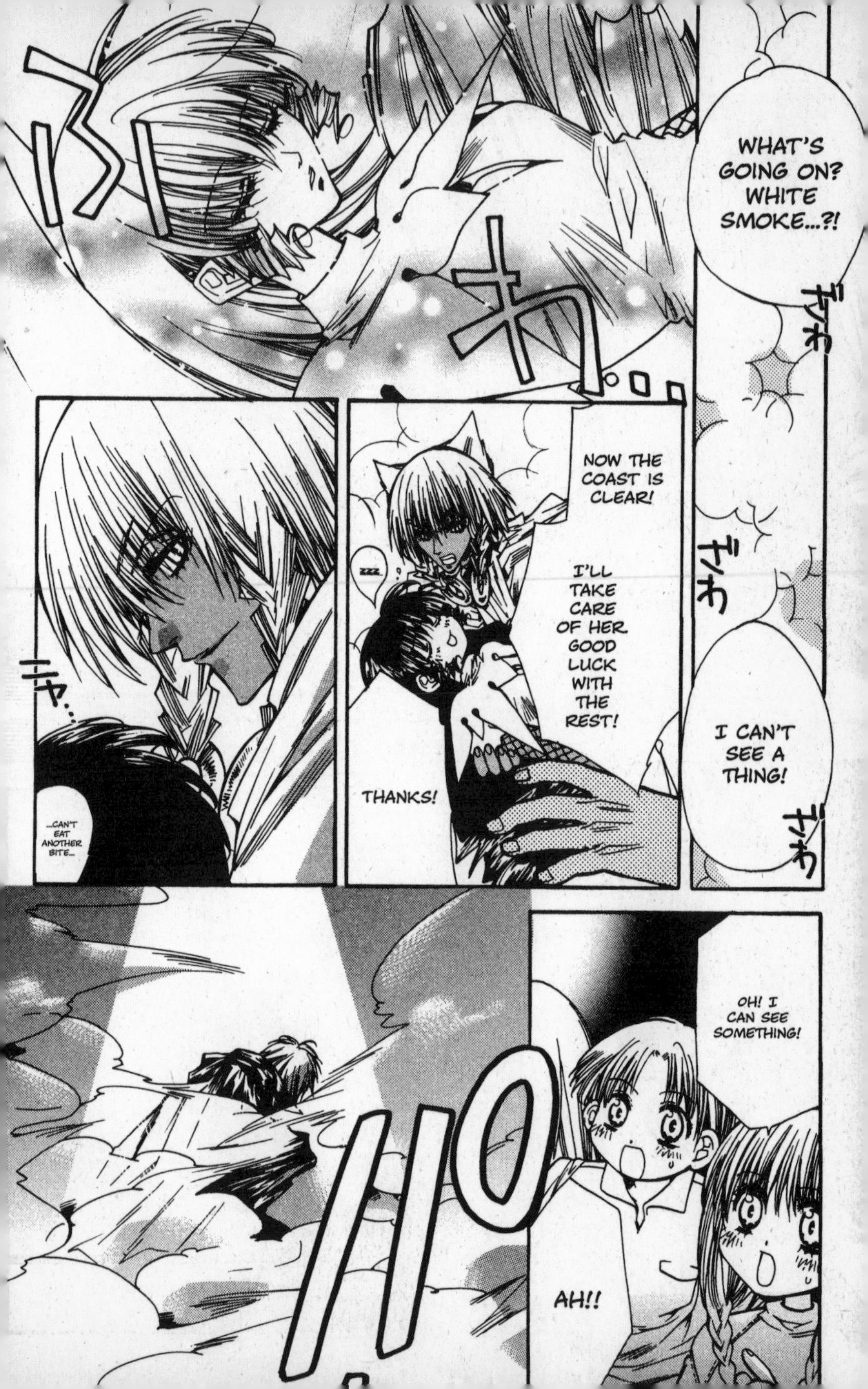
WHAT'S GOING ON? WHITE SMOKE...?!
ざわ
ざわ
I CAN'T SEE A THING!
ざわ
NOW THE COAST IS CLEAR!
I'LL TAKE CARE OF HER GOOD LUCK WITH THE REST!
ZZZ..
THANKS!
ニャ...
...CAN'T EAT ANOTHER BITE...
OH! I CAN SEE SOMETHING!
AH!!

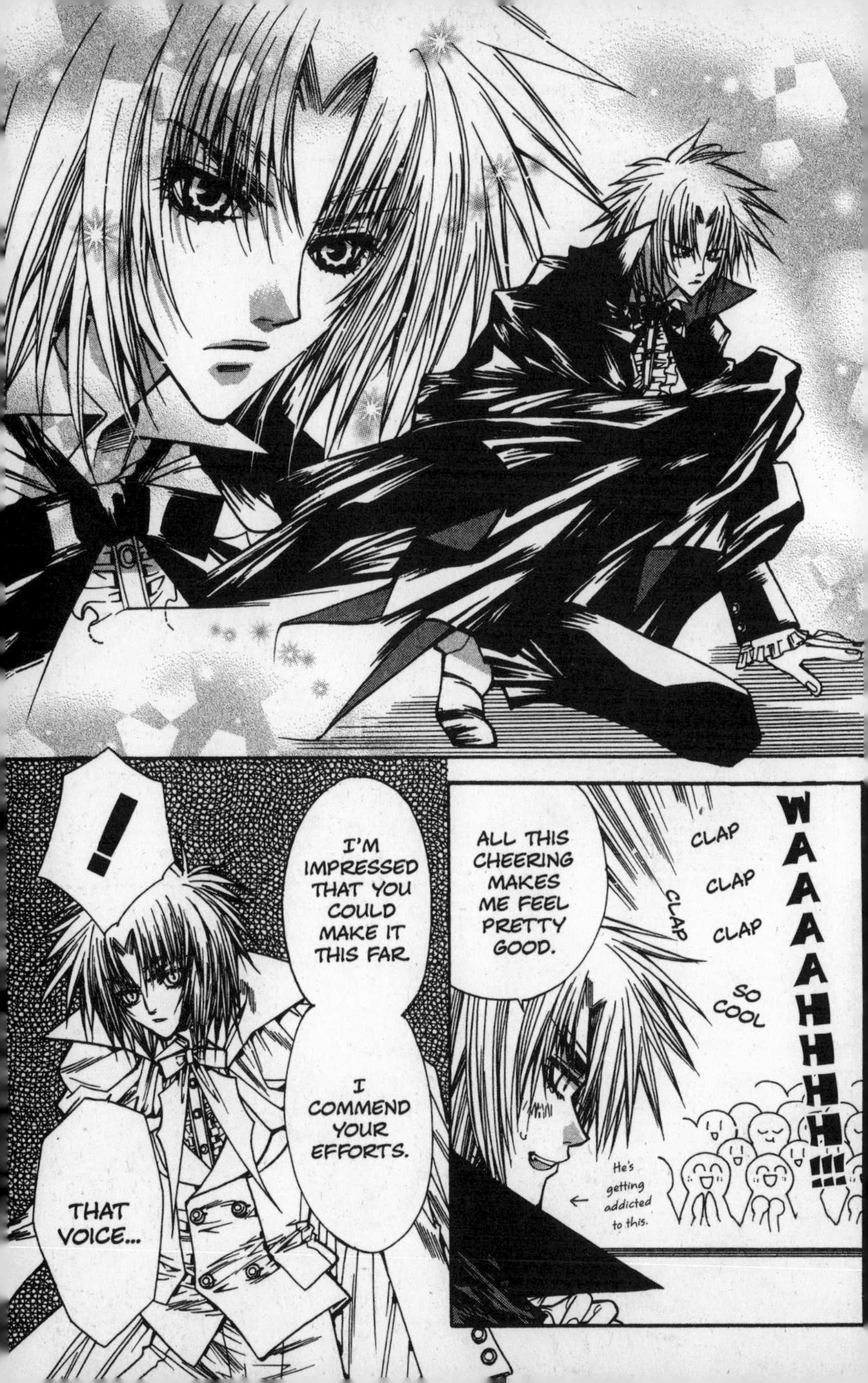
WAAAAHHHH!!!
CLAP
CLAP
CLAP
CLAP
SO COOL
ALL THIS CHEERING MAKES ME FEEL PRETTY GOOD.
He's getting addicted to this.
!
I'M IMPRESSED THAT YOU COULD MAKE IT THIS FAR.
I COMMEND YOUR EFFORTS.
THAT VOICE...

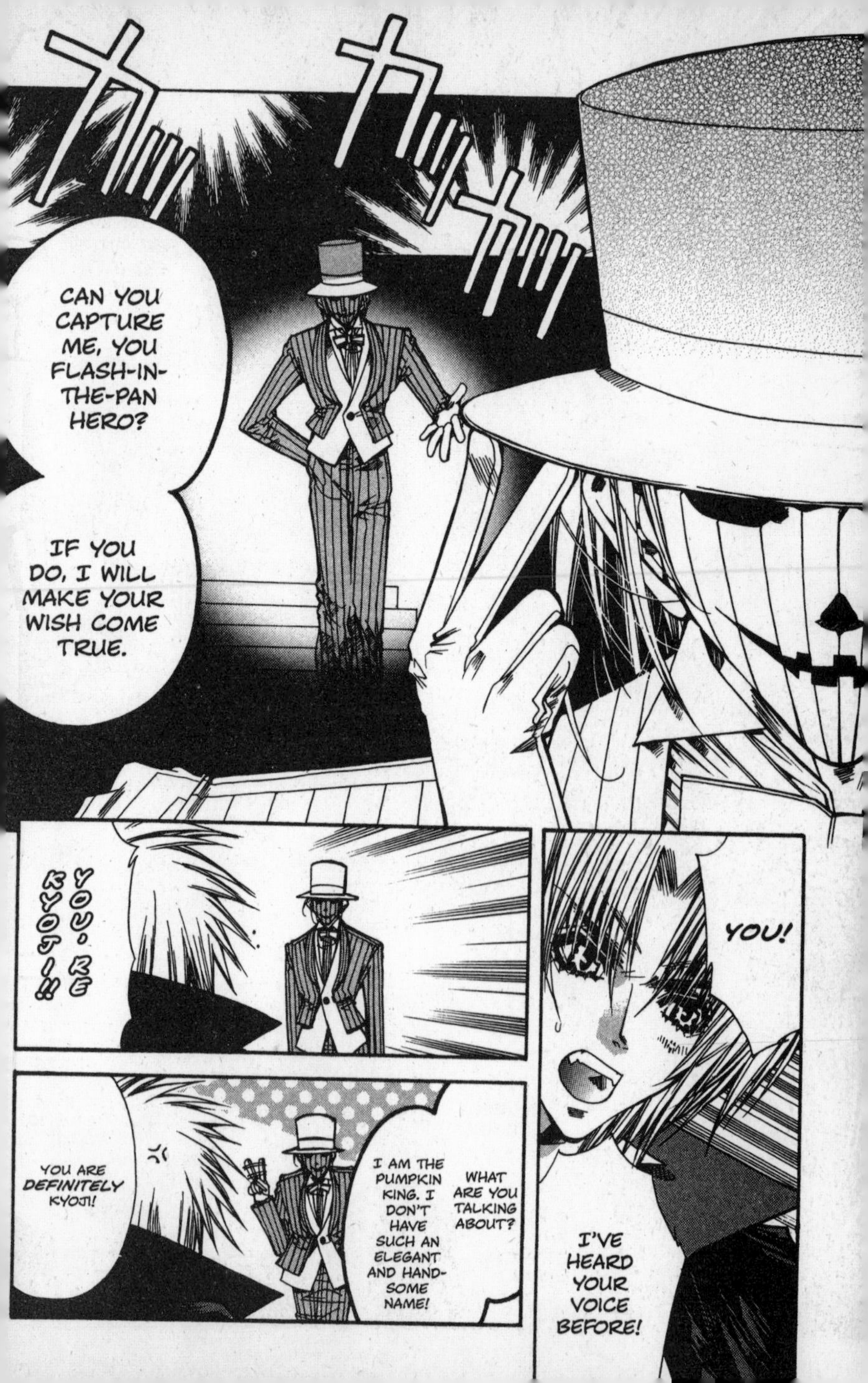
カッ
カッカッ
CAN YOU CAPTURE ME, YOU FLASH-IN-THE-PAN HERO?
IF YOU DO, I WILL MAKE YOUR WISH COME TRUE.
YOU!
I'VE HEARD YOUR VOICE BEFORE!
YOU'RE KYOJI!!
WHAT ARE YOU TALKING ABOUT?
I AM THE PUMPKIN KING. I DON'T HAVE SUCH AN ELEGANT AND HAND-SOME NAME!
YOU ARE DEFINITELY KYOJI!

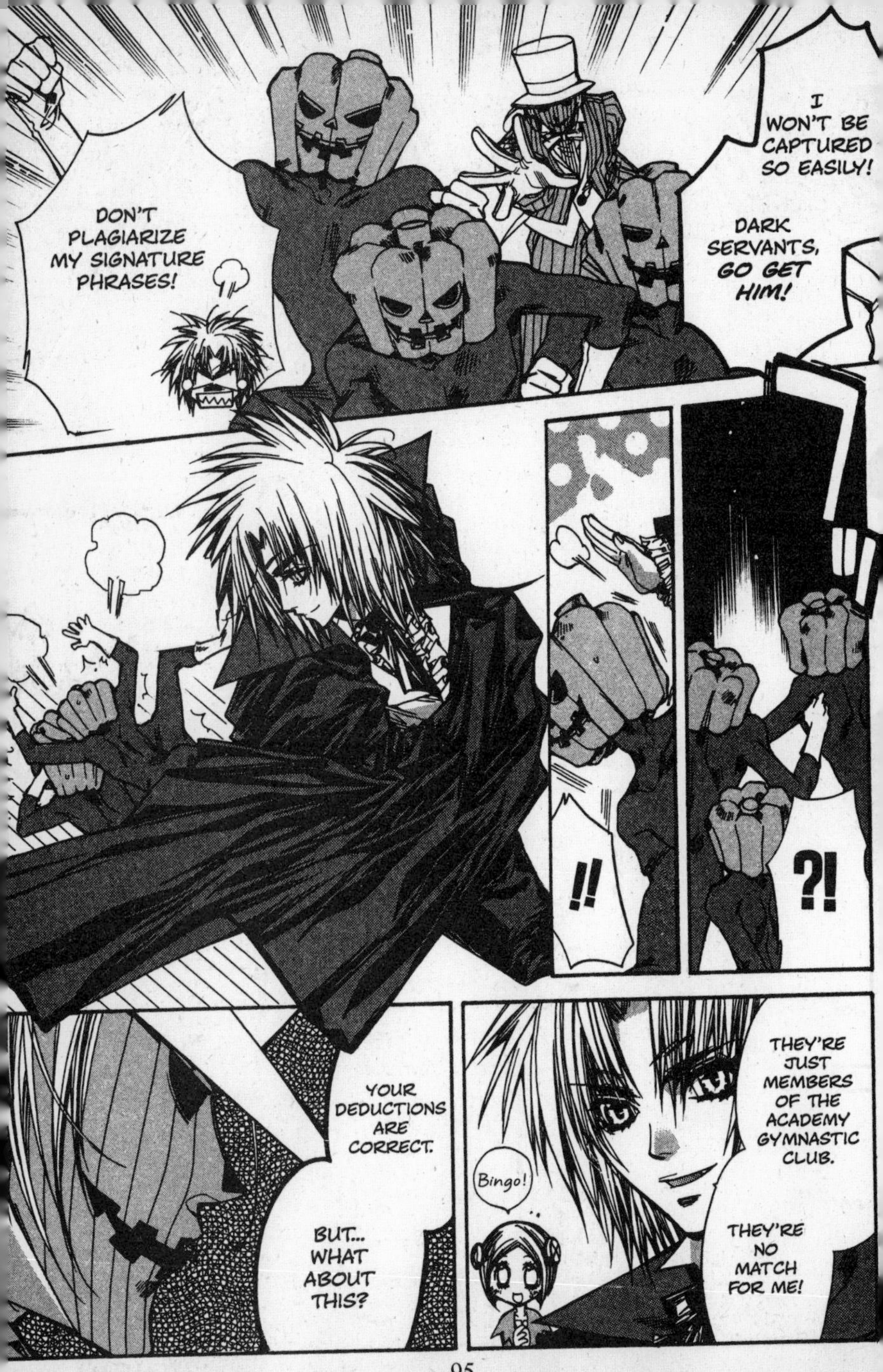
I WON'T BE CAPTURED SO EASILY!
DARK SERVANTS, GO GET HIM!
DON'T PLAGIARIZE MY SIGNATURE PHRASES!
?!
!!
THEY'RE JUST MEMBERS OF THE ACADEMY GYMNASTIC CLUB.
Bingo!
THEY'RE NO MATCH FOR ME!
YOUR DEDUCTIONS ARE CORRECT.
BUT... WHAT ABOUT THIS?

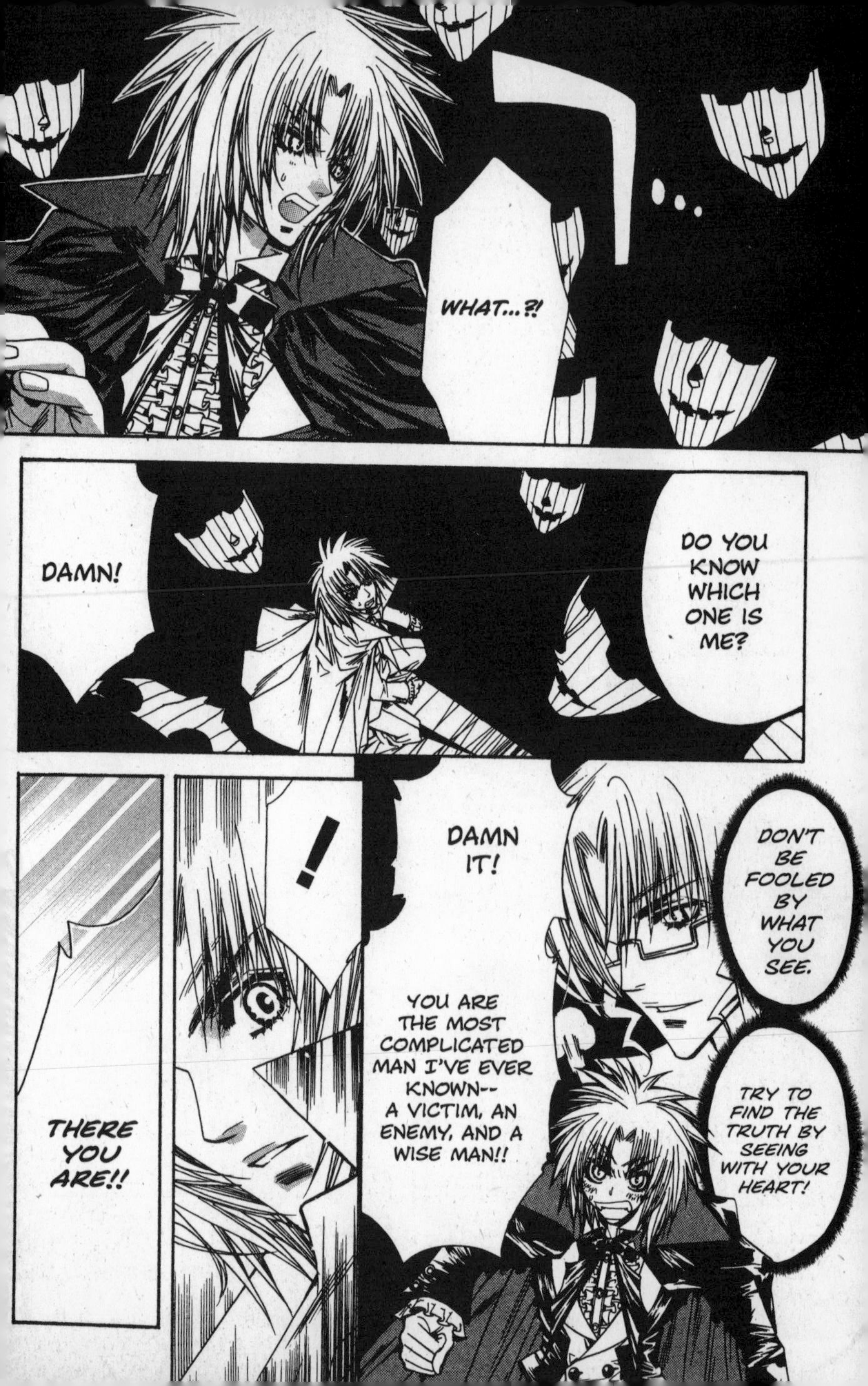
WHAT...?!
DO YOU KNOW WHICH ONE IS ME?
DAMN!
DON'T BE FOOLED BY WHAT YOU SEE.
DAMN IT!
TRY TO FIND THE TRUTH BY SEEING WITH YOUR HEART!
YOU ARE THE MOST COMPLICATED MAN I'VE EVER KNOWN-- A VICTIM, AN ENEMY, AND A WISE MAN!!
!
THERE YOU ARE!!

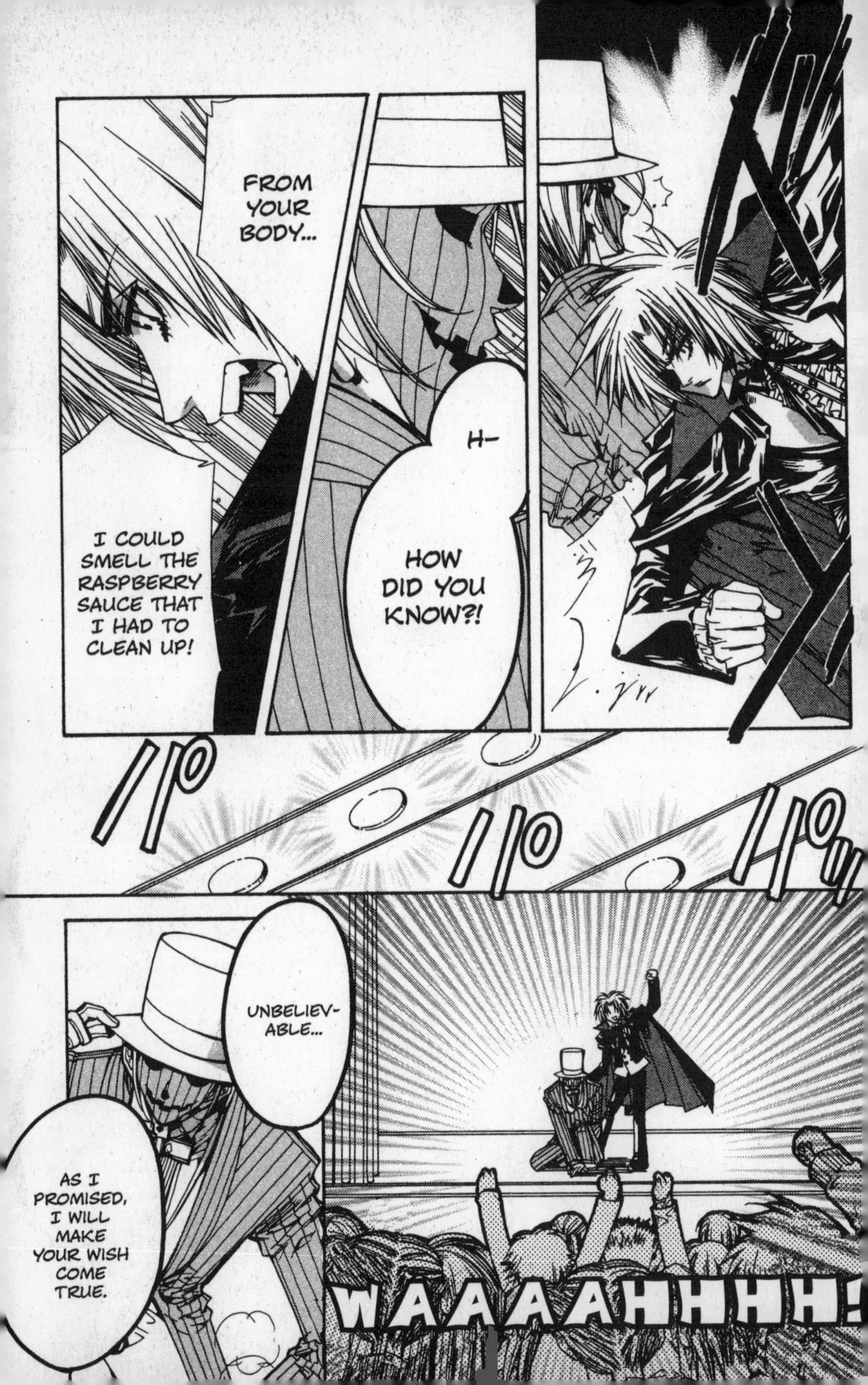
H-
HOW DID YOU KNOW?!
FROM YOUR BODY...
I COULD SMELL THE RASPBERRY SAUCE THAT I HAD TO CLEAN UP!
WAAAAAHHHH!
UNBELIEV-ABLE...
AS I PROMISED, I WILL MAKE YOUR WISH COME TRUE.

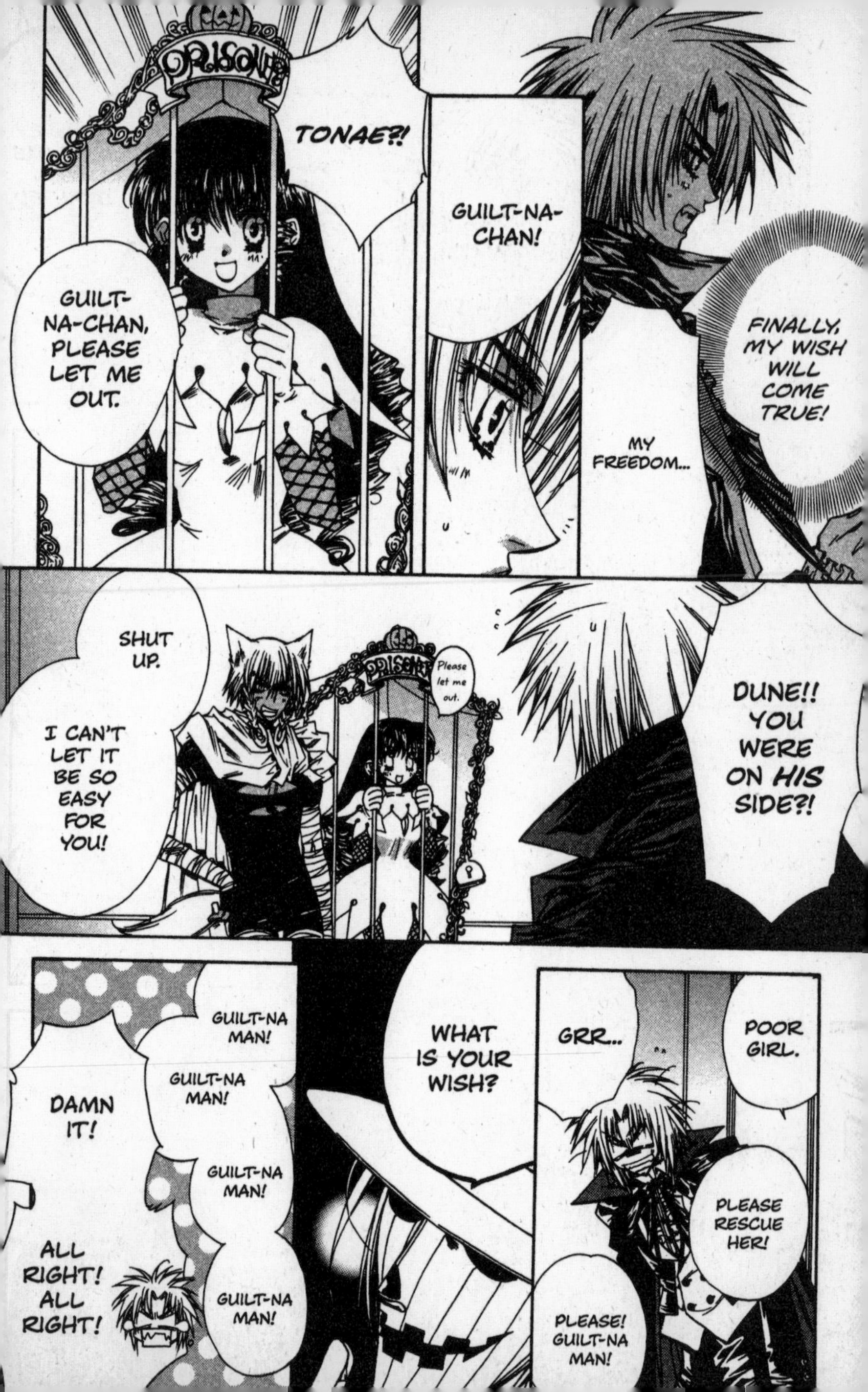
FINALLY, MY WISH WILL COME TRUE!
MY FREEDOM...
GUILT-NA-CHAN!
TONAE?!
GUILT-NA-CHAN, PLEASE LET ME OUT.
DUNE!! YOU WERE ON HIS SIDE?!
Please let me out.
SHUT UP.
I CAN'T LET IT BE SO EASY FOR YOU!
POOR GIRL.
GRR...
PLEASE RESCUE HER!
PLEASE! GUILT-NA MAN!
WHAT IS YOUR WISH?
GUILT-NA MAN!
GUILT-NA MAN!
DAMN IT!
GUILT-NA MAN!
GUILT-NA MAN!
ALL RIGHT! ALL RIGHT!

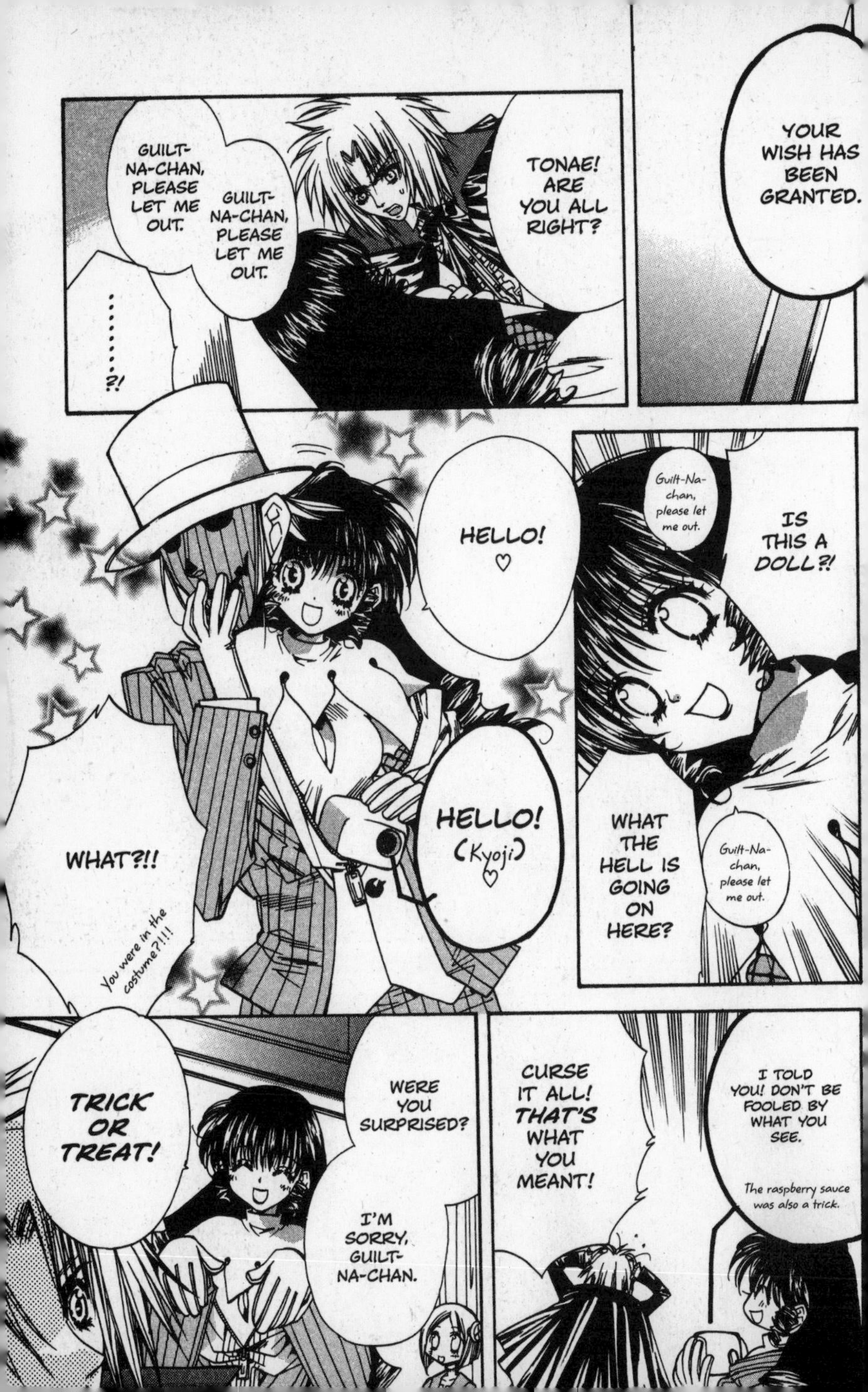
YOUR WISH HAS BEEN GRANTED.
TONAE! ARE YOU ALL RIGHT?
GUILT-NA-CHAN, PLEASE LET ME OUT.
GUILT-NA-CHAN, PLEASE LET ME OUT.
......?!
IS THIS A DOLL?!
Guilt-Na-chan, please let me out.
WHAT THE HELL IS GOING ON HERE?
Guilt-Na-chan, please let me out.
HELLO! ♡
HELLO! (Kyoji) ♡
WHAT?!!
You were in the costume?!!!
I TOLD YOU! DON'T BE FOOLED BY WHAT YOU SEE.
The raspberry sauce was also a trick.
CURSE IT ALL! THAT'S WHAT YOU MEANT!
WERE YOU SURPRISED?
I'M SORRY, GUILT-NA-CHAN.
TRICK OR TREAT!

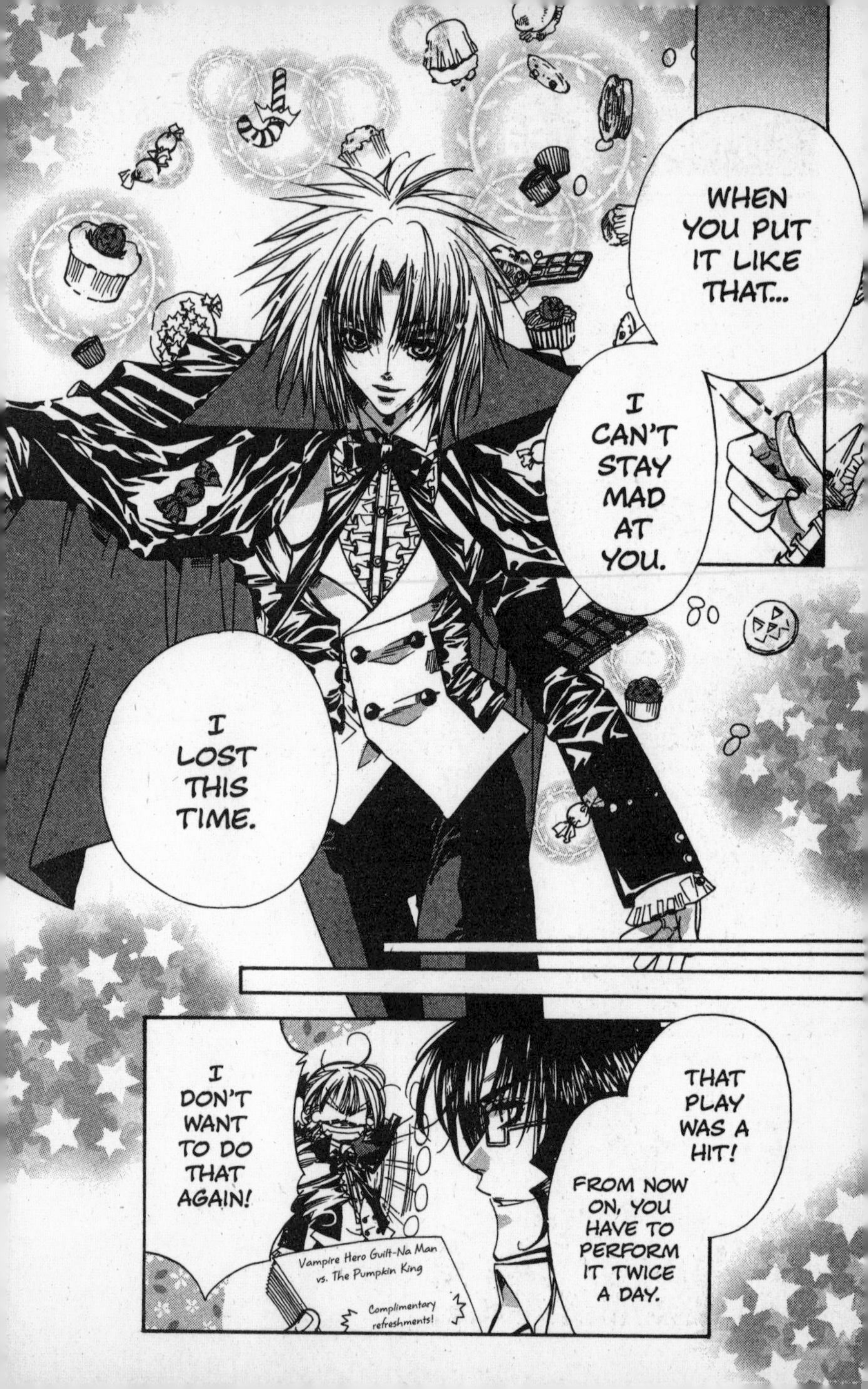
WHEN YOU PUT IT LIKE THAT...
I CAN'T STAY MAD AT YOU.
I LOST THIS TIME.
THAT PLAY WAS A HIT!
FROM NOW ON, YOU HAVE TO PERFORM IT TWICE A DAY.
I DON'T WANT TO DO THAT AGAIN!
Vampire Hero Guilt-Na Man vs. The Pumpkin King
Complimentary refreshments!

BONUS COMIC STRIP

VAMPIRE DOLL REFLECTIONS

Trick or Treat

QUESTION: WHAT OTHER MONSTERS BESIDES WEREWOLVES HAVE UNIQUE ATTRIBUTES TO THEIR SPEECH?
I REMEMBER NOW!!
YOU CAN'T SAY THE LETTER "W"!
WHA...
Dracula
EH...
AH...
GRR... ARG...
THAT'S IT!!
WAY TO GO!!
Frankenstein

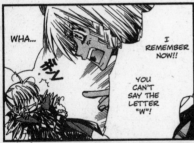

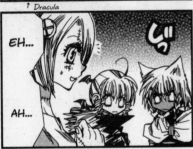

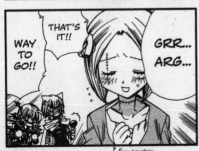

デューン

Dune
male
tribe: nomad of desert
attribute: evil
job: malice absorber
height: 160~182
eyes: ocher
hair: ivy green

三ツ蜂志づ香

Shizuka Mitsuhachi
female
tribe: human
attribute: good
job: chairperson
height: 156
eyes: ivory
hair: pale sepia

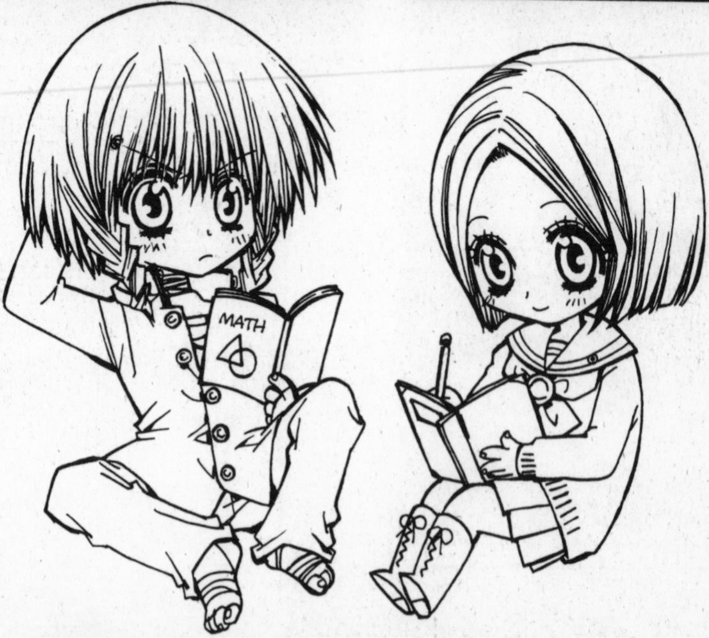
MATH

People from Mitsuhachi are thinking. What do you do?

#12 DOLL

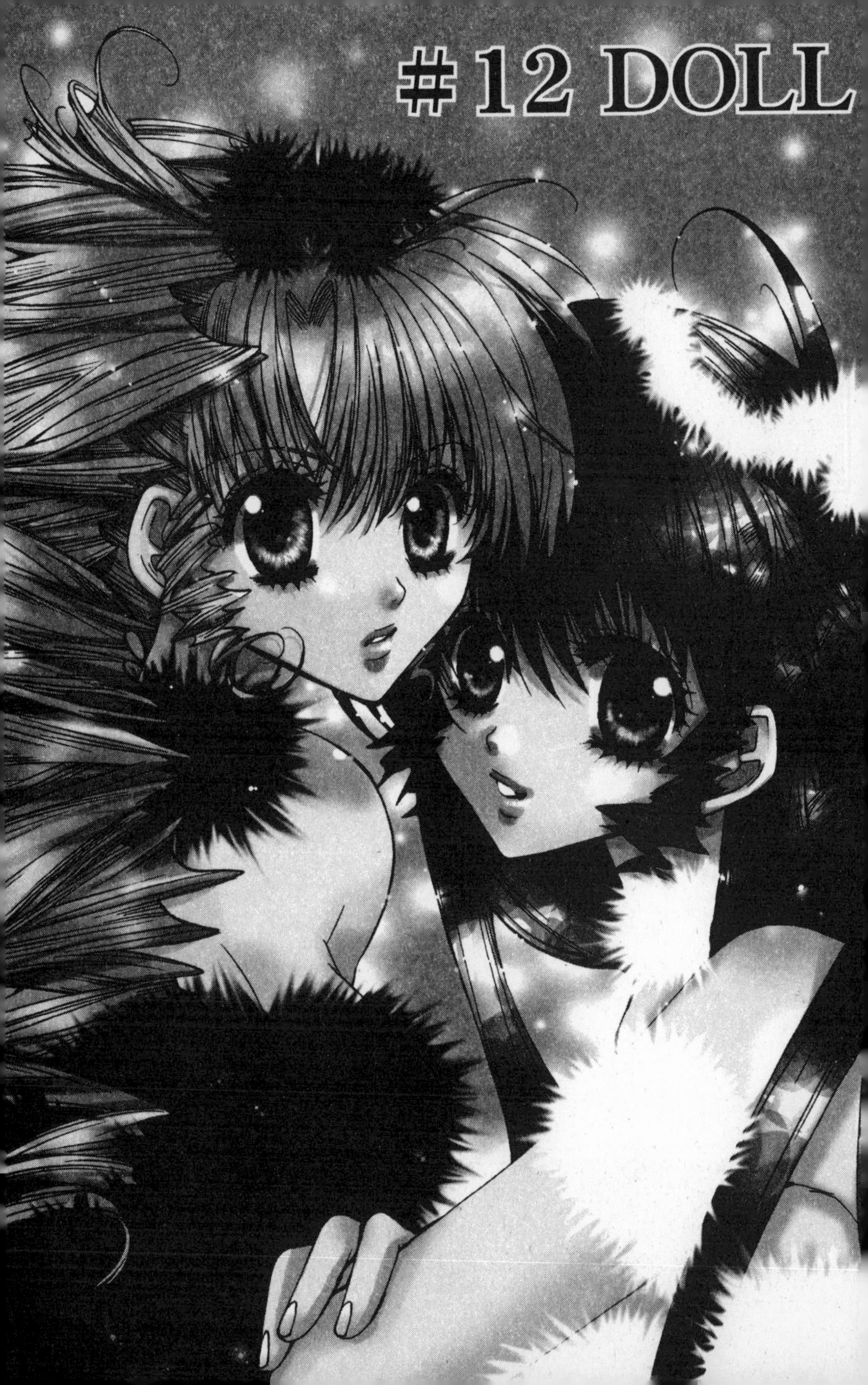

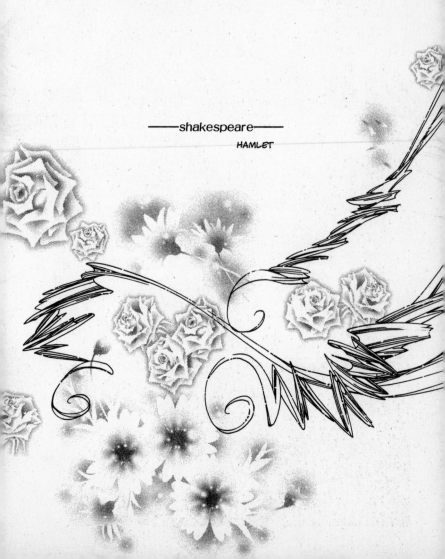

O rose of May!
Dear maid, kind sister,
sweet Ophelia!

——shakespeare——

HAMLET

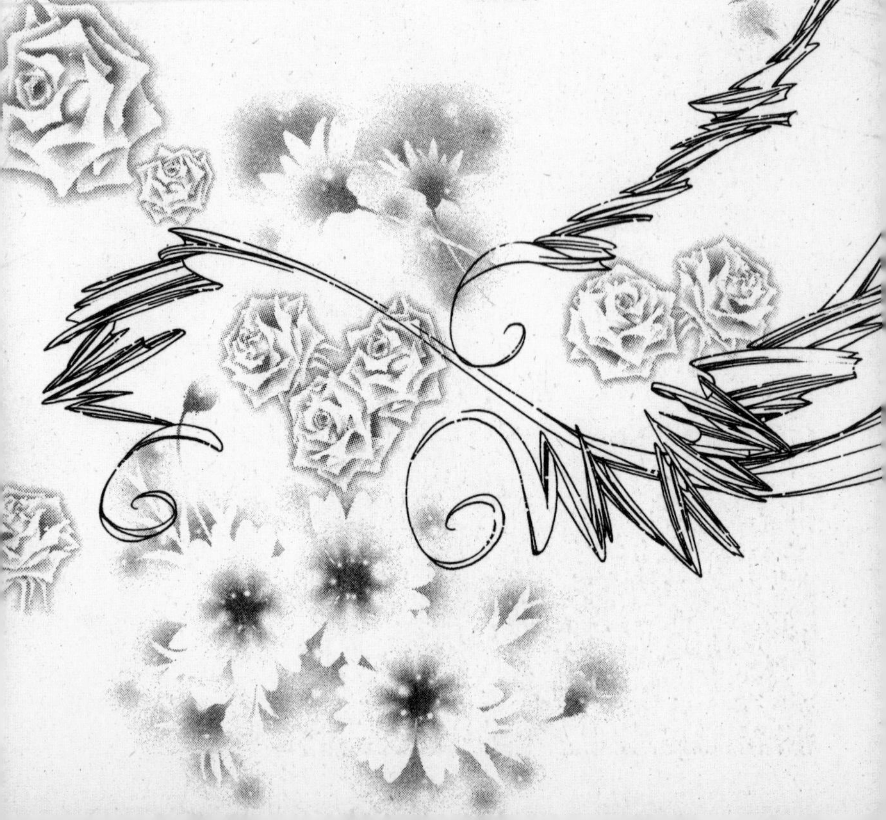

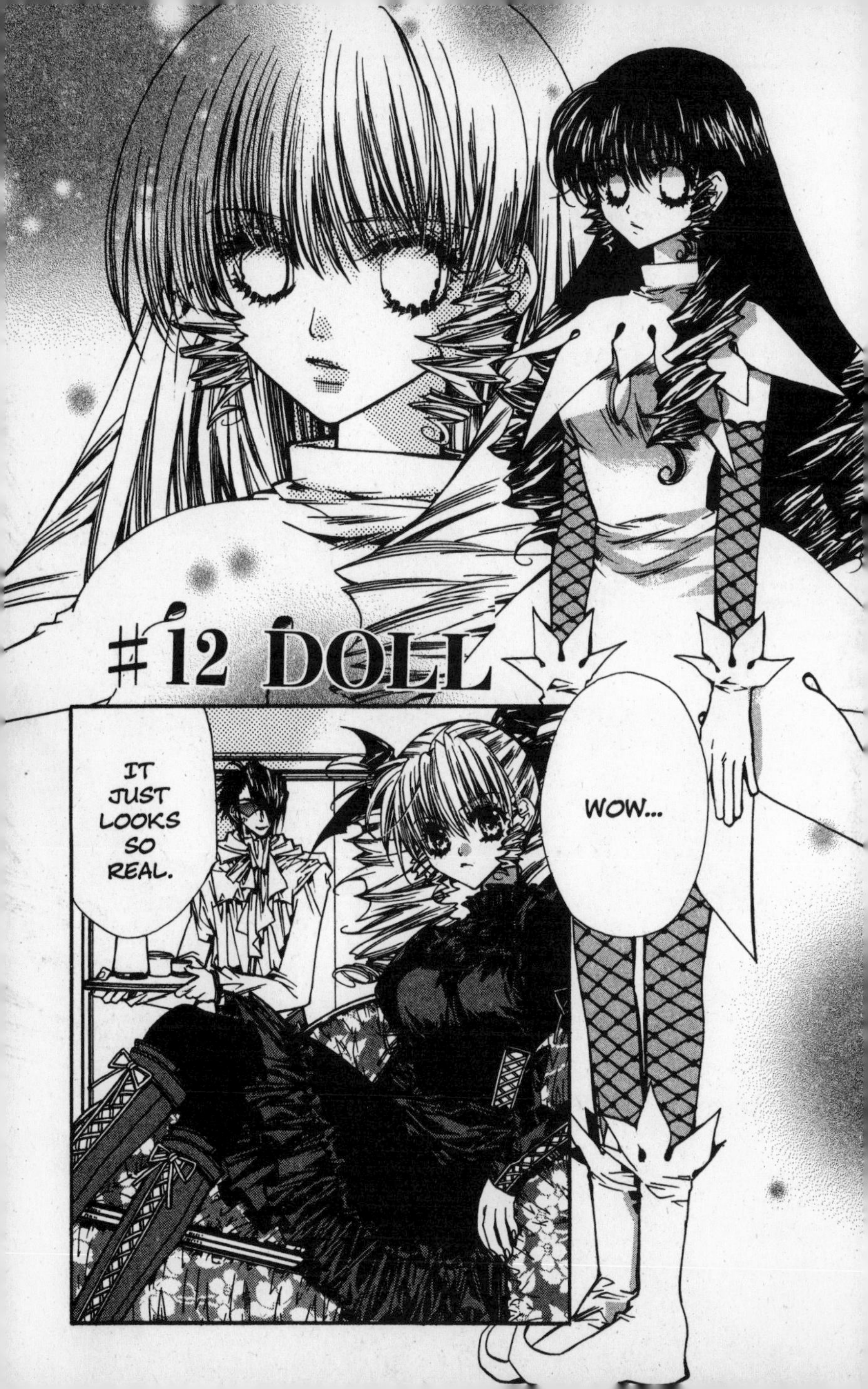
#12 DOLL
WOW...
IT JUST LOOKS SO REAL.

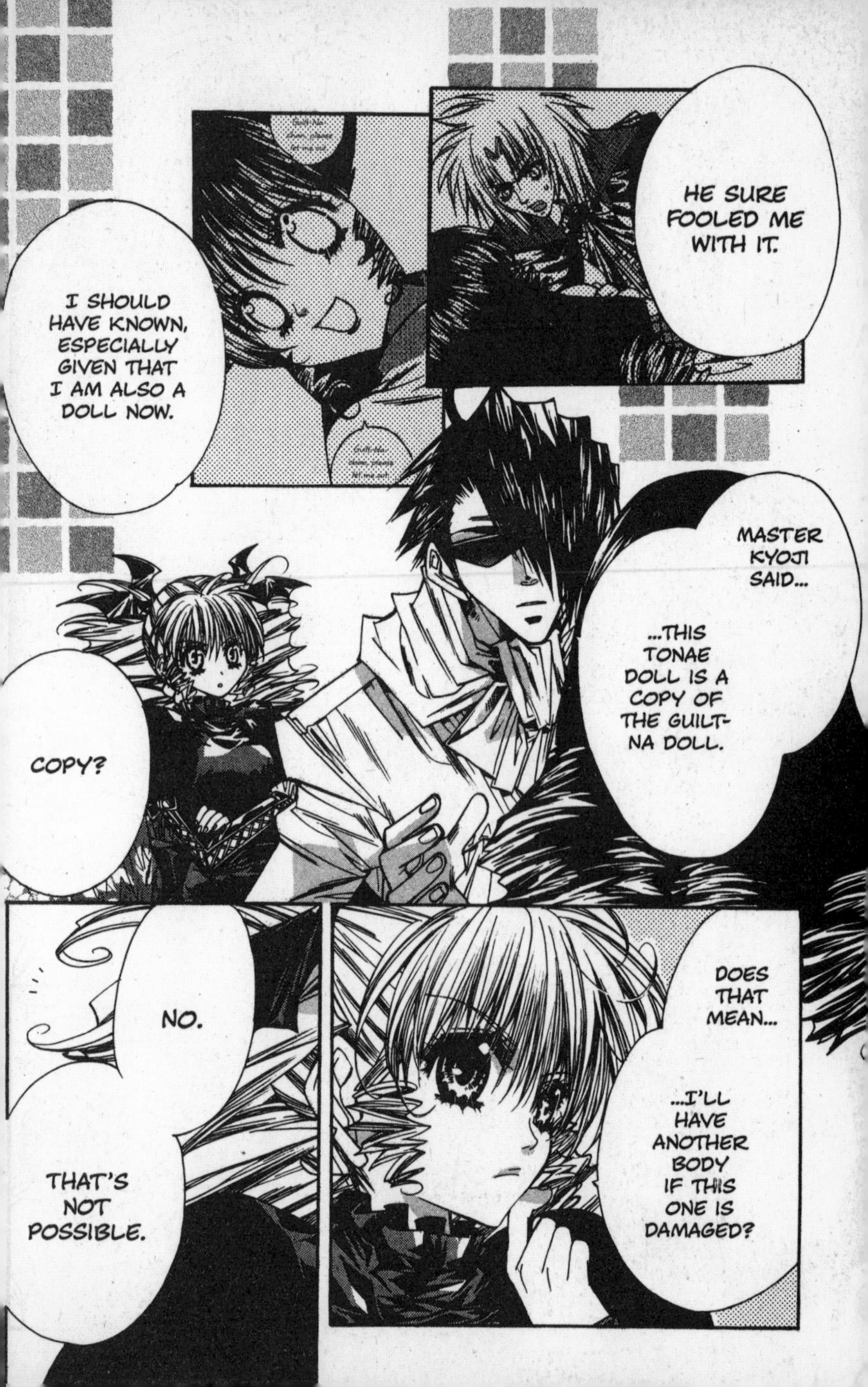
HE SURE FOOLED ME WITH IT.
Guilt-Na-chan, please let me out.
I SHOULD HAVE KNOWN, ESPECIALLY GIVEN THAT I AM ALSO A DOLL NOW.
Guilt-Na-chan, please let me out.
MASTER KYOJI SAID...
...THIS TONAE DOLL IS A COPY OF THE GUILT-NA DOLL.
COPY?
DOES THAT MEAN...
...I'LL HAVE ANOTHER BODY IF THIS ONE IS DAMAGED?
NO.
THAT'S NOT POSSIBLE.

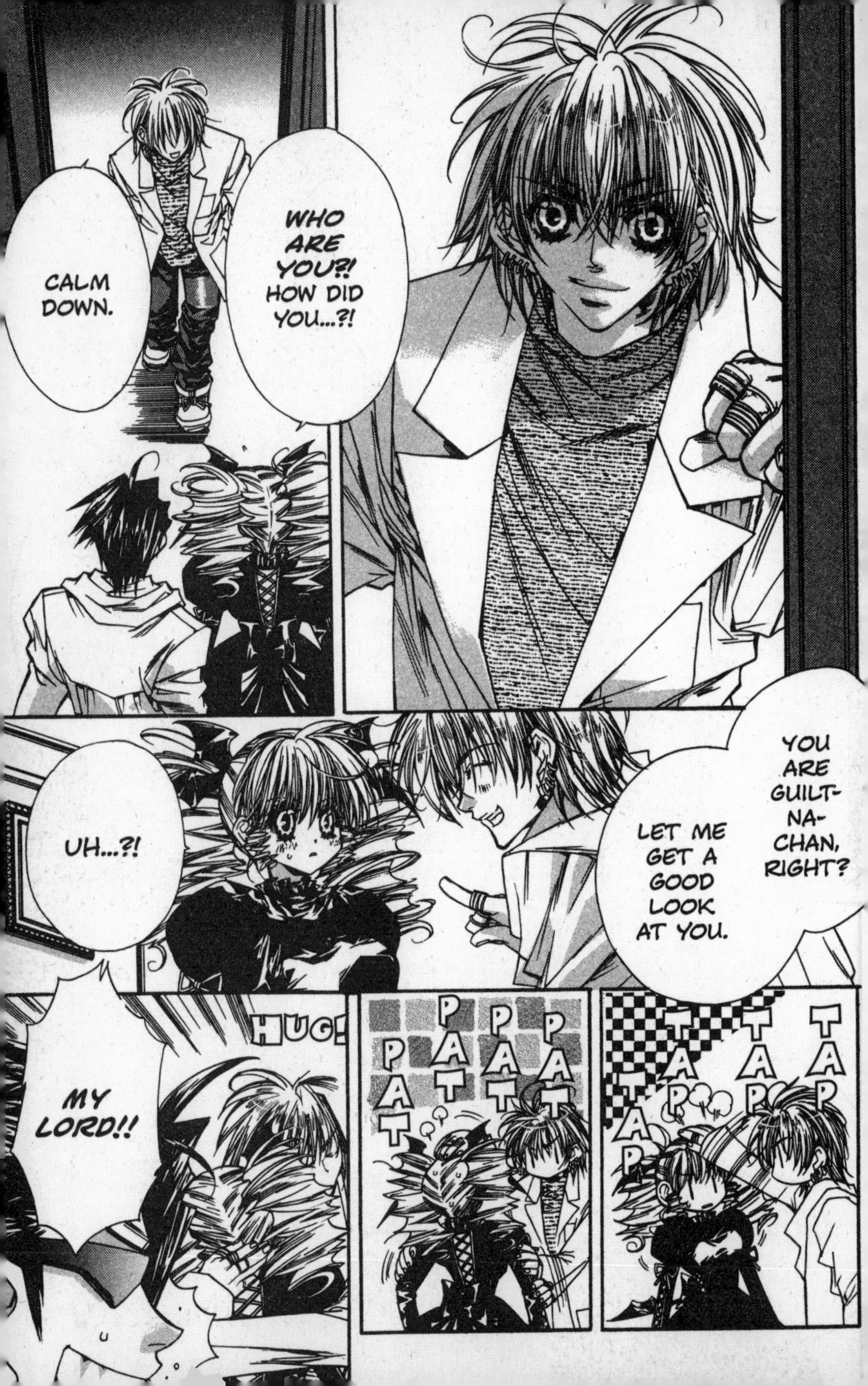
WHO ARE YOU?! HOW DID YOU...?!
CALM DOWN.
YOU ARE GUILT-NA-CHAN, RIGHT?
LET ME GET A GOOD LOOK AT YOU.
UH...?!
TAP TAP TAP TAP
PAT PAT PAT PAT
HUG!
MY LORD!!

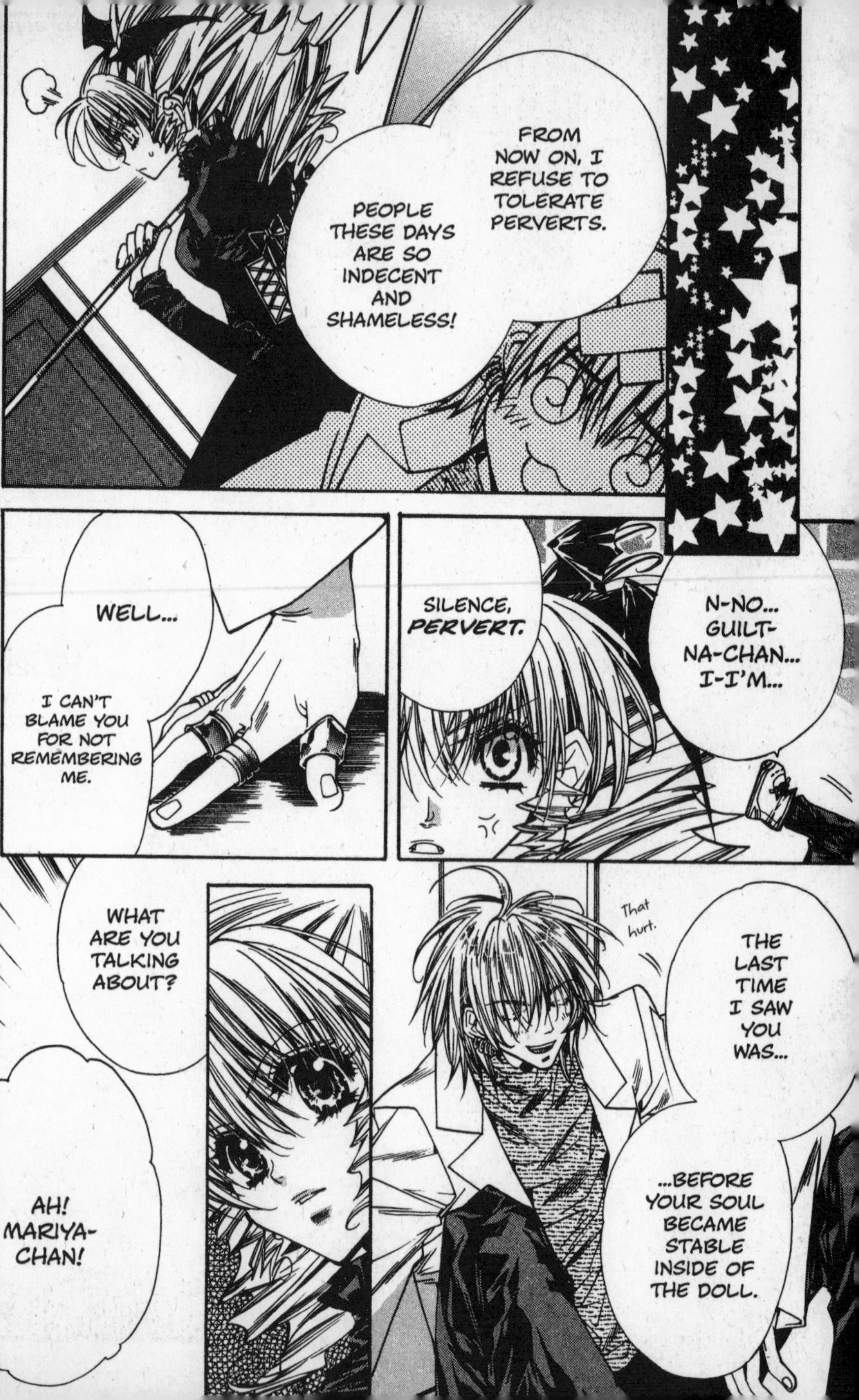
FROM NOW ON, I REFUSE TO TOLERATE PERVERTS.
PEOPLE THESE DAYS ARE SO INDECENT AND SHAMELESS!
N-NO... GUILT-NA-CHAN... I-I'M...
SILENCE, ***PERVERT.***
WELL...
I CAN'T BLAME YOU FOR NOT REMEMBERING ME.
That hurt.
THE LAST TIME I SAW YOU WAS...
...BEFORE YOUR SOUL BECAME STABLE INSIDE OF THE DOLL.
WHAT ARE YOU TALKING ABOUT?
AH! MARIYA-CHAN!

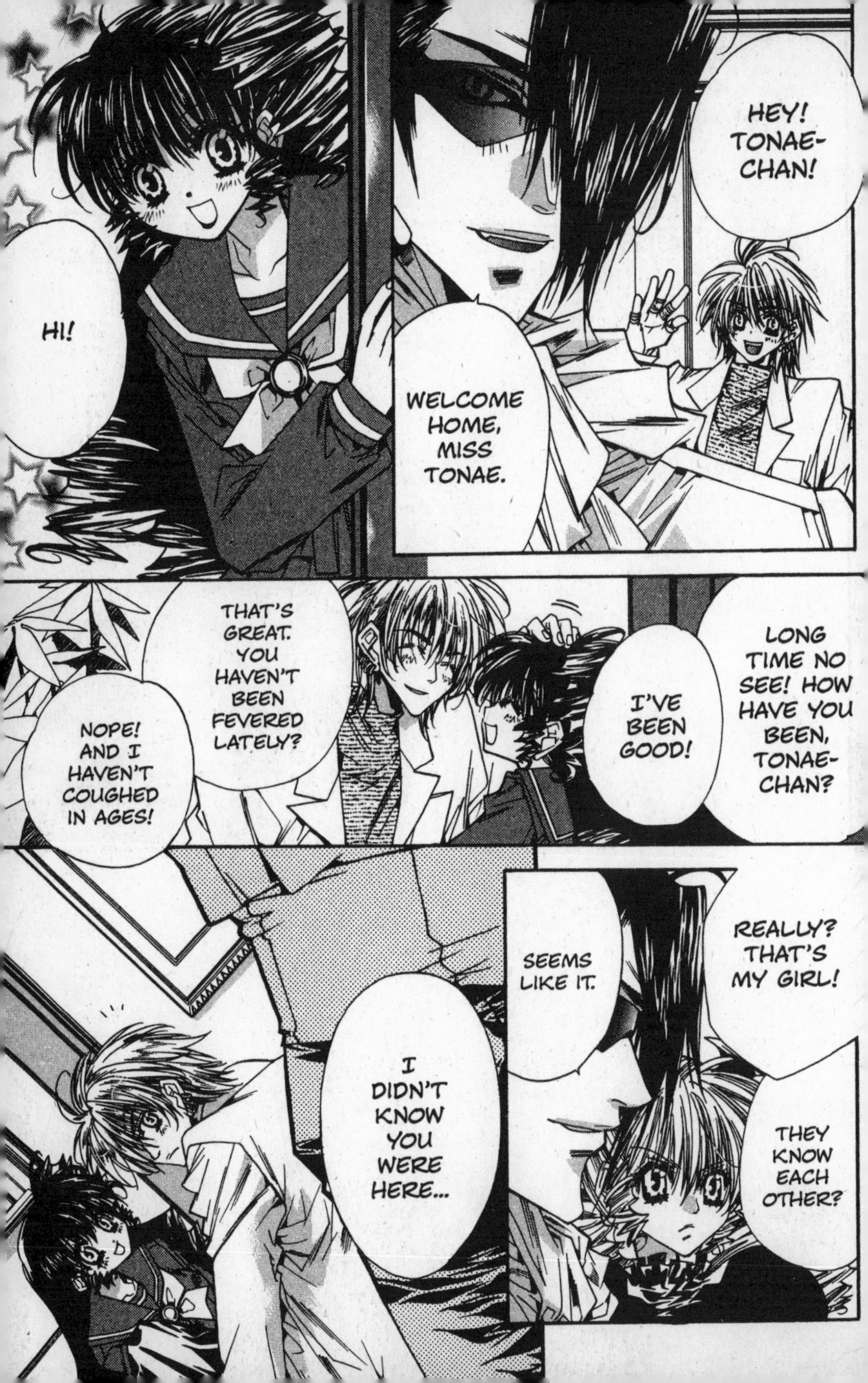
HEY! TONAE-CHAN!
WELCOME HOME, MISS TONAE.
HI!
LONG TIME NO SEE! HOW HAVE YOU BEEN, TONAE-CHAN?
I'VE BEEN GOOD!
THAT'S GREAT. YOU HAVEN'T BEEN FEVERED LATELY?
NOPE! AND I HAVEN'T COUGHED IN AGES!
REALLY? THAT'S MY GIRL!
SEEMS LIKE IT.
THEY KNOW EACH OTHER?
I DIDN'T KNOW YOU WERE HERE...

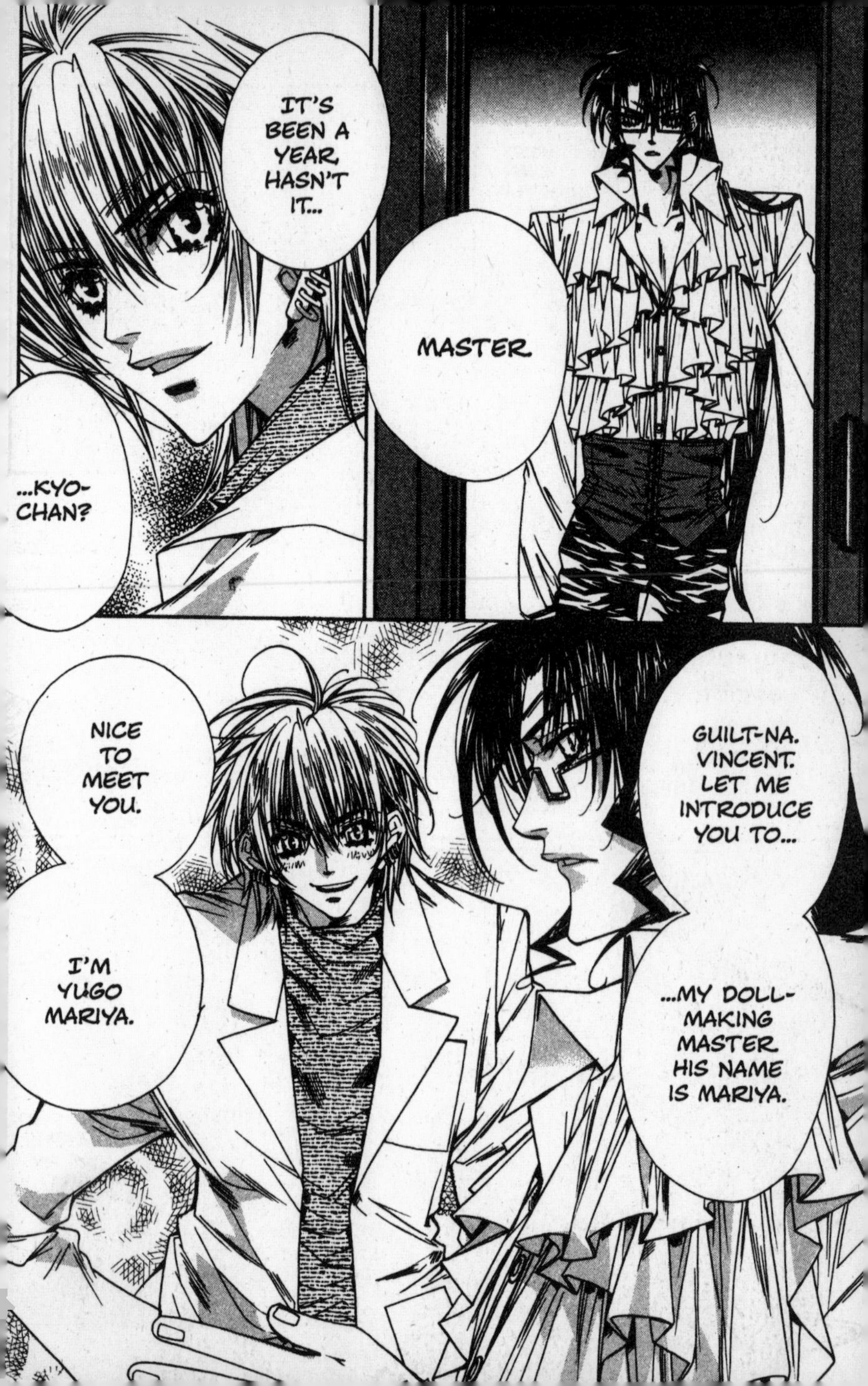
MASTER
IT'S BEEN A YEAR HASN'T IT...
...KYO-CHAN?
GUILT-NA. VINCENT. LET ME INTRODUCE YOU TO...
...MY DOLL-MAKING MASTER HIS NAME IS MARIYA.
NICE TO MEET YOU.
I'M YUGO MARIYA.

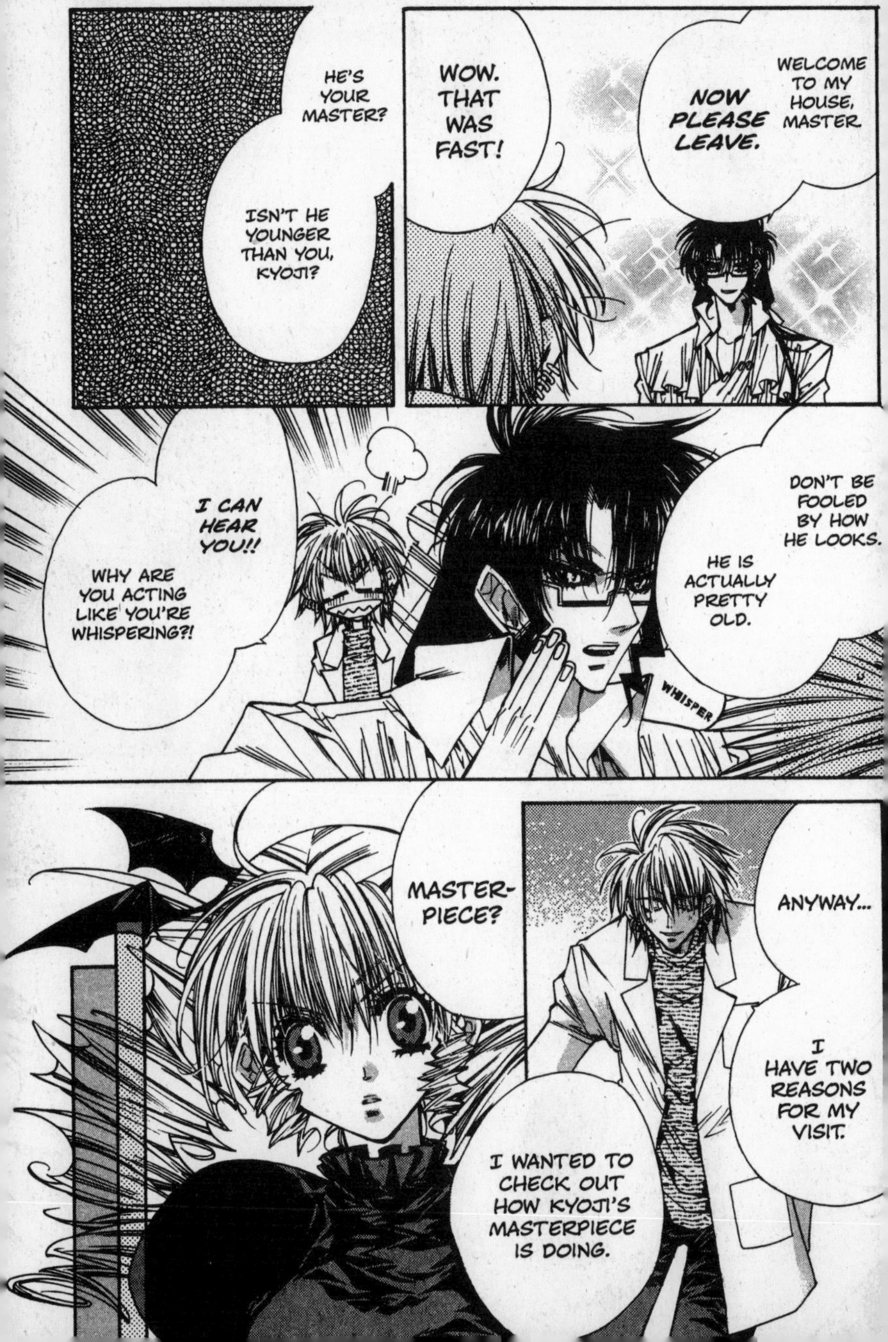
WELCOME TO MY HOUSE, MASTER
NOW PLEASE LEAVE.
WOW. THAT WAS FAST!
HE'S YOUR MASTER?
ISN'T HE YOUNGER THAN YOU, KYOJI?
DON'T BE FOOLED BY HOW HE LOOKS.
HE IS ACTUALLY PRETTY OLD.
WHISPER
I CAN HEAR YOU!!
WHY ARE YOU ACTING LIKE YOU'RE WHISPERING?!
ANYWAY...
I HAVE TWO REASONS FOR MY VISIT.
I WANTED TO CHECK OUT HOW KYOJI'S MASTERPIECE IS DOING.
MASTER-PIECE?

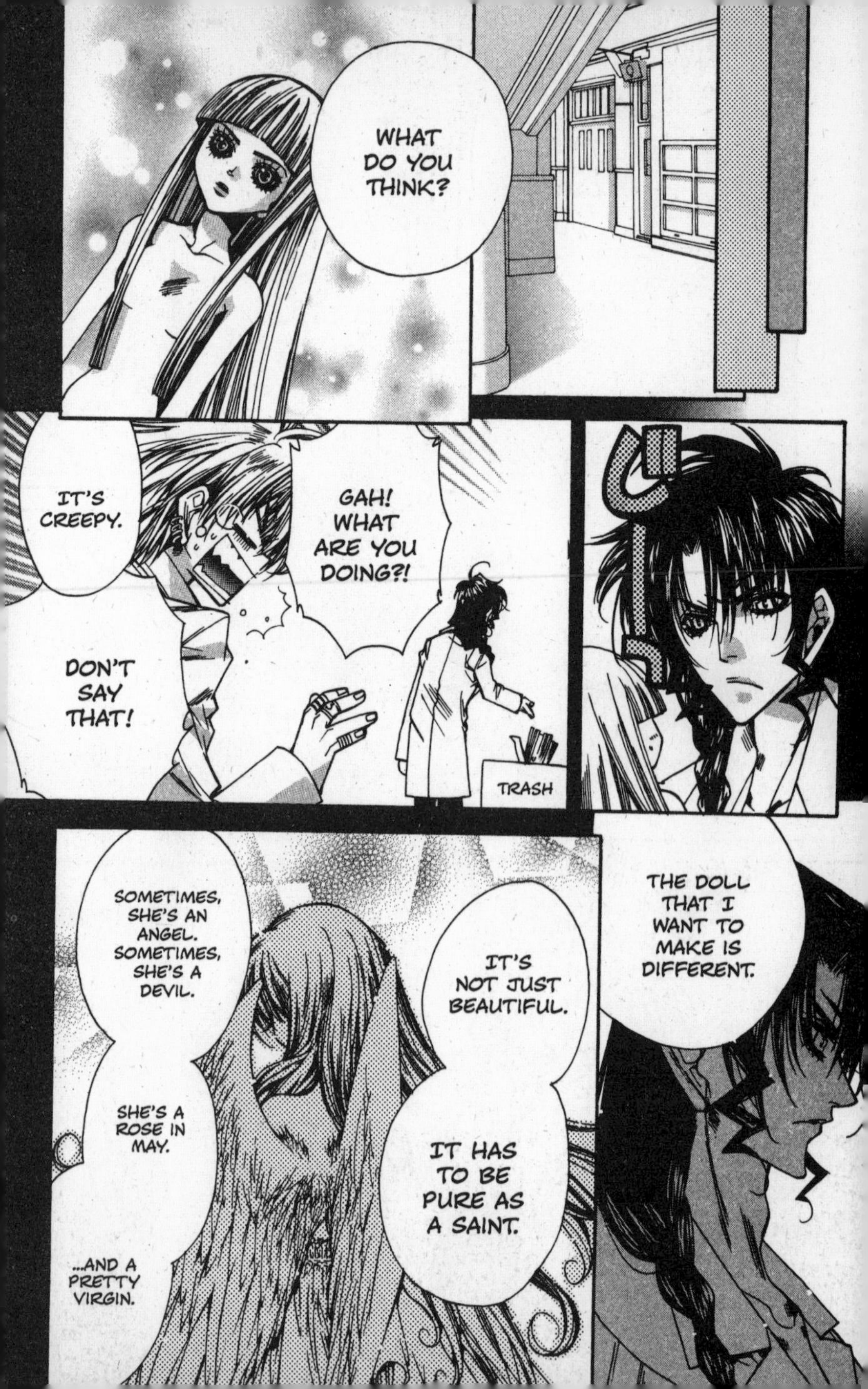
WHAT DO YOU THINK?
GAH! WHAT ARE YOU DOING?!
IT'S CREEPY.
DON'T SAY THAT!
TRASH
THE DOLL THAT I WANT TO MAKE IS DIFFERENT.
IT'S NOT JUST BEAUTIFUL.
IT HAS TO BE PURE AS A SAINT.
SOMETIMES, SHE'S AN ANGEL. SOMETIMES, SHE'S A DEVIL.
SHE'S A ROSE IN MAY.
...AND A PRETTY VIRGIN.

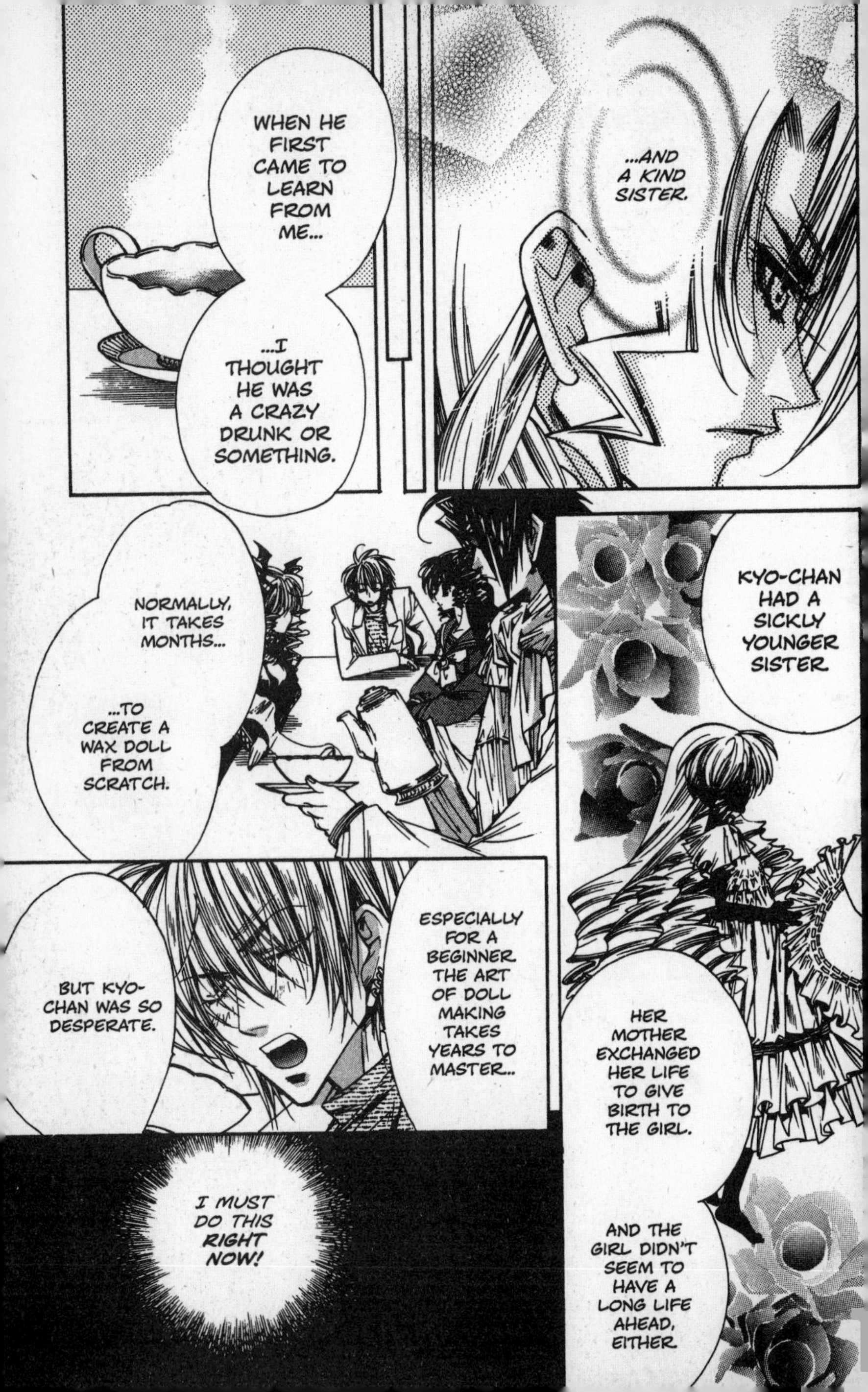
...AND A KIND SISTER.
WHEN HE FIRST CAME TO LEARN FROM ME...
...I THOUGHT HE WAS A CRAZY DRUNK OR SOMETHING.
KYO-CHAN HAD A SICKLY YOUNGER SISTER
HER MOTHER EXCHANGED HER LIFE TO GIVE BIRTH TO THE GIRL.
AND THE GIRL DIDN'T SEEM TO HAVE A LONG LIFE AHEAD, EITHER
NORMALLY, IT TAKES MONTHS...
...TO CREATE A WAX DOLL FROM SCRATCH.
ESPECIALLY FOR A BEGINNER THE ART OF DOLL MAKING TAKES YEARS TO MASTER...
BUT KYO-CHAN WAS SO DESPERATE.
I MUST DO THIS RIGHT NOW!

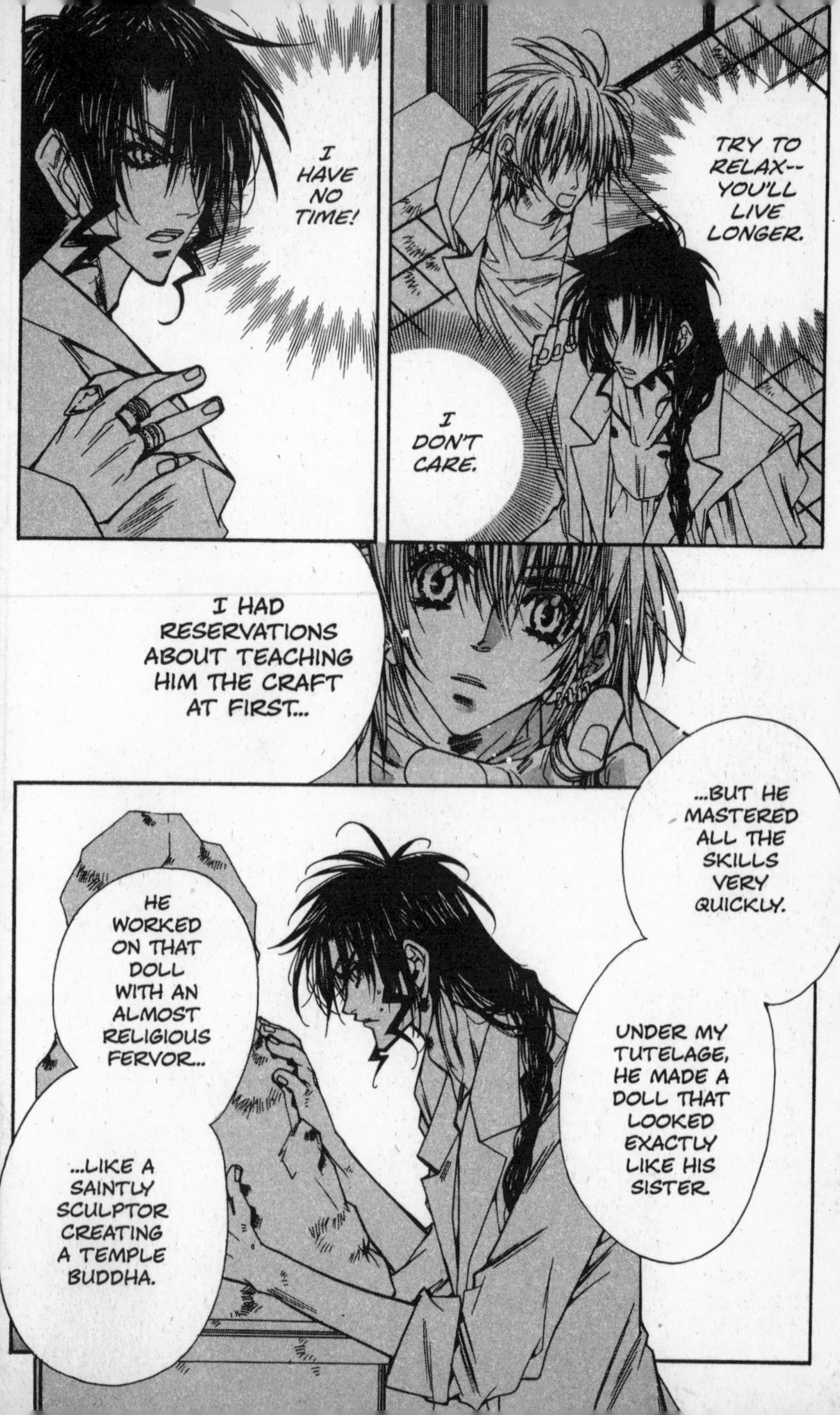
TRY TO RELAX--YOU'LL LIVE LONGER.
I DON'T CARE.
I HAVE NO TIME!
I HAD RESERVATIONS ABOUT TEACHING HIM THE CRAFT AT FIRST...
...BUT HE MASTERED ALL THE SKILLS VERY QUICKLY.
UNDER MY TUTELAGE, HE MADE A DOLL THAT LOOKED EXACTLY LIKE HIS SISTER.
HE WORKED ON THAT DOLL WITH AN ALMOST RELIGIOUS FERVOR...
...LIKE A SAINTLY SCULPTOR CREATING A TEMPLE BUDDHA.

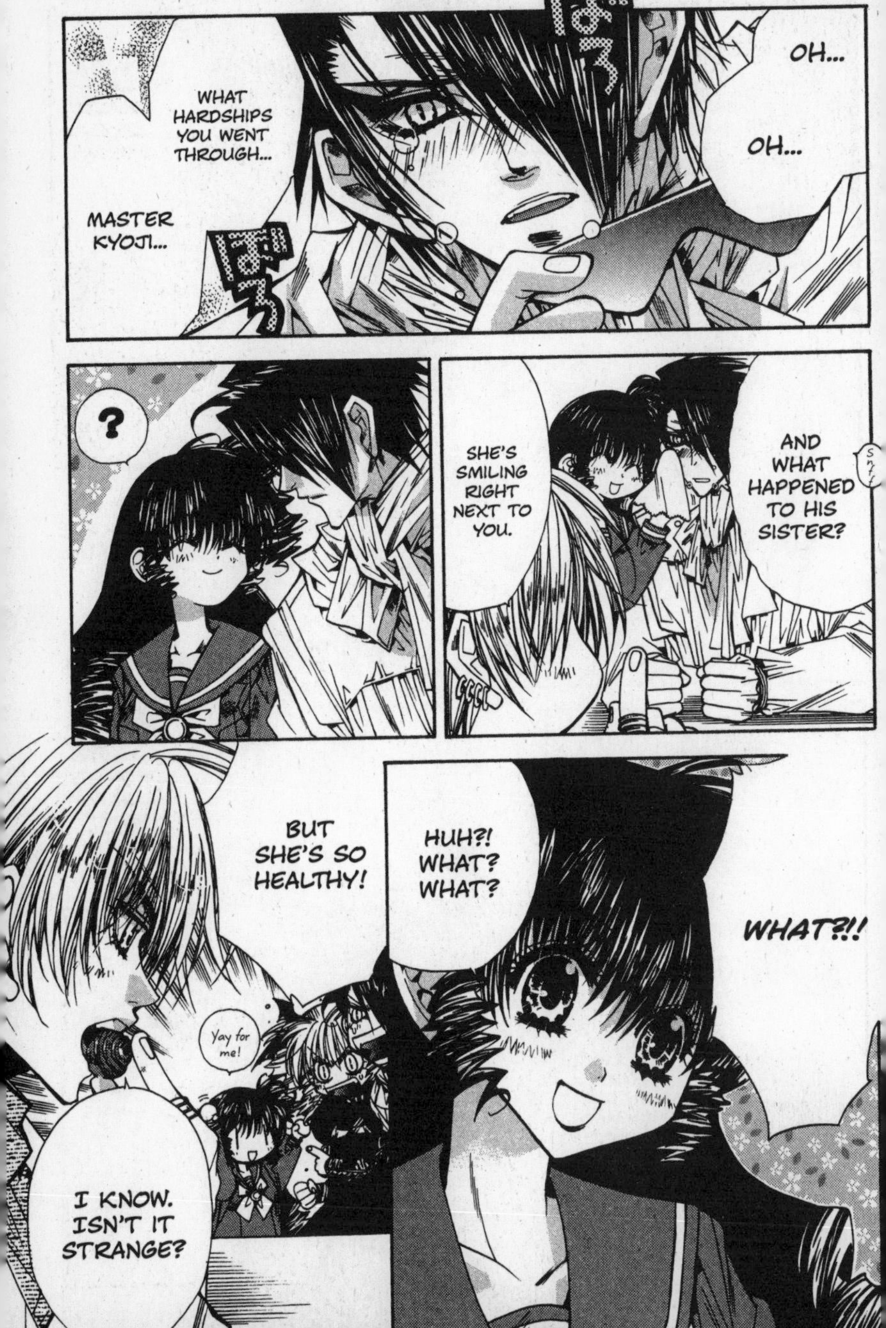

OH...
OH...
ぽろ
WHAT HARDSHIPS YOU WENT THROUGH...
MASTER KYOJI...
ぽろ
Sniff
AND WHAT HAPPENED TO HIS SISTER?
SHE'S SMILING RIGHT NEXT TO YOU.
?
WHAT?!!
HUH?! WHAT? WHAT?
BUT SHE'S SO HEALTHY!
Yay for me!
I KNOW. ISN'T IT STRANGE?

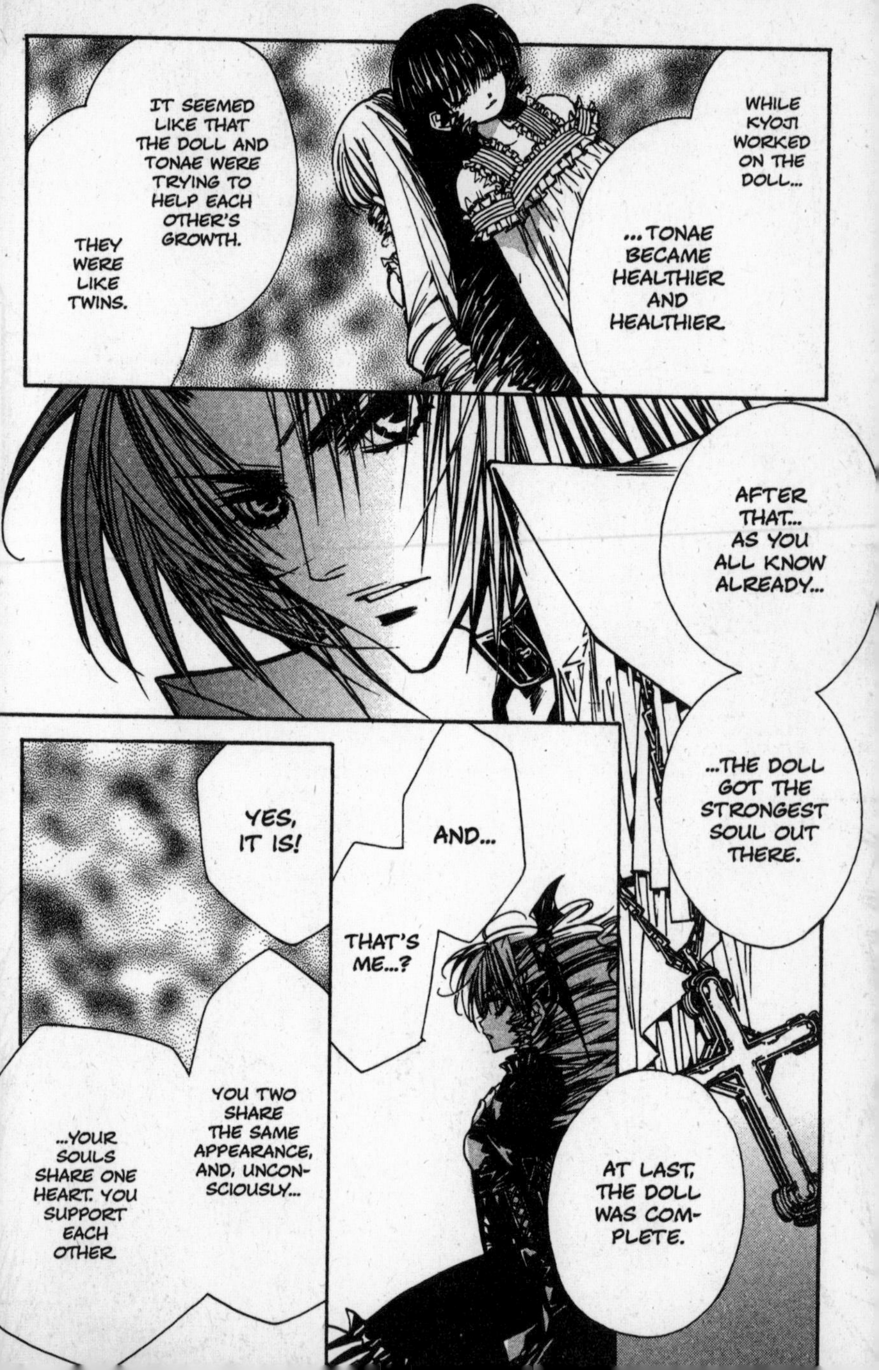
WHILE KYOJI WORKED ON THE DOLL...
...TONAE BECAME HEALTHIER AND HEALTHIER
IT SEEMED LIKE THAT THE DOLL AND TONAE WERE TRYING TO HELP EACH OTHER'S GROWTH.
THEY WERE LIKE TWINS.
AFTER THAT... AS YOU ALL KNOW ALREADY...
...THE DOLL GOT THE STRONGEST SOUL OUT THERE.
AT LAST, THE DOLL WAS COMPLETE.
AND...
THAT'S ME...?
YES, IT IS!
YOU TWO SHARE THE SAME APPEARANCE, AND, UNCONSCIOUSLY...
...YOUR SOULS SHARE ONE HEART. YOU SUPPORT EACH OTHER

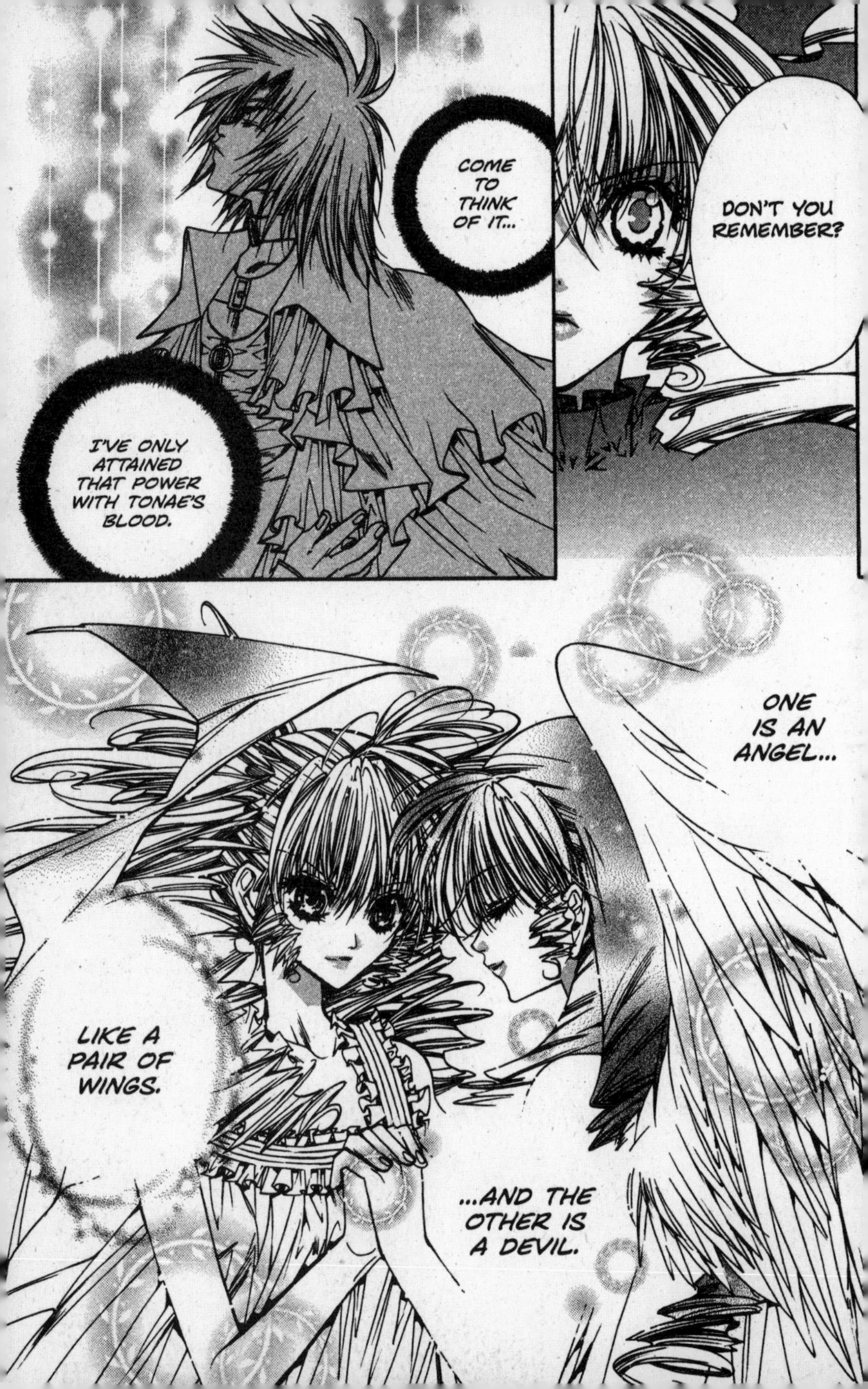
DON'T YOU REMEMBER?
COME TO THINK OF IT...
I'VE ONLY ATTAINED THAT POWER WITH TONAE'S BLOOD.
ONE IS AN ANGEL...
LIKE A PAIR OF WINGS.
...AND THE OTHER IS A DEVIL.

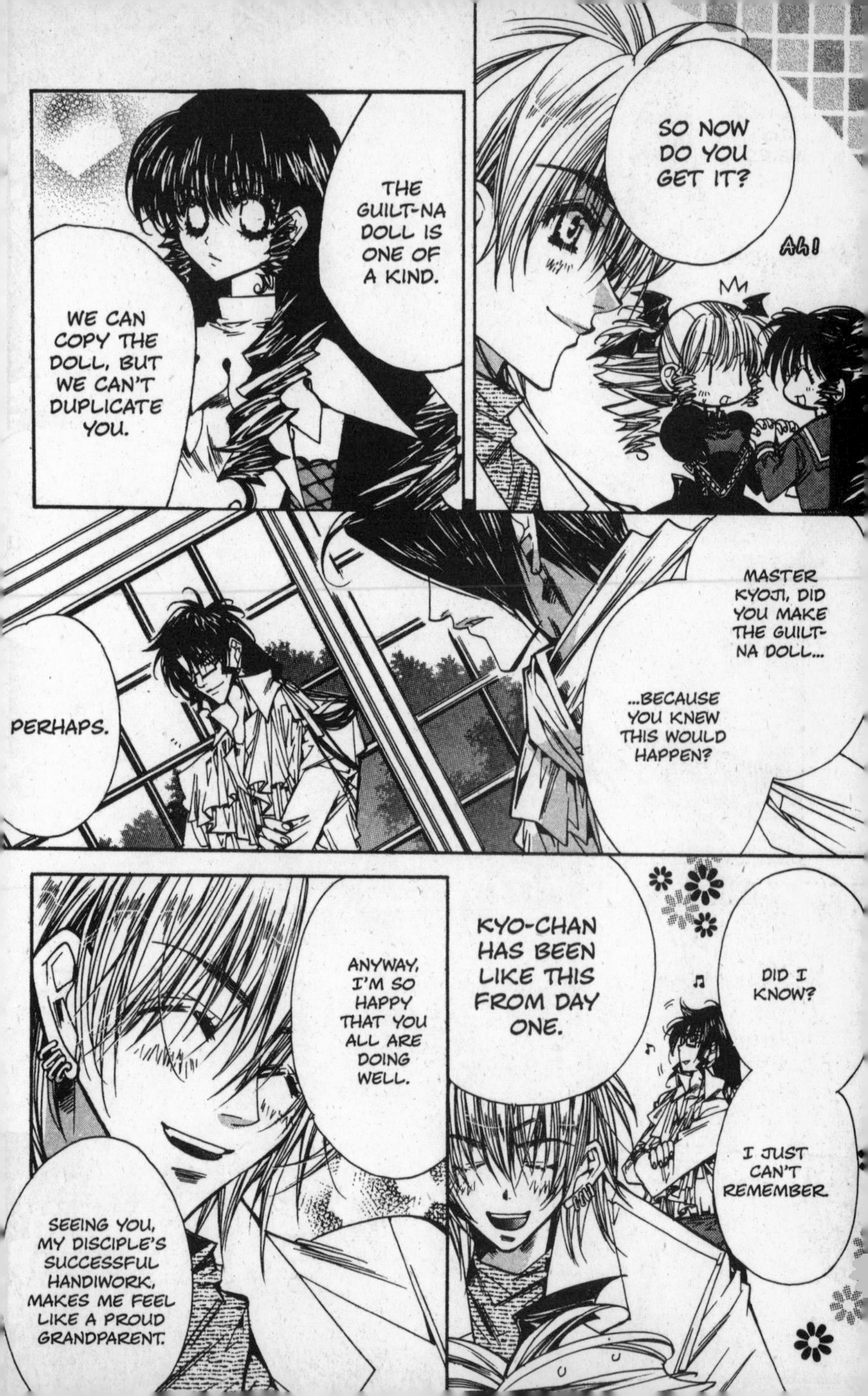
SO NOW DO YOU GET IT?
Ah!
THE GUILT-NA DOLL IS ONE OF A KIND.
WE CAN COPY THE DOLL, BUT WE CAN'T DUPLICATE YOU.
MASTER KYOJI, DID YOU MAKE THE GUILT-NA DOLL...
...BECAUSE YOU KNEW THIS WOULD HAPPEN?
PERHAPS.
DID I KNOW?
I JUST CAN'T REMEMBER.
KYO-CHAN HAS BEEN LIKE THIS FROM DAY ONE.
ANYWAY, I'M SO HAPPY THAT YOU ALL ARE DOING WELL.
SEEING YOU, MY DISCIPLE'S SUCCESSFUL HANDIWORK, MAKES ME FEEL LIKE A PROUD GRANDPARENT.

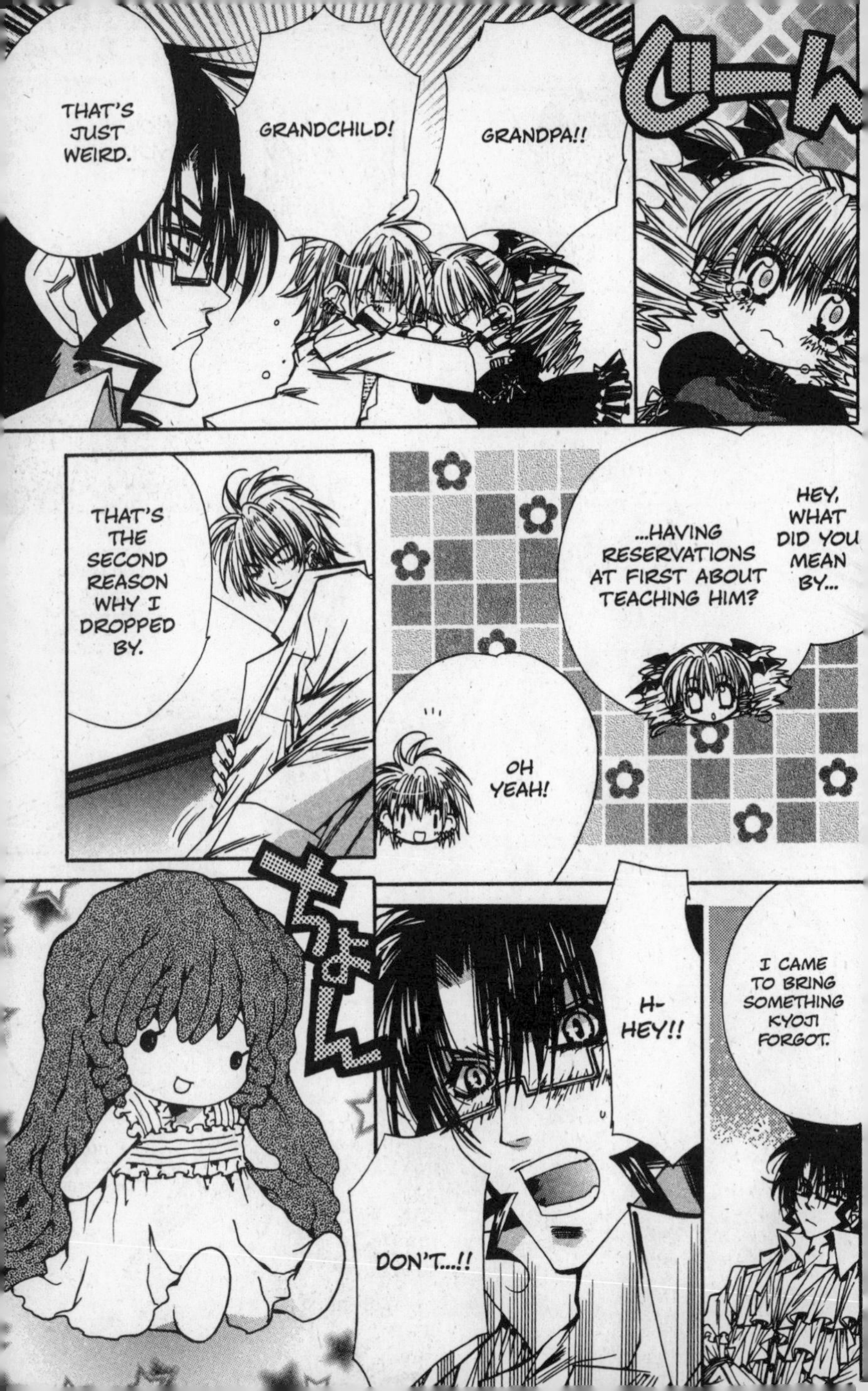
じーん
GRANDPA!!
GRANDCHILD!
THAT'S JUST WEIRD.
HEY, WHAT DID YOU MEAN BY...
...HAVING RESERVATIONS AT FIRST ABOUT TEACHING HIM?
OH YEAH!
THAT'S THE SECOND REASON WHY I DROPPED BY.
I CAME TO BRING SOMETHING KYOJI FORGOT.
H- HEY!!
DON'T...!!

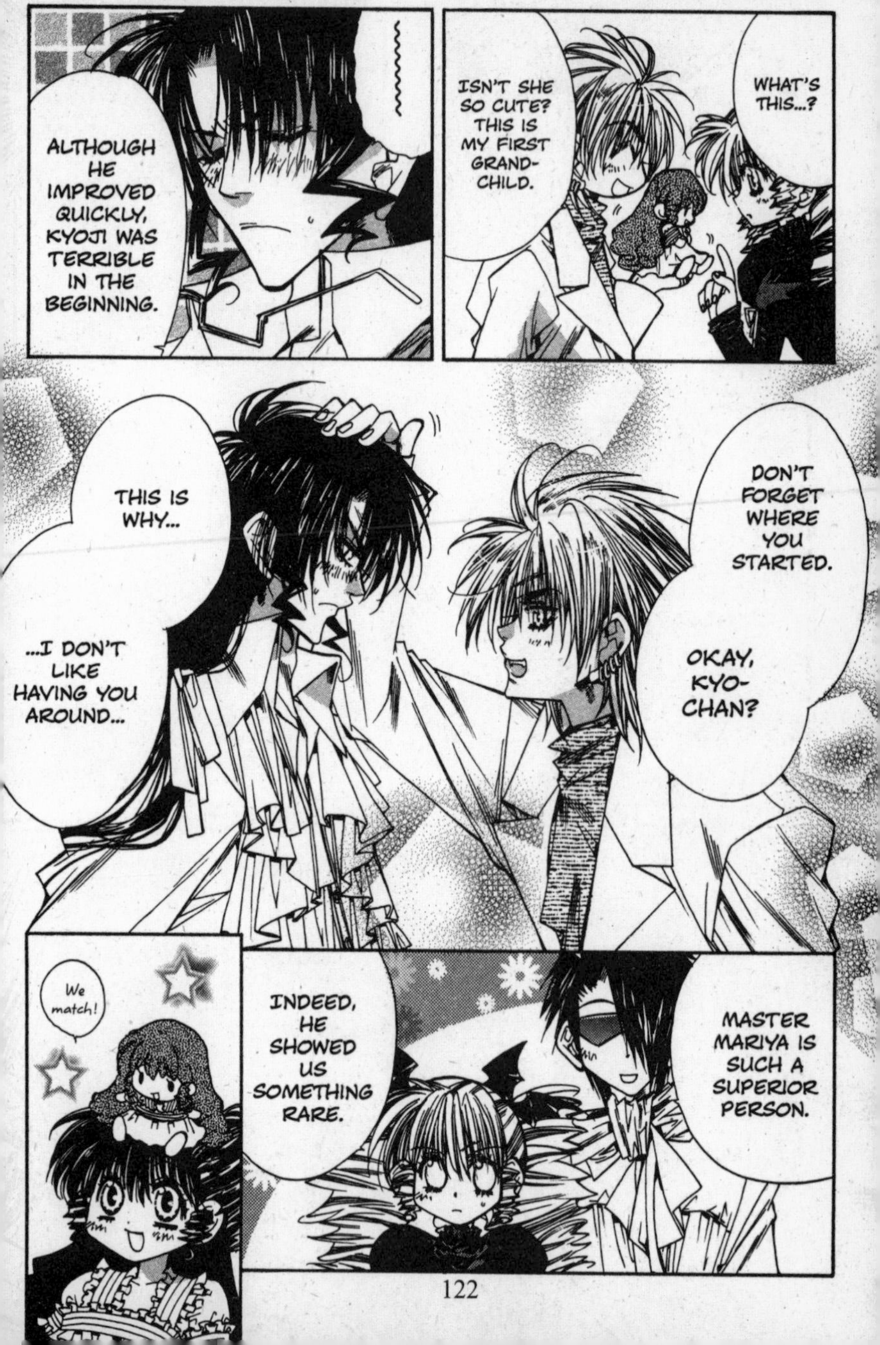
WHAT'S THIS...?
ISN'T SHE SO CUTE? THIS IS MY FIRST GRAND-CHILD.
......
ALTHOUGH HE IMPROVED QUICKLY, KYOJI WAS TERRIBLE IN THE BEGINNING.
DON'T FORGET WHERE YOU STARTED.
OKAY, KYO-CHAN?
THIS IS WHY...
...I DON'T LIKE HAVING YOU AROUND...
MASTER MARIYA IS SUCH A SUPERIOR PERSON.
INDEED, HE SHOWED US SOMETHING RARE.
We match!

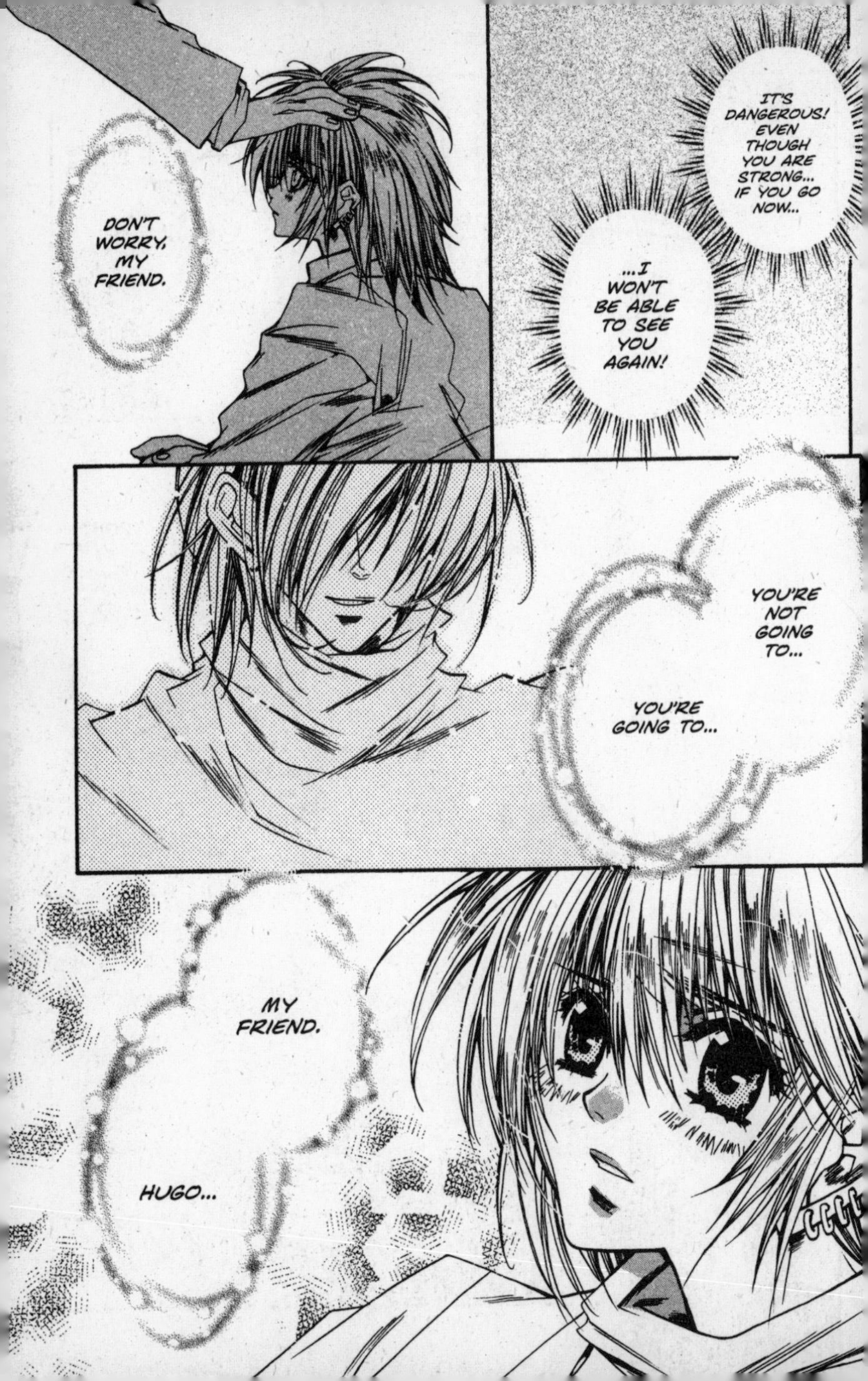
IT'S DANGEROUS! EVEN THOUGH YOU ARE STRONG... IF YOU GO NOW...
...I WON'T BE ABLE TO SEE YOU AGAIN!
DON'T WORRY, MY FRIEND.
YOU'RE NOT GOING TO...
YOU'RE GOING TO...
MY FRIEND.
HUGO...

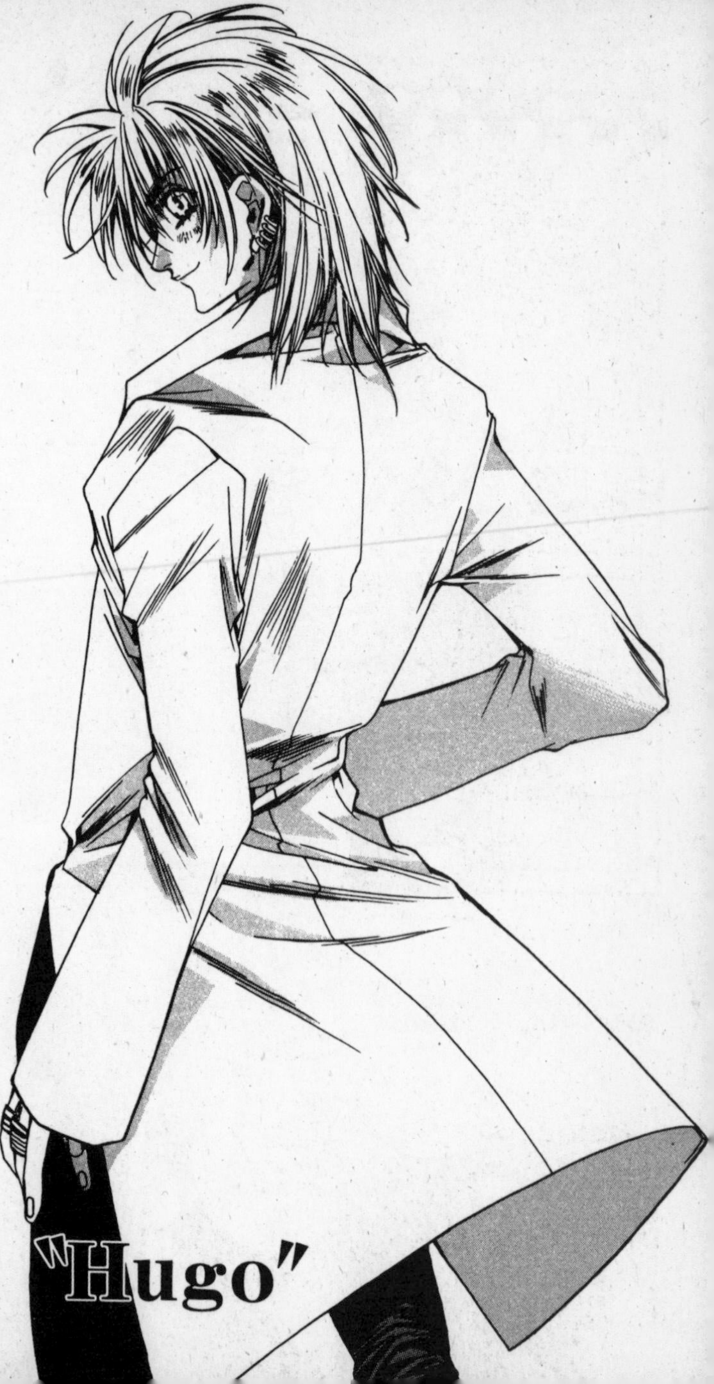

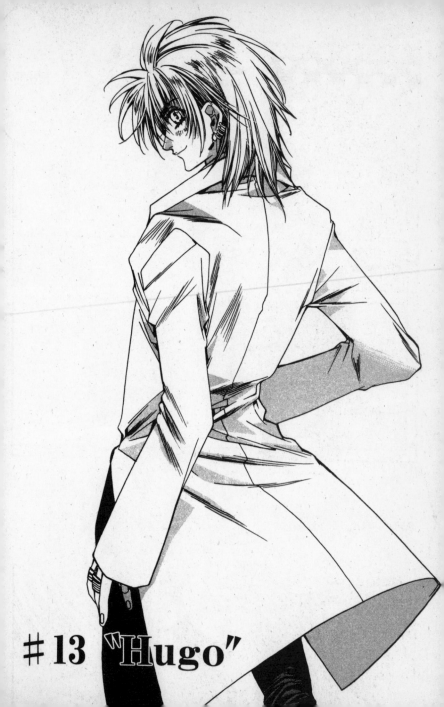

♯13 "Hugo"

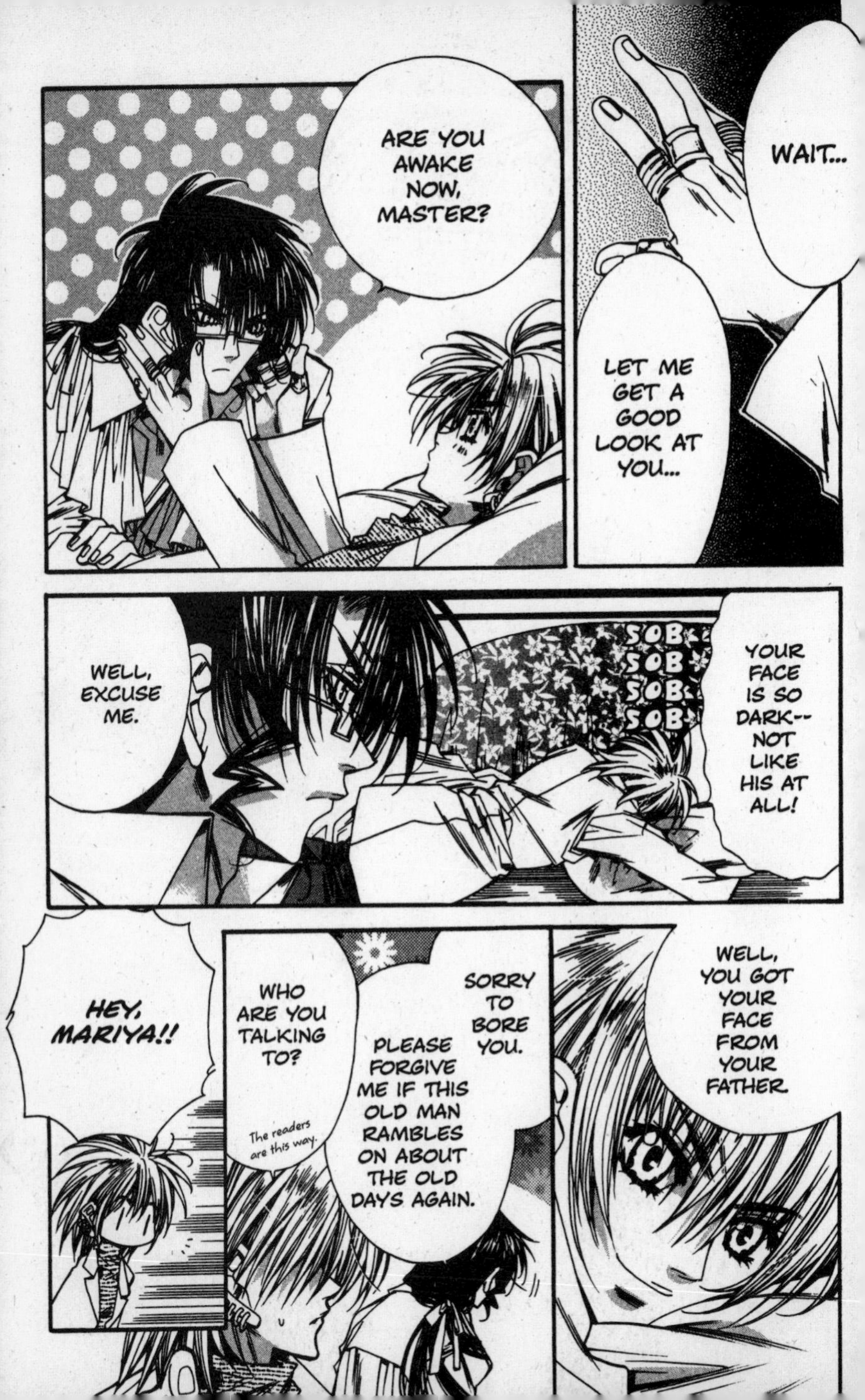
WAIT...
LET ME GET A GOOD LOOK AT YOU...
ARE YOU AWAKE NOW, MASTER?
YOUR FACE IS SO DARK--NOT LIKE HIS AT ALL!
SOB SOB SOB SOB
WELL, EXCUSE ME.
WELL, YOU GOT YOUR FACE FROM YOUR FATHER.
SORRY TO BORE YOU.
PLEASE FORGIVE ME IF THIS OLD MAN RAMBLES ON ABOUT THE OLD DAYS AGAIN.
WHO ARE YOU TALKING TO?
The readers are this way.
HEY, MARIYA!!

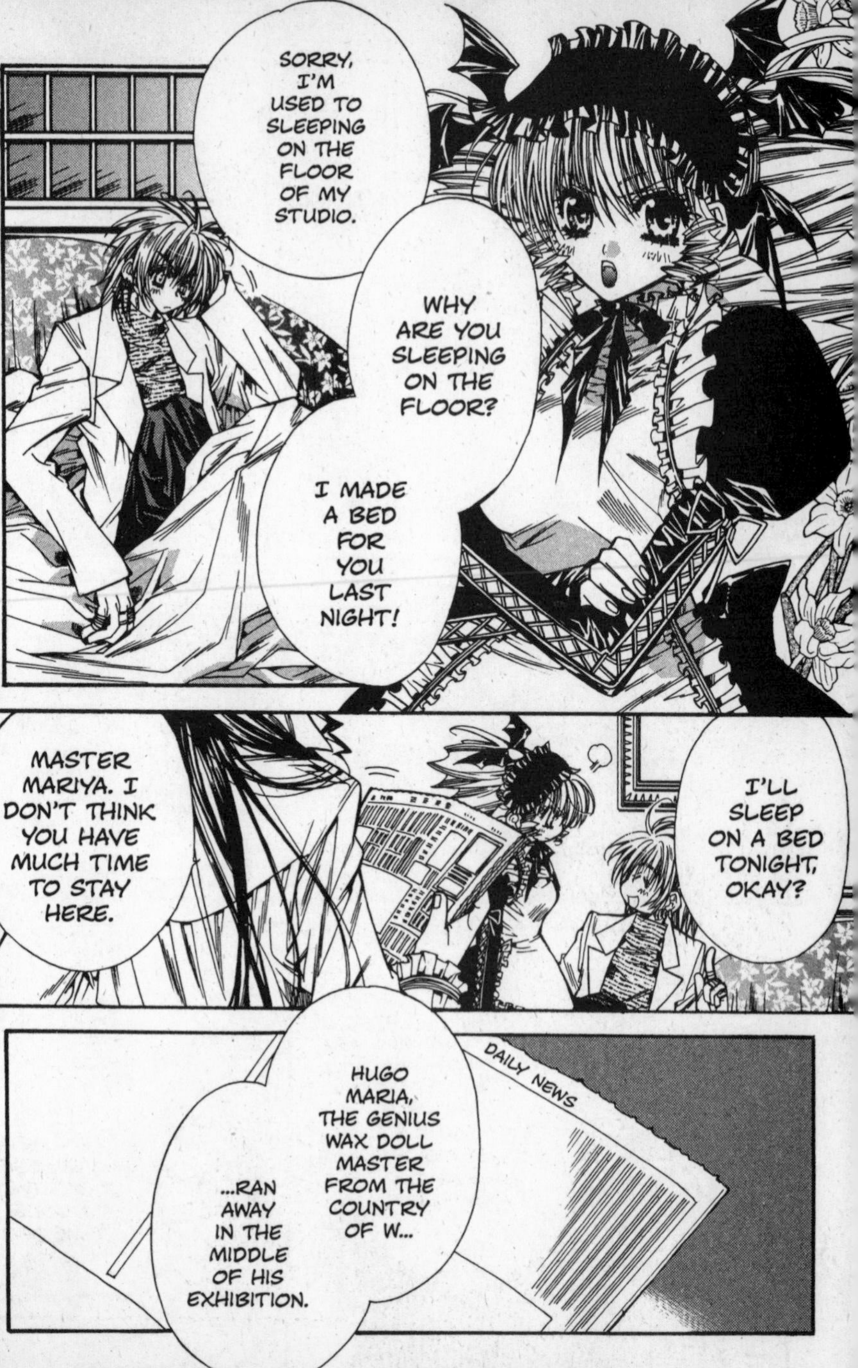
WHY ARE YOU SLEEPING ON THE FLOOR?
I MADE A BED FOR YOU LAST NIGHT!
SORRY, I'M USED TO SLEEPING ON THE FLOOR OF MY STUDIO.
I'LL SLEEP ON A BED TONIGHT, OKAY?
MASTER MARIYA. I DON'T THINK YOU HAVE MUCH TIME TO STAY HERE.
DAILY NEWS
HUGO MARIA, THE GENIUS WAX DOLL MASTER FROM THE COUNTRY OF W...
...RAN AWAY IN THE MIDDLE OF HIS EXHIBITION.

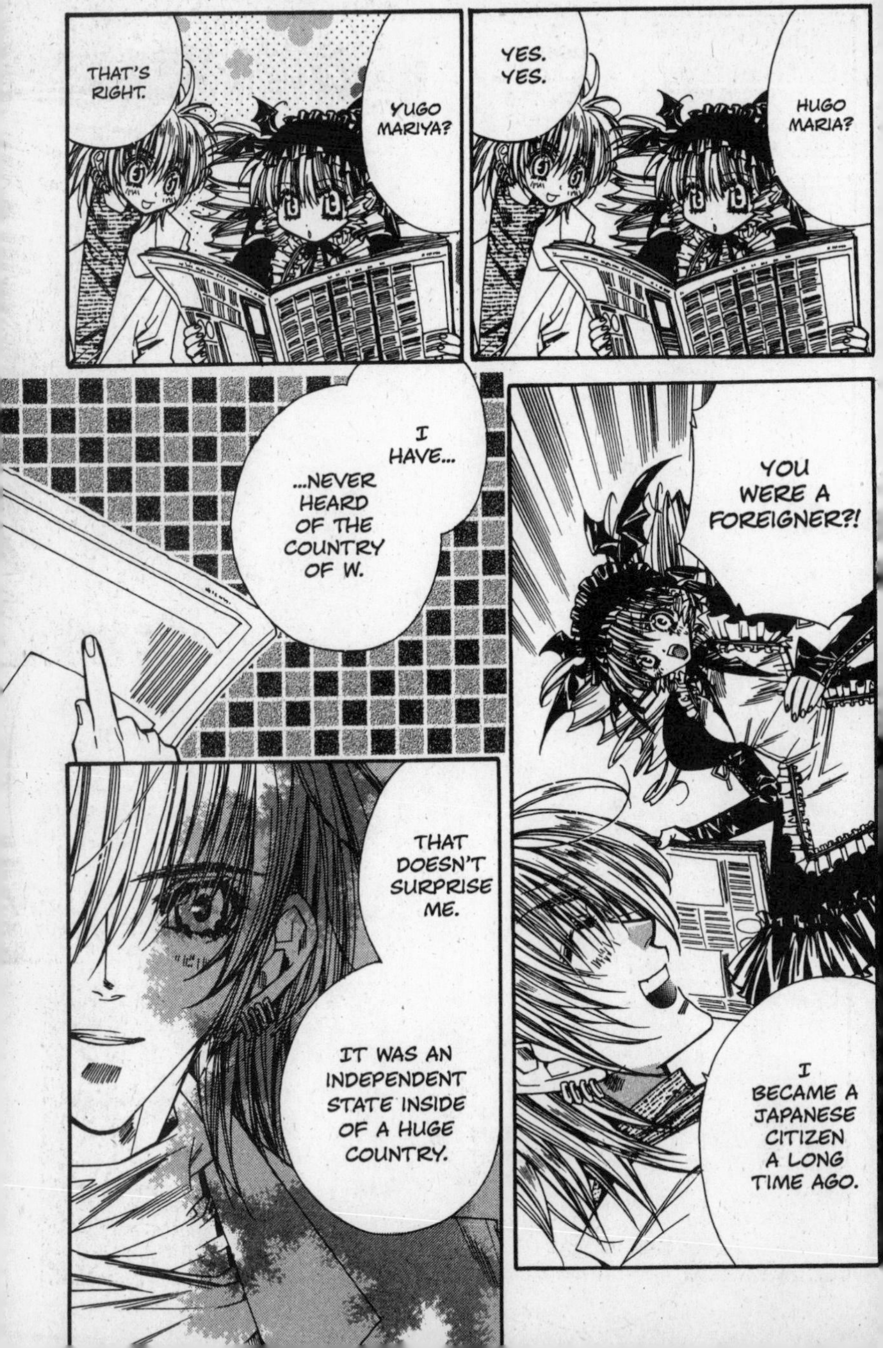
HUGO MARIA?
YES. YES.
YUGO MARIYA?
THAT'S RIGHT.
YOU WERE A FOREIGNER?!
I BECAME A JAPANESE CITIZEN A LONG TIME AGO.
I HAVE...
...NEVER HEARD OF THE COUNTRY OF W.
THAT DOESN'T SURPRISE ME.
IT WAS AN INDEPENDENT STATE INSIDE OF A HUGE COUNTRY.

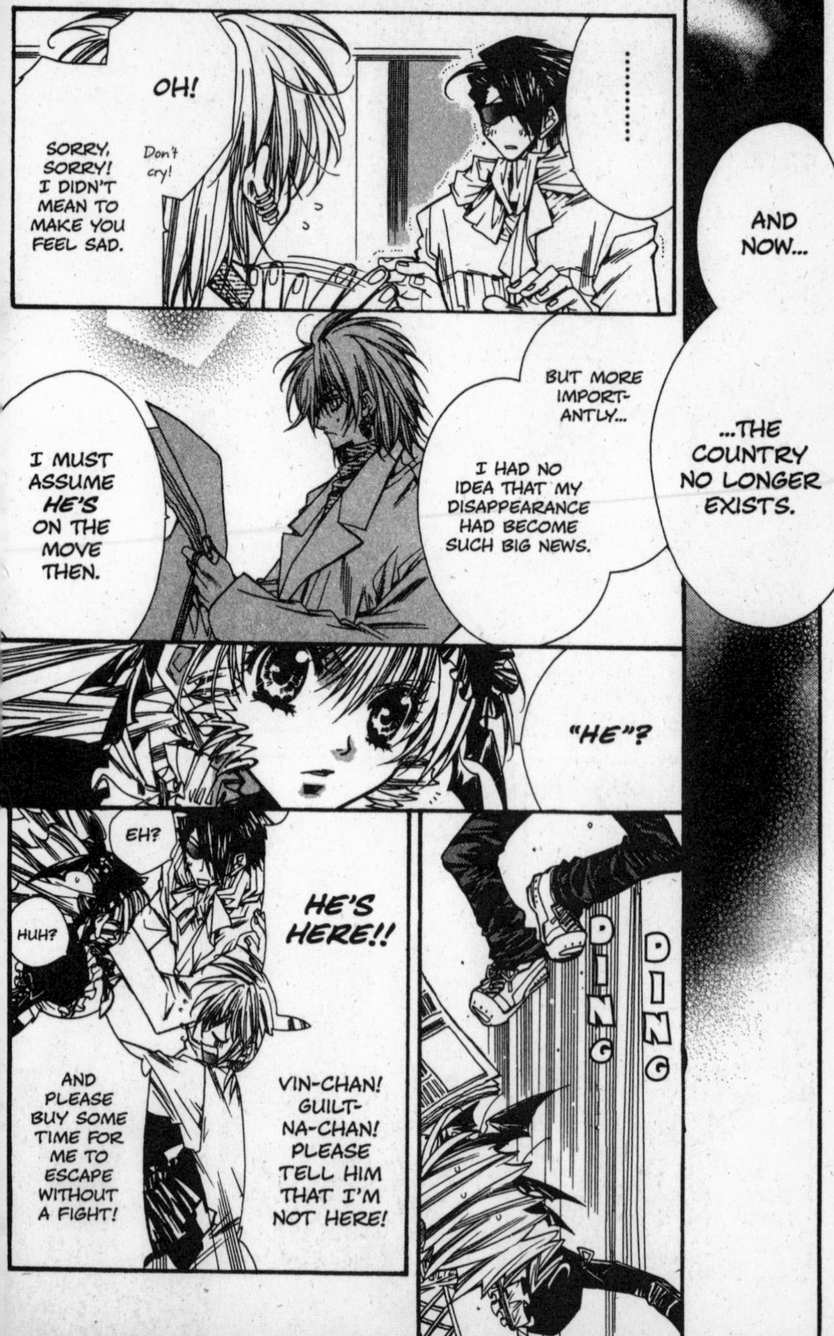
AND NOW...
...THE COUNTRY NO LONGER EXISTS.
......
OH!
SORRY, SORRY! I DIDN'T MEAN TO MAKE YOU FEEL SAD.
Don't cry!
BUT MORE IMPORT-ANTLY...
I HAD NO IDEA THAT MY DISAPPEARANCE HAD BECOME SUCH BIG NEWS.
I MUST ASSUME *HE'S* ON THE MOVE THEN.
"HE"?
DING
DING
HE'S HERE!!
EH?
HUH?
VIN-CHAN! GUILT-NA-CHAN! PLEASE TELL HIM THAT I'M NOT HERE!
AND PLEASE BUY SOME TIME FOR ME TO ESCAPE WITHOUT A FIGHT!

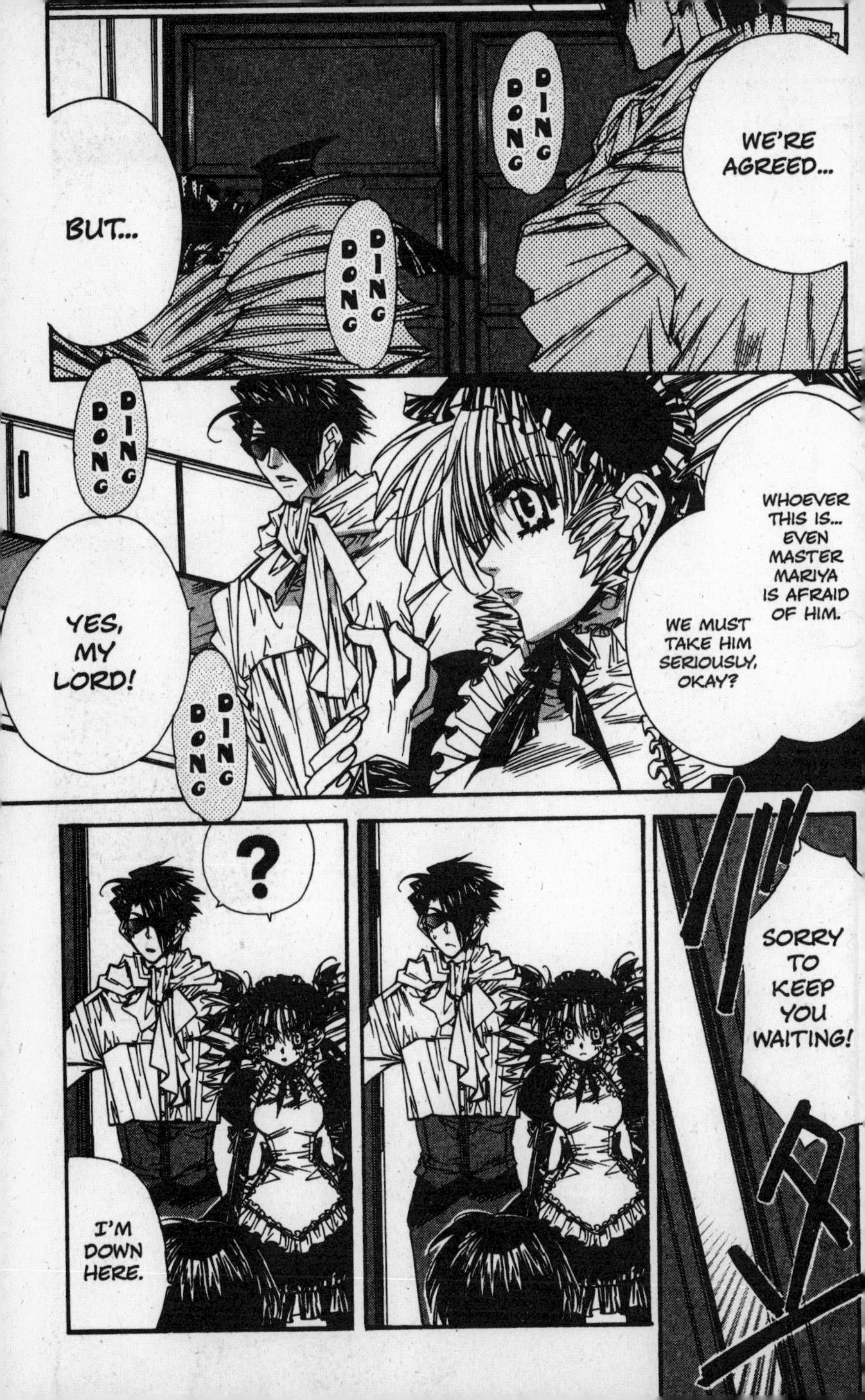
WE'RE AGREED...
DING DONG
DING DONG
BUT...
WHOEVER THIS IS... EVEN MASTER MARIYA IS AFRAID OF HIM.
WE MUST TAKE HIM SERIOUSLY, OKAY?
DING DONG
YES, MY LORD!
DING DONG
SORRY TO KEEP YOU WAITING!
?
I'M DOWN HERE.

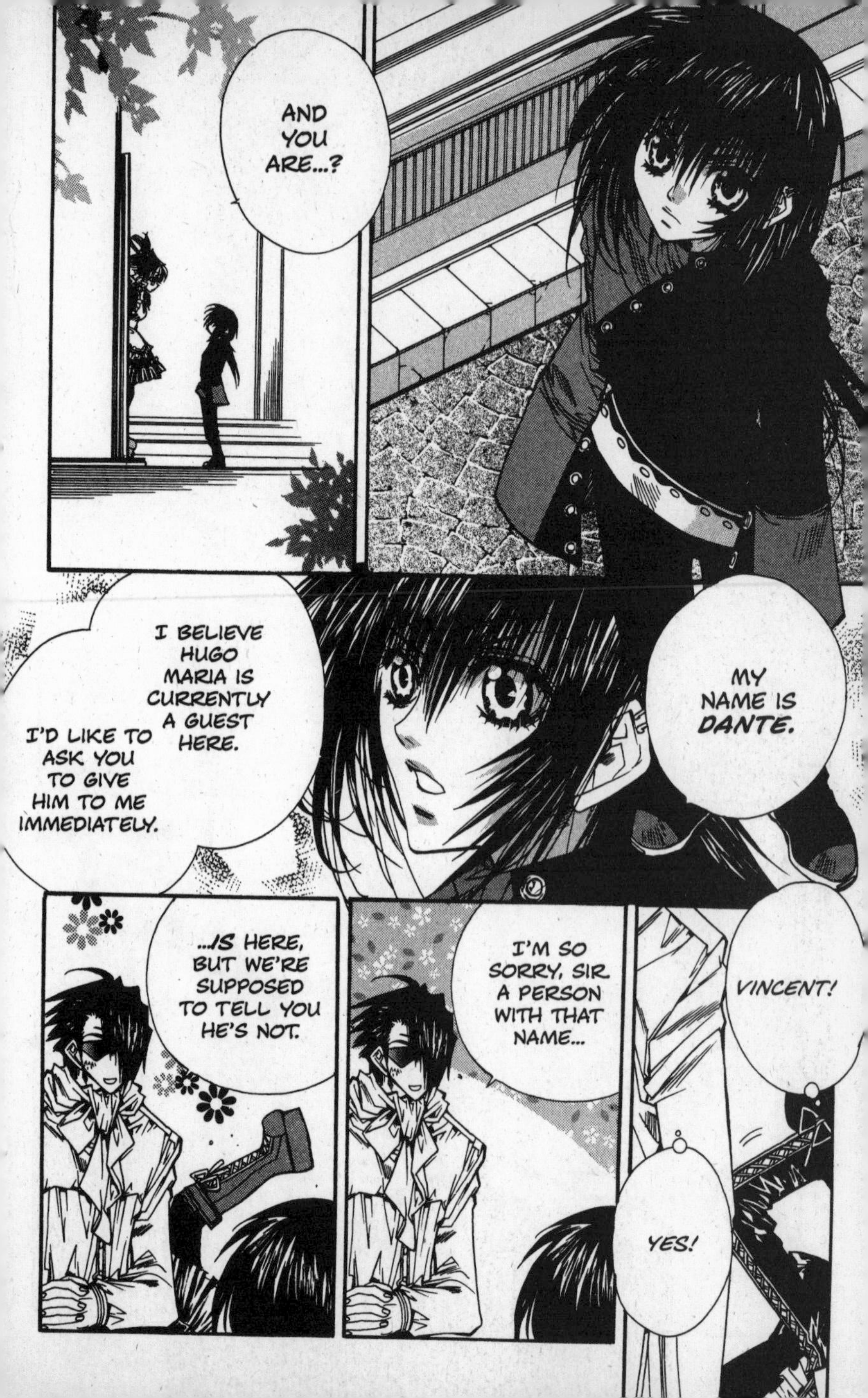
AND YOU ARE...?
MY NAME IS DANTE.
I BELIEVE HUGO MARIA IS CURRENTLY A GUEST HERE.
I'D LIKE TO ASK YOU TO GIVE HIM TO ME IMMEDIATELY.
VINCENT!
YES!
I'M SO SORRY, SIR A PERSON WITH THAT NAME...
...IS HERE, BUT WE'RE SUPPOSED TO TELL YOU HE'S NOT.

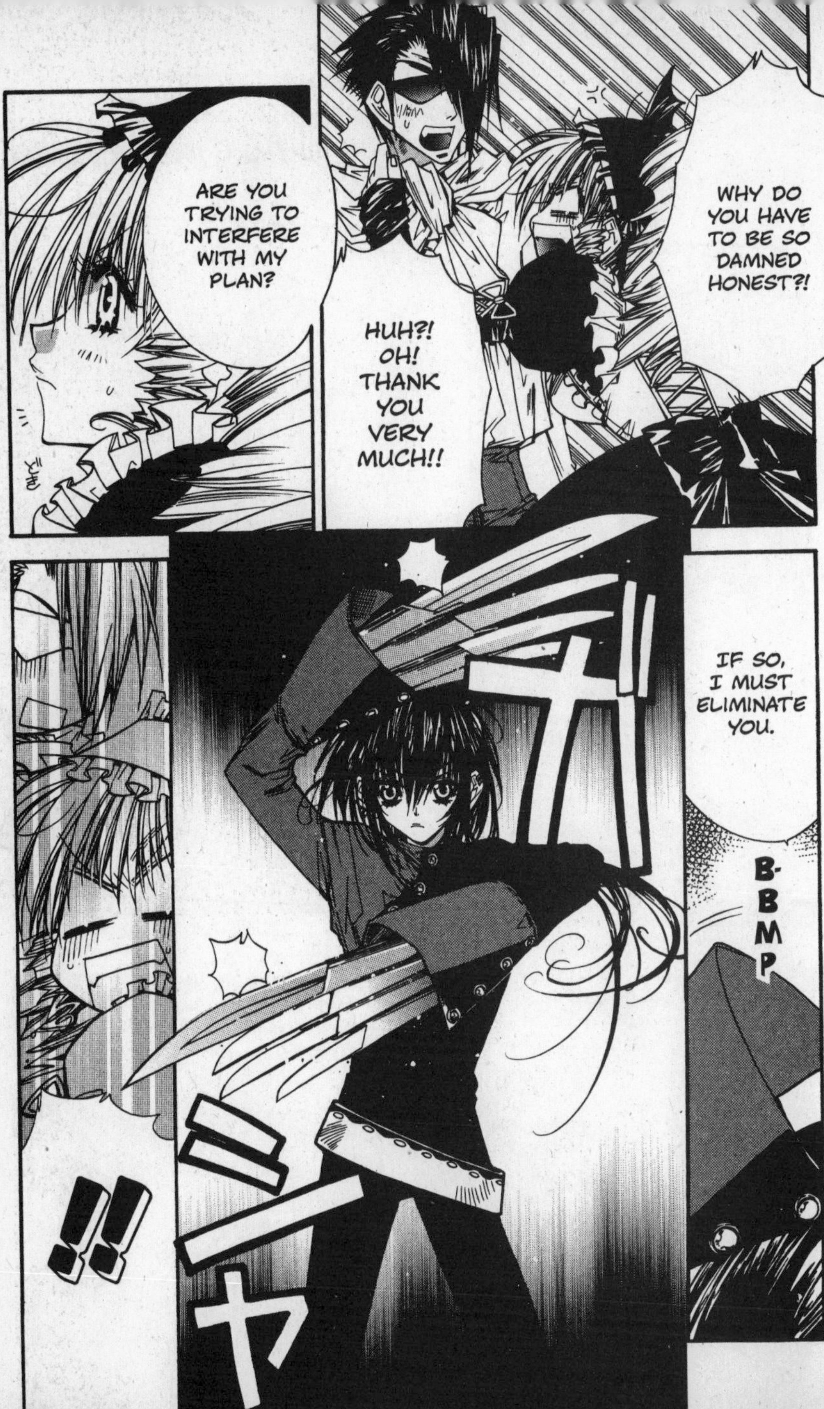
WHY DO YOU HAVE TO BE SO DAMNED HONEST?!
HUH?! OH! THANK YOU VERY MUCH!!
ARE YOU TRYING TO INTERFERE WITH MY PLAN?
IF SO, I MUST ELIMINATE YOU.
B-BMP
!!

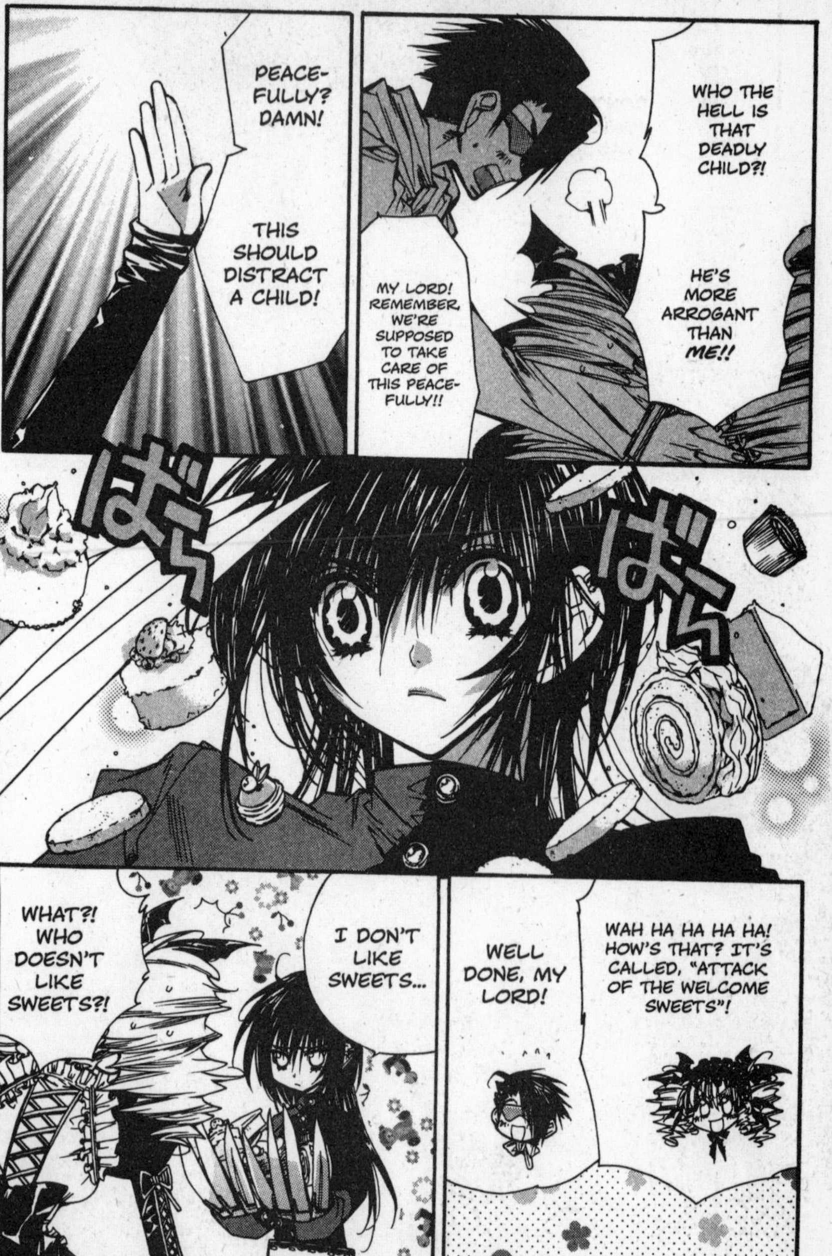
WHO THE HELL IS THAT DEADLY CHILD?!
HE'S MORE ARROGANT THAN *ME!!*
MY LORD! REMEMBER, WE'RE SUPPOSED TO TAKE CARE OF THIS PEACE-FULLY!!
PEACE-FULLY? DAMN!
THIS SHOULD DISTRACT A CHILD!
ばら
ばら
WAH HA HA HA HA! HOW'S THAT? IT'S CALLED, "ATTACK OF THE WELCOME SWEETS"!
WELL DONE, MY LORD!
I DON'T LIKE SWEETS...
WHAT?! WHO DOESN'T LIKE SWEETS?!

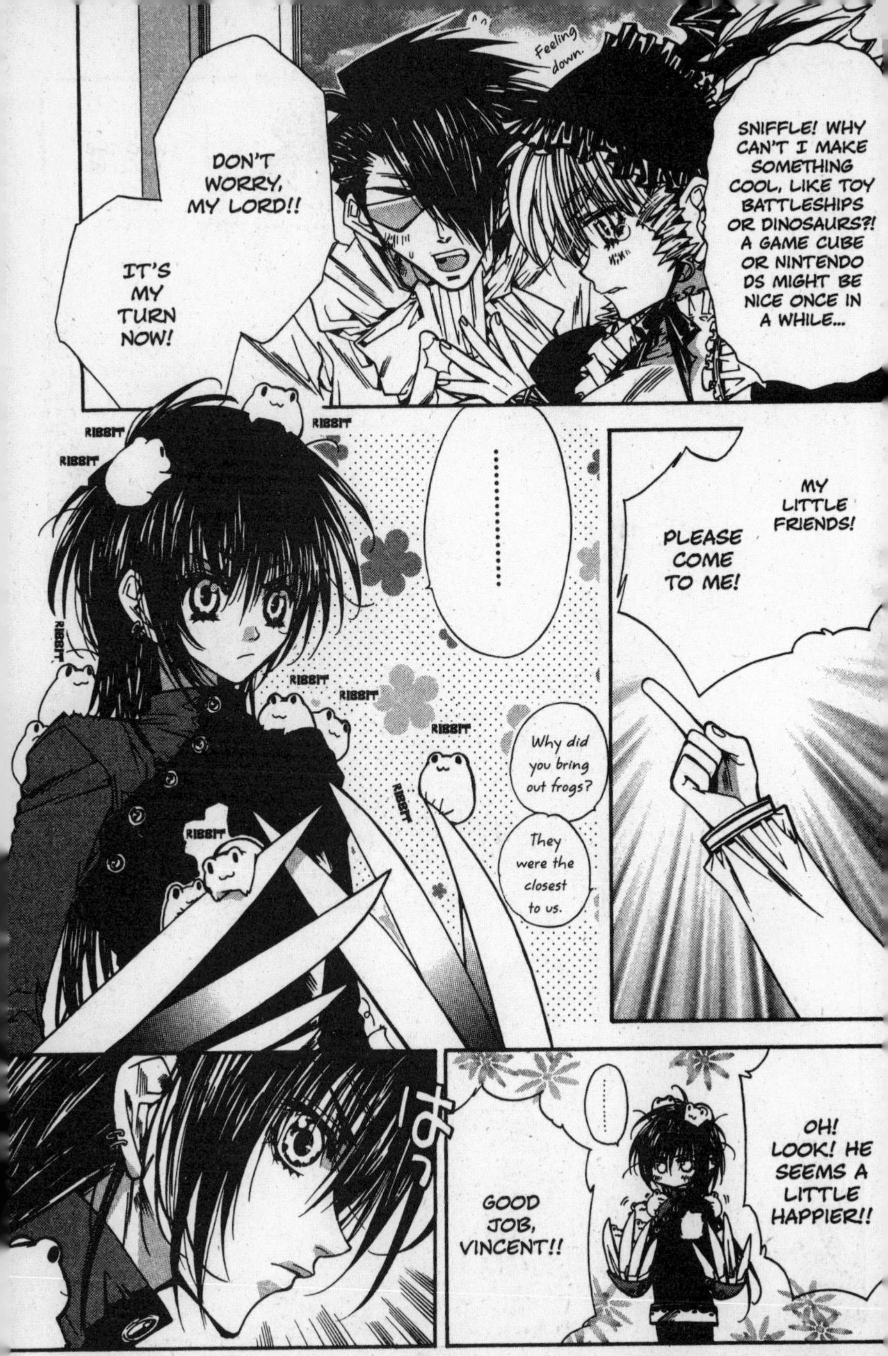
SNIFFLE! WHY CAN'T I MAKE SOMETHING COOL, LIKE TOY BATTLESHIPS OR DINOSAURS?! A GAME CUBE OR NINTENDO DS MIGHT BE NICE ONCE IN A WHILE...
Feeling down.
DON'T WORRY, MY LORD!!
IT'S MY TURN NOW!
MY LITTLE FRIENDS!
PLEASE COME TO ME!
......
RIBBIT
RIBBIT
RIBBIT
RIBBIT
RIBBIT
RIBBIT
RIBBIT
RIBBIT
RIBBIT
Why did you bring out frogs?
They were the closest to us.
OH! LOOK! HE SEEMS A LITTLE HAPPIER!!
......
GOOD JOB, VINCENT!!

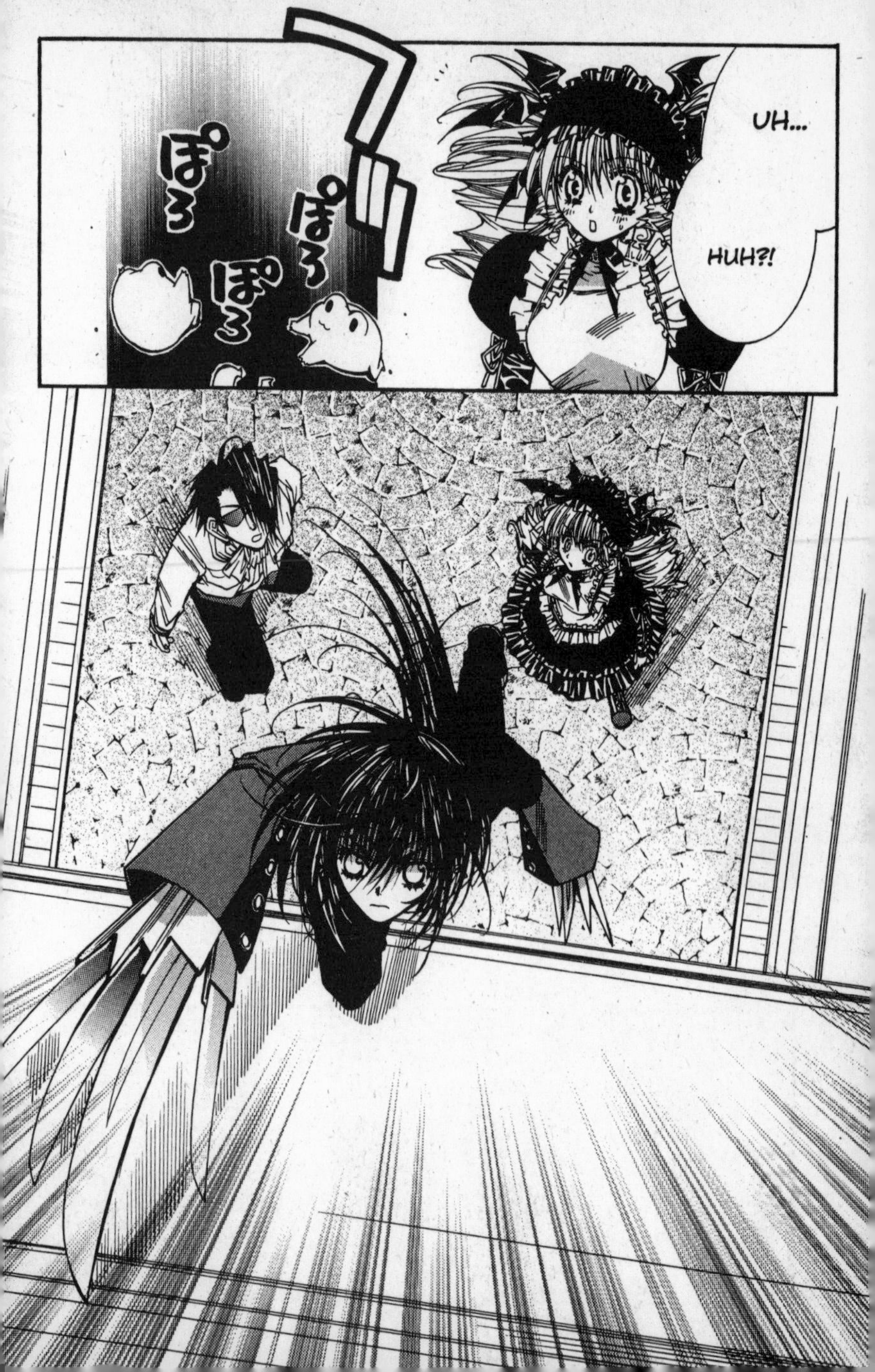
UH... HUH?!
ぽろ
ぽろ
ぽろ

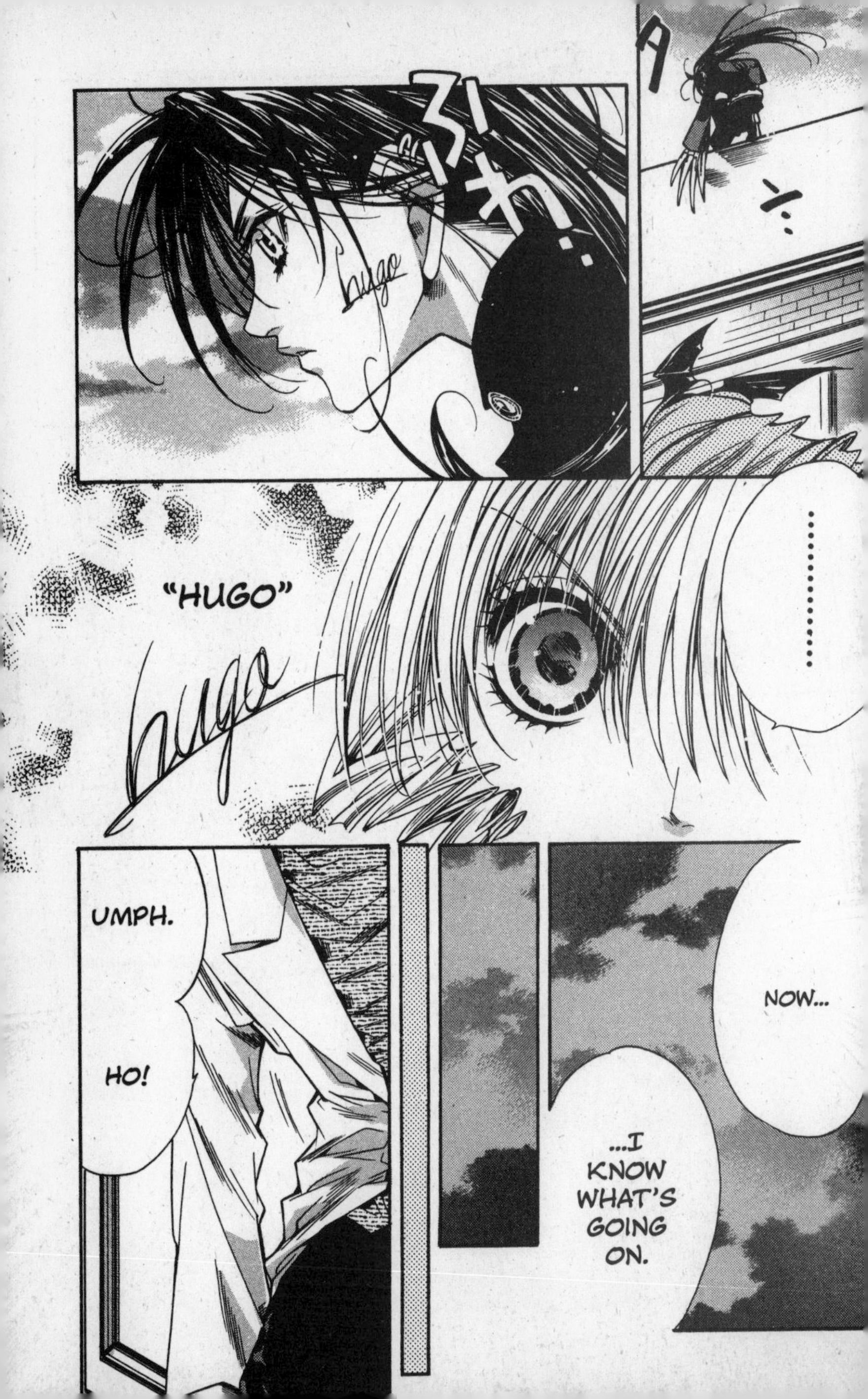
hugo
......
"HUGO"
hugo
NOW...
...I KNOW WHAT'S GOING ON.
UMPH.
HO!

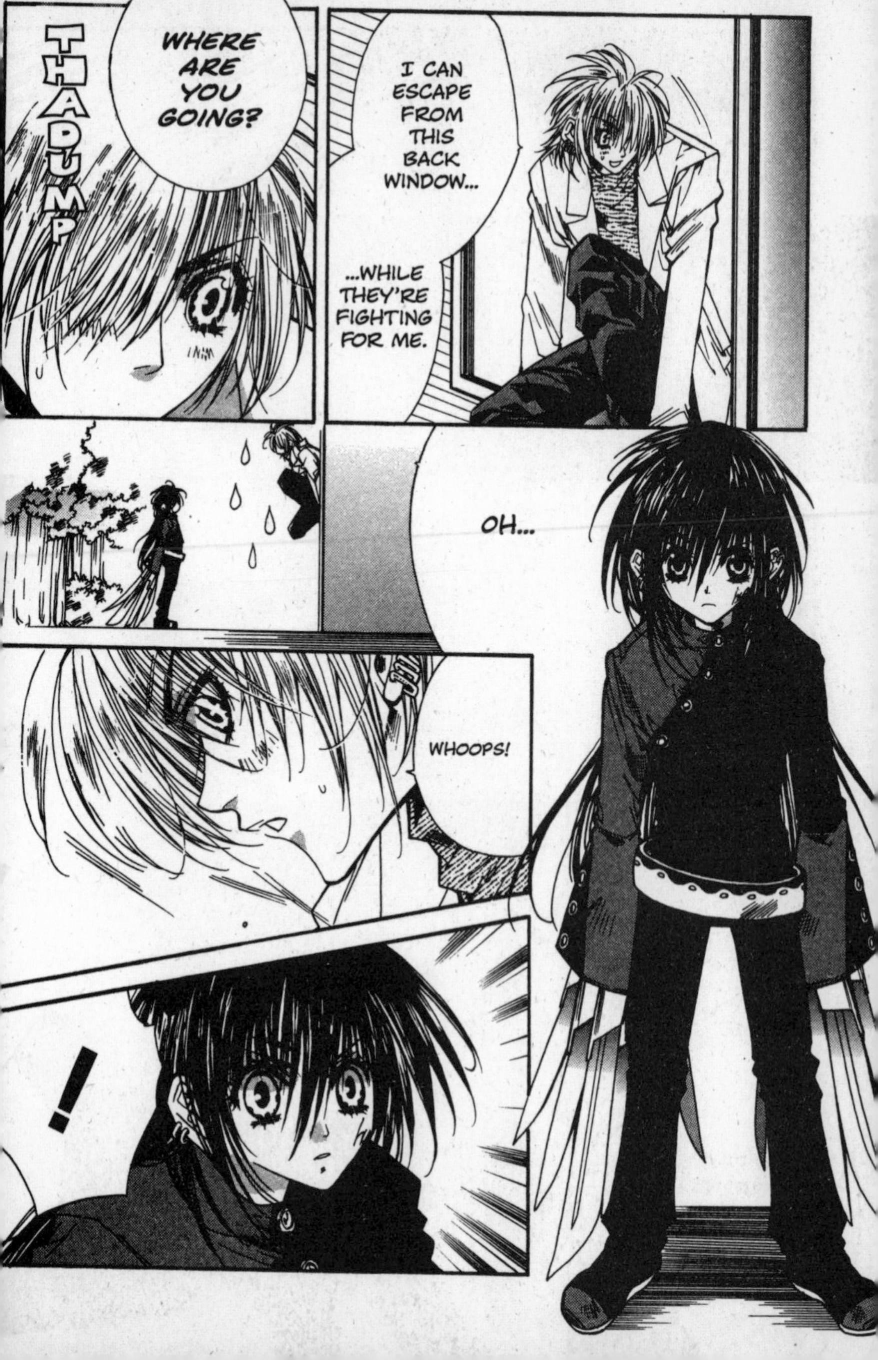

I CAN ESCAPE FROM THIS BACK WINDOW...
...WHILE THEY'RE FIGHTING FOR ME.
WHERE ARE YOU GOING?
THADUMP
OH...
WHOOPS!
!

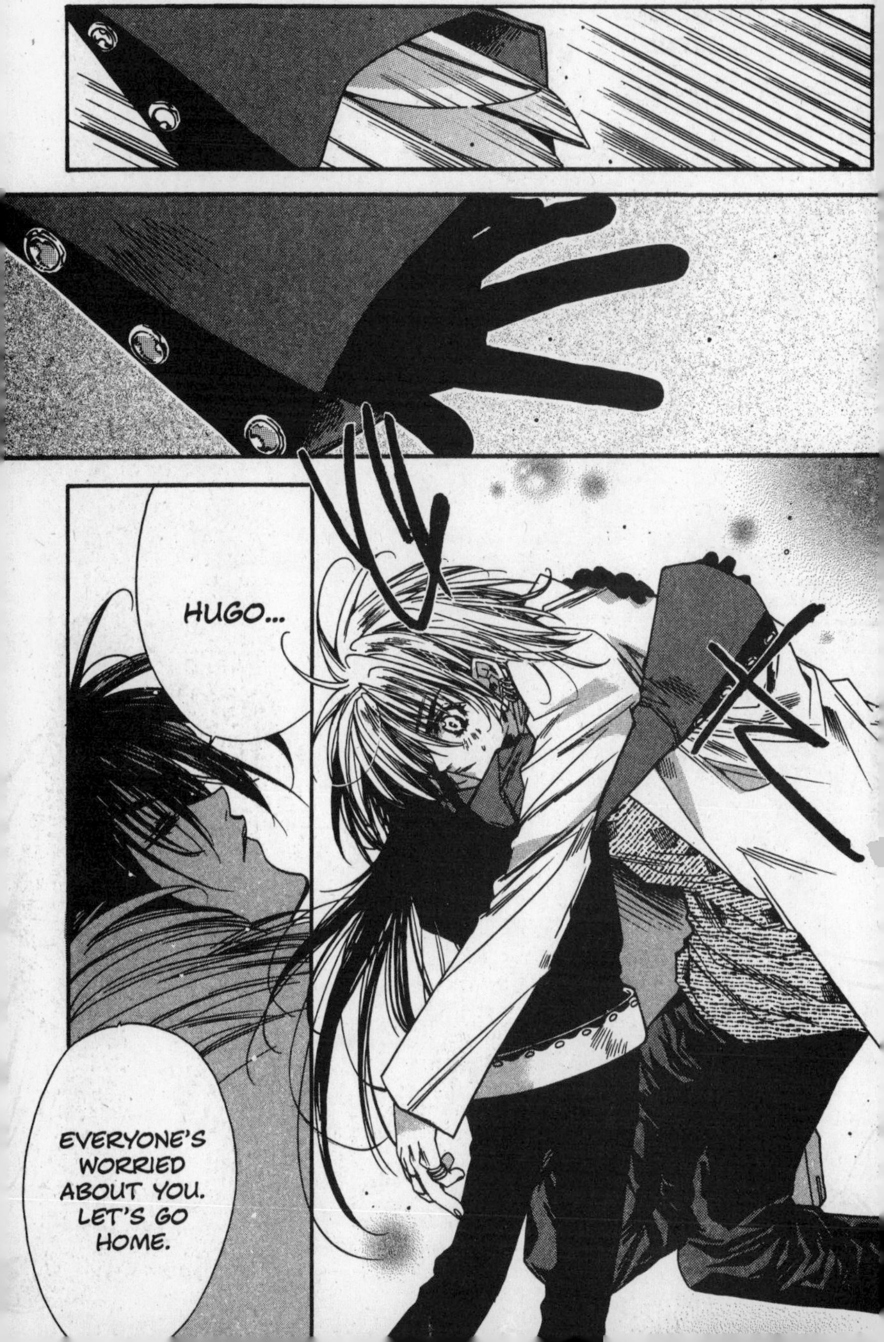
HUGO...
EVERYONE'S WORRIED ABOUT YOU. LET'S GO HOME.

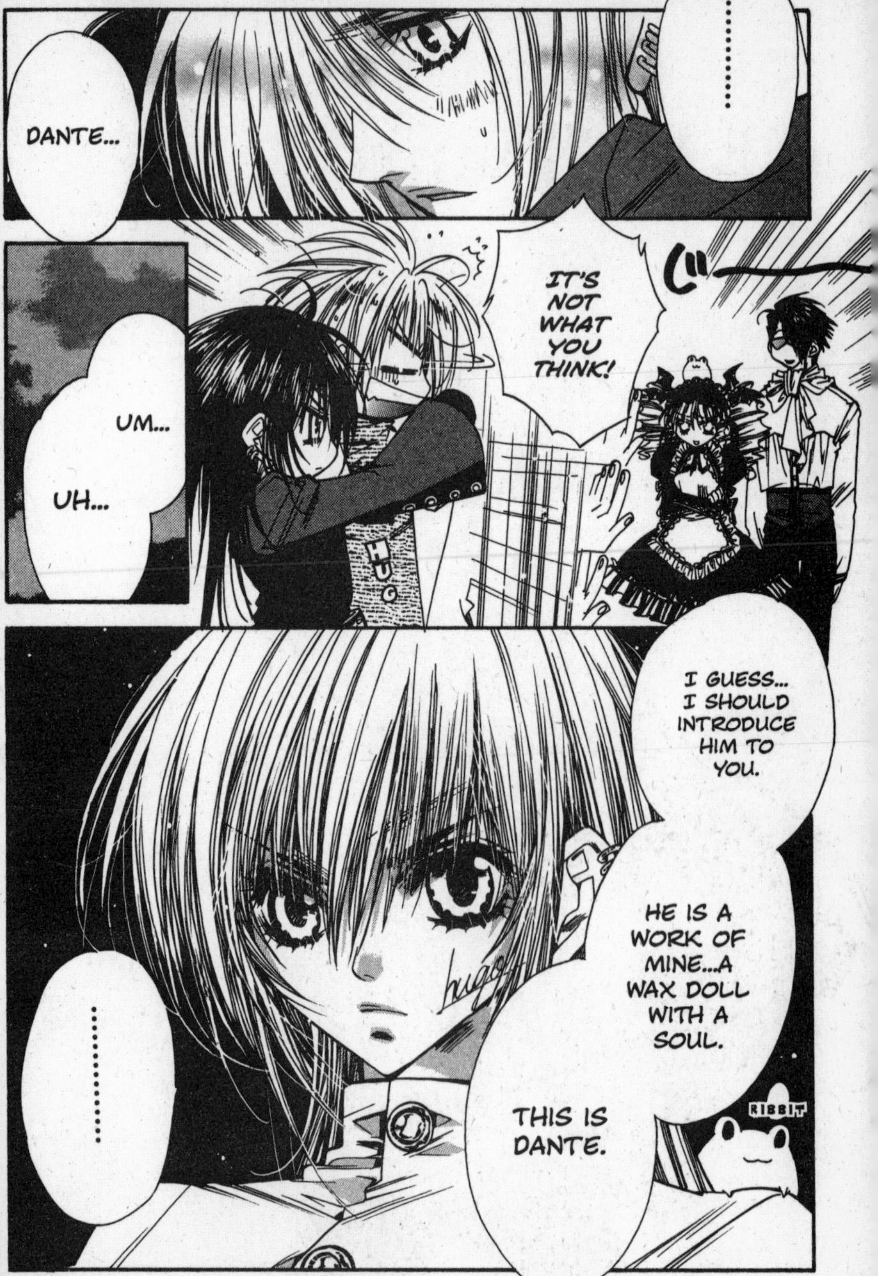
......
DANTE...
IT'S NOT WHAT YOU THINK!
HUG
UM...
UH...
I GUESS... I SHOULD INTRODUCE HIM TO YOU.
HE IS A WORK OF MINE...A WAX DOLL WITH A SOUL.
THIS IS DANTE.
RIBBIT
....

♯14 "Dante"

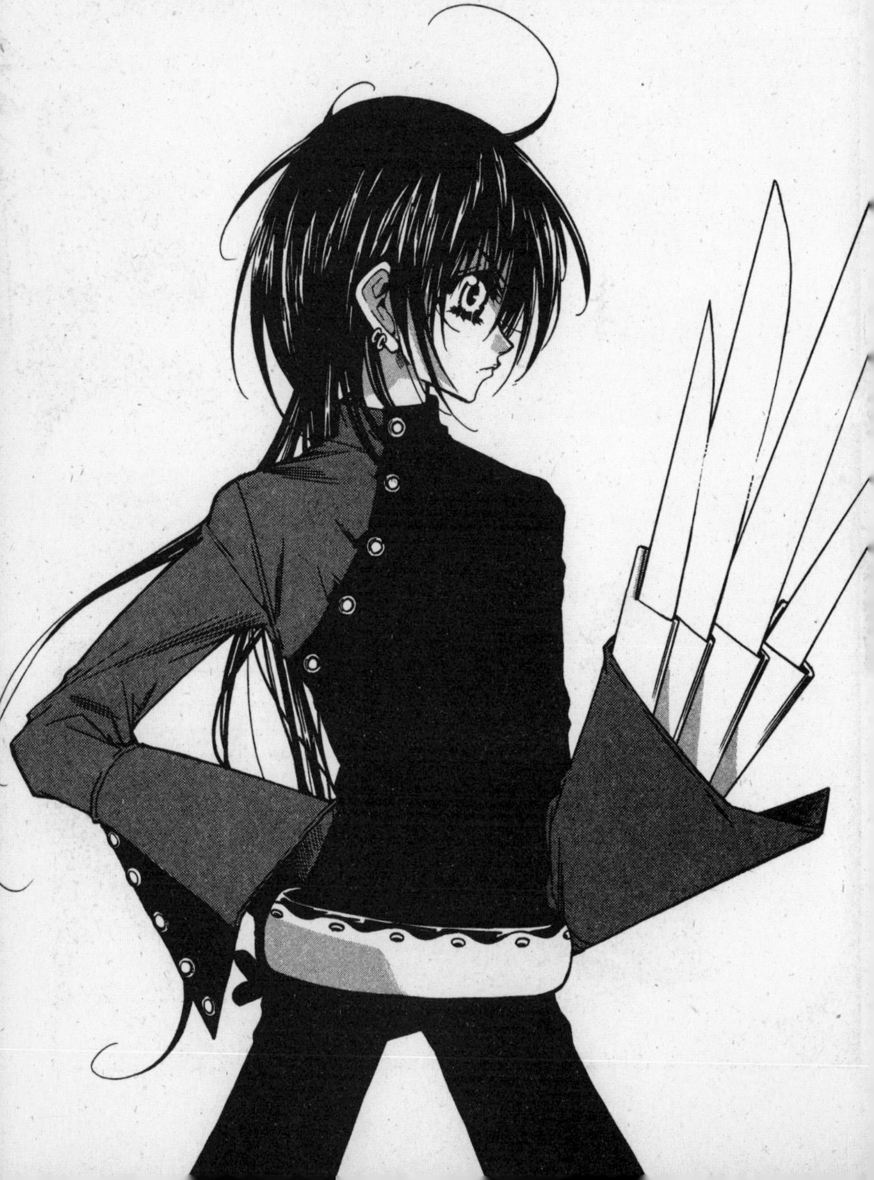

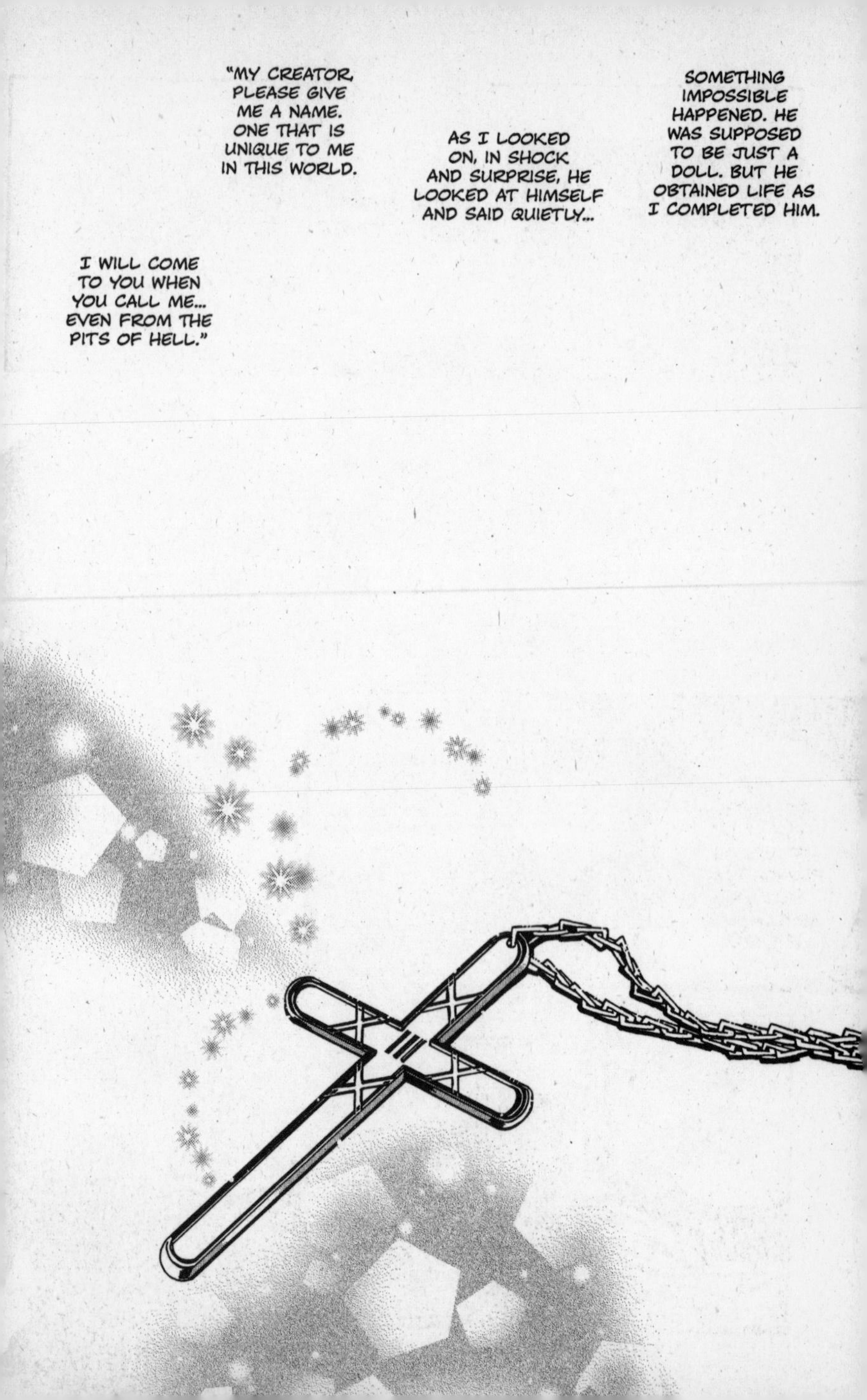
SOMETHING IMPOSSIBLE HAPPENED. HE WAS SUPPOSED TO BE JUST A DOLL. BUT HE OBTAINED LIFE AS I COMPLETED HIM.
AS I LOOKED ON, IN SHOCK AND SURPRISE, HE LOOKED AT HIMSELF AND SAID QUIETLY...
"MY CREATOR, PLEASE GIVE ME A NAME. ONE THAT IS UNIQUE TO ME IN THIS WORLD.
I WILL COME TO YOU WHEN YOU CALL ME... EVEN FROM THE PITS OF HELL."

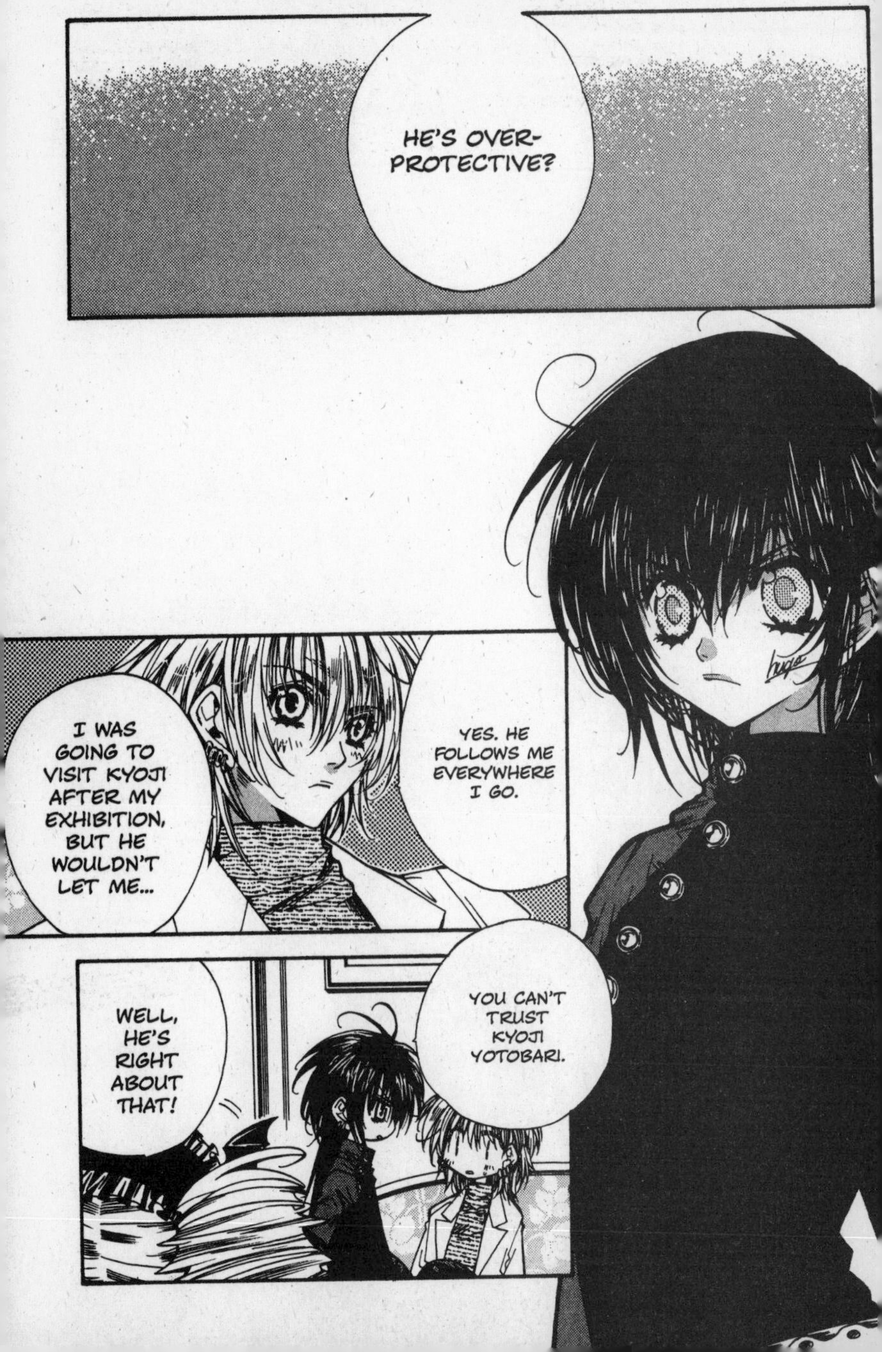
HE'S OVER-PROTECTIVE?
YES. HE FOLLOWS ME EVERYWHERE I GO.
I WAS GOING TO VISIT KYOJI AFTER MY EXHIBITION, BUT HE WOULDN'T LET ME...
YOU CAN'T TRUST KYOJI YOTOBARI.
WELL, HE'S RIGHT ABOUT THAT!

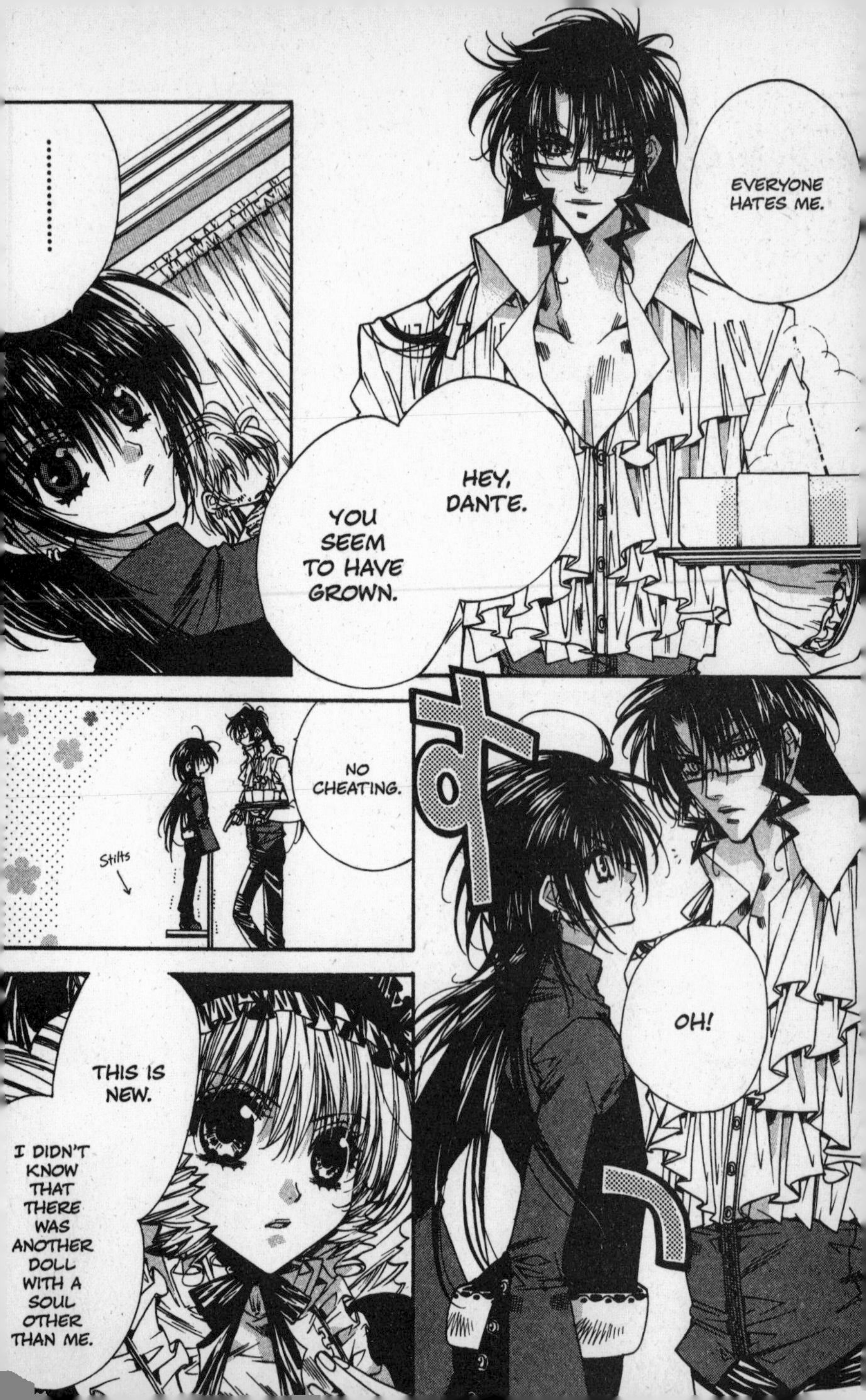
EVERYONE HATES ME.
HEY, DANTE.
YOU SEEM TO HAVE GROWN.
……
す
OH!
っ
NO CHEATING.
Stilts
THIS IS NEW.
I DIDN'T KNOW THAT THERE WAS ANOTHER DOLL WITH A SOUL OTHER THAN ME.

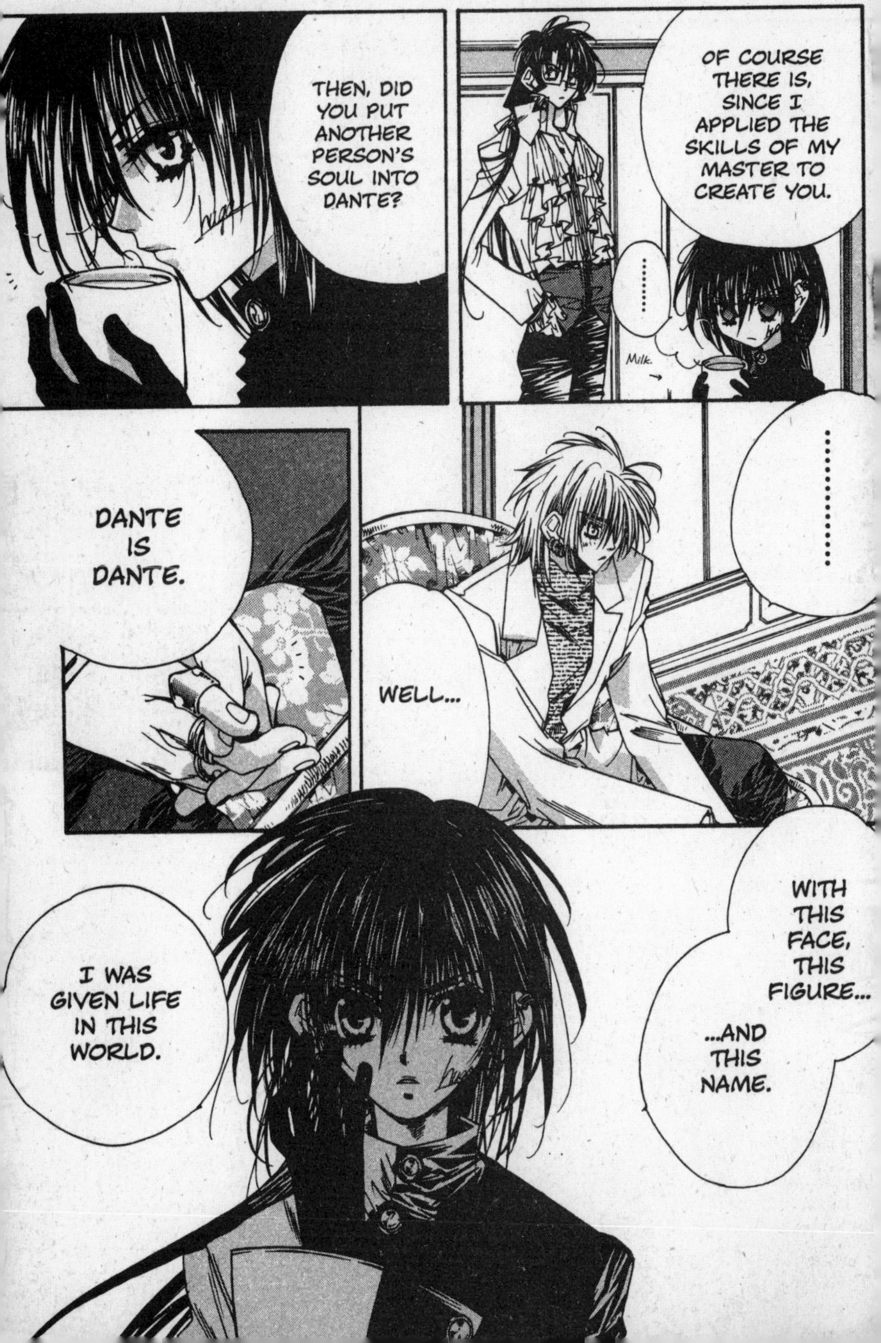
OF COURSE THERE IS, SINCE I APPLIED THE SKILLS OF MY MASTER TO CREATE YOU.
......
Milk.
THEN, DID YOU PUT ANOTHER PERSON'S SOUL INTO DANTE?
......
WELL...
DANTE IS DANTE.
WITH THIS FACE, THIS FIGURE...
...AND THIS NAME.
I WAS GIVEN LIFE IN THIS WORLD.

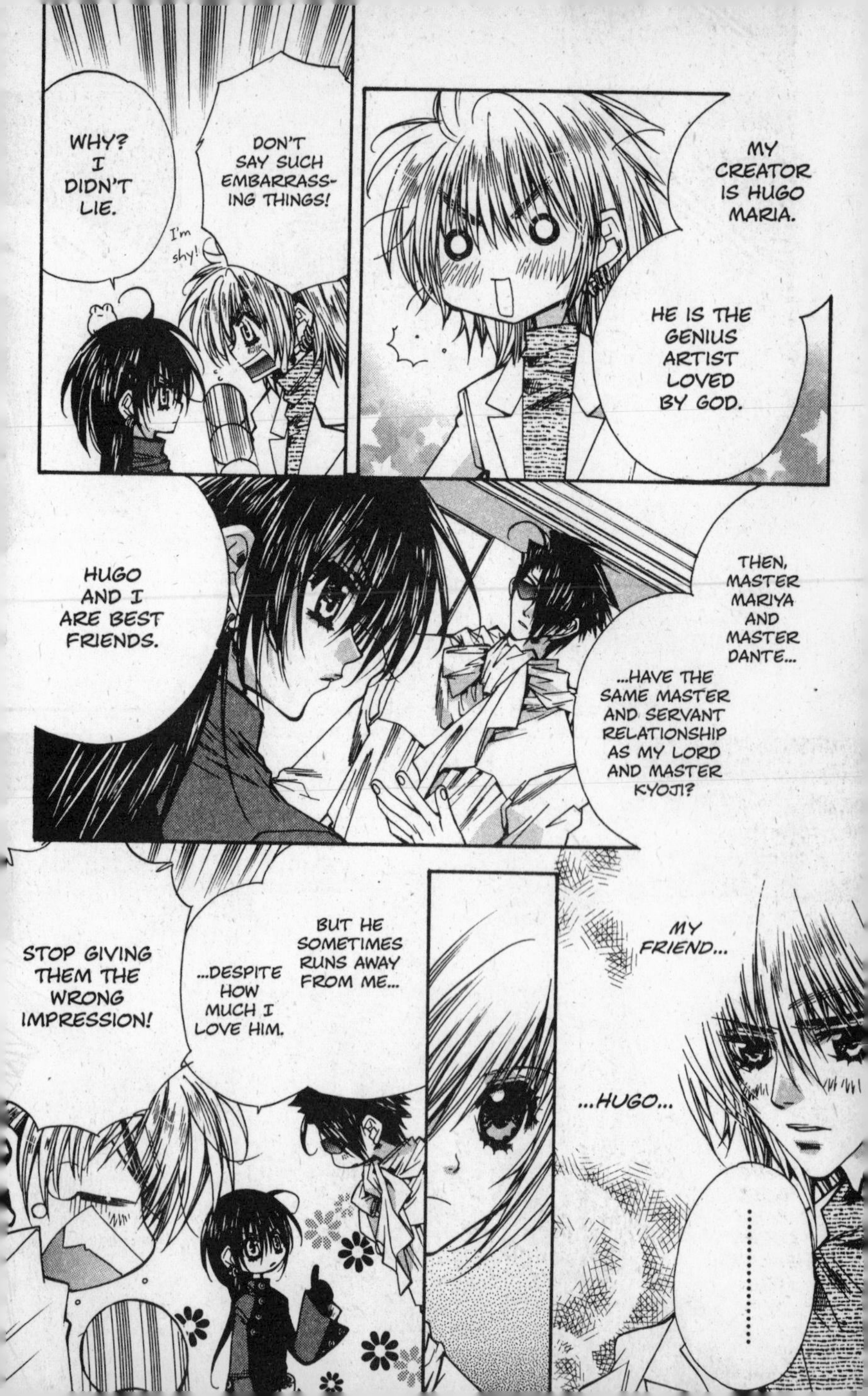
MY CREATOR IS HUGO MARIA.
HE IS THE GENIUS ARTIST LOVED BY GOD.
DON'T SAY SUCH EMBARRASS-ING THINGS!
I'm shy!
WHY? I DIDN'T LIE.
THEN, MASTER MARIYA AND MASTER DANTE...
...HAVE THE SAME MASTER AND SERVANT RELATIONSHIP AS MY LORD AND MASTER KYOJI?
HUGO AND I ARE BEST FRIENDS.
MY FRIEND...
...HUGO...
......
BUT HE SOMETIMES RUNS AWAY FROM ME...
...DESPITE HOW MUCH I LOVE HIM.
STOP GIVING THEM THE WRONG IMPRESSION!

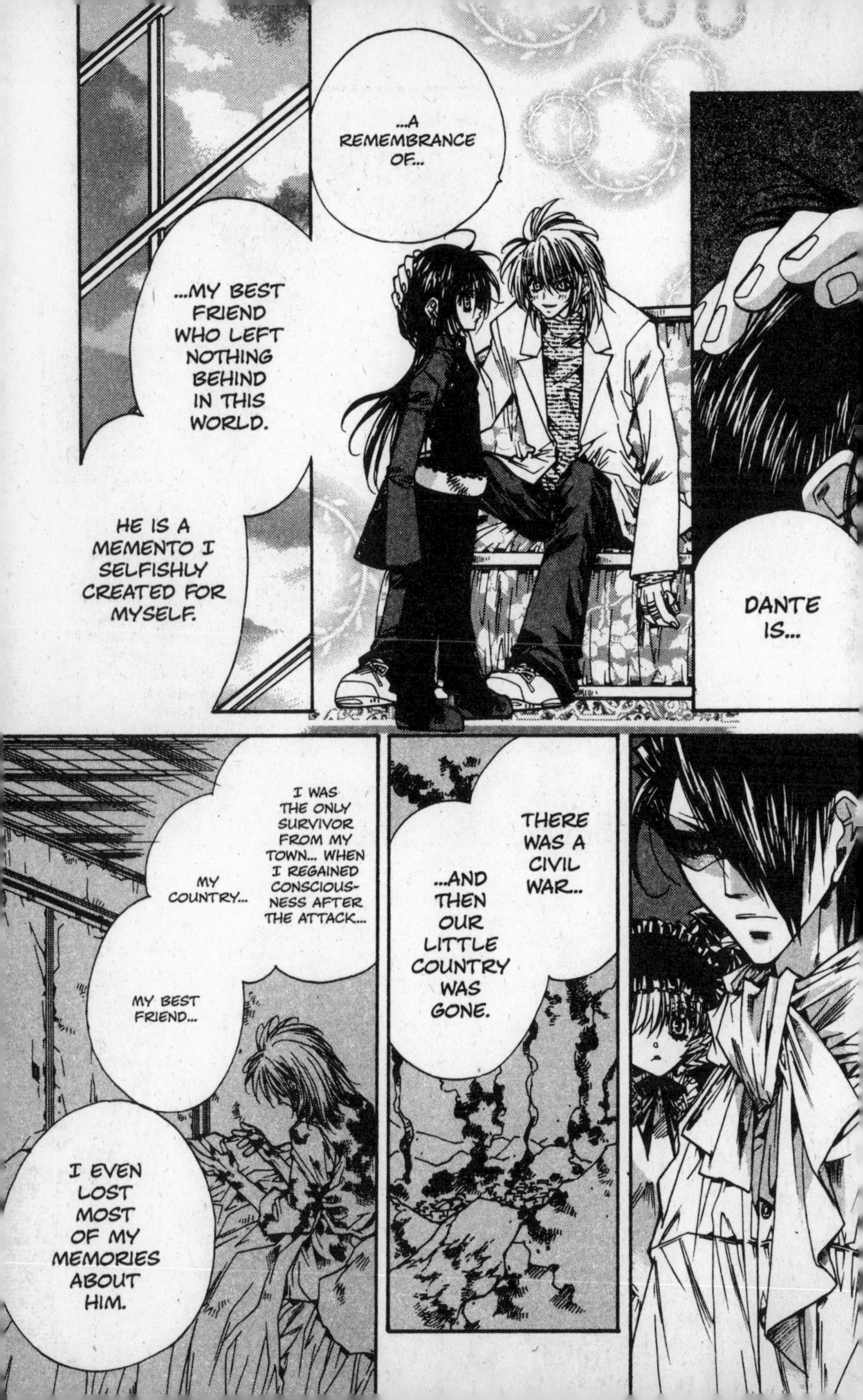
DANTE IS...
...A REMEMBRANCE OF...
...MY BEST FRIEND WHO LEFT NOTHING BEHIND IN THIS WORLD.
HE IS A MEMENTO I SELFISHLY CREATED FOR MYSELF.
THERE WAS A CIVIL WAR...
...AND THEN OUR LITTLE COUNTRY WAS GONE.
I WAS THE ONLY SURVIVOR FROM MY TOWN... WHEN I REGAINED CONSCIOUSNESS AFTER THE ATTACK...
MY COUNTRY...
MY BEST FRIEND...
I EVEN LOST MOST OF MY MEMORIES ABOUT HIM.

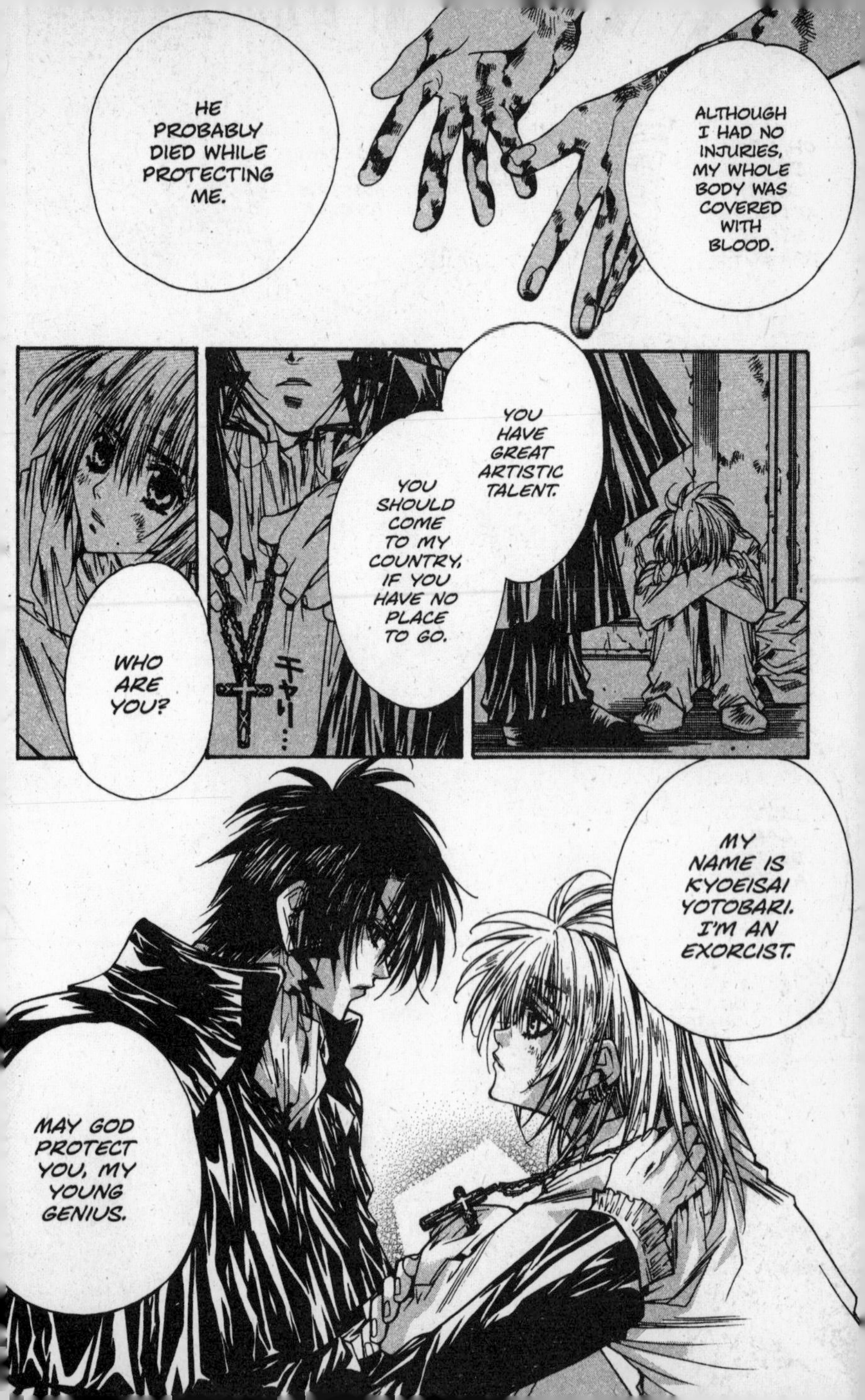
ALTHOUGH I HAD NO INJURIES, MY WHOLE BODY WAS COVERED WITH BLOOD.
HE PROBABLY DIED WHILE PROTECTING ME.
YOU HAVE GREAT ARTISTIC TALENT.
YOU SHOULD COME TO MY COUNTRY, IF YOU HAVE NO PLACE TO GO.
キャリ…
WHO ARE YOU?
MY NAME IS KYOEISAI YOTOBARI. I'M AN EXORCIST.
MAY GOD PROTECT YOU, MY YOUNG GENIUS.

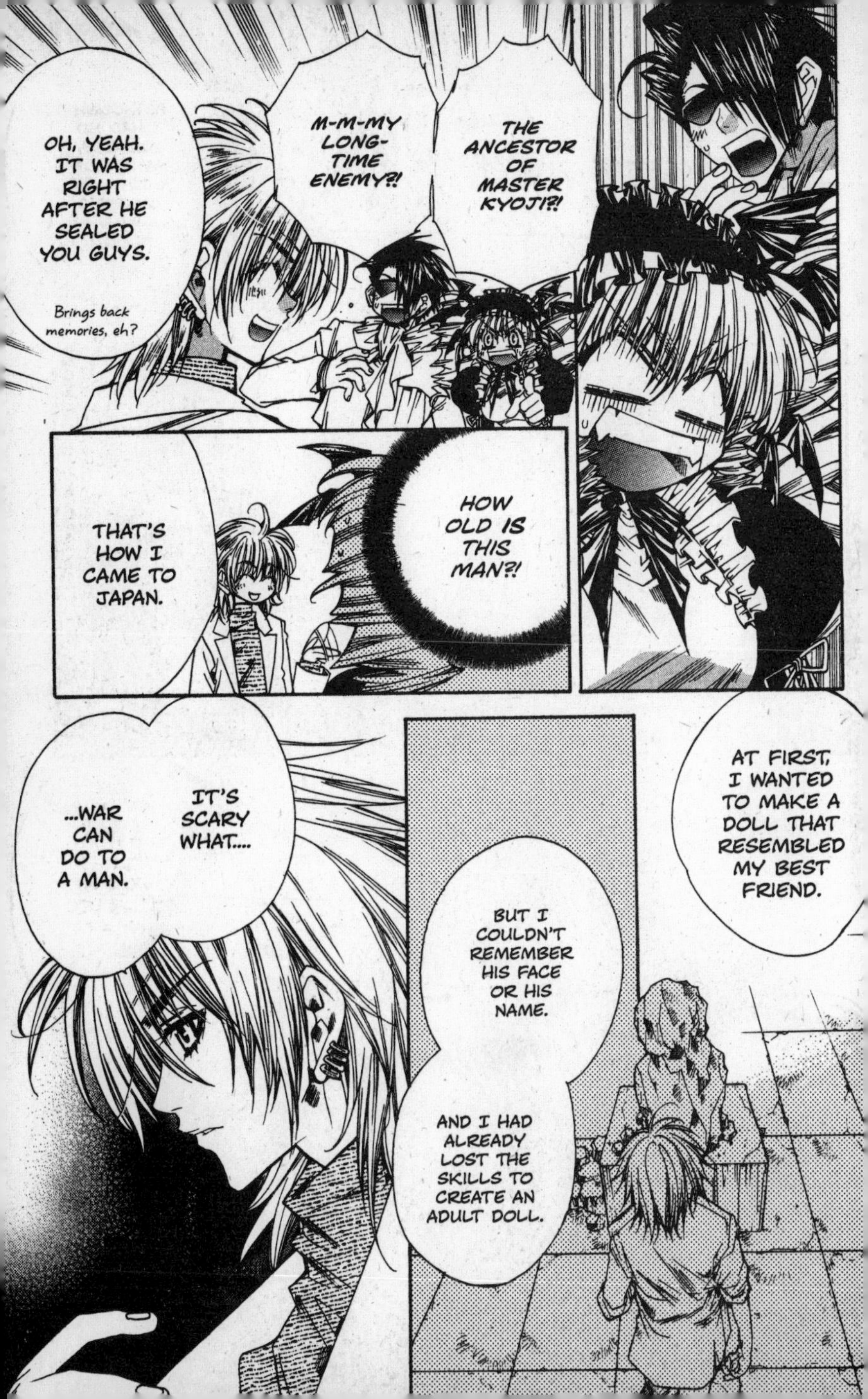
THE ANCESTOR OF MASTER KYOJI?!
M-M-MY LONG-TIME ENEMY?!
OH, YEAH. IT WAS RIGHT AFTER HE SEALED YOU GUYS.
Brings back memories, eh?
HOW OLD IS THIS MAN?!
THAT'S HOW I CAME TO JAPAN.
AT FIRST, I WANTED TO MAKE A DOLL THAT RESEMBLED MY BEST FRIEND.
BUT I COULDN'T REMEMBER HIS FACE OR HIS NAME.
AND I HAD ALREADY LOST THE SKILLS TO CREATE AN ADULT DOLL.
IT'S SCARY WHAT....
...WAR CAN DO TO A MAN.

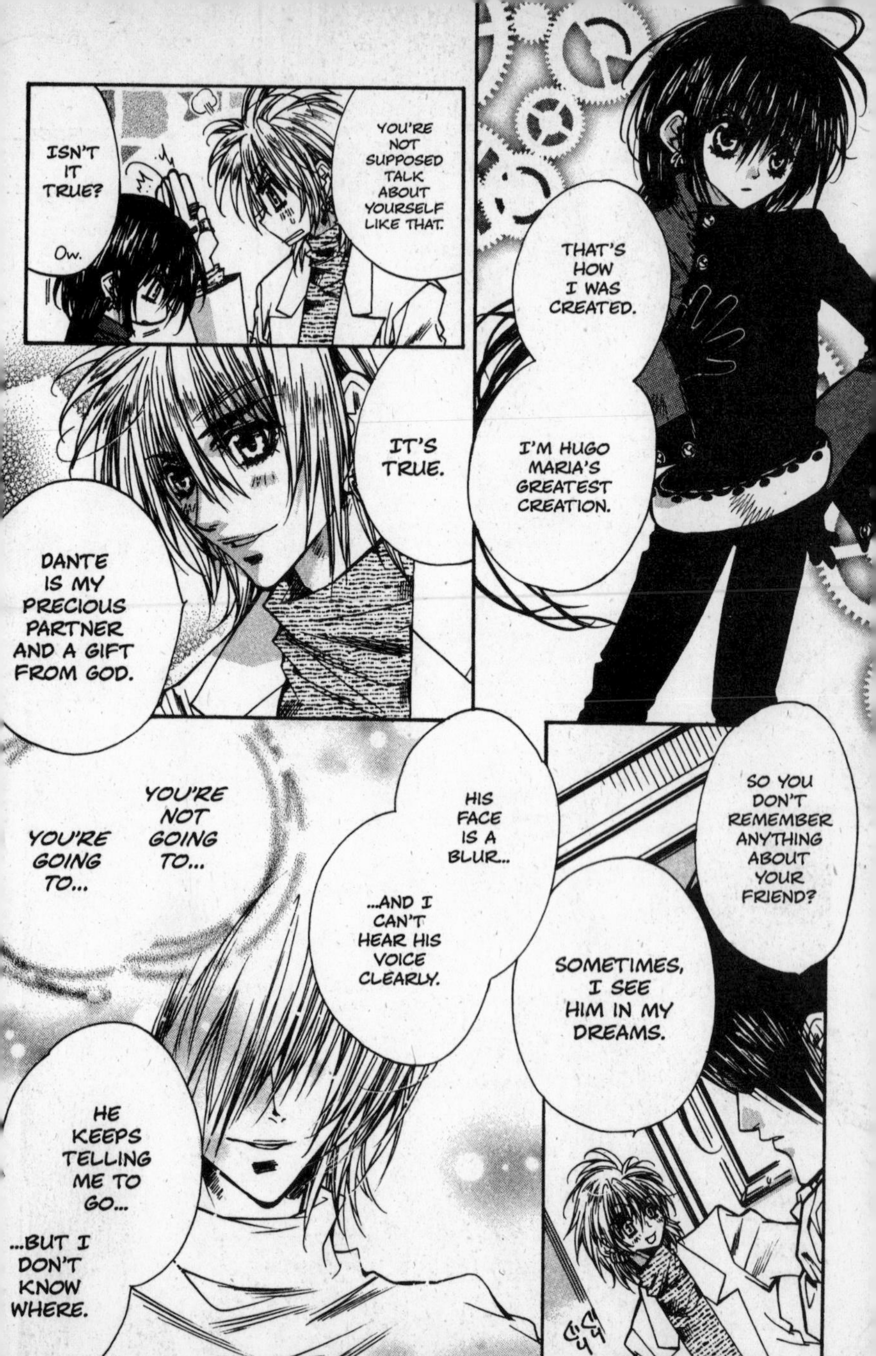
THAT'S HOW I WAS CREATED.
I'M HUGO MARIA'S GREATEST CREATION.
YOU'RE NOT SUPPOSED TALK ABOUT YOURSELF LIKE THAT.
ISN'T IT TRUE?
Ow.
IT'S TRUE.
DANTE IS MY PRECIOUS PARTNER AND A GIFT FROM GOD.
SO YOU DON'T REMEMBER ANYTHING ABOUT YOUR FRIEND?
SOMETIMES, I SEE HIM IN MY DREAMS.
HIS FACE IS A BLUR...
...AND I CAN'T HEAR HIS VOICE CLEARLY.
YOU'RE NOT GOING TO...
YOU'RE GOING TO...
HE KEEPS TELLING ME TO GO...
...BUT I DON'T KNOW WHERE.

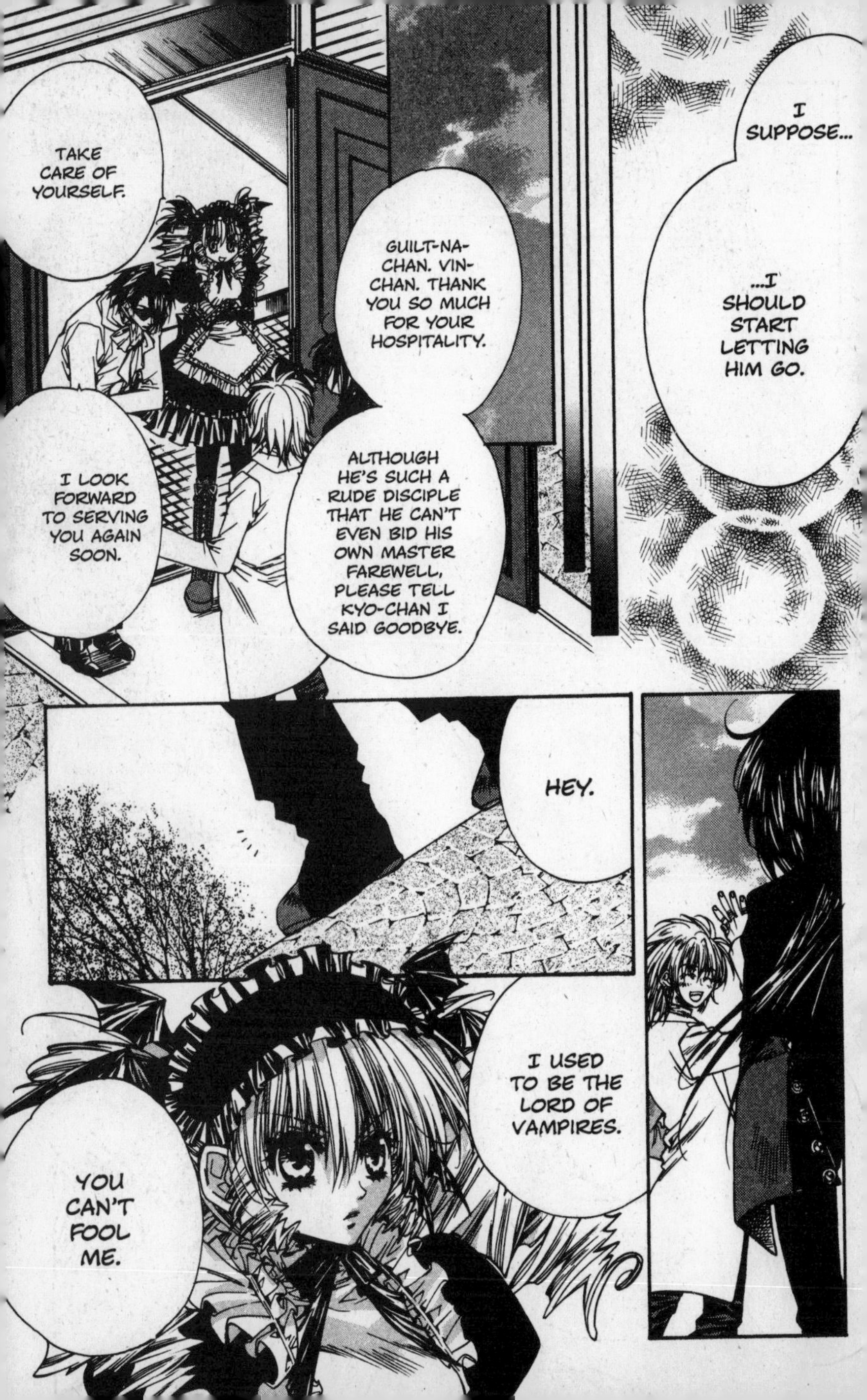
I SUPPOSE...
...I SHOULD START LETTING HIM GO.
GUILT-NA-CHAN. VIN-CHAN. THANK YOU SO MUCH FOR YOUR HOSPITALITY.
ALTHOUGH HE'S SUCH A RUDE DISCIPLE THAT HE CAN'T EVEN BID HIS OWN MASTER FAREWELL, PLEASE TELL KYO-CHAN I SAID GOODBYE.
TAKE CARE OF YOURSELF.
I LOOK FORWARD TO SERVING YOU AGAIN SOON.
HEY.
I USED TO BE THE LORD OF VAMPIRES.
YOU CAN'T FOOL ME.

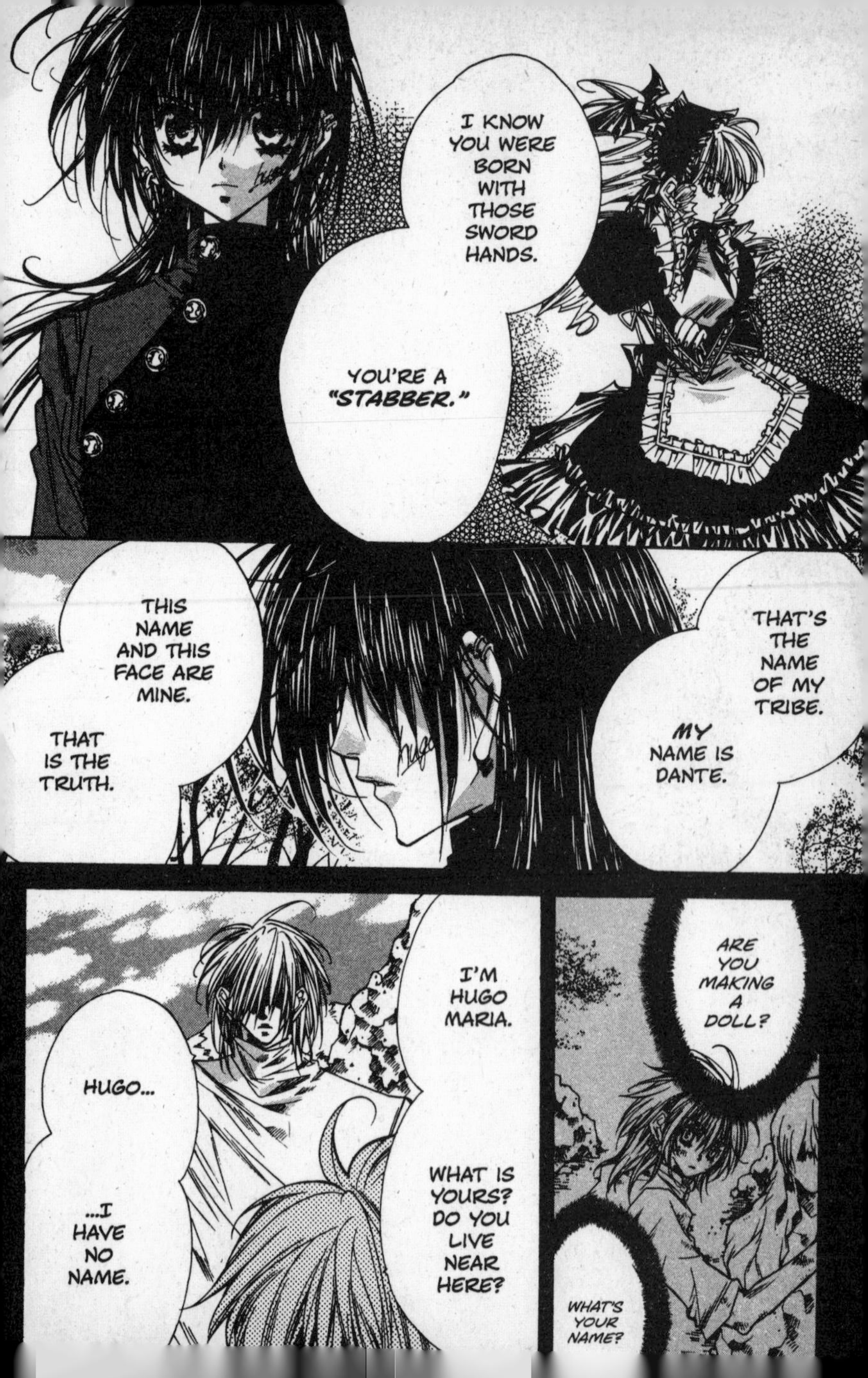
I KNOW YOU WERE BORN WITH THOSE SWORD HANDS.
YOU'RE A "STABBER."
THAT'S THE NAME OF MY TRIBE.
MY NAME IS DANTE.
THIS NAME AND THIS FACE ARE MINE.
THAT IS THE TRUTH.
ARE YOU MAKING A DOLL?
WHAT'S YOUR NAME?
I'M HUGO MARIA.
WHAT IS YOURS? DO YOU LIVE NEAR HERE?
HUGO...
...I HAVE NO NAME.

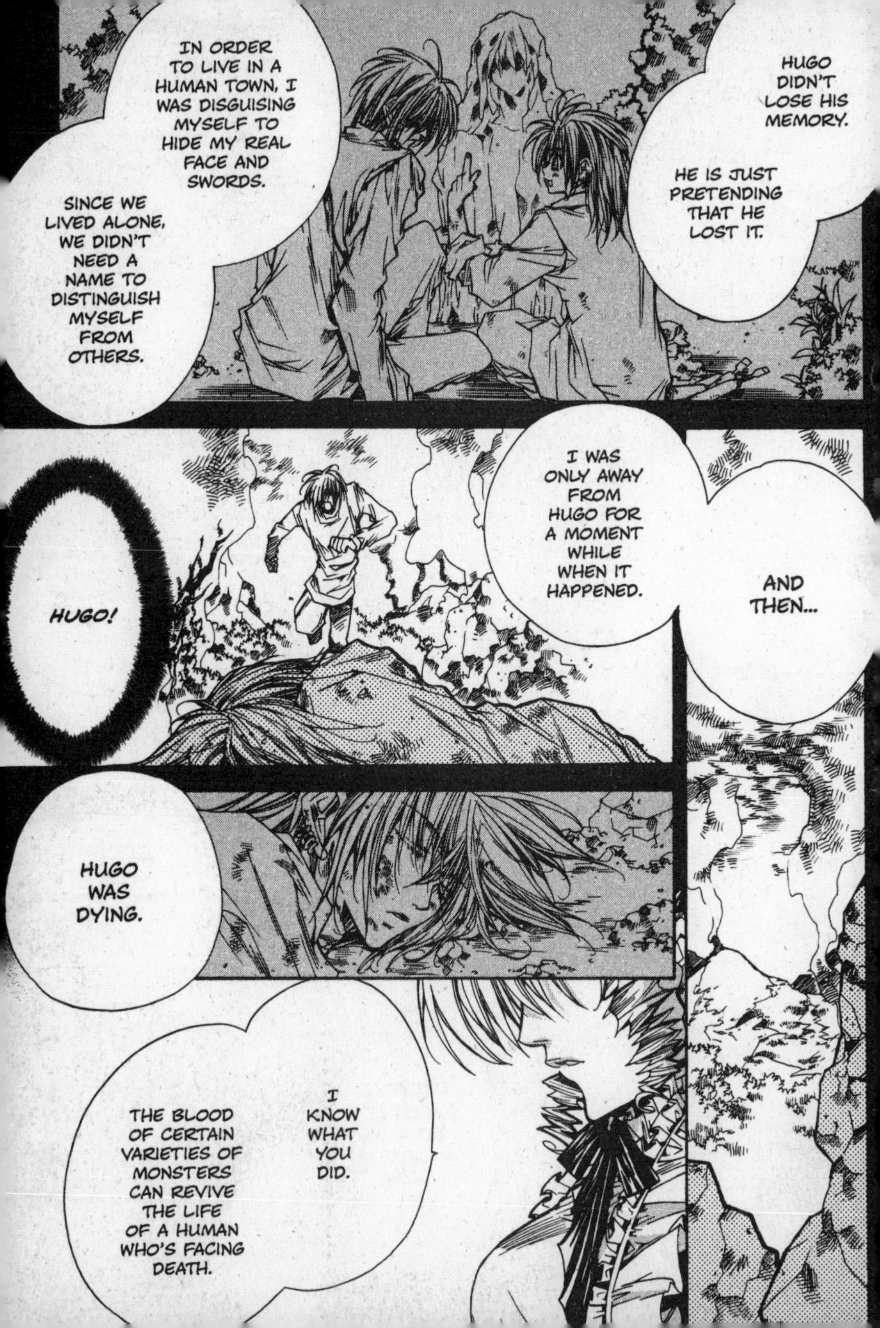
HUGO DIDN'T LOSE HIS MEMORY.
HE IS JUST PRETENDING THAT HE LOST IT.
IN ORDER TO LIVE IN A HUMAN TOWN, I WAS DISGUISING MYSELF TO HIDE MY REAL FACE AND SWORDS.
SINCE WE LIVED ALONE, WE DIDN'T NEED A NAME TO DISTINGUISH MYSELF FROM OTHERS.
I WAS ONLY AWAY FROM HUGO FOR A MOMENT WHILE WHEN IT HAPPENED.
AND THEN...
HUGO!
HUGO WAS DYING.
I KNOW WHAT YOU DID.
THE BLOOD OF CERTAIN VARIETIES OF MONSTERS CAN REVIVE THE LIFE OF A HUMAN WHO'S FACING DEATH.

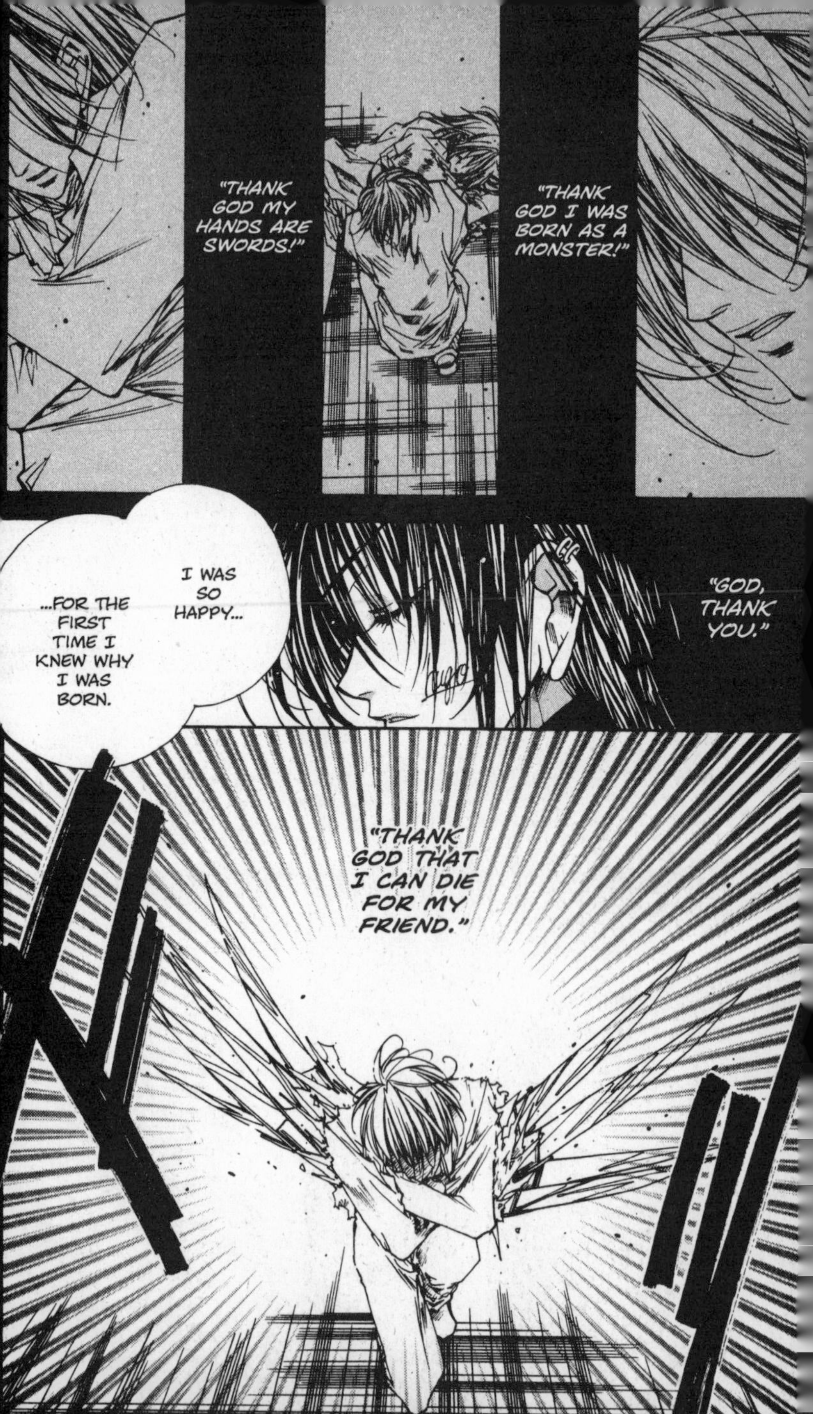
"THANK GOD I WAS BORN AS A MONSTER!"
"THANK GOD MY HANDS ARE SWORDS!"
"GOD, THANK YOU."
I WAS SO HAPPY...
...FOR THE FIRST TIME I KNEW WHY I WAS BORN.
"THANK GOD THAT I CAN DIE FOR MY FRIEND."

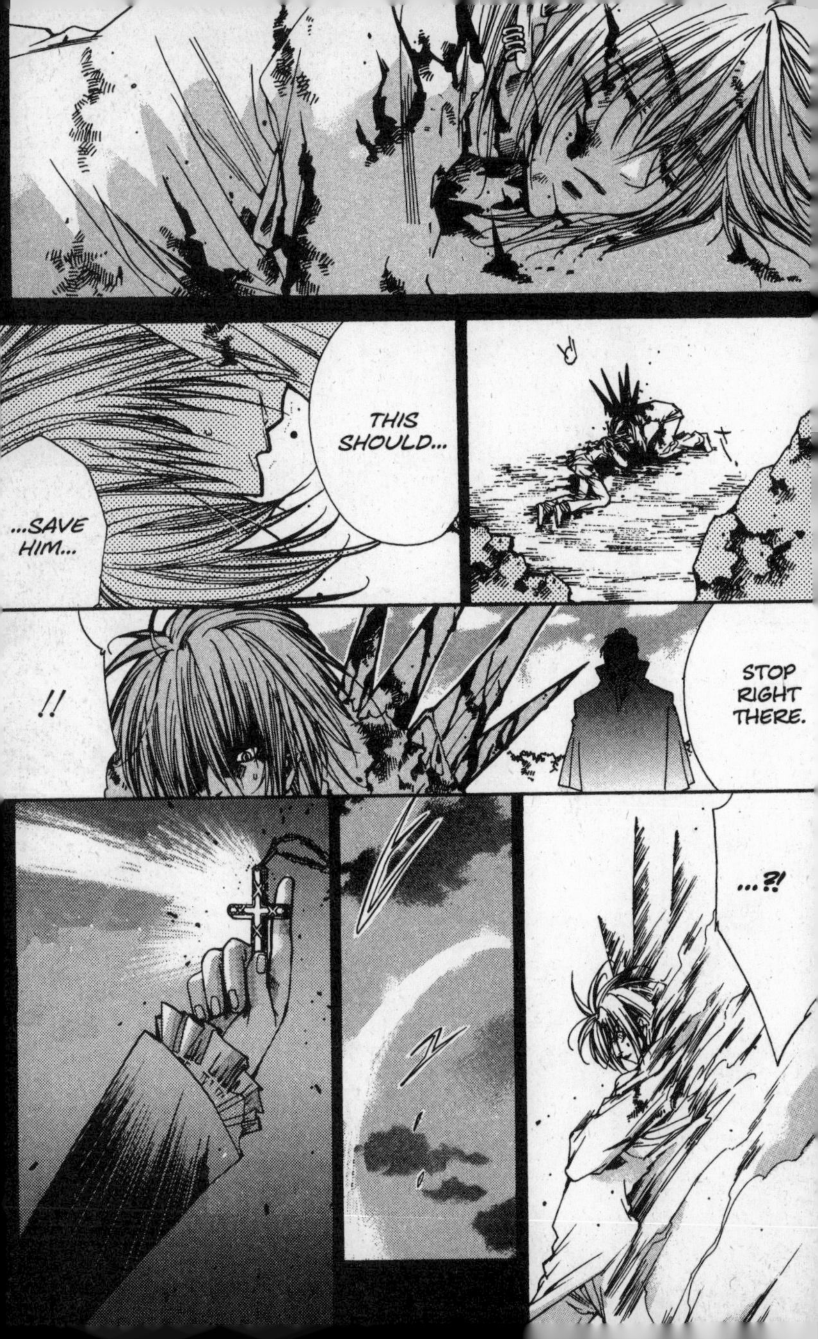
THIS SHOULD...
...SAVE HIM...
STOP RIGHT THERE.
!!
...?!

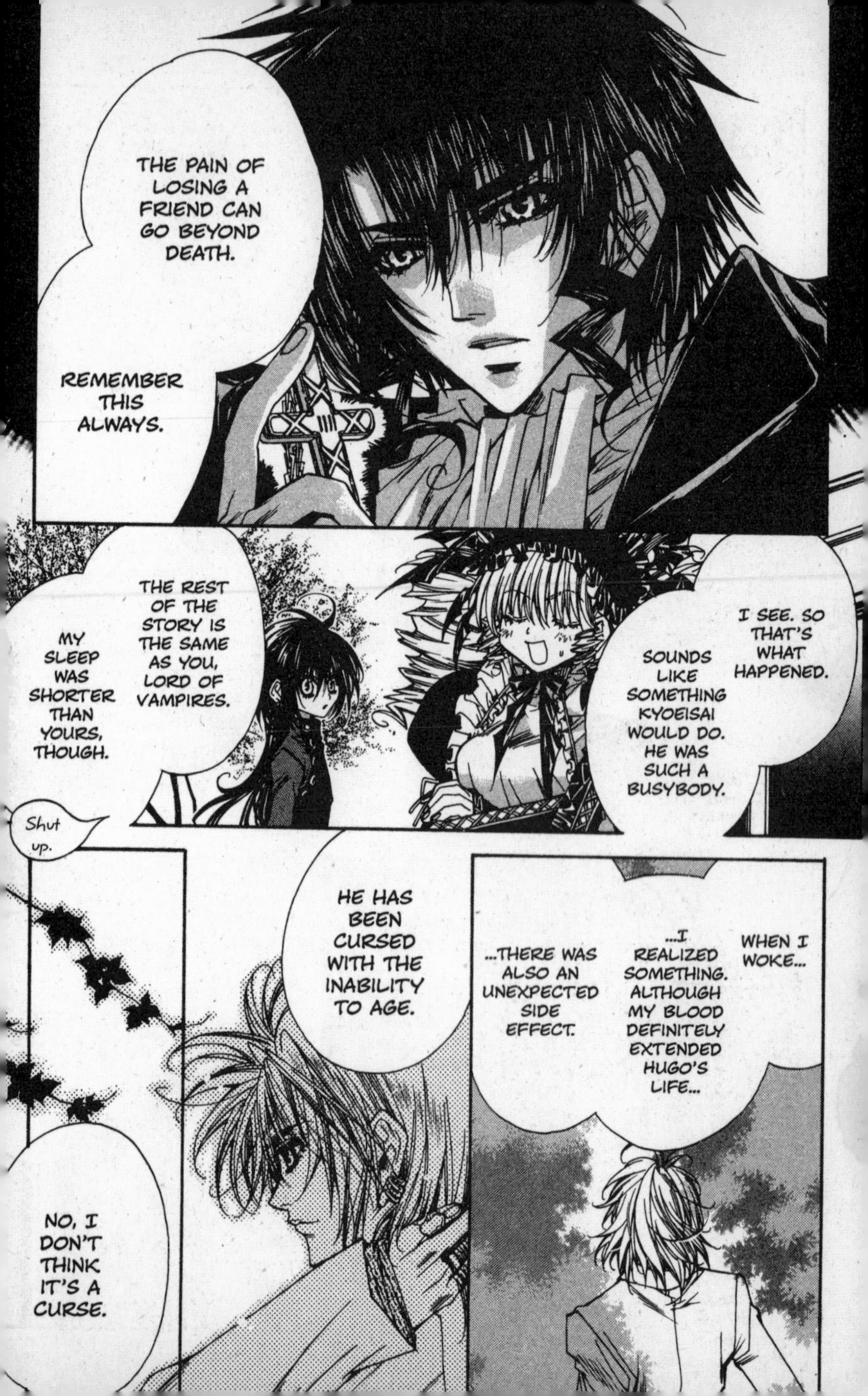
THE PAIN OF LOSING A FRIEND CAN GO BEYOND DEATH.
REMEMBER THIS ALWAYS.
I SEE. SO THAT'S WHAT HAPPENED.
SOUNDS LIKE SOMETHING KYOEISAI WOULD DO. HE WAS SUCH A BUSYBODY.
THE REST OF THE STORY IS THE SAME AS YOU, LORD OF VAMPIRES.
MY SLEEP WAS SHORTER THAN YOURS, THOUGH.
Shut up.
WHEN I WOKE...
...I REALIZED SOMETHING. ALTHOUGH MY BLOOD DEFINITELY EXTENDED HUGO'S LIFE...
...THERE WAS ALSO AN UNEXPECTED SIDE EFFECT.
HE HAS BEEN CURSED WITH THE INABILITY TO AGE.
NO, I DON'T THINK IT'S A CURSE.

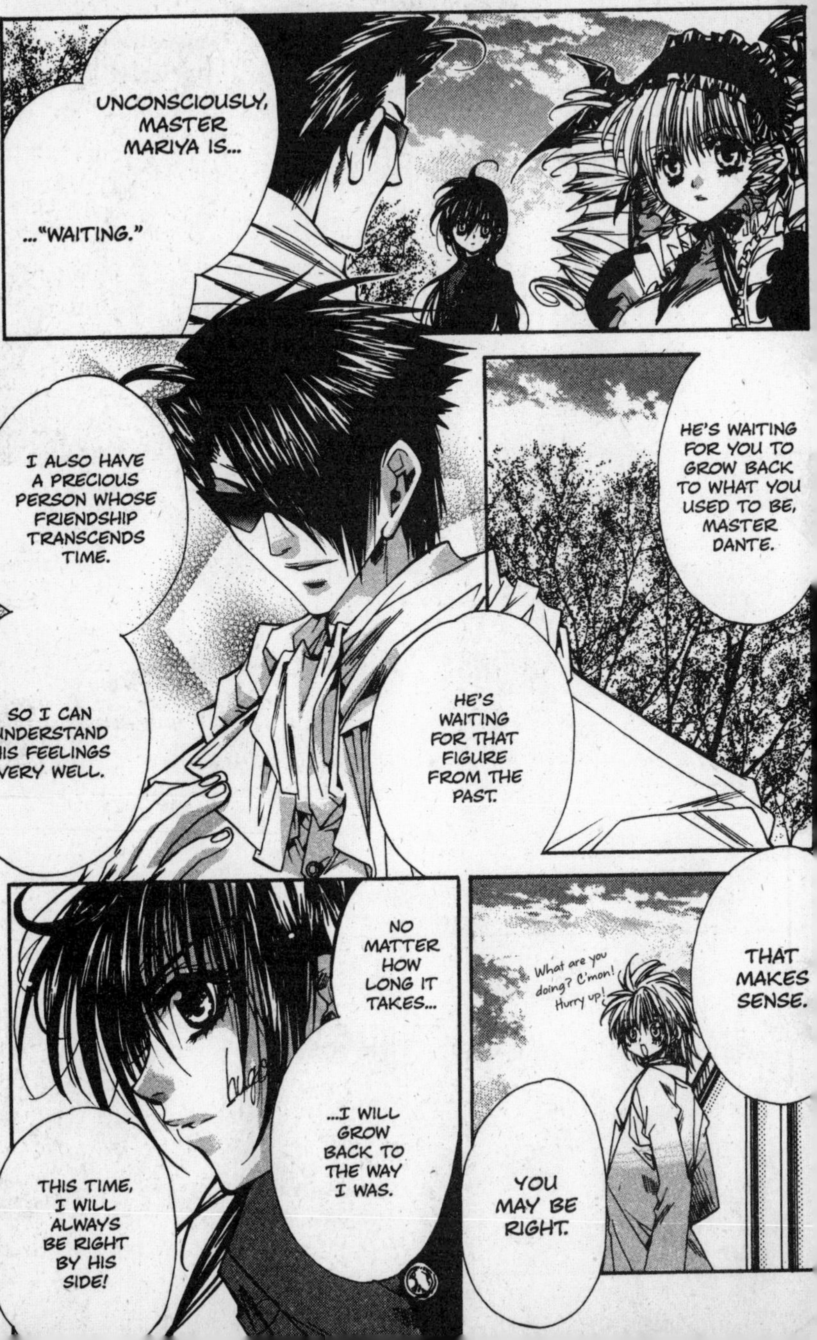
UNCONSCIOUSLY, MASTER MARIYA IS...
..."WAITING."
HE'S WAITING FOR YOU TO GROW BACK TO WHAT YOU USED TO BE, MASTER DANTE.
HE'S WAITING FOR THAT FIGURE FROM THE PAST.
I ALSO HAVE A PRECIOUS PERSON WHOSE FRIENDSHIP TRANSCENDS TIME.
SO I CAN UNDERSTAND HIS FEELINGS VERY WELL.
THAT MAKES SENSE.
What are you doing? C'mon! Hurry up!
YOU MAY BE RIGHT.
NO MATTER HOW LONG IT TAKES...
...I WILL GROW BACK TO THE WAY I WAS.
THIS TIME, I WILL ALWAYS BE RIGHT BY HIS SIDE!

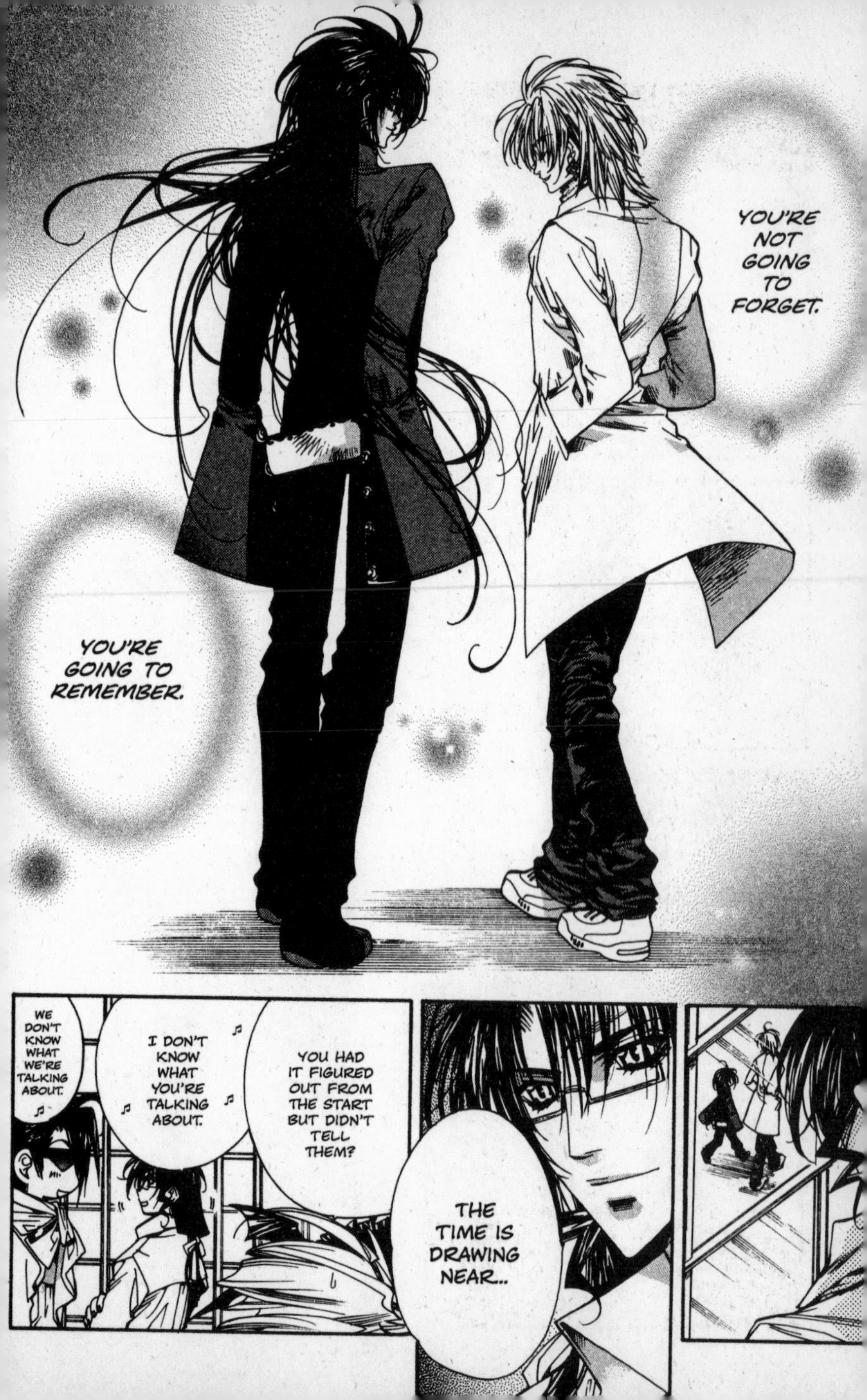
YOU'RE NOT GOING TO FORGET.
YOU'RE GOING TO REMEMBER.
THE TIME IS DRAWING NEAR..
YOU HAD IT FIGURED OUT FROM THE START BUT DIDN'T TELL THEM?
I DON'T KNOW WHAT YOU'RE TALKING ABOUT.
WE DON'T KNOW WHAT WE'RE TALKING ABOUT.

Bonus Comic Strip

Vampire Doll Reflections

Doll~"Hugo"~"Dante"

QUESTION: WHY IS HUGO'S NAME WRITTEN ON DANTE'S CHEEK?
IT'S LIKE A TATTOO TO SHOW HIS LOVE FOR MMF...
NO IT'S NOT!
ばふっ
BECAUSE HE'S A DOLL THAT CAN WALK AROUND BY HIMSELF.
hugo
I SIGNED HIS CHEEK SO I WOULDN'T LOSE HIM.
BUT NOW HE'S THE ONE WHO FINDS ME.
がっちり
SO THERE'S NO POINT TO IT?

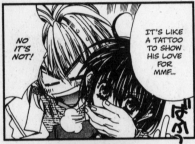

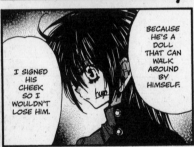

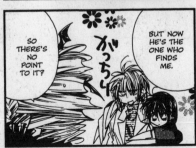

ダンテ

dante
male
tribe: stabber
attribute: evil
job: Hugo's assistant
height: 142～?
eyes: ice blue
hair: black

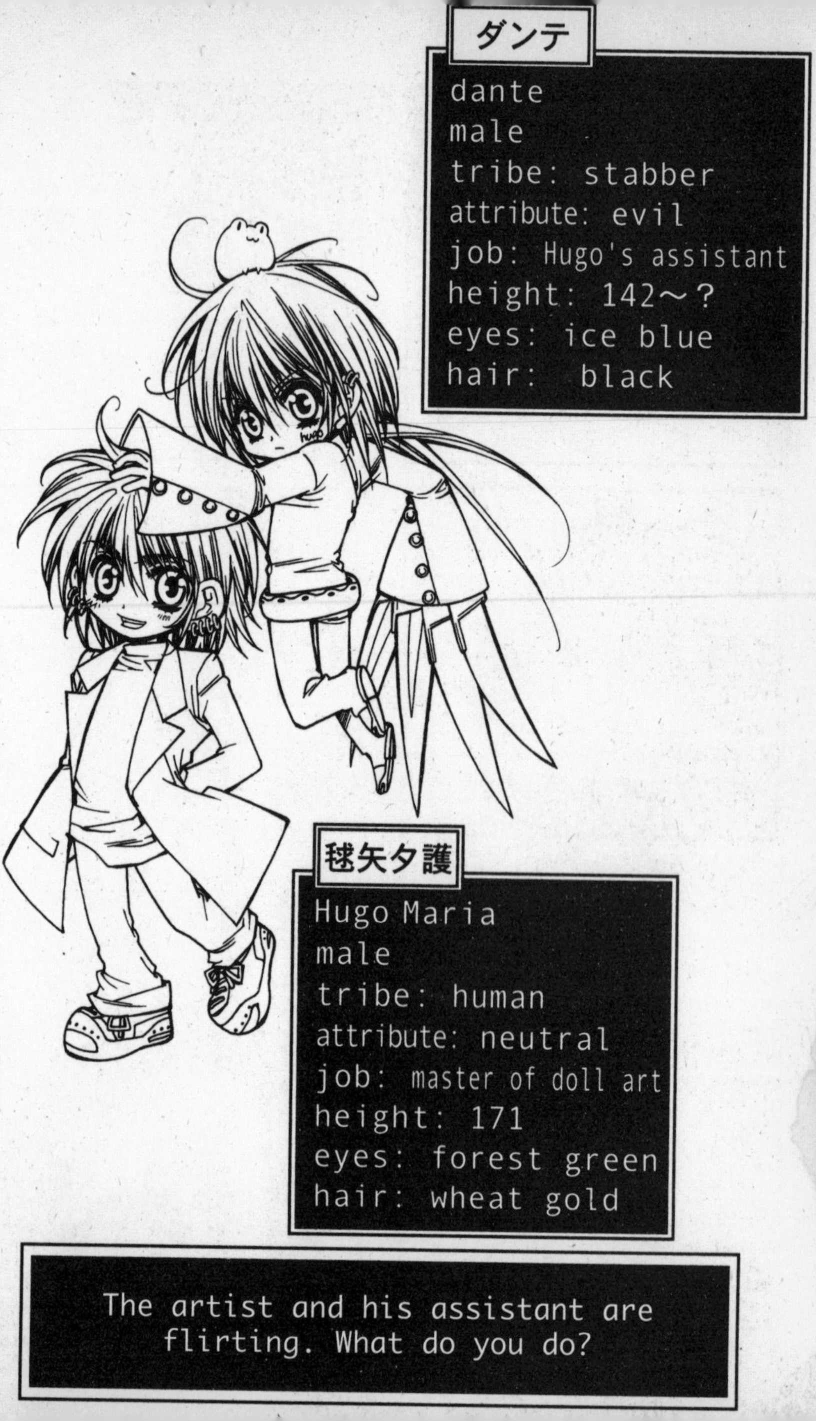
hugo

毬矢夕護

Hugo Maria
male
tribe: human
attribute: neutral
job: master of doll art
height: 171
eyes: forest green
hair: wheat gold

The artist and his assistant are flirting. What do you do?

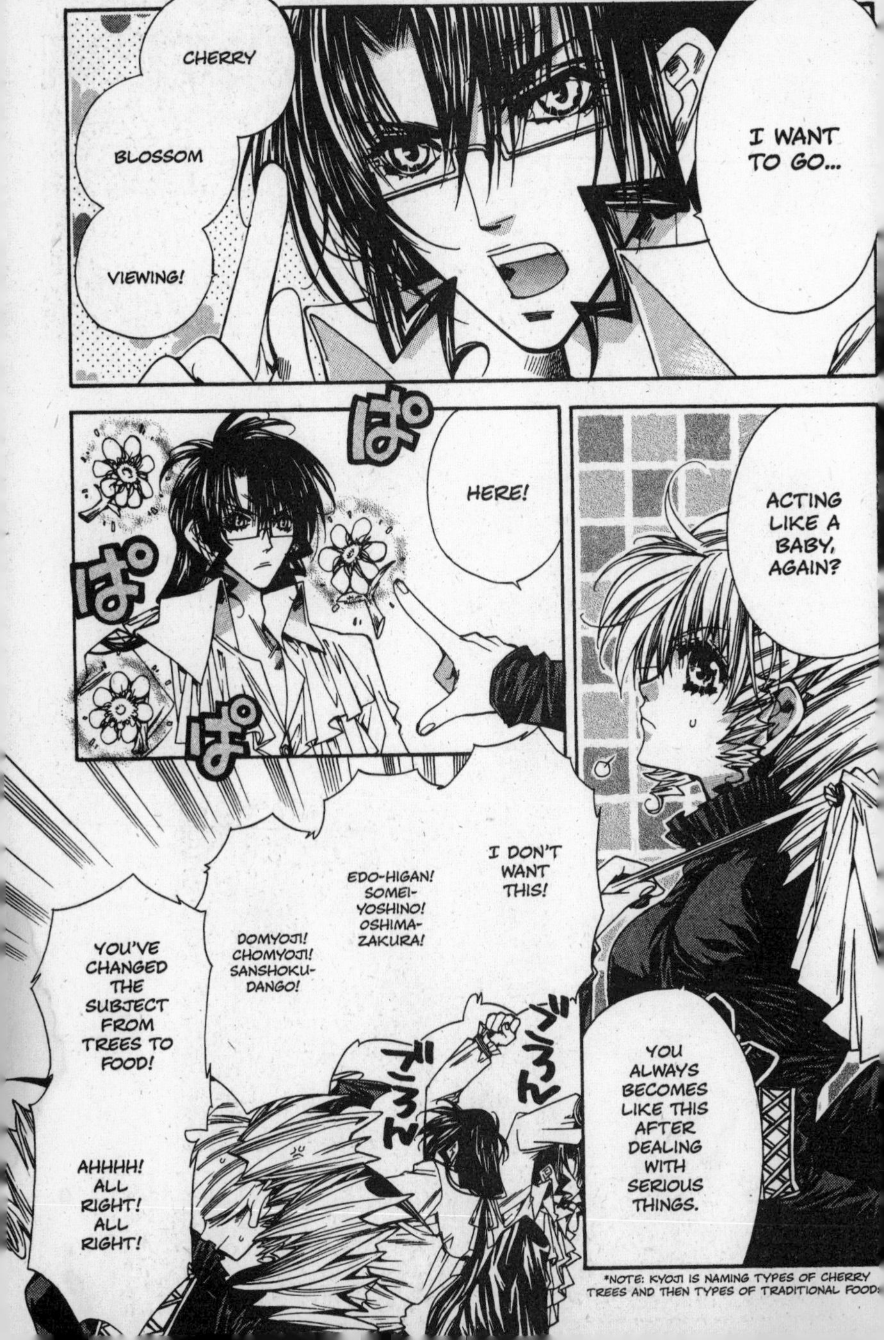
I WANT TO GO...
CHERRY
BLOSSOM
VIEWING!
ACTING LIKE A BABY, AGAIN?
HERE!
ぱ
ぱ
ぱ
YOU ALWAYS BECOMES LIKE THIS AFTER DEALING WITH SERIOUS THINGS.
ごろん
ごろん
I DON'T WANT THIS!
EDO-HIGAN! SOMEI-YOSHINO! OSHIMA-ZAKURA!
DOMYOJI! CHOMYOJI! SANSHOKU-DANGO!
YOU'VE CHANGED THE SUBJECT FROM TREES TO FOOD!
AHHHH! ALL RIGHT! ALL RIGHT!

*NOTE: KYOJI IS NAMING TYPES OF CHERRY TREES AND THEN TYPES OF TRADITIONAL FOOD.

#15 UNDER THE CHERRY BLOSSOMS

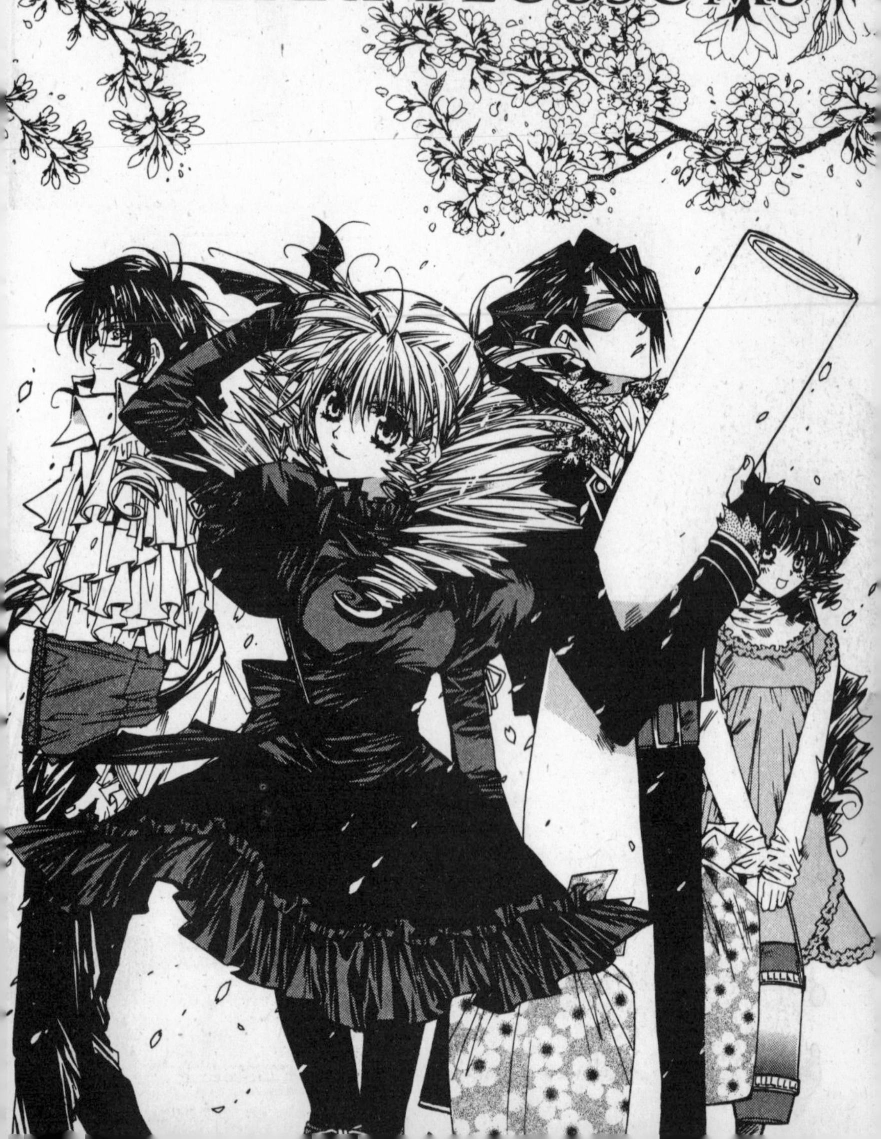

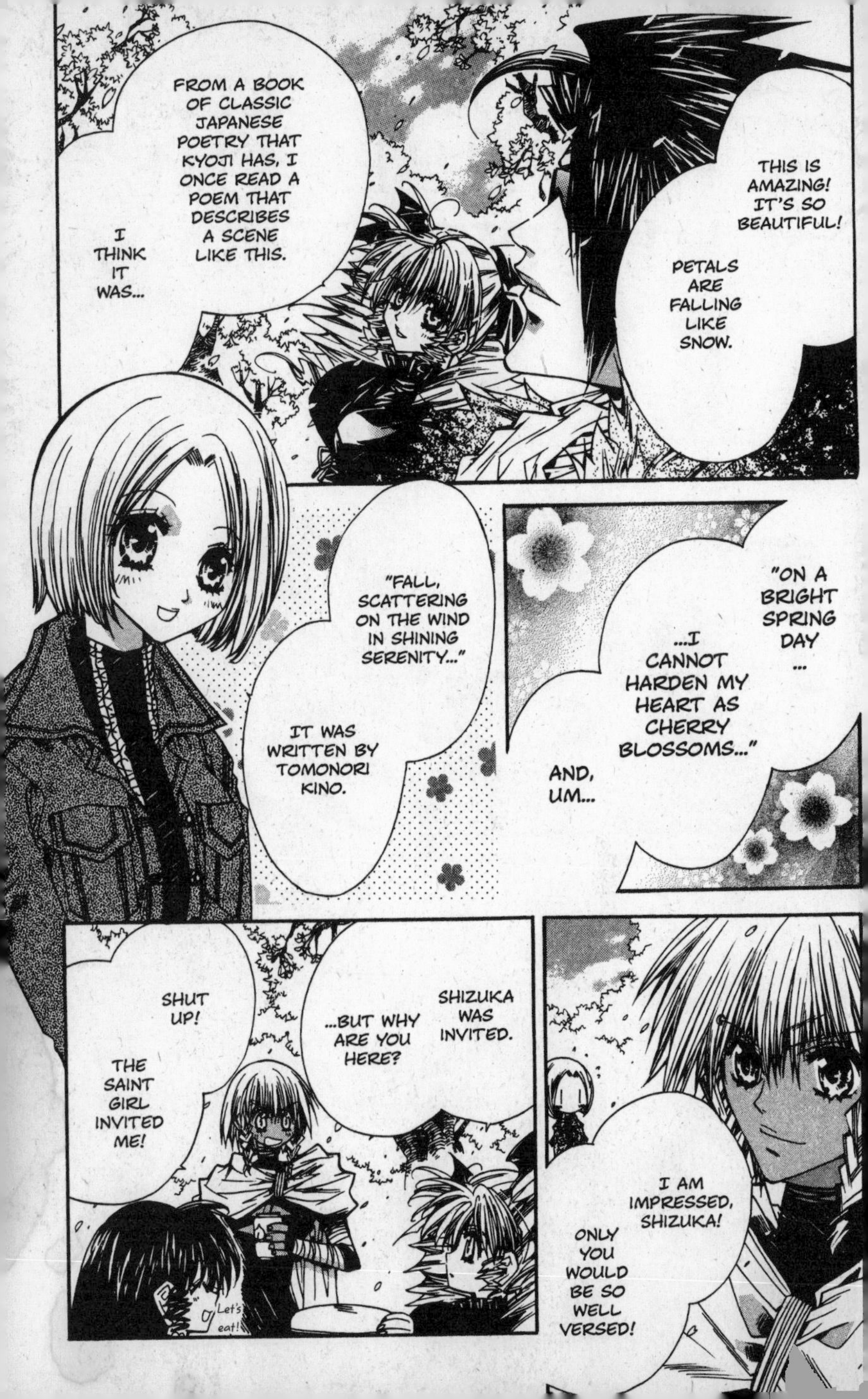
THIS IS AMAZING! IT'S SO BEAUTIFUL!
PETALS ARE FALLING LIKE SNOW.
FROM A BOOK OF CLASSIC JAPANESE POETRY THAT KYOJI HAS, I ONCE READ A POEM THAT DESCRIBES A SCENE LIKE THIS.
I THINK IT WAS...
"ON A BRIGHT SPRING DAY ...
...I CANNOT HARDEN MY HEART AS CHERRY BLOSSOMS..."
AND, UM...
"FALL, SCATTERING ON THE WIND IN SHINING SERENITY..."
IT WAS WRITTEN BY TOMONORI KINO.
I AM IMPRESSED, SHIZUKA!
ONLY YOU WOULD BE SO WELL VERSED!
SHIZUKA WAS INVITED.
...BUT WHY ARE YOU HERE?
SHUT UP!
THE SAINT GIRL INVITED ME!
Let's eat!

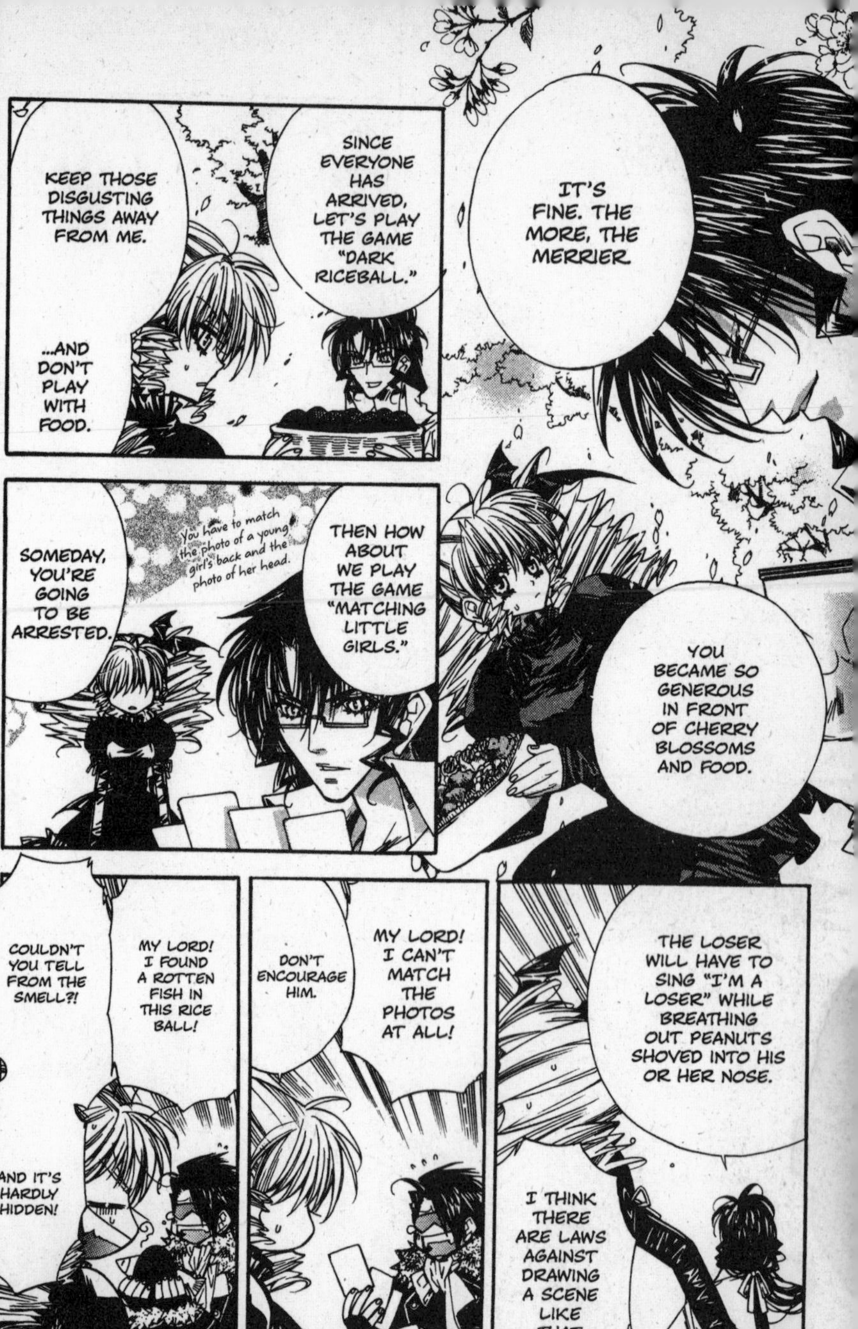
IT'S FINE. THE MORE, THE MERRIER
YOU BECAME SO GENEROUS IN FRONT OF CHERRY BLOSSOMS AND FOOD.
SINCE EVERYONE HAS ARRIVED, LET'S PLAY THE GAME "DARK RICEBALL."
KEEP THOSE DISGUSTING THINGS AWAY FROM ME.
...AND DON'T PLAY WITH FOOD.
THEN HOW ABOUT WE PLAY THE GAME "MATCHING LITTLE GIRLS."
You have to match the photo of a young girl's back and the photo of her head.
SOMEDAY, YOU'RE GOING TO BE ARRESTED.
THE LOSER WILL HAVE TO SING "I'M A LOSER" WHILE BREATHING OUT PEANUTS SHOVED INTO HIS OR HER NOSE.
I THINK THERE ARE LAWS AGAINST DRAWING A SCENE LIKE THAT.
MY LORD! I CAN'T MATCH THE PHOTOS AT ALL!
DON'T ENCOURAGE HIM.
MY LORD! I FOUND A ROTTEN FISH IN THIS RICE BALL!
COULDN'T YOU TELL FROM THE SMELL?!
AND IT'S HARDLY HIDDEN!

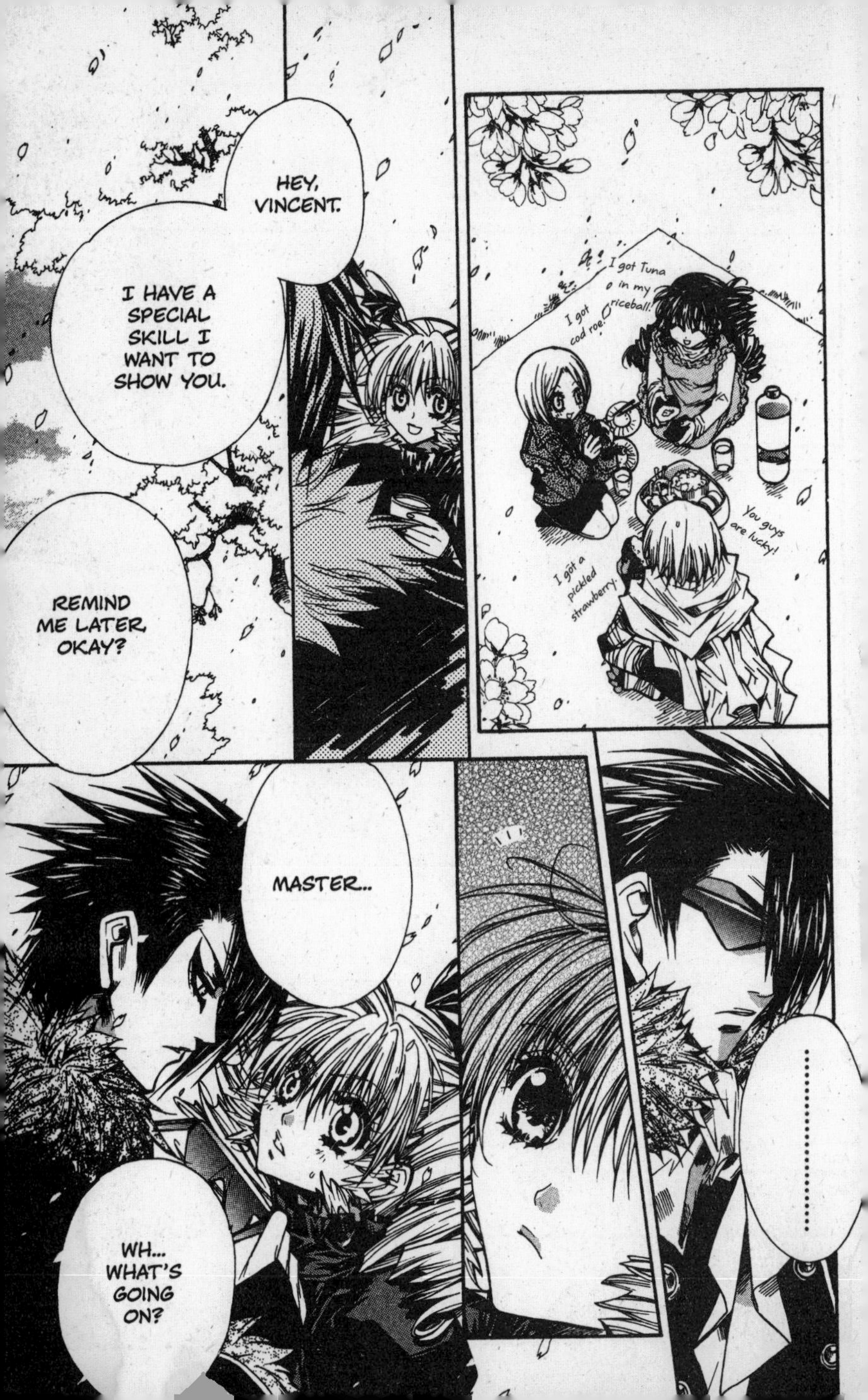
I got Tuna in my riceball!
I got cod roe.
You guys are lucky!
I got a pickled strawberry.
HEY, VINCENT.
I HAVE A SPECIAL SKILL I WANT TO SHOW YOU.
REMIND ME LATER, OKAY?
......
MASTER..
WH... WHAT'S GOING ON?

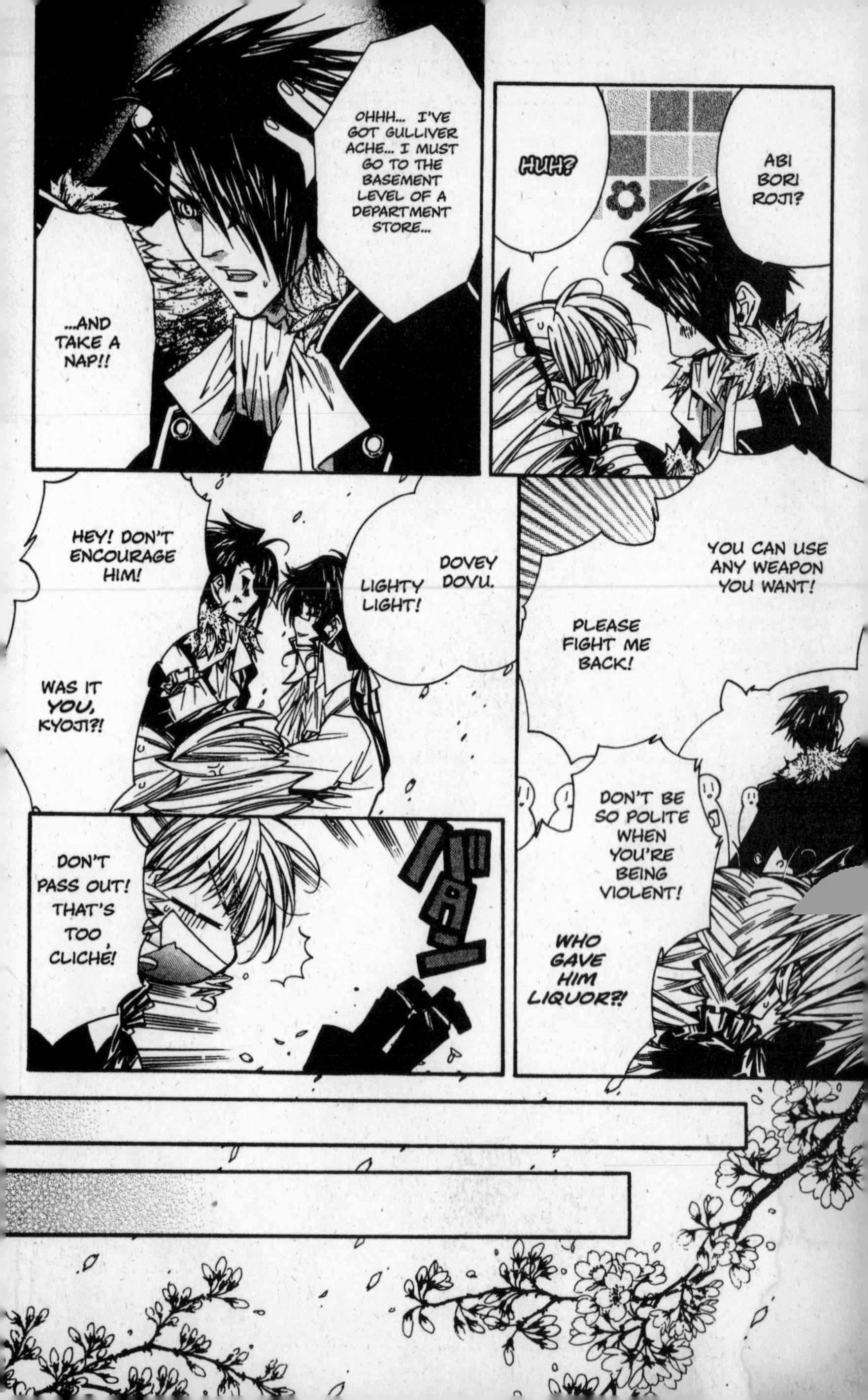
ABI BORI ROJI?
HUH?
OHHH... I'VE GOT GULLIVER ACHE... I MUST GO TO THE BASEMENT LEVEL OF A DEPARTMENT STORE...
...AND TAKE A NAP!!
YOU CAN USE ANY WEAPON YOU WANT!
PLEASE FIGHT ME BACK!
DON'T BE SO POLITE WHEN YOU'RE BEING VIOLENT!
WHO GAVE HIM LIQUOR?!
DOVEY DOVU.
LIGHTY LIGHT!
HEY! DON'T ENCOURAGE HIM!
WAS IT YOU, KYOJI?!
DON'T PASS OUT! THAT'S TOO CLICHÉ!

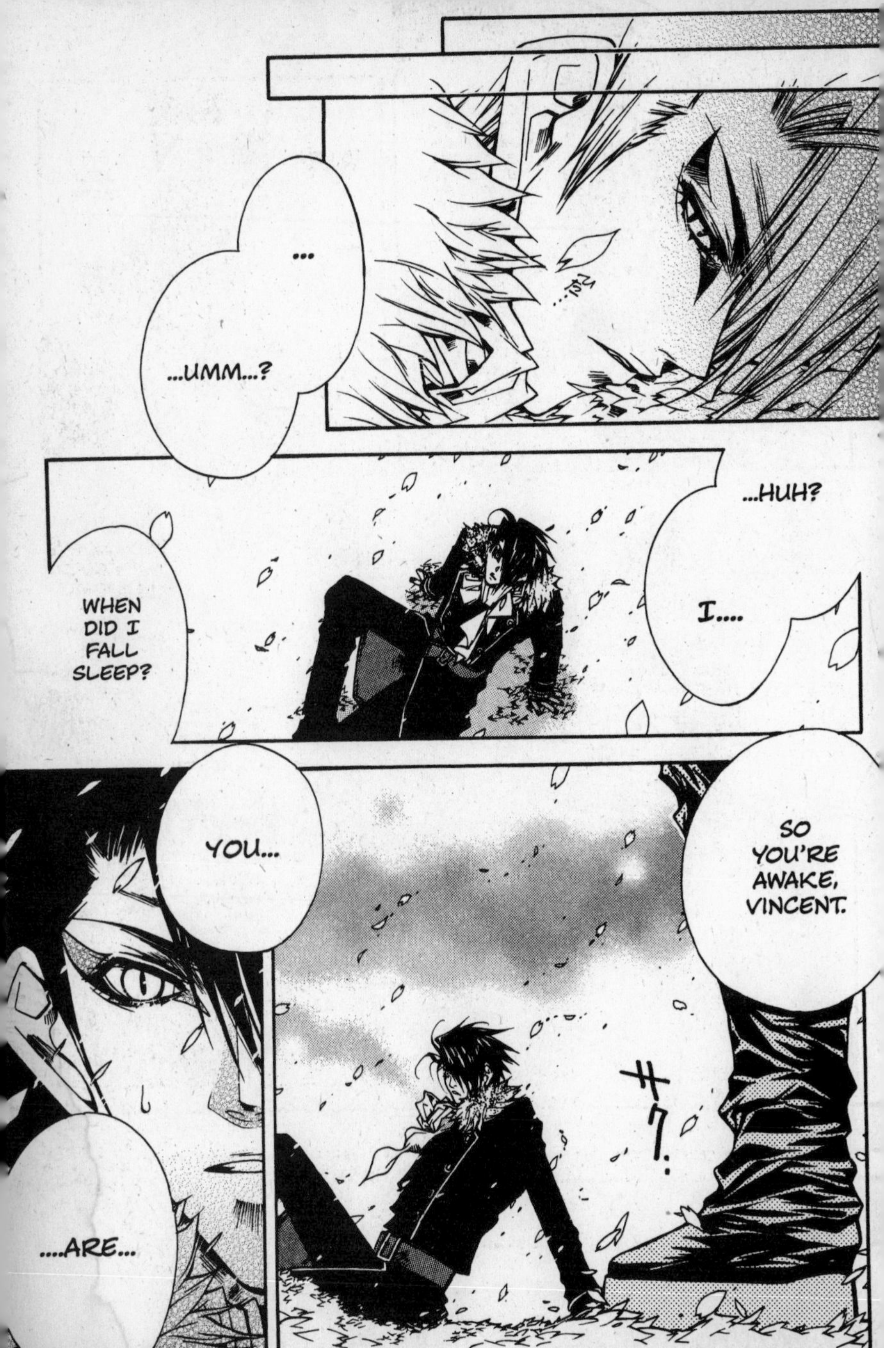
...
...UMM...?
...HUH?
I....
WHEN DID I FALL SLEEP?
SO YOU'RE AWAKE, VINCENT.
ギク
YOU...
....ARE...

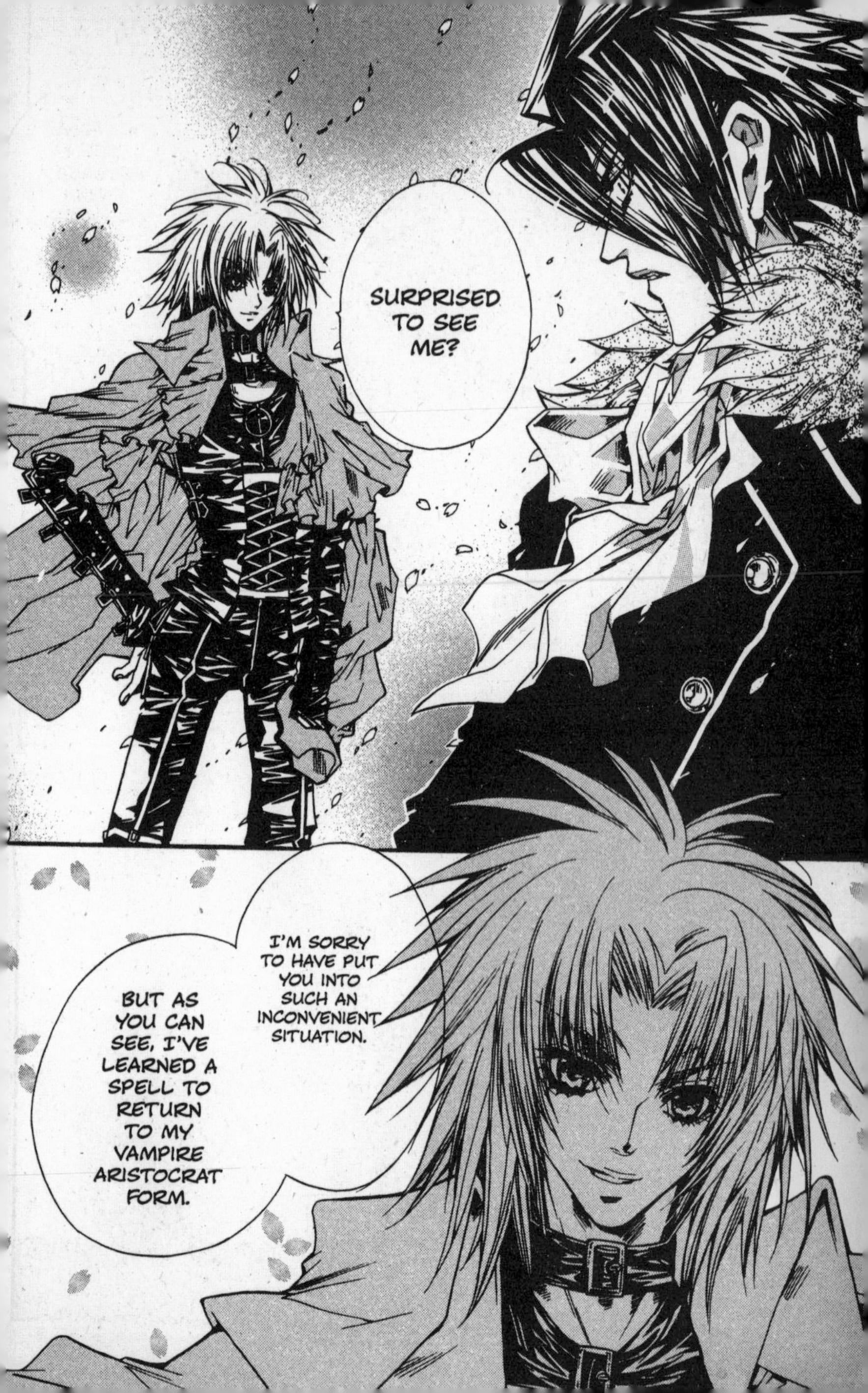
SURPRISED TO SEE ME?
I'M SORRY TO HAVE PUT YOU INTO SUCH AN INCONVENIENT SITUATION.
BUT AS YOU CAN SEE, I'VE LEARNED A SPELL TO RETURN TO MY VAMPIRE ARISTOCRAT FORM.

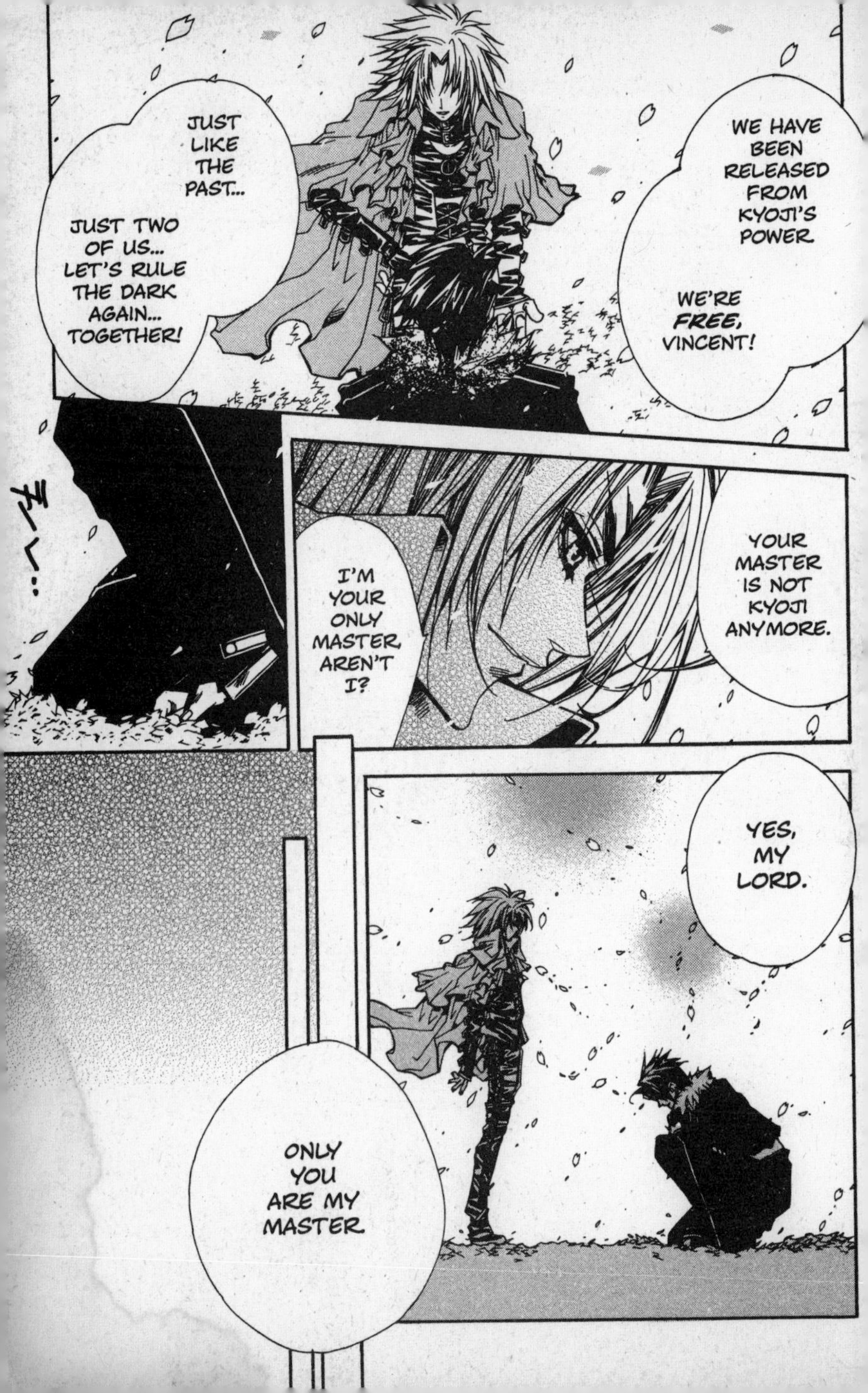
WE HAVE BEEN RELEASED FROM KYOJI'S POWER
WE'RE FREE, VINCENT!
JUST LIKE THE PAST...
JUST TWO OF US... LET'S RULE THE DARK AGAIN... TOGETHER!
YOUR MASTER IS NOT KYOJI ANYMORE.
I'M YOUR ONLY MASTER AREN'T I?
YES, MY LORD.
ONLY YOU ARE MY MASTER

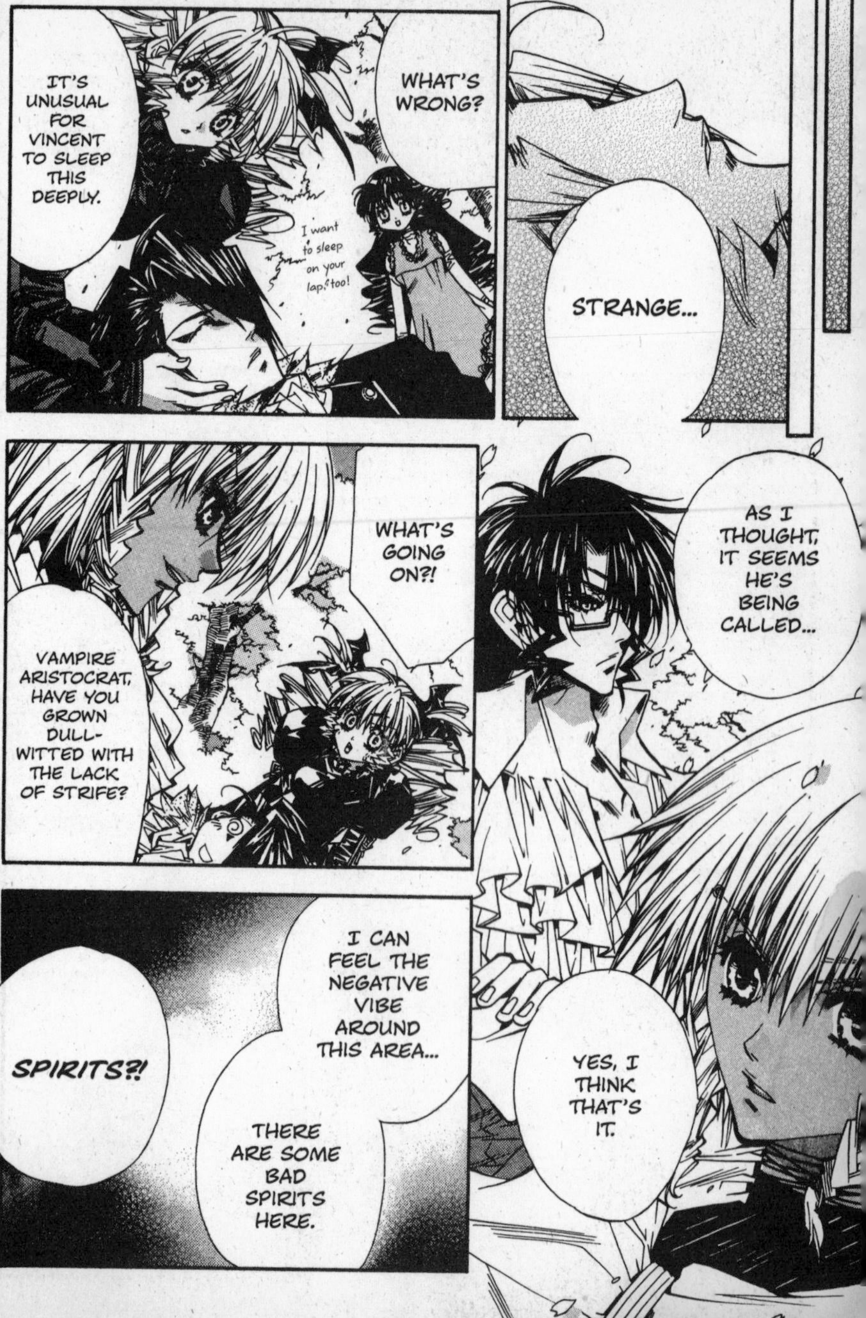
STRANGE...
WHAT'S WRONG?
IT'S UNUSUAL FOR VINCENT TO SLEEP THIS DEEPLY.
I want to sleep on your lap, too!
AS I THOUGHT, IT SEEMS HE'S BEING CALLED...
YES, I THINK THAT'S IT.
WHAT'S GOING ON?!
VAMPIRE ARISTOCRAT, HAVE YOU GROWN DULL-WITTED WITH THE LACK OF STRIFE?
I CAN FEEL THE NEGATIVE VIBE AROUND THIS AREA...
THERE ARE SOME BAD SPIRITS HERE.
SPIRITS?!

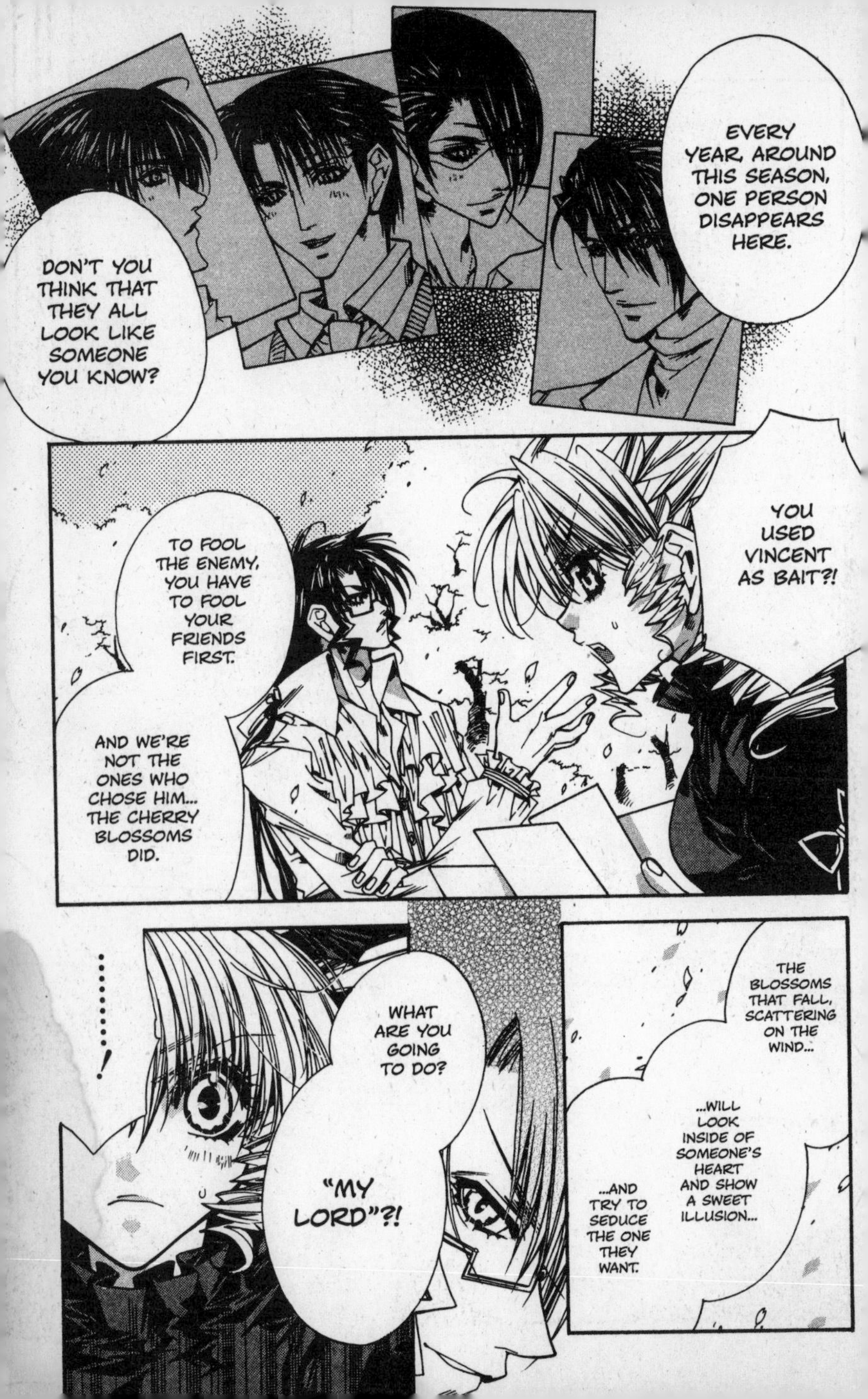
EVERY YEAR, AROUND THIS SEASON, ONE PERSON DISAPPEARS HERE.
DON'T YOU THINK THAT THEY ALL LOOK LIKE SOMEONE YOU KNOW?
YOU USED VINCENT AS BAIT?!
TO FOOL THE ENEMY, YOU HAVE TO FOOL YOUR FRIENDS FIRST.
AND WE'RE NOT THE ONES WHO CHOSE HIM... THE CHERRY BLOSSOMS DID.
THE BLOSSOMS THAT FALL, SCATTERING ON THE WIND...
...WILL LOOK INSIDE OF SOMEONE'S HEART AND SHOW A SWEET ILLUSION...
...AND TRY TO SEDUCE THE ONE THEY WANT.
WHAT ARE YOU GOING TO DO?
"MY LORD"?!
......!

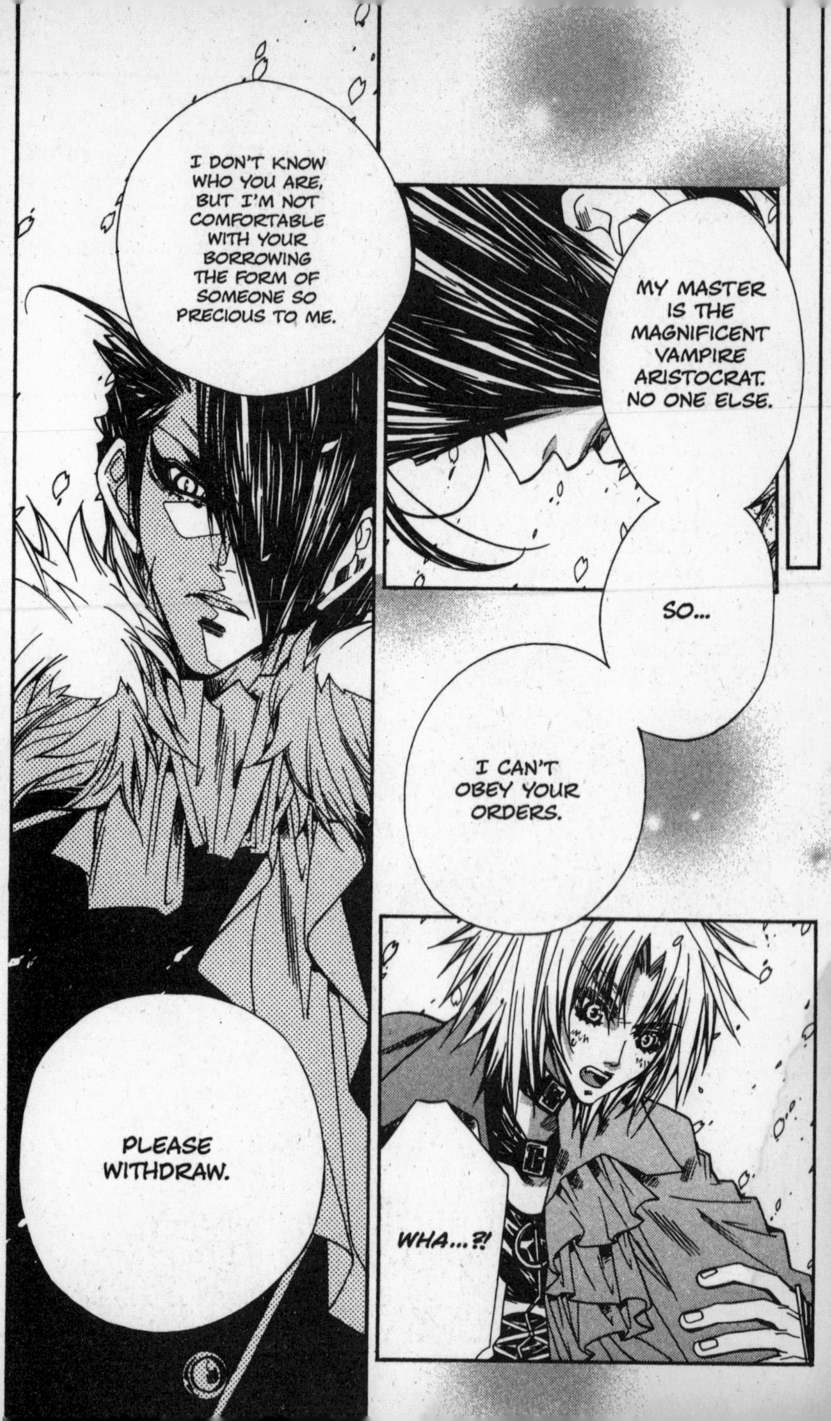
MY MASTER IS THE MAGNIFICENT VAMPIRE ARISTOCRAT. NO ONE ELSE.
SO...
I CAN'T OBEY YOUR ORDERS.
WHA...?!
I DON'T KNOW WHO YOU ARE, BUT I'M NOT COMFORTABLE WITH YOUR BORROWING THE FORM OF SOMEONE SO PRECIOUS TO ME.
PLEASE WITHDRAW.

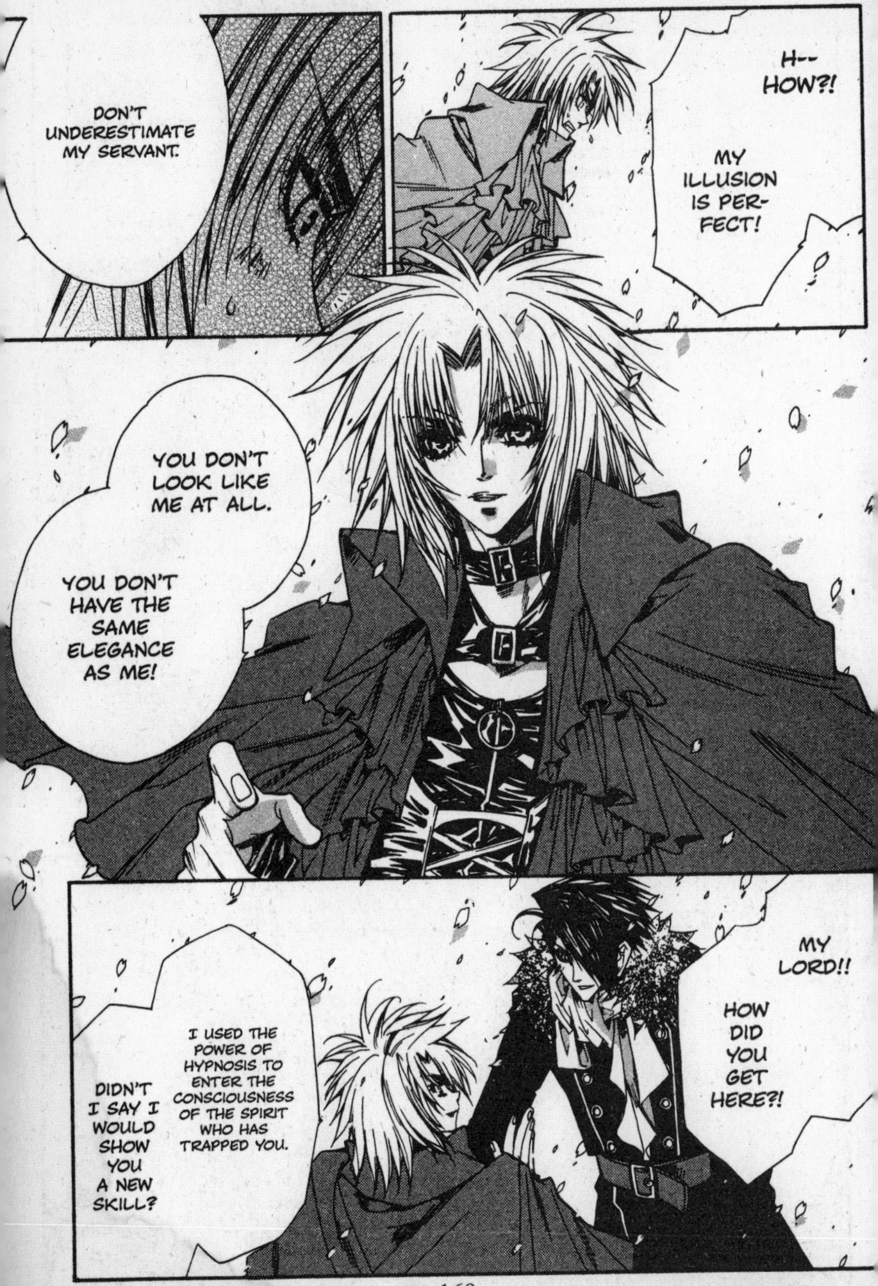
H-- HOW?!
MY ILLUSION IS PER- FECT!
DON'T UNDERESTIMATE MY SERVANT.
YOU DON'T LOOK LIKE ME AT ALL.
YOU DON'T HAVE THE SAME ELEGANCE AS ME!
MY LORD!!
HOW DID YOU GET HERE?!
I USED THE POWER OF HYPNOSIS TO ENTER THE CONSCIOUSNESS OF THE SPIRIT WHO HAS TRAPPED YOU.
DIDN'T I SAY I WOULD SHOW YOU A NEW SKILL?

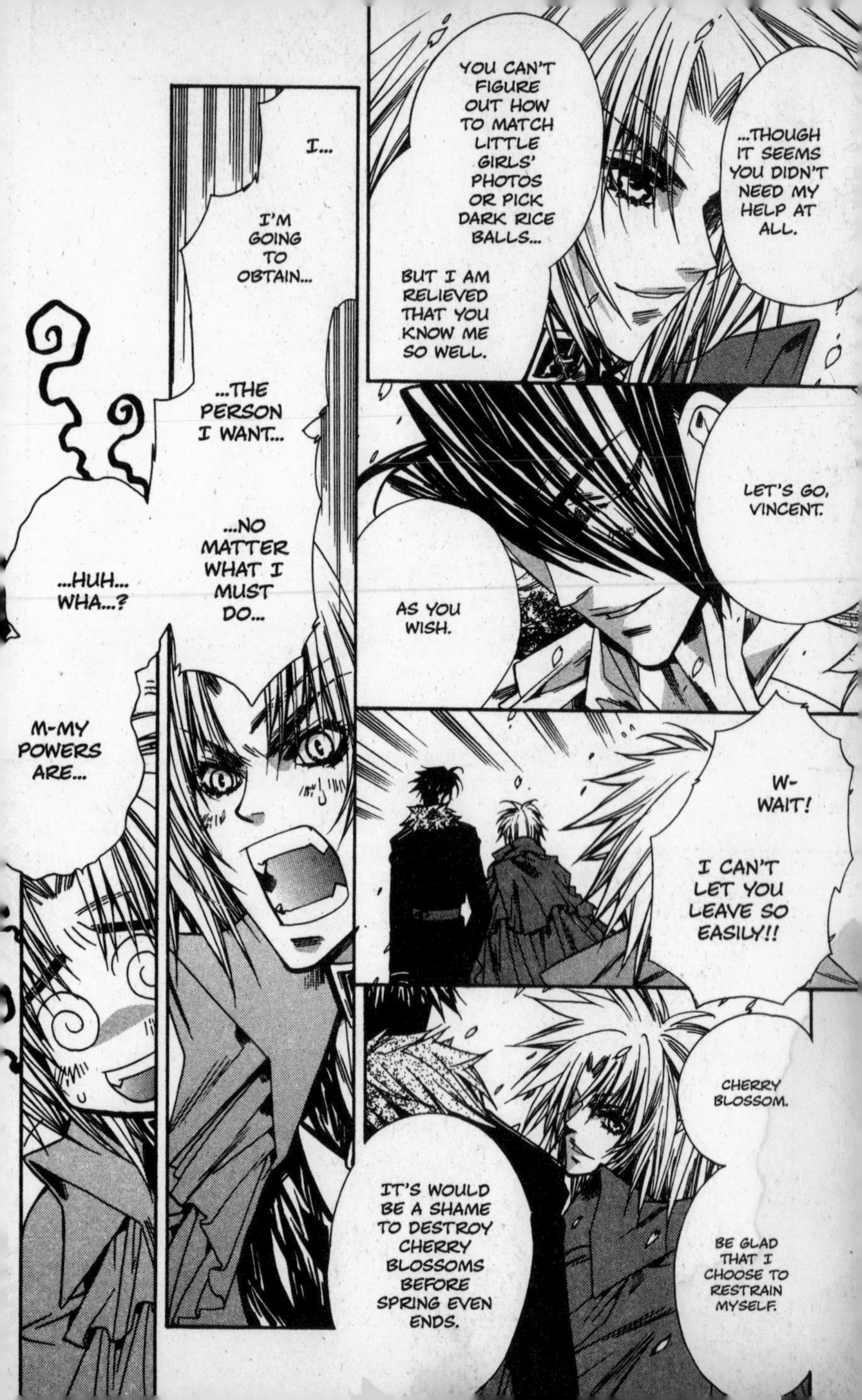
...THOUGH IT SEEMS YOU DIDN'T NEED MY HELP AT ALL.
YOU CAN'T FIGURE OUT HOW TO MATCH LITTLE GIRLS' PHOTOS OR PICK DARK RICE BALLS...
BUT I AM RELIEVED THAT YOU KNOW ME SO WELL.
I...
I'M GOING TO OBTAIN...
...THE PERSON I WANT...
...NO MATTER WHAT I MUST DO...
LET'S GO, VINCENT.
AS YOU WISH.
W- WAIT!
I CAN'T LET YOU LEAVE SO EASILY!!
CHERRY BLOSSOM.
BE GLAD THAT I CHOOSE TO RESTRAIN MYSELF.
IT'S WOULD BE A SHAME TO DESTROY CHERRY BLOSSOMS BEFORE SPRING EVEN ENDS.
...HUH... WHA...?
M-MY POWERS ARE...

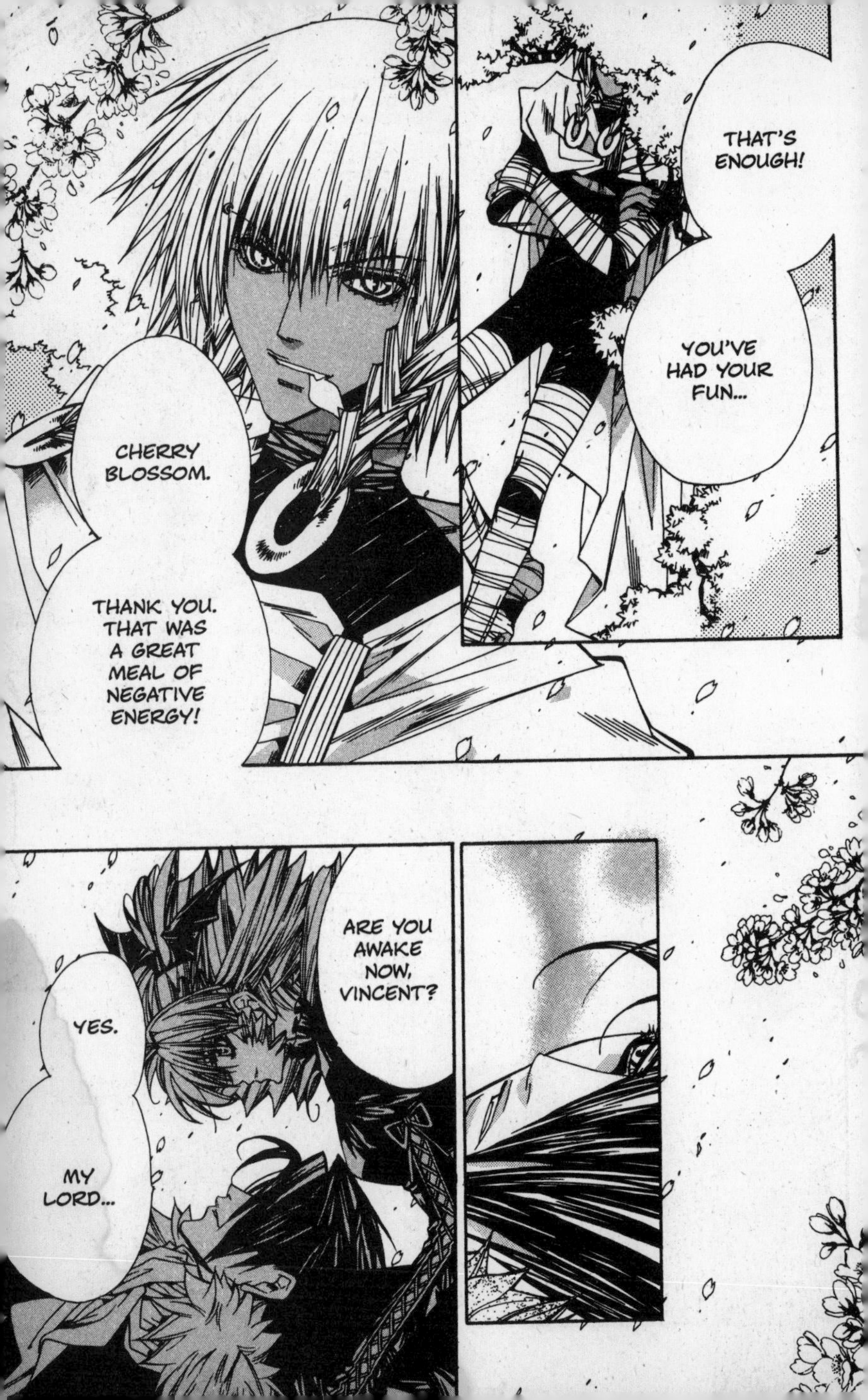
THAT'S ENOUGH!
YOU'VE HAD YOUR FUN...
CHERRY BLOSSOM.
THANK YOU. THAT WAS A GREAT MEAL OF NEGATIVE ENERGY!
ARE YOU AWAKE NOW, VINCENT?
YES.
MY LORD...

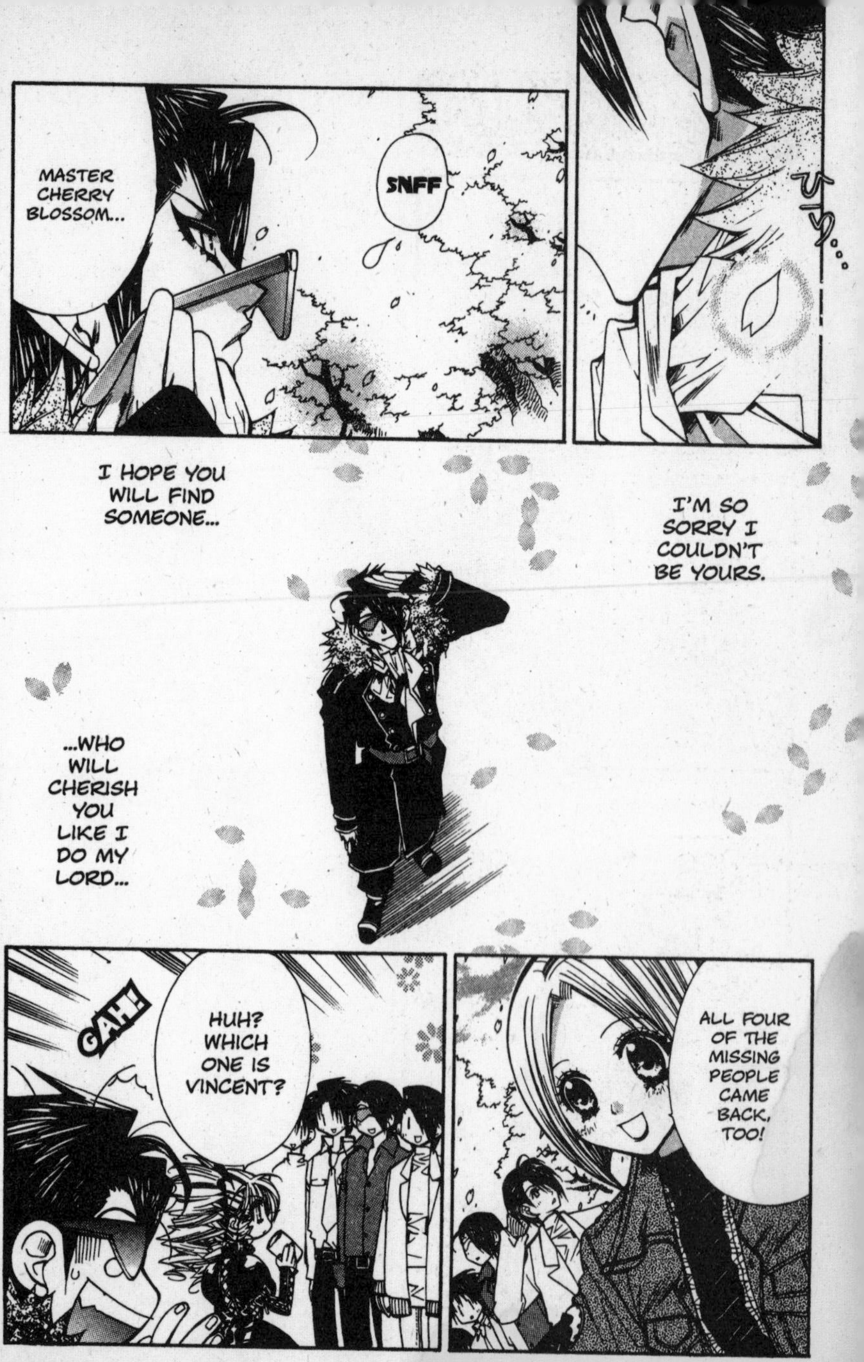
MASTER CHERRY BLOSSOM...
SNFF
I'M SO SORRY I COULDN'T BE YOURS.
I HOPE YOU WILL FIND SOMEONE...
...WHO WILL CHERISH YOU LIKE I DO MY LORD...
ALL FOUR OF THE MISSING PEOPLE CAME BACK, TOO!
GAH!
HUH? WHICH ONE IS VINCENT?

BONUS COMIC STRIP

VAMPIRE DOLL REFLECTIONS

Under the Cherry Blossoms

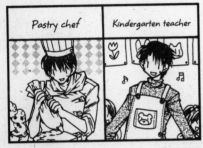

QUESTION: WHAT ARE THE JOBS OF THOSE PEOPLE WHO LOOK LIKE VINCENT?
Kindergarten teacher
Pastry chef
Florist
Pet store owner
AND UNEMPLOYED.
EH?! AREN'T I A BUTLER?!

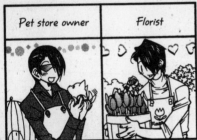

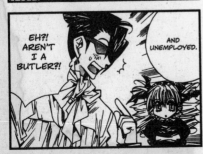

ギルナザン

Guilt-na-Zan
male
tribe: vampire aristocrat
attribute: evil
job: young noble
height: 172
eyes: pigeon blood ruby
hair: silver

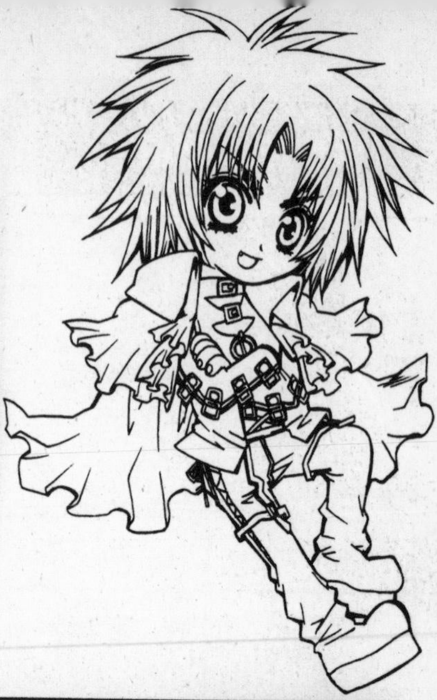

Evil creatures appear! What do you do?

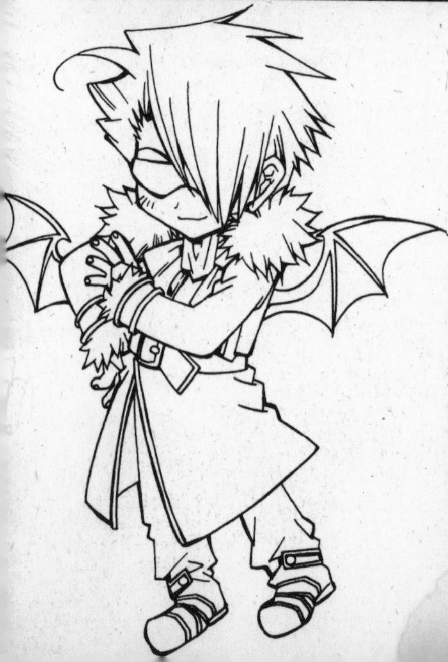

ビンセント

vincent
male
tribe: the incarnation of bat
attribute: good
job: butler
height: 189
eyes: gold
hair: black

BONUS COMIC STRIP

ROLE PLAYING GUILT-NA-ZAN

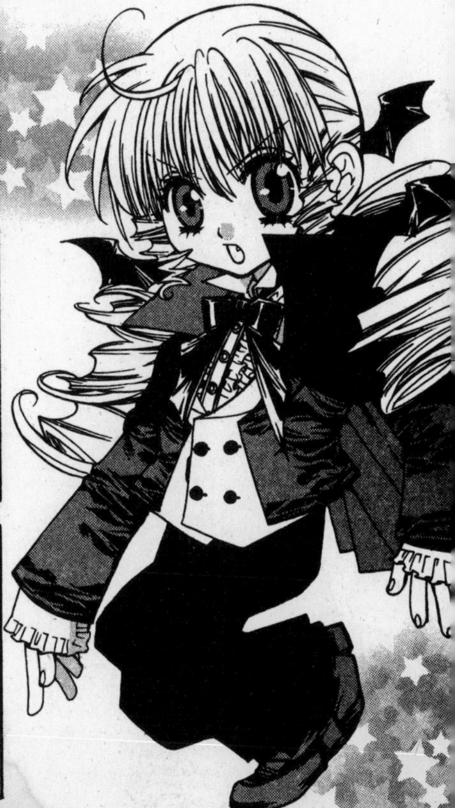

At the Bar

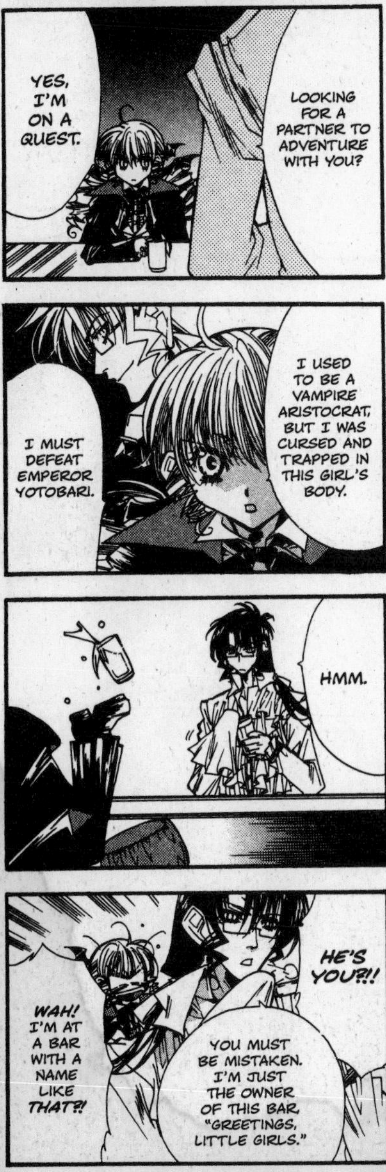
LOOKING FOR A PARTNER TO ADVENTURE WITH YOU?
YES, I'M ON A QUEST.
I USED TO BE A VAMPIRE ARISTOCRAT, BUT I WAS CURSED AND TRAPPED IN THIS GIRL'S BODY.
I MUST DEFEAT EMPEROR YOTOBARI.
HMM.
HE'S YOU?!!
YOU MUST BE MISTAKEN. I'M JUST THE OWNER OF THIS BAR "GREETINGS, LITTLE GIRLS."
WAH! I'M AT A BAR WITH A NAME LIKE THAT?!

In Sweetish

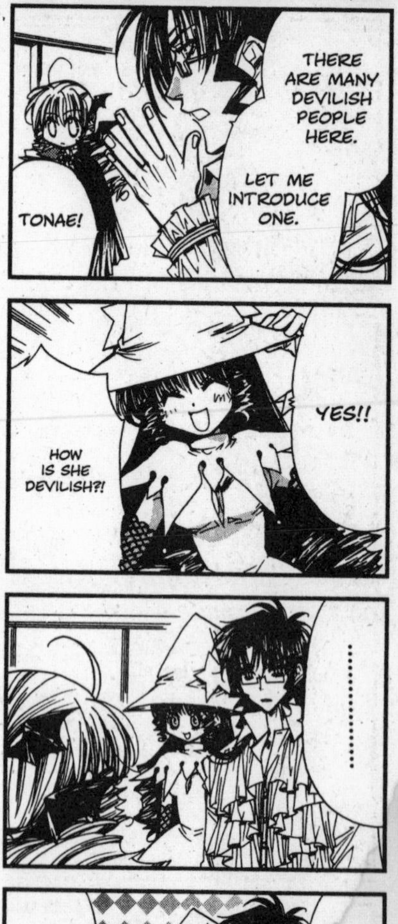
THERE ARE MANY DEVILISH PEOPLE HERE.
LET ME INTRODUCE ONE.
TONAE!
YES!!
HOW IS SHE DEVILISH?!
......
SHE LOVES DEVIL'S FOOD CAKE.
YOU WASTED A PANEL IN SILENCE, JUST TO SAY A BAD PUN?

Commercial

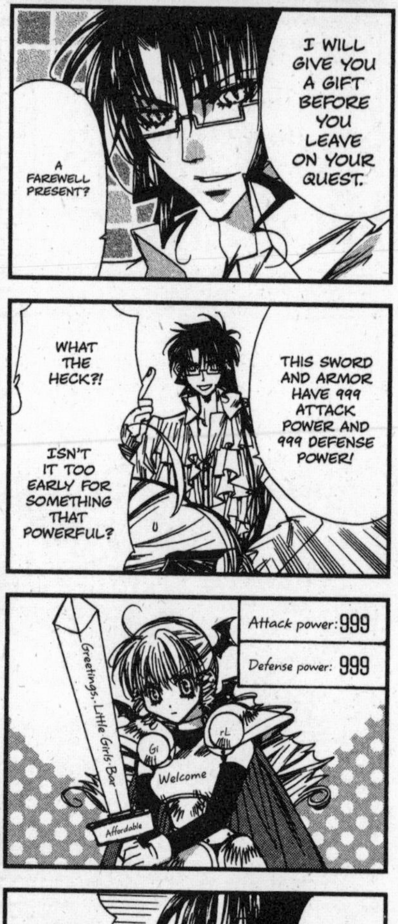
I WILL GIVE YOU A GIFT BEFORE YOU LEAVE ON YOUR QUEST.
A FAREWELL PRESENT?
THIS SWORD AND ARMOR HAVE 999 ATTACK POWER AND 999 DEFENSE POWER!
WHAT THE HECK?!
ISN'T IT TOO EARLY FOR SOMETHING THAT POWERFUL?
Attack power: 999
Defense power: 999
Greetings...Little Girls Bar
rL
Gi
Welcome
Affordable
YOU DON'T WANT THEM?
THEY'RE OF THE BEST QUALITY.
LEAVE ME ALONE!
rL

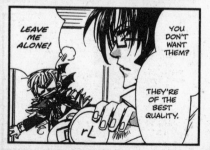

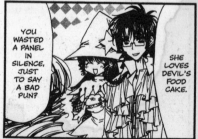

Weapon Shop

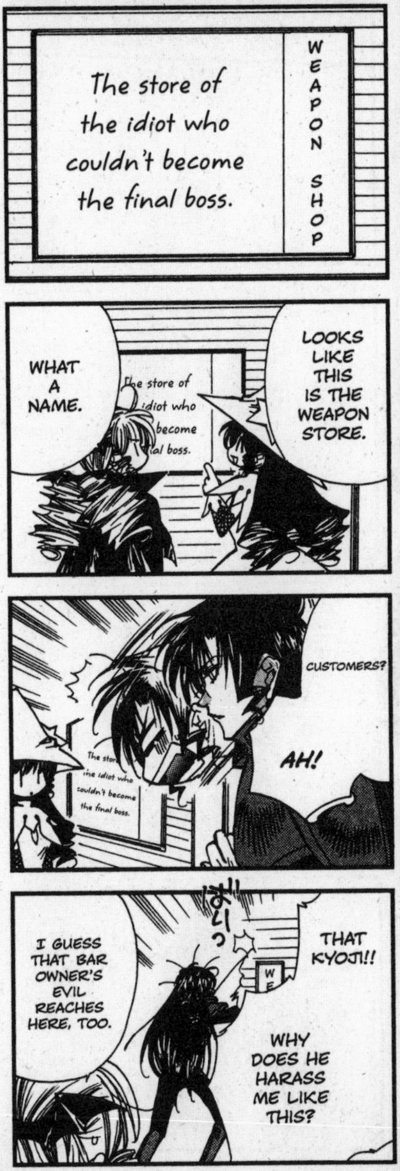
WEAPON SHOP
The store of the idiot who couldn't become the final boss.
LOOKS LIKE THIS IS THE WEAPON STORE.
WHAT A NAME.
CUSTOMERS?
AH!
THAT KYOJI!!
I GUESS THAT BAR OWNER'S EVIL REACHES HERE, TOO.
WHY DOES HE HARASS ME LIKE THIS?

Restart

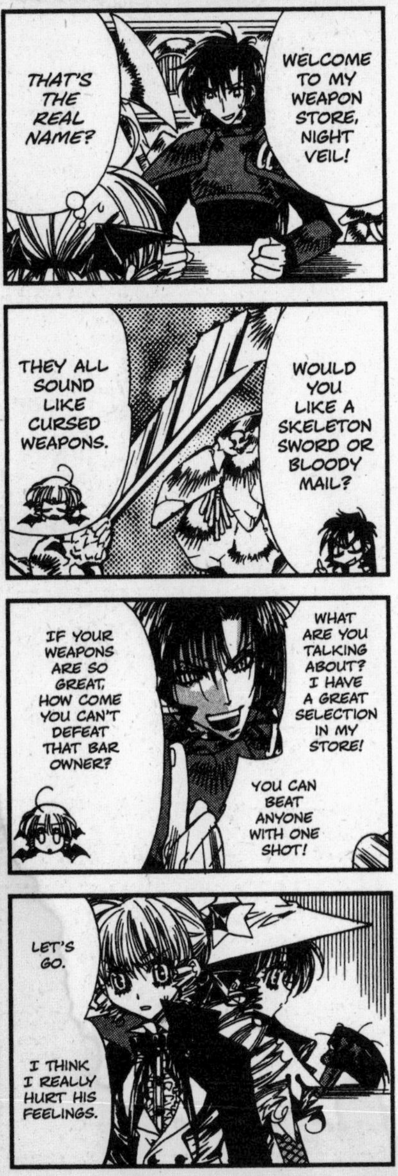
WELCOME TO MY WEAPON STORE, NIGHT VEIL!
THAT'S THE REAL NAME?
WOULD YOU LIKE A SKELETON SWORD OR BLOODY MAIL?
THEY ALL SOUND LIKE CURSED WEAPONS.
WHAT ARE YOU TALKING ABOUT? I HAVE A GREAT SELECTION IN MY STORE!
IF YOUR WEAPONS ARE SO GREAT, HOW COME YOU CAN'T DEFEAT THAT BAR OWNER?
YOU CAN BEAT ANYONE WITH ONE SHOT!
LET'S GO.
I THINK I REALLY HURT HIS FEELINGS.

Special Skill

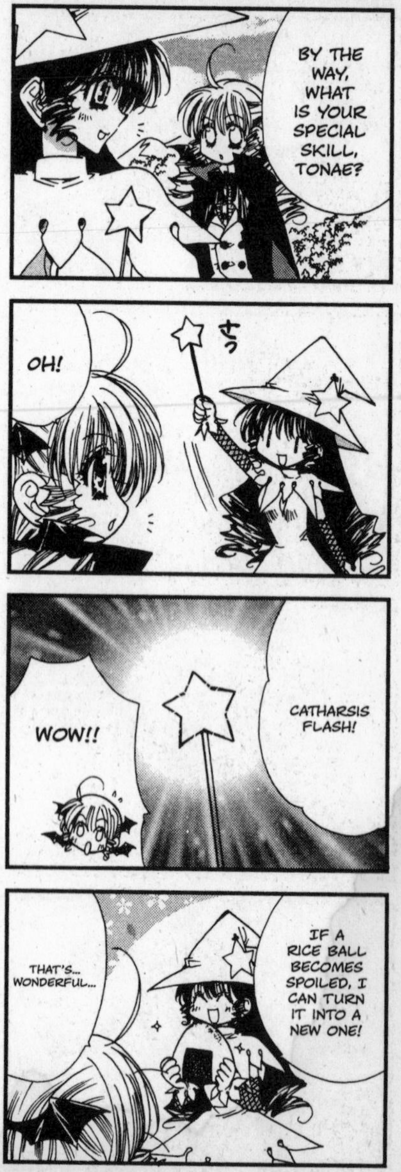
BY THE WAY, WHAT IS YOUR SPECIAL SKILL, TONAE?
さっ
OH!
CATHARSIS FLASH!
WOW!!
IF A RICE BALL BECOMES SPOILED, I CAN TURN IT INTO A NEW ONE!
THAT'S... WONDERFUL...

Father Yotobari

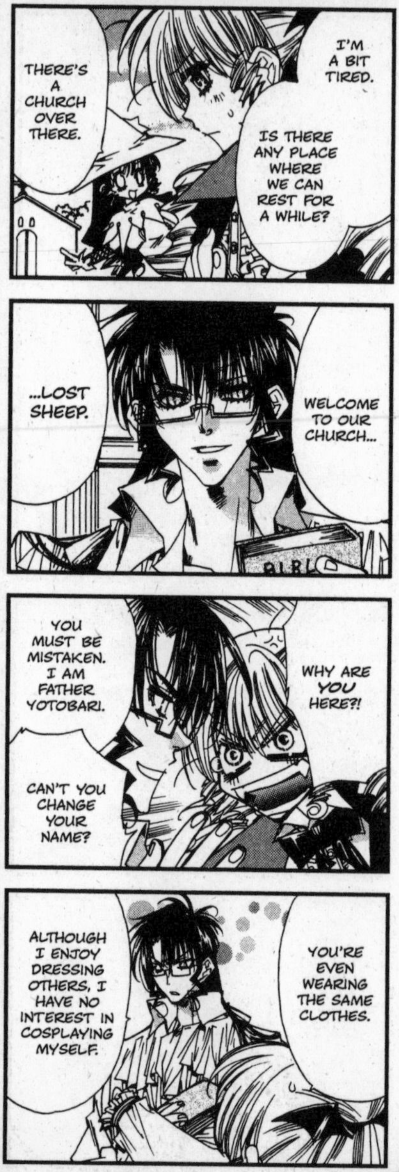
I'M A BIT TIRED.
IS THERE ANY PLACE WHERE WE CAN REST FOR A WHILE?
THERE'S A CHURCH OVER THERE.
WELCOME TO OUR CHURCH...
...LOST SHEEP.
WHY ARE YOU HERE?!
YOU MUST BE MISTAKEN. I AM FATHER YOTOBARI.
CAN'T YOU CHANGE YOUR NAME?
YOU'RE EVEN WEARING THE SAME CLOTHES.
ALTHOUGH I ENJOY DRESSING OTHERS, I HAVE NO INTEREST IN COSPLAYING MYSELF.

Meeting

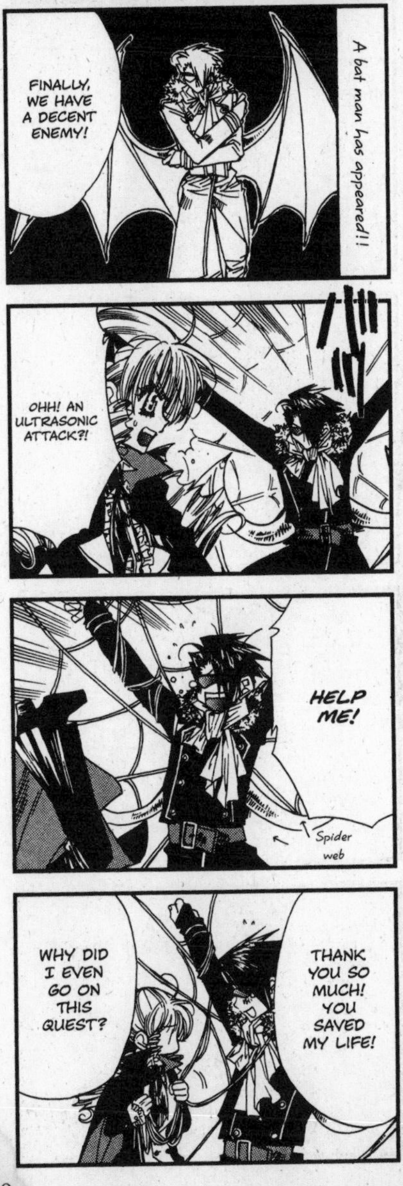
A bat man has appeared!!
FINALLY, WE HAVE A DECENT ENEMY!
OHH! AN ULTRASONIC ATTACK?!
HELP ME!
Spider web
THANK YOU SO MUCH! YOU SAVED MY LIFE!
WHY DID I EVEN GO ON THIS QUEST?

The Grateful Bat

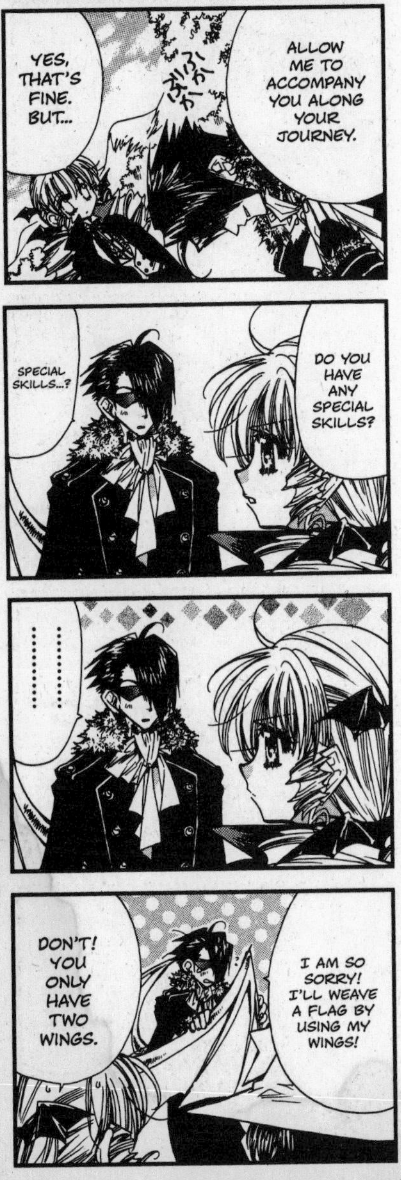
ALLOW ME TO ACCOMPANY YOU ALONG YOUR JOURNEY.
YES, THAT'S FINE. BUT...
DO YOU HAVE ANY SPECIAL SKILLS?
SPECIAL SKILLS...?
....
I AM SO SORRY! I'LL WEAVE A FLAG BY USING MY WINGS!
DON'T! YOU ONLY HAVE TWO WINGS.

True Special Skill

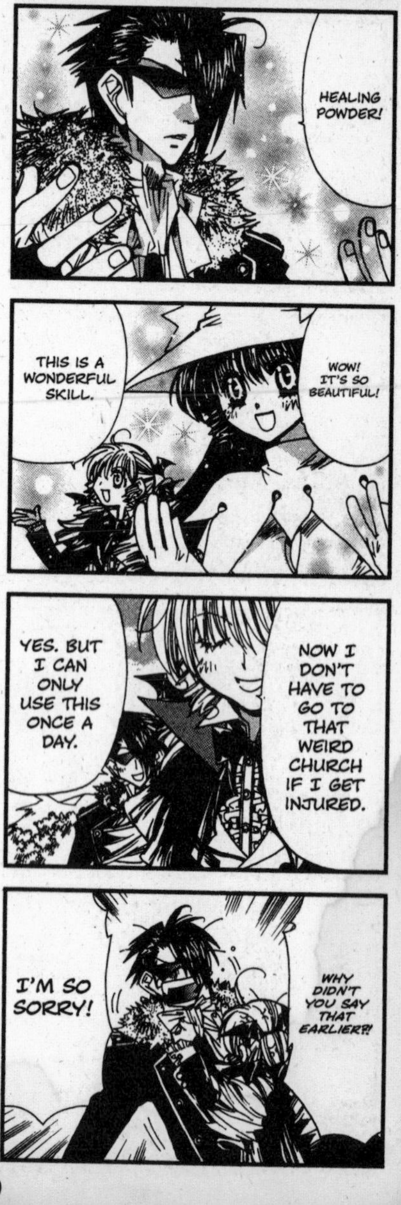
HEALING POWDER!
WOW! IT'S SO BEAUTIFUL!
THIS IS A WONDERFUL SKILL.
NOW I DON'T HAVE TO GO TO THAT WEIRD CHURCH IF I GET INJURED.
YES. BUT I CAN ONLY USE THIS ONCE A DAY.
WHY DIDN'T YOU SAY THAT EARLIER?!
I'M SO SORRY!

Punchline

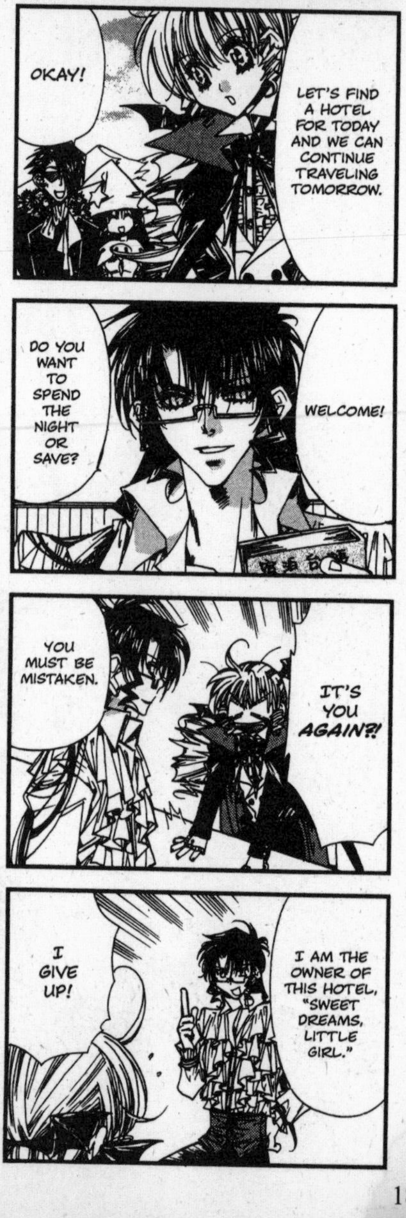
LET'S FIND A HOTEL FOR TODAY AND WE CAN CONTINUE TRAVELING TOMORROW.
OKAY!
WELCOME!
DO YOU WANT TO SPEND THE NIGHT OR SAVE?
IT'S YOU AGAIN?!
YOU MUST BE MISTAKEN.
I AM THE OWNER OF THIS HOTEL, "SWEET DREAMS, LITTLE GIRL."
I GIVE UP!

Bonus Comic Strip

Role-Playing Guilt-na-Zan Part 2

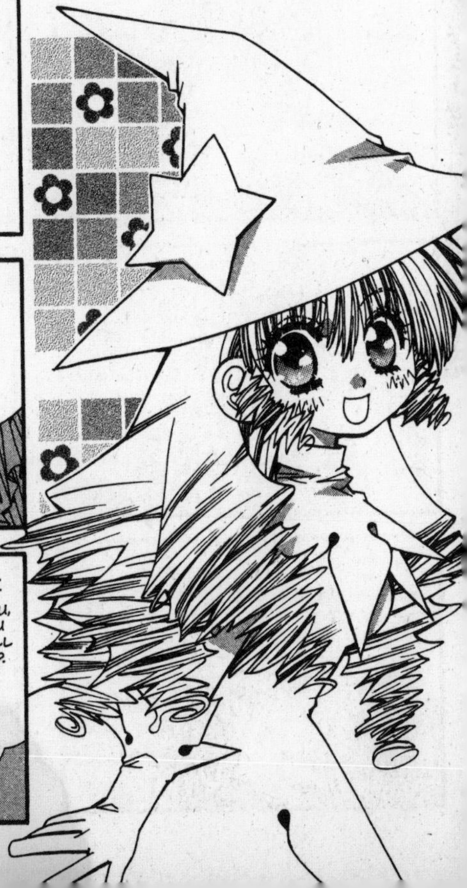

Sheep

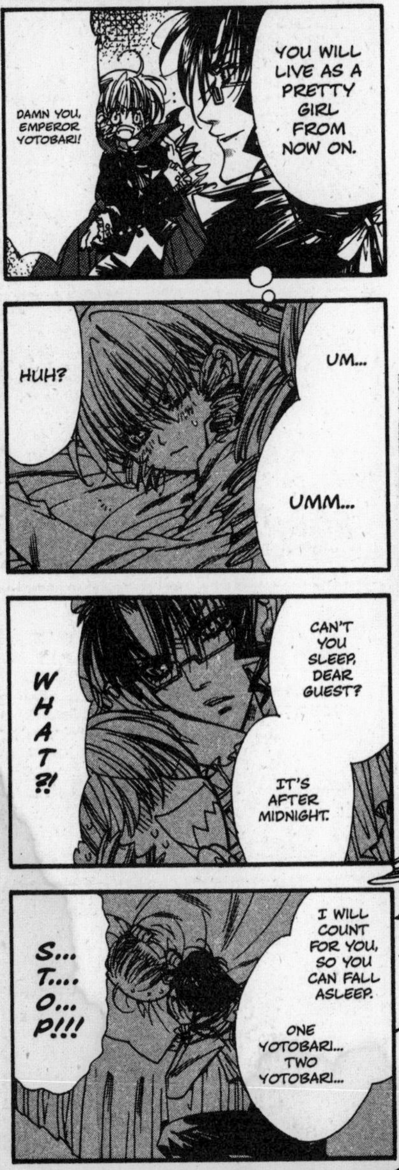
YOU WILL LIVE AS A PRETTY GIRL FROM NOW ON.
DAMN YOU, EMPEROR YOTOBARI!
UM...
UMM...
HUH?
CAN'T YOU SLEEP, DEAR GUEST?
IT'S AFTER MIDNIGHT.
WHAT?!
I WILL COUNT FOR YOU, SO YOU CAN FALL ASLEEP.
ONE YOTOBARI... TWO YOTOBARI...
S... T... O... P!!!

Carbohydrates

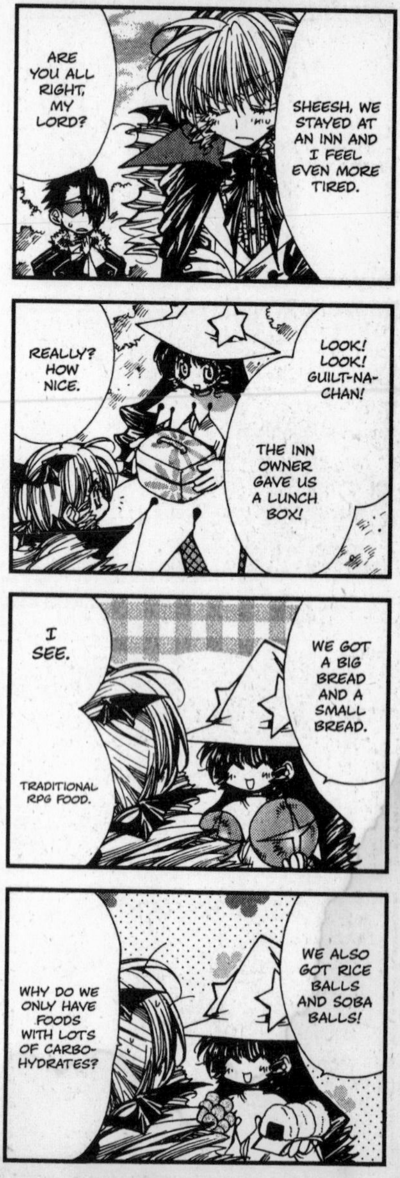
SHEESH, WE STAYED AT AN INN AND I FEEL EVEN MORE TIRED.
ARE YOU ALL RIGHT, MY LORD?
LOOK! LOOK! GUILT-NA-CHAN!
THE INN OWNER GAVE US A LUNCH BOX!
REALLY? HOW NICE.
WE GOT A BIG BREAD AND A SMALL BREAD.
I SEE.
TRADITIONAL RPG FOOD.
WE ALSO GOT RICE BALLS AND SOBA BALLS!
WHY DO WE ONLY HAVE FOODS WITH LOTS OF CARBOHYDRATES?

Carbohydrates 2

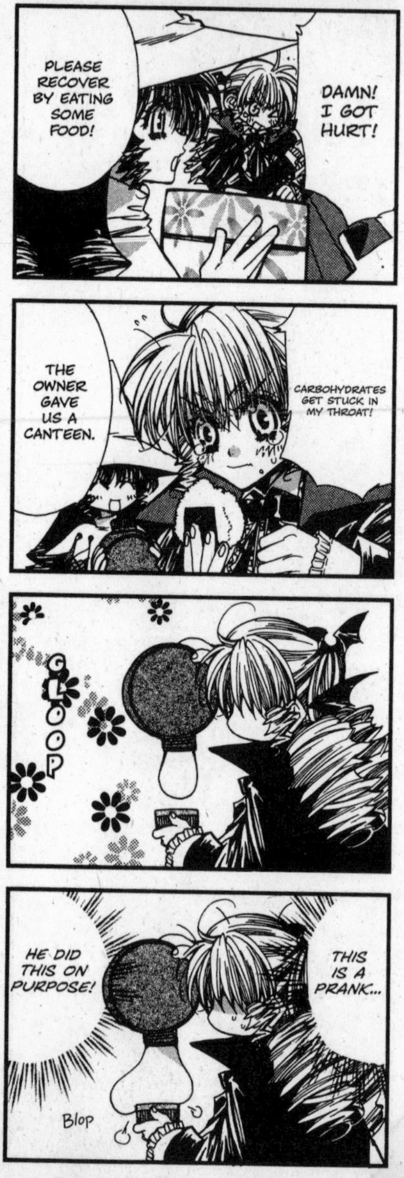
DAMN! I GOT HURT!
PLEASE RECOVER BY EATING SOME FOOD!
CARBOHYDRATES GET STUCK IN MY THROAT!
THE OWNER GAVE US A CANTEEN.
GLOOP
THIS IS A PRANK...
HE DID THIS ON PURPOSE!
Blop

Spring

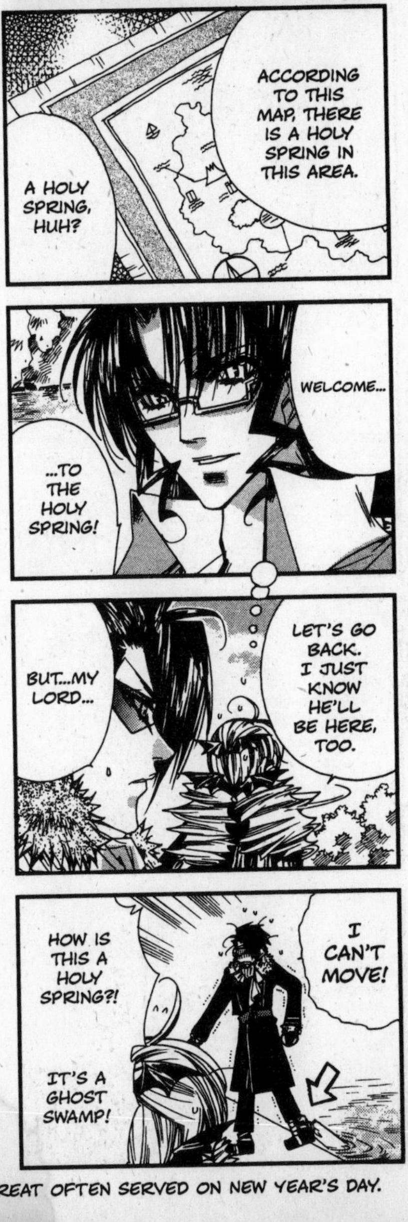
ACCORDING TO THIS MAP, THERE IS A HOLY SPRING IN THIS AREA.
A HOLY SPRING, HUH?
WELCOME...
...TO THE HOLY SPRING!
LET'S GO BACK. I JUST KNOW HE'LL BE HERE, TOO.
BUT...MY LORD...
I CAN'T MOVE!
HOW IS THIS A HOLY SPRING?!
IT'S A GHOST SWAMP!

Double

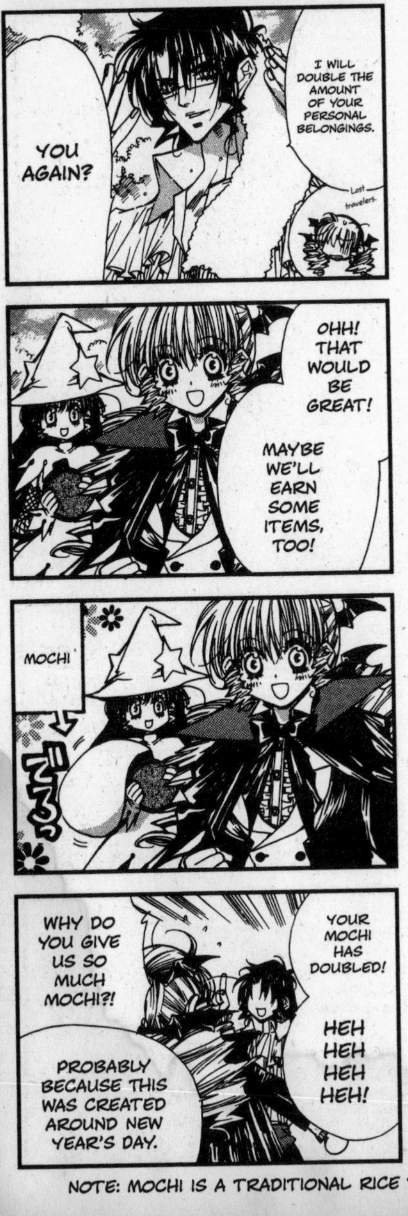
I WILL DOUBLE THE AMOUNT OF YOUR PERSONAL BELONGINGS.
Lost travelers.
YOU AGAIN?
OHH! THAT WOULD BE GREAT!
MAYBE WE'LL EARN SOME ITEMS, TOO!
MOCHI
YOUR MOCHI HAS DOUBLED!
HEH HEH HEH HEH!
WHY DO YOU GIVE US SO MUCH MOCHI?!
PROBABLY BECAUSE THIS WAS CREATED AROUND NEW YEAR'S DAY.

NOTE: MOCHI IS A TRADITIONAL RICE TREAT OFTEN SERVED ON NEW YEAR'S DAY.

Shrinking

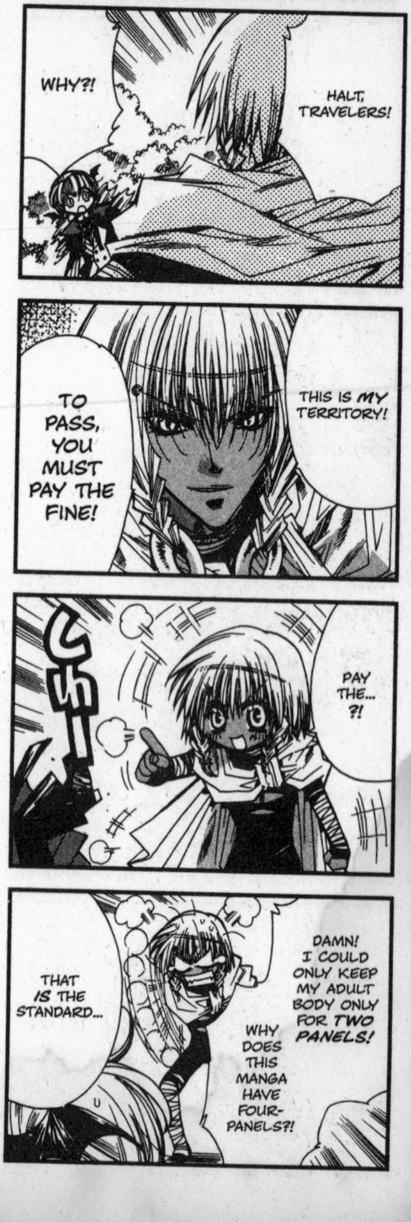
HALT, TRAVELERS!
WHY?!
THIS IS *MY* TERRITORY!
TO PASS, YOU MUST PAY THE FINE!
PAY THE... ?!
DAMN! I COULD ONLY KEEP MY ADULT BODY ONLY FOR *TWO PANELS!*
WHY DOES THIS MANGA HAVE FOUR-PANELS?!
THAT *IS* THE STANDARD...

Priest

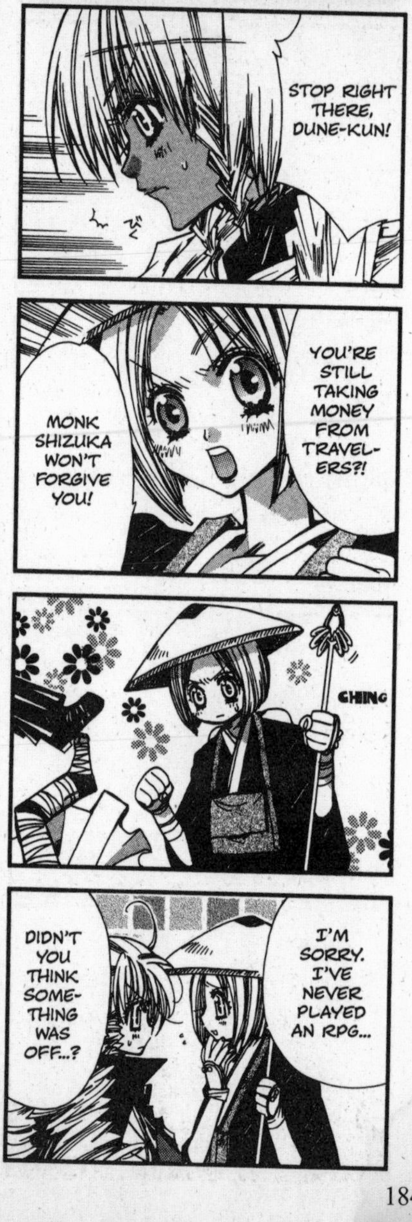
STOP RIGHT THERE, DUNE-KUN!
YOU'RE STILL TAKING MONEY FROM TRAVEL-ERS?!
MONK SHIZUKA WON'T FORGIVE YOU!
CHING
I'M SORRY. I'VE NEVER PLAYED AN RPG...
DIDN'T YOU THINK SOME-THING WAS OFF...?

Costume Change

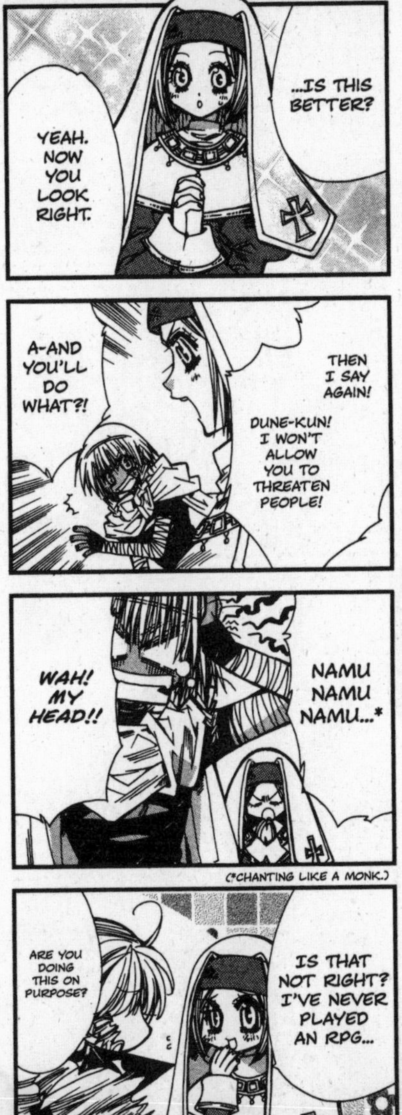
...IS THIS BETTER?
YEAH. NOW YOU LOOK RIGHT.
THEN I SAY AGAIN!
DUNE-KUN! I WON'T ALLOW YOU TO THREATEN PEOPLE!
A-AND YOU'LL DO WHAT?!
NAMU NAMU NAMU...*
WAH! MY HEAD!!
(*CHANTING LIKE A MONK.)
IS THAT NOT RIGHT? I'VE NEVER PLAYED AN RPG...
ARE YOU DOING THIS ON PURPOSE?

Special Skills

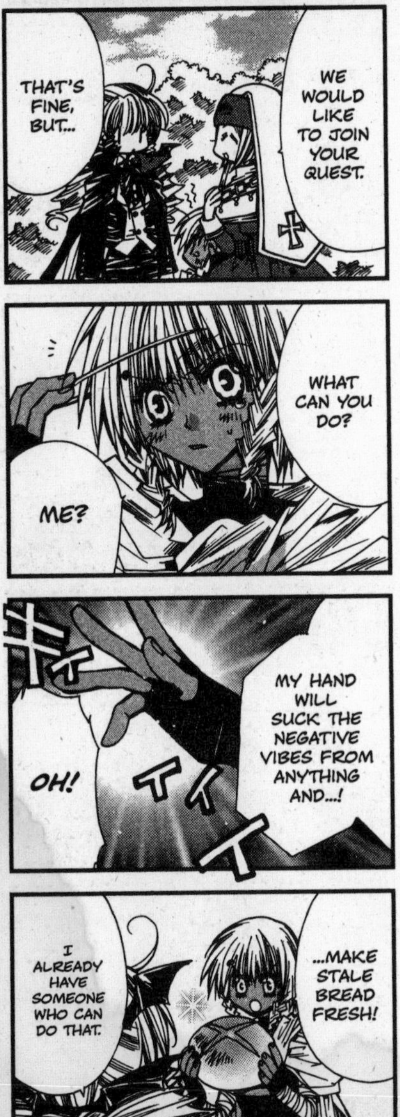
WE WOULD LIKE TO JOIN YOUR QUEST.
THAT'S FINE, BUT...
WHAT CAN YOU DO?
ME?
MY HAND WILL SUCK THE NEGATIVE VIBES FROM ANYTHING AND...!
OH!
...MAKE STALE BREAD FRESH!
I ALREADY HAVE SOMEONE WHO CAN DO THAT.

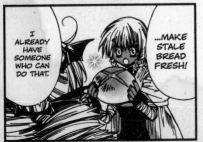

Venerable Sage

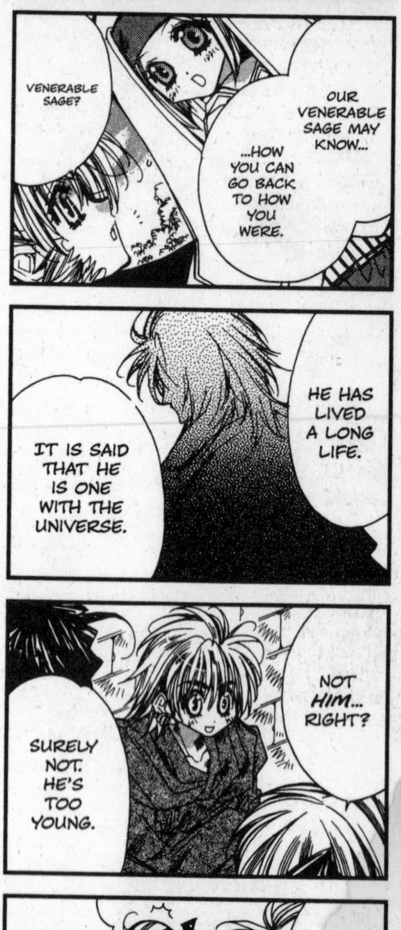
OUR VENERABLE SAGE MAY KNOW...
...HOW YOU CAN GO BACK TO HOW YOU WERE.
VENERABLE SAGE?
HE HAS LIVED A LONG LIFE.
IT IS SAID THAT HE IS ONE WITH THE UNIVERSE.
NOT *HIM*... RIGHT?
SURELY NOT. HE'S TOO YOUNG.
HELLO, DOLLY!
YOU *ARE* THE ONE!

Patriarch

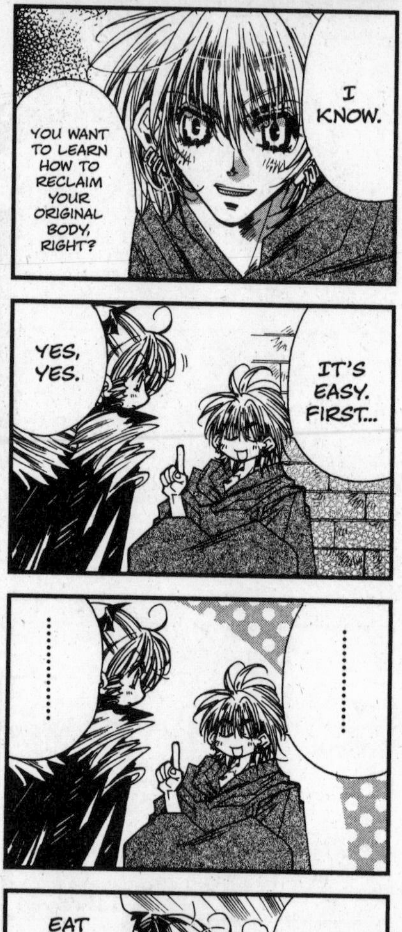
I KNOW.
YOU WANT TO LEARN HOW TO RECLAIM YOUR ORIGINAL BODY, RIGHT?
IT'S EASY. FIRST...
YES, YES.
......
......
...I HAVEN'T EATEN LUNCH YET.
EAT THIS MOCHI! EAT IT!
MY LORD, IT'S NOT SAFE TO FEED MOCHI TO AN OLD PERSON.

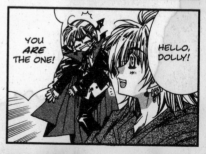

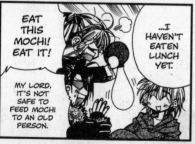

VAMPIRE DOLL GUILT-NA-ZAN VOLUME 2/END

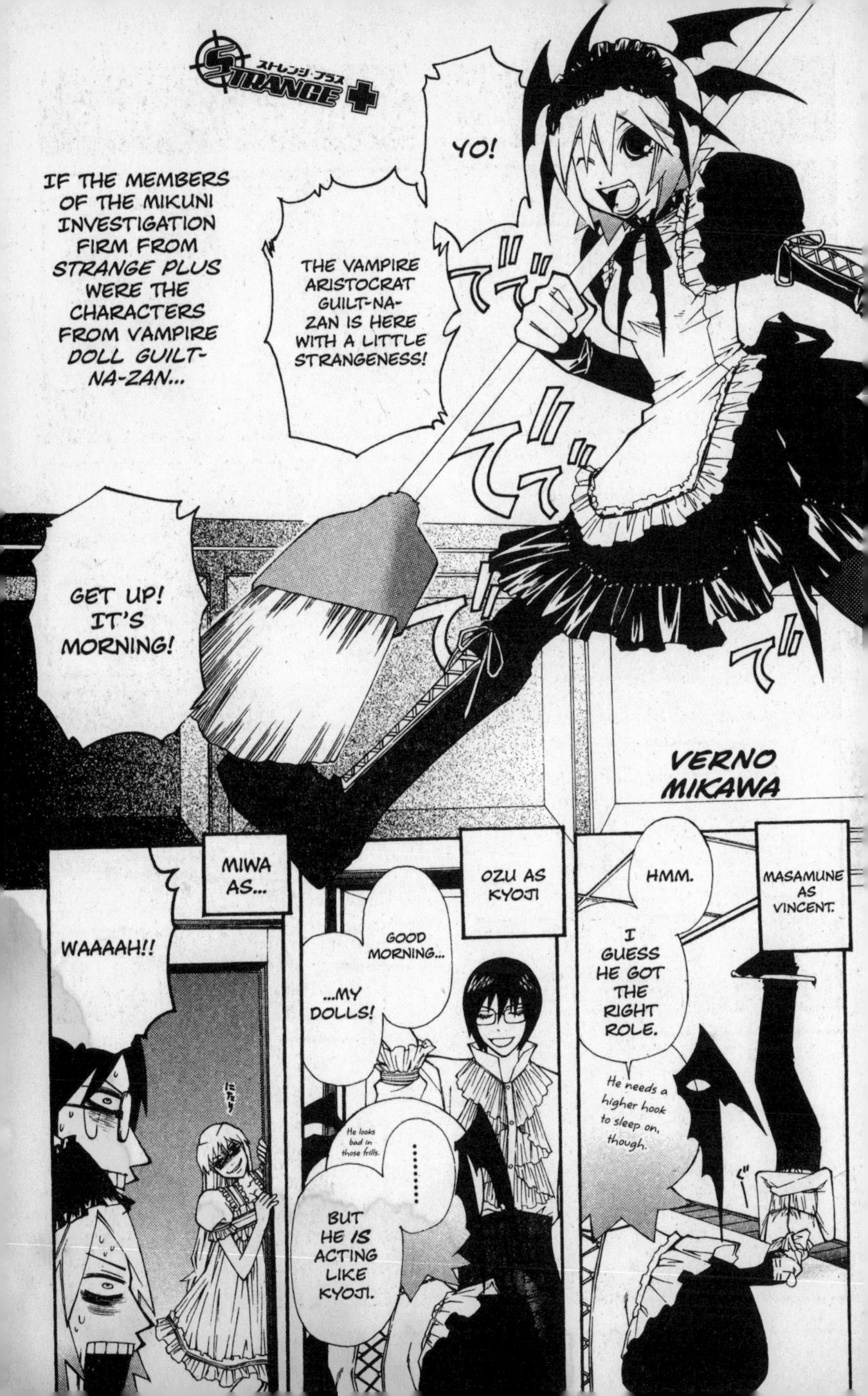

STRANGE+
YO!
THE VAMPIRE ARISTOCRAT GUILT-NA-ZAN IS HERE WITH A LITTLE STRANGENESS!
IF THE MEMBERS OF THE MIKUNI INVESTIGATION FIRM FROM STRANGE PLUS WERE THE CHARACTERS FROM VAMPIRE DOLL GUILT-NA-ZAN...
GET UP! IT'S MORNING!
VERNO MIKAWA
MASAMUNE AS VINCENT.
HMM.
I GUESS HE GOT THE RIGHT ROLE.
He needs a higher hook to sleep on, though.
OZU AS KYOJI
GOOD MORNING...
...MY DOLLS!
......
He looks bad in those frills.
BUT HE IS ACTING LIKE KYOJI.
MIWA AS...
WAAAAH!!

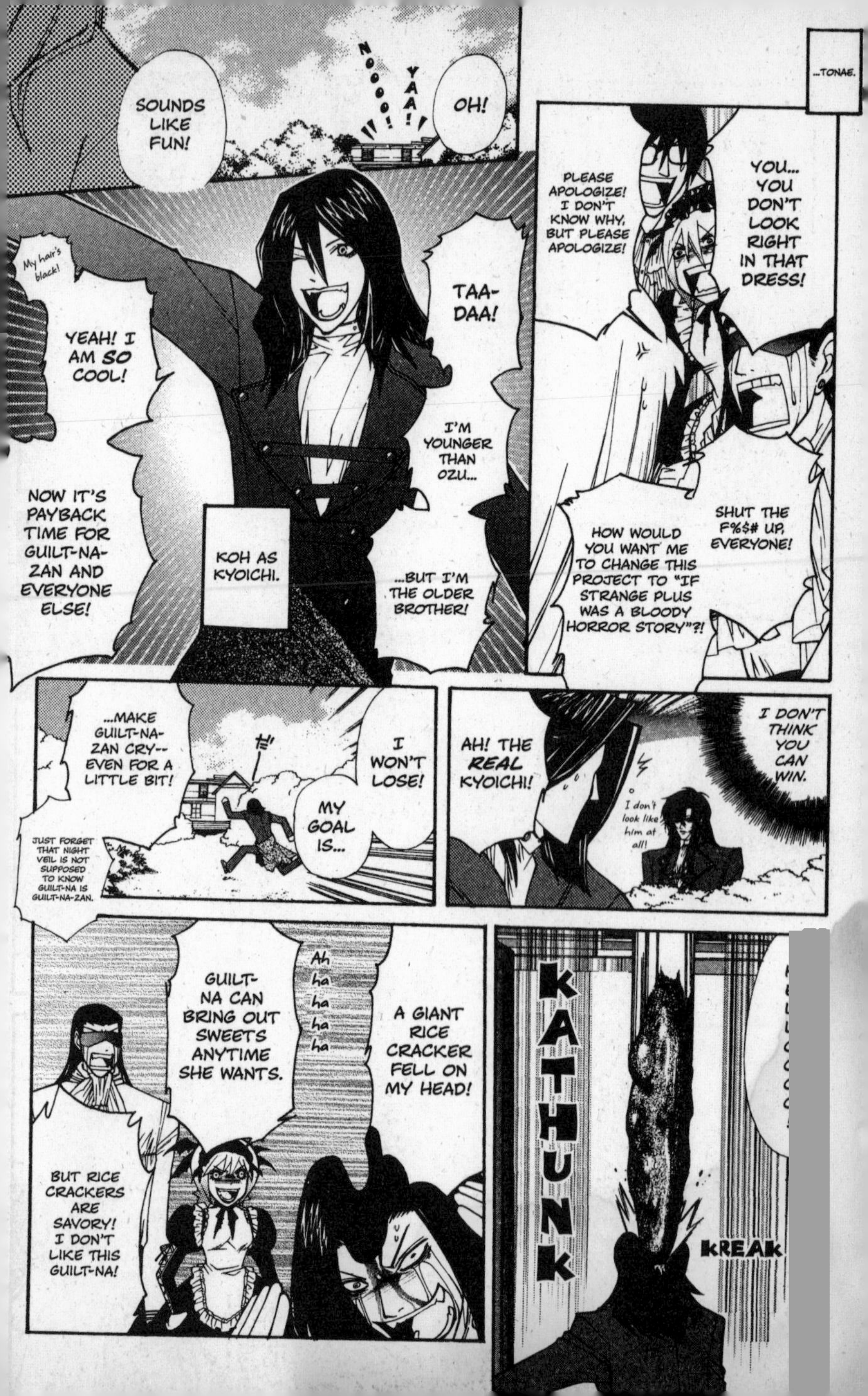
...TONAE.
YOU... YOU DON'T LOOK RIGHT IN THAT DRESS!
PLEASE APOLOGIZE! I DON'T KNOW WHY, BUT PLEASE APOLOGIZE!
SHUT THE F%$# UP, EVERYONE!
HOW WOULD YOU WANT ME TO CHANGE THIS PROJECT TO "IF STRANGE PLUS WAS A BLOODY HORROR STORY"?!
OH!
NOOOO! YAAA!
SOUNDS LIKE FUN!
TAA-DAA!
My hair's black!
YEAH! I AM SO COOL!
I'M YOUNGER THAN OZU...
...BUT I'M THE OLDER BROTHER!
KOH AS KYOICHI.
NOW IT'S PAYBACK TIME FOR GUILT-NA-ZAN AND EVERYONE ELSE!
I DON'T THINK YOU CAN WIN.
AH! THE REAL KYOICHI!
I don't look like him at all!
I WON'T LOSE!
MY GOAL IS...
...MAKE GUILT-NA-ZAN CRY-- EVEN FOR A LITTLE BIT!
JUST FORGET THAT NIGHT VEIL IS NOT SUPPOSED TO KNOW GUILT-NA IS GUILT-NA-ZAN.
KATHUNK
KREAK
A GIANT RICE CRACKER FELL ON MY HEAD!
Ah ha ha ha ha
GUILT-NA CAN BRING OUT SWEETS ANYTIME SHE WANTS.
BUT RICE CRACKERS ARE SAVORY! I DON'T LIKE THIS GUILT-NA!

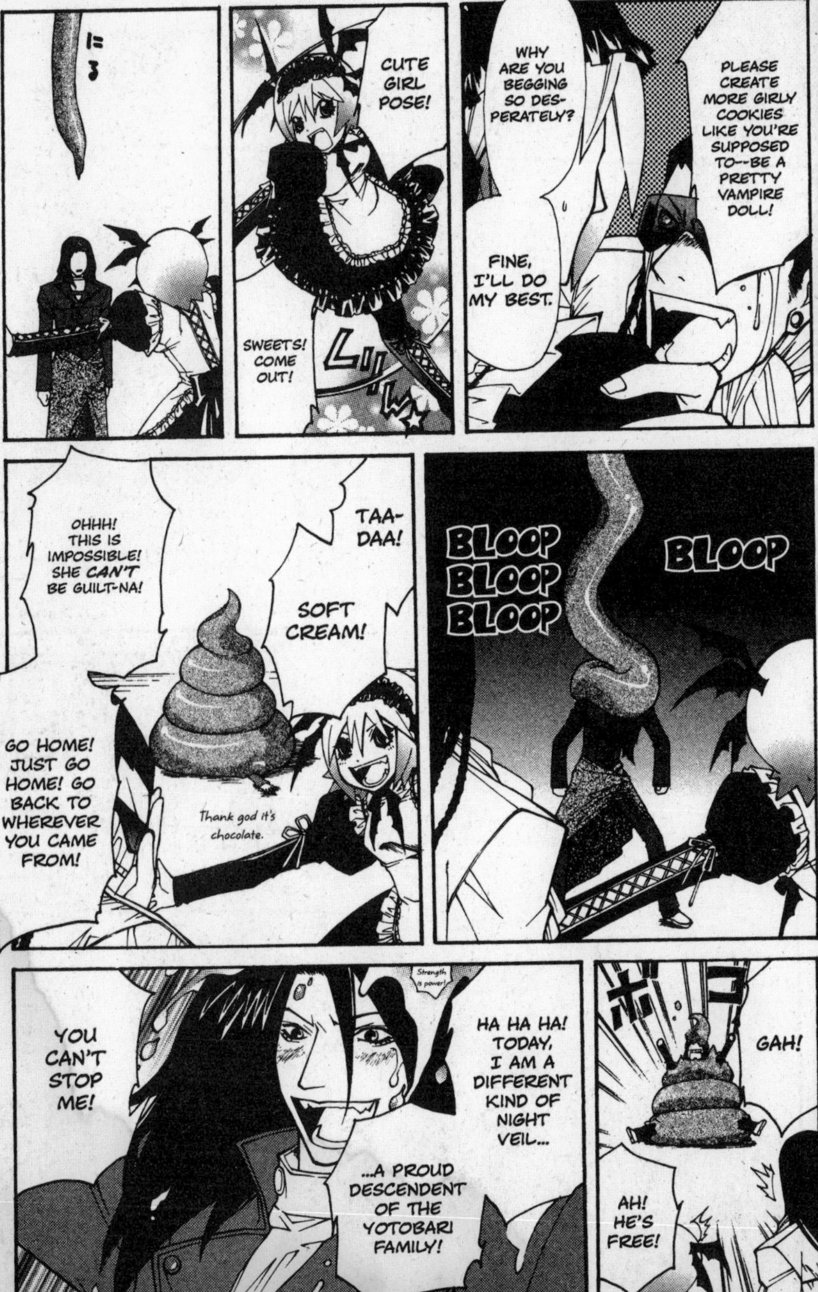
PLEASE CREATE MORE GIRLY COOKIES LIKE YOU'RE SUPPOSED TO--BE A PRETTY VAMPIRE DOLL!
WHY ARE YOU BEGGING SO DES-PERATELY?
FINE, I'LL DO MY BEST.
CUTE GIRL POSE!
SWEETS! COME OUT!
BLOOP
BLOOP BLOOP BLOOP
TAA-DAA!
SOFT CREAM!
OHHH! THIS IS IMPOSSIBLE! SHE *CAN'T* BE GUILT-NA!
GO HOME! JUST GO HOME! GO BACK TO WHEREVER YOU CAME FROM!
Thank god it's chocolate.
GAH!
AH! HE'S FREE!
Strength is power!
HA HA HA! TODAY, I AM A DIFFERENT KIND OF NIGHT VEIL...
...A PROUD DESCENDENT OF THE YOTOBARI FAMILY!
YOU CAN'T STOP ME!

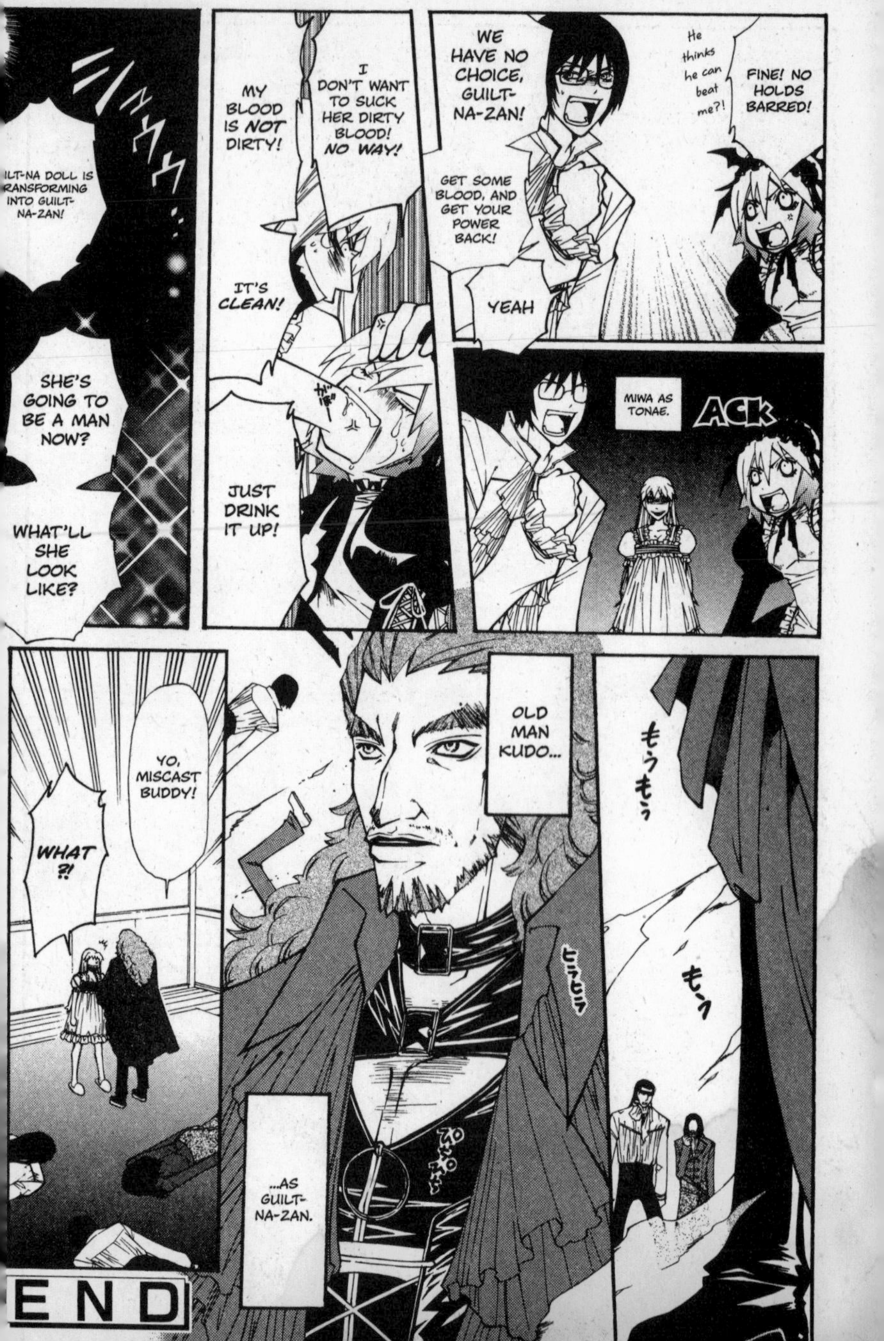

FINE! NO HOLDS BARRED!
He thinks he can beat me?!
WE HAVE NO CHOICE, GUILT-NA-ZAN!
GET SOME BLOOD, AND GET YOUR POWER BACK!
YEAH
MIWA AS TONAE.
ACK
I DON'T WANT TO SUCK HER DIRTY BLOOD! NO WAY!
MY BLOOD IS NOT DIRTY!
IT'S CLEAN!
JUST DRINK IT UP!
ILT-NA DOLL IS RANSFORMING INTO GUILT-NA-ZAN!
SHE'S GOING TO BE A MAN NOW?
WHAT'LL SHE LOOK LIKE?
もうもう
もぅ
OLD MAN KUDO...
ヒラヒラ
...AS GUILT-NA-ZAN.
YO, MISCAST BUDDY!
WHAT?!
END

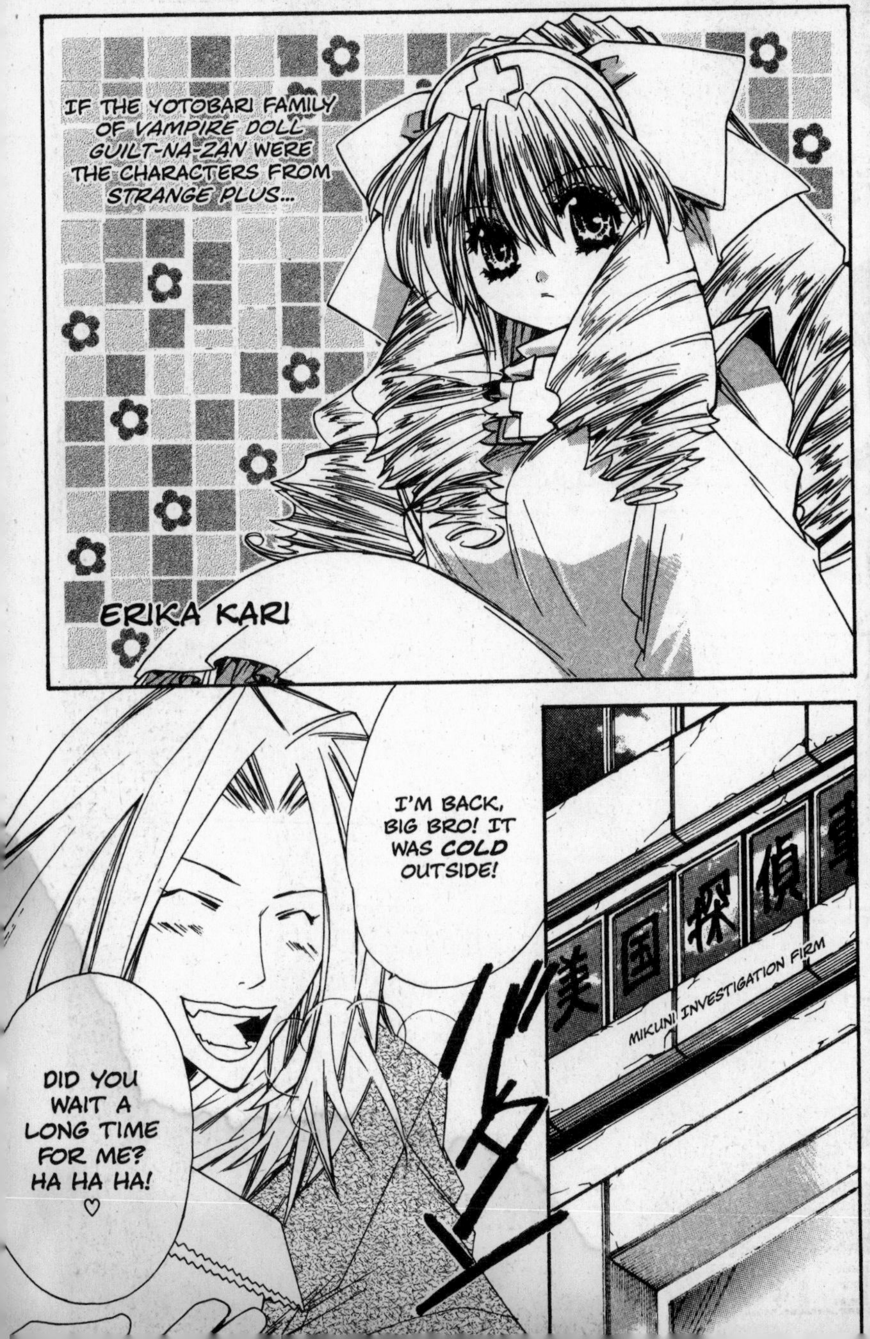
IF THE YOTOBARI FAMILY OF VAMPIRE DOLL GUILT-NA-ZAN WERE THE CHARACTERS FROM STRANGE PLUS...
ERIKA KARI
美国探偵
MIKUNI INVESTIGATION FIRM
I'M BACK, BIG BRO! IT WAS COLD OUTSIDE!
DID YOU WAIT A LONG TIME FOR ME? HA HA HA! ♡

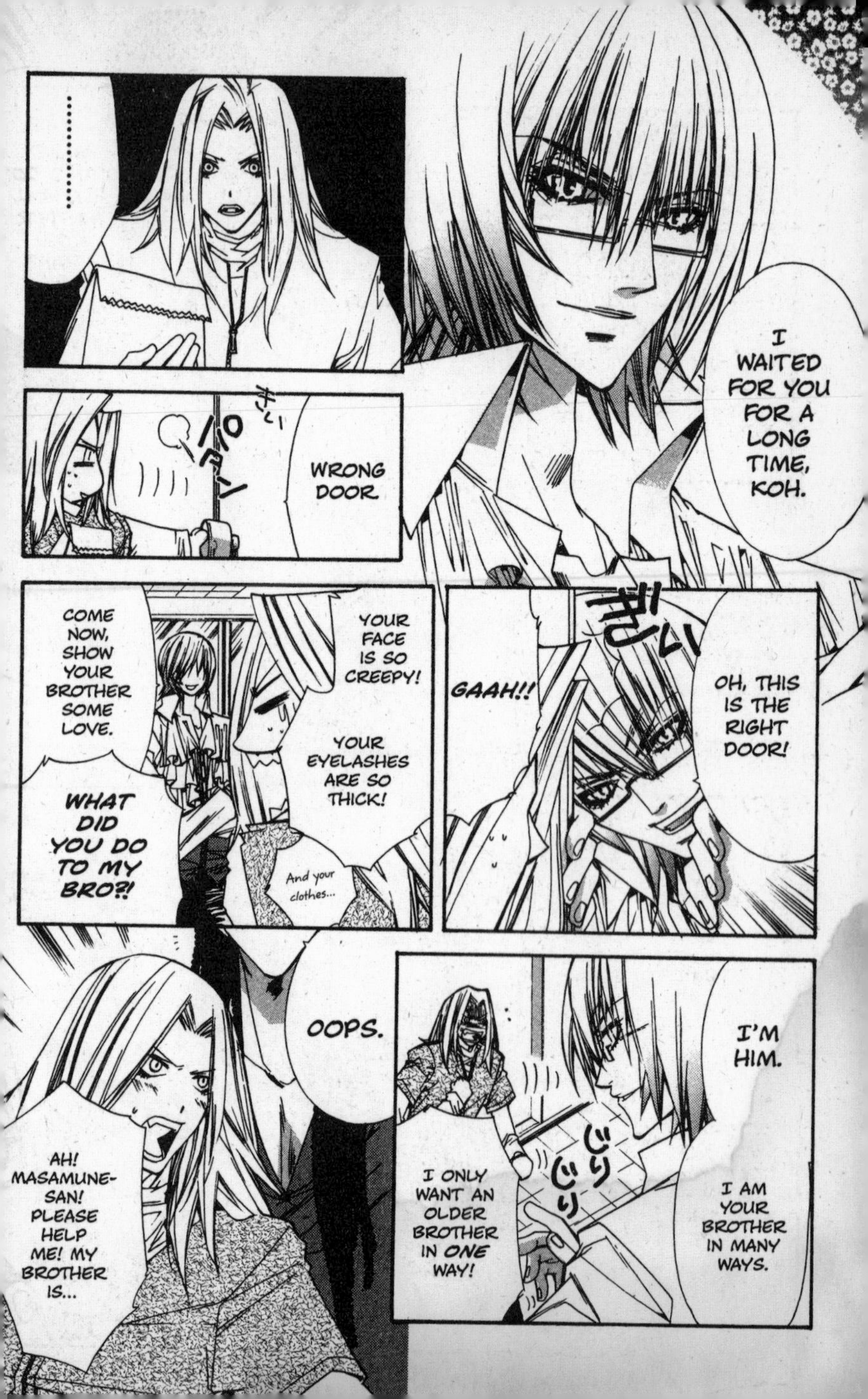
I WAITED FOR YOU FOR A LONG TIME, KOH.
……
きぃ
バタン
WRONG DOOR
きぃ
OH, THIS IS THE RIGHT DOOR!
GAAH!!
YOUR FACE IS SO CREEPY!
YOUR EYELASHES ARE SO THICK!
And your clothes...
COME NOW, SHOW YOUR BROTHER SOME LOVE.
WHAT DID YOU DO TO MY BRO?!
I'M HIM.
I AM YOUR BROTHER IN MANY WAYS.
じり じり
I ONLY WANT AN OLDER BROTHER IN *ONE* WAY!
OOPS.
AH! MASAMUNE-SAN! PLEASE HELP ME! MY BROTHER IS...

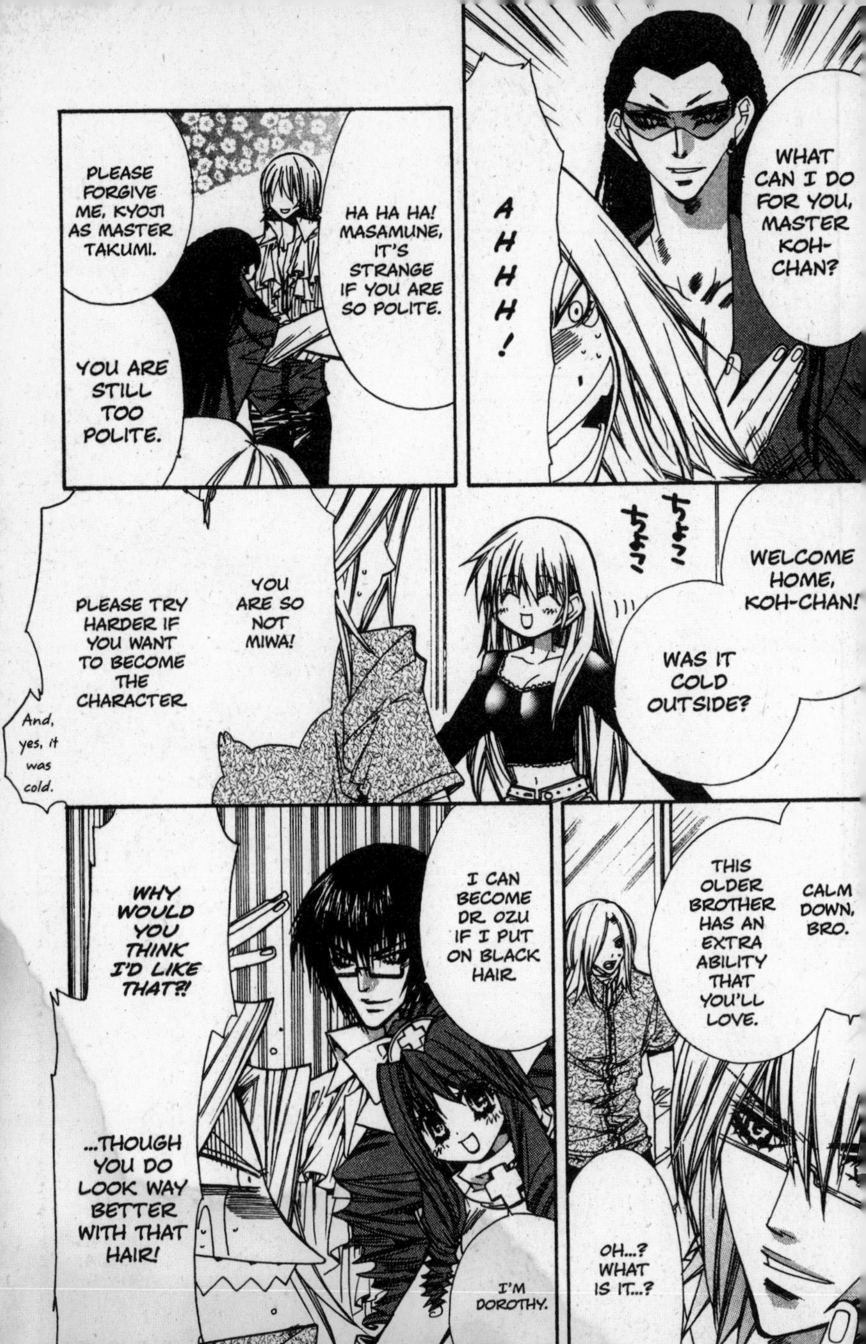
WHAT CAN I DO FOR YOU, MASTER KOH-CHAN?
AHHH!
HA HA HA! MASAMUNE, IT'S STRANGE IF YOU ARE SO POLITE.
PLEASE FORGIVE ME, KYOJI AS MASTER TAKUMI.
YOU ARE STILL TOO POLITE.
WELCOME HOME, KOH-CHAN!
WAS IT COLD OUTSIDE?
ちょこちょこ
YOU ARE SO NOT MIWA!
PLEASE TRY HARDER IF YOU WANT TO BECOME THE CHARACTER
And, yes, it was cold.
CALM DOWN, BRO.
THIS OLDER BROTHER HAS AN EXTRA ABILITY THAT YOU'LL LOVE.
OH...? WHAT IS IT...?
I CAN BECOME DR. OZU IF I PUT ON BLACK HAIR
WHY WOULD YOU THINK I'D LIKE THAT?!
I'M DOROTHY.
...THOUGH YOU DO LOOK WAY BETTER WITH THAT HAIR!

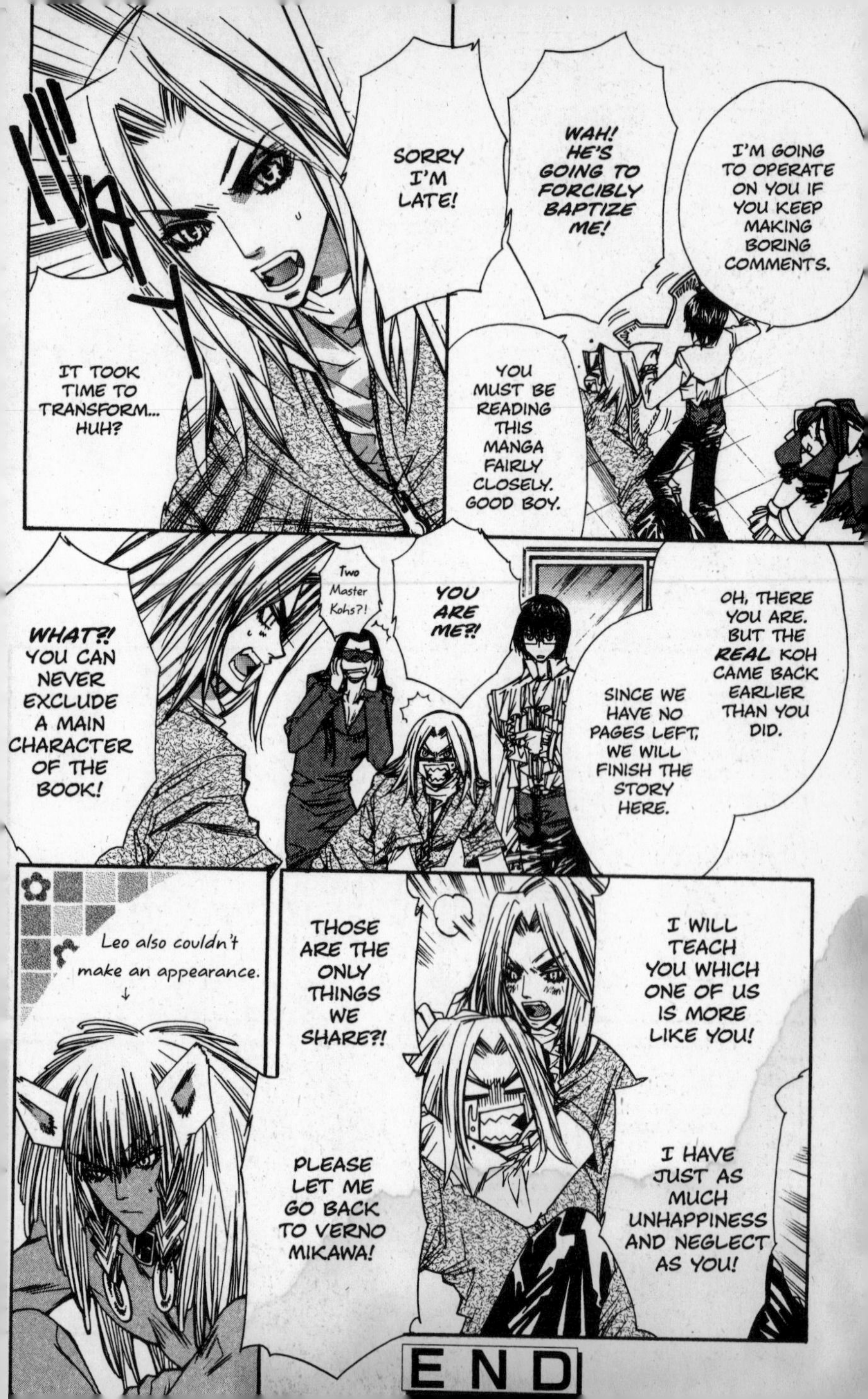
I'M GOING TO OPERATE ON YOU IF YOU KEEP MAKING BORING COMMENTS.
WAH! HE'S GOING TO FORCIBLY BAPTIZE ME!
YOU MUST BE READING THIS MANGA FAIRLY CLOSELY. GOOD BOY.
SORRY I'M LATE!
IT TOOK TIME TO TRANSFORM... HUH?
OH, THERE YOU ARE. BUT THE REAL KOH CAME BACK EARLIER THAN YOU DID.
SINCE WE HAVE NO PAGES LEFT, WE WILL FINISH THE STORY HERE.
YOU ARE ME?!
Two Master Kohs?!
WHAT?! YOU CAN NEVER EXCLUDE A MAIN CHARACTER OF THE BOOK!
I WILL TEACH YOU WHICH ONE OF US IS MORE LIKE YOU!
THOSE ARE THE ONLY THINGS WE SHARE?!
I HAVE JUST AS MUCH UNHAPPINESS AND NEGLECT AS YOU!
PLEASE LET ME GO BACK TO VERNO MIKAWA!
Leo also couldn't make an appearance.
END

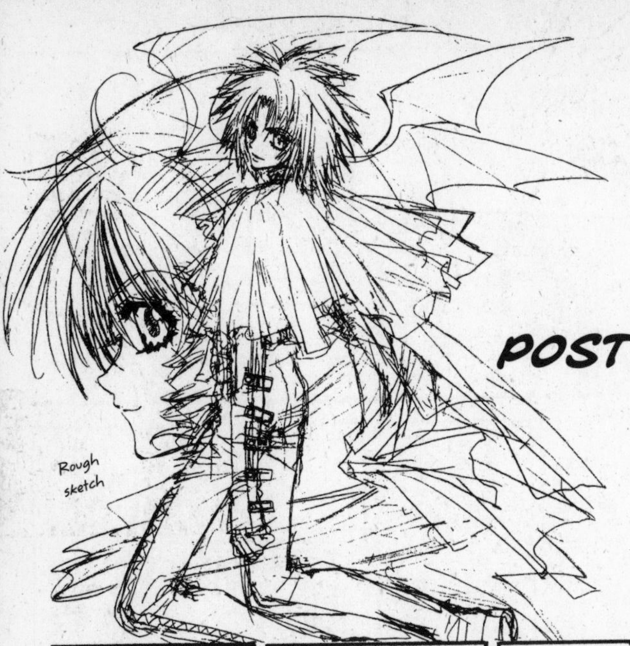
Rough sketch

POSTSCRIPT

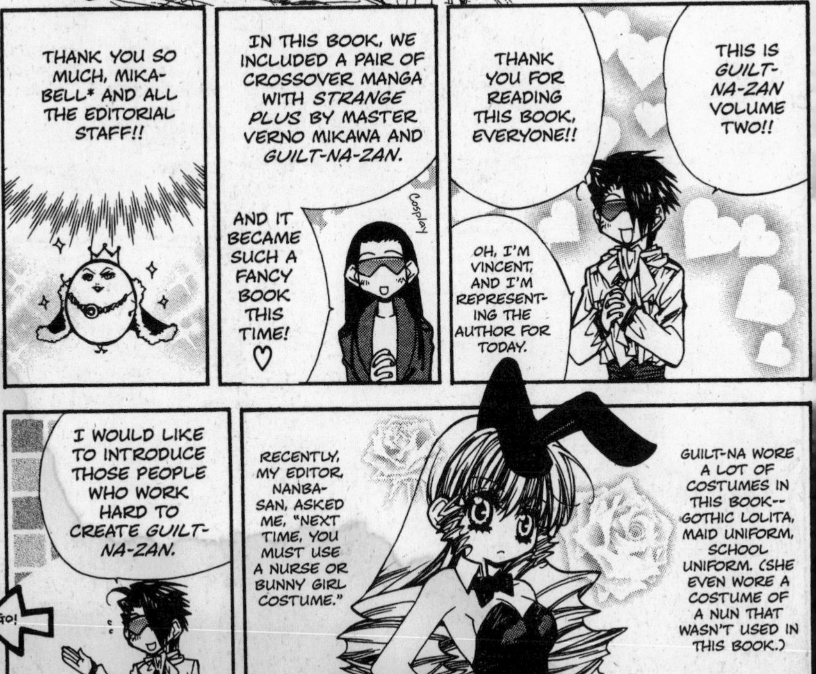
THIS IS GUILT-NA-ZAN VOLUME TWO!!
THANK YOU FOR READING THIS BOOK, EVERYONE!!
OH, I'M VINCENT, AND I'M REPRESENTING THE AUTHOR FOR TODAY.
IN THIS BOOK, WE INCLUDED A PAIR OF CROSSOVER MANGA WITH *STRANGE PLUS* BY MASTER VERNO MIKAWA AND *GUILT-NA-ZAN*.
Cosplay
AND IT BECAME SUCH A FANCY BOOK THIS TIME! ♡
THANK YOU SO MUCH, MIKA-BELL* AND ALL THE EDITORIAL STAFF!!
GUILT-NA WORE A LOT OF COSTUMES IN THIS BOOK-- GOTHIC LOLITA, MAID UNIFORM, SCHOOL UNIFORM. (SHE EVEN WORE A COSTUME OF A NUN THAT WASN'T USED IN THIS BOOK.)
RECENTLY, MY EDITOR, NANBA-SAN, ASKED ME, "NEXT TIME, YOU MUST USE A NURSE OR BUNNY GIRL COSTUME."
I WOULD LIKE TO INTRODUCE THOSE PEOPLE WHO WORK HARD TO CREATE *GUILT-NA-ZAN*.
GO!

*VERNO MIKAWA'S NICKNAME.

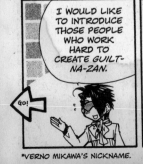

THIS IS THE CREATIVE TEAM OF *GUILT-NA-ZAN!* WOOT!

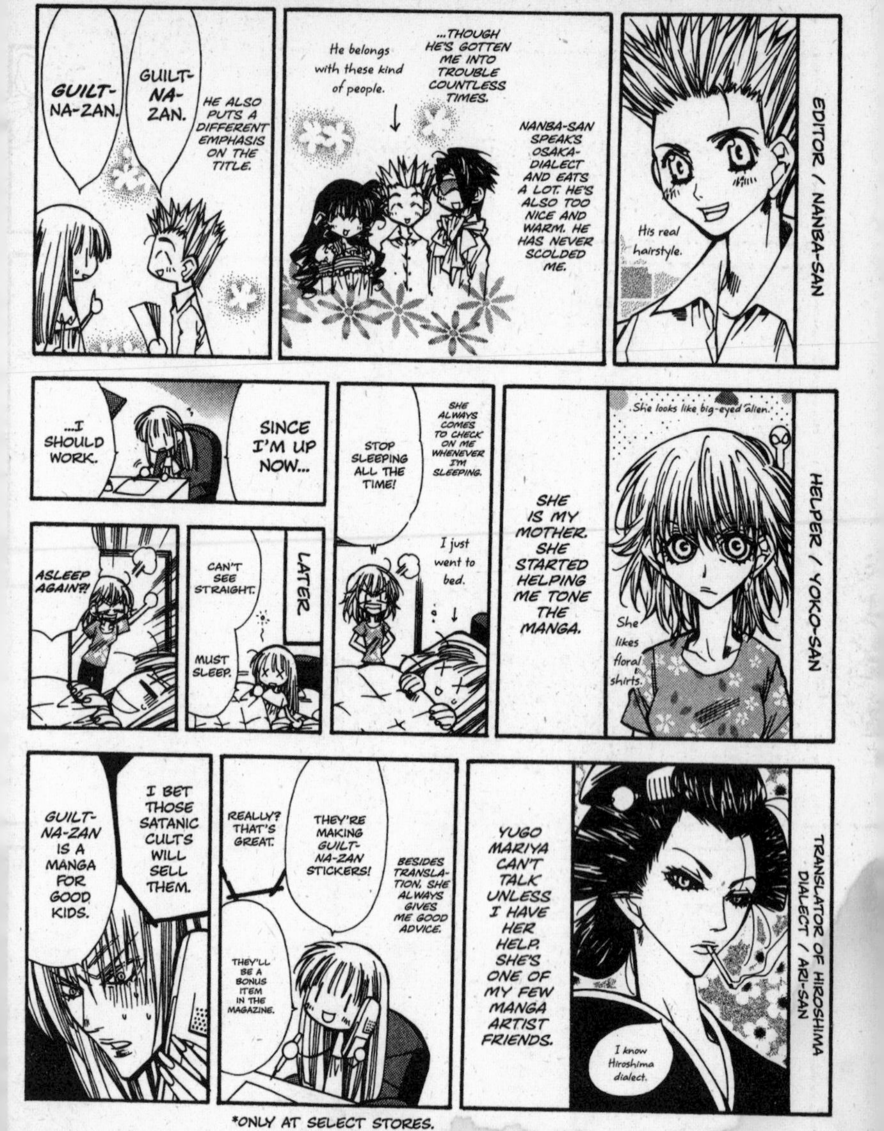
EDITOR / NANBA-SAN
His real hairstyle.
NANBA-SAN SPEAKS OSAKA-DIALECT AND EATS A LOT. HE'S ALSO TOO NICE AND WARM. HE HAS NEVER SCOLDED ME.
...THOUGH HE'S GOTTEN ME INTO TROUBLE COUNTLESS TIMES.
He belongs with these kind of people.
HE ALSO PUTS A DIFFERENT EMPHASIS ON THE TITLE.
GUILT-NA-ZAN.
GUILT-NA-ZAN.
HELPER / YOKO-SAN
She looks like big-eyed alien.
She likes floral shirts.
SHE IS MY MOTHER. SHE STARTED HELPING ME TONE THE MANGA.
SHE ALWAYS COMES TO CHECK ON ME WHENEVER I'M SLEEPING.
STOP SLEEPING ALL THE TIME!
I just went to bed.
SINCE I'M UP NOW...
...I SHOULD WORK.
LATER
CAN'T SEE STRAIGHT.
MUST SLEEP.
ASLEEP AGAIN?!
TRANSLATOR OF HIROSHIMA DIALECT / ARI-SAN
YUGO MARIYA CAN'T TALK UNLESS I HAVE HER HELP. SHE'S ONE OF MY FEW MANGA ARTIST FRIENDS.
I know Hiroshima dialect.
BESIDES TRANSLATION, SHE ALWAYS GIVES ME GOOD ADVICE.
THEY'RE MAKING GUILT-NA-ZAN STICKERS!
REALLY? THAT'S GREAT.
THEY'LL BE A BONUS ITEM IN THE MAGAZINE.
I BET THOSE SATANIC CULTS WILL SELL THEM.
GUILT-NA-ZAN IS A MANGA FOR GOOD KIDS.

*ONLY AT SELECT STORES.

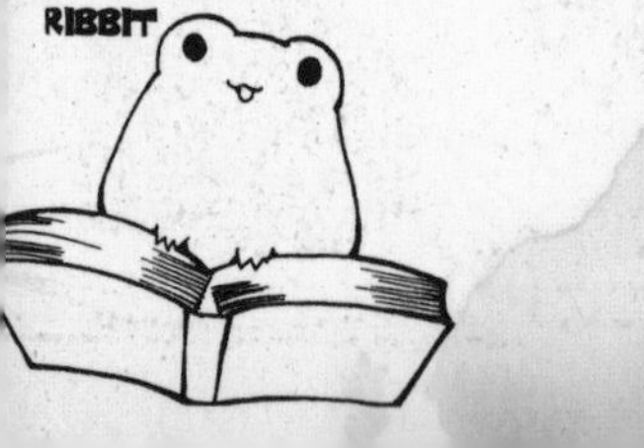
RIBBIT

SEE YOU IN VOLUME THREE!

ERIKA KARI, MAY 2005

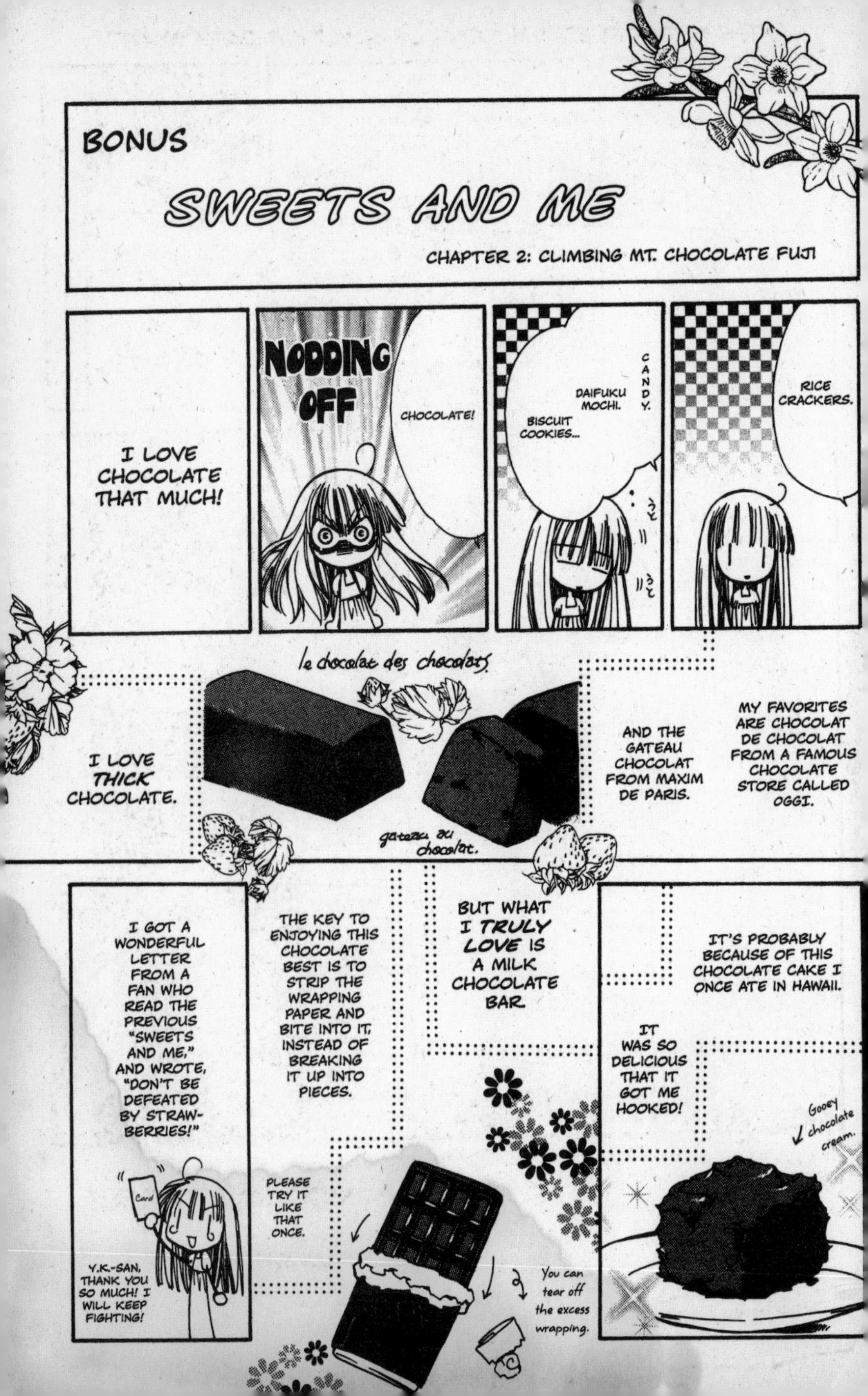
BONUS
SWEETS AND ME
CHAPTER 2: CLIMBING MT. CHOCOLATE FUJI
RICE CRACKERS.
CANDY.
DAIFUKU MOCHI.
BISCUIT COOKIES...
NODDING OFF
CHOCOLATE!
I LOVE CHOCOLATE THAT MUCH!
MY FAVORITES ARE CHOCOLAT DE CHOCOLAT FROM A FAMOUS CHOCOLATE STORE CALLED OGGI.
AND THE GATEAU CHOCOLAT FROM MAXIM DE PARIS.
le chocolat des chocolats.
gateau au chocolat.
I LOVE THICK CHOCOLATE.
IT'S PROBABLY BECAUSE OF THIS CHOCOLATE CAKE I ONCE ATE IN HAWAII.
IT WAS SO DELICIOUS THAT IT GOT ME HOOKED!
Gooey chocolate cream.
BUT WHAT I TRULY LOVE IS A MILK CHOCOLATE BAR.
THE KEY TO ENJOYING THIS CHOCOLATE BEST IS TO STRIP THE WRAPPING PAPER AND BITE INTO IT, INSTEAD OF BREAKING IT UP INTO PIECES.
PLEASE TRY IT LIKE THAT ONCE.
You can tear off the excess wrapping.
I GOT A WONDERFUL LETTER FROM A FAN WHO READ THE PREVIOUS "SWEETS AND ME," AND WROTE, "DON'T BE DEFEATED BY STRAW-BERRIES!"
Card
Y.K.-SAN, THANK YOU SO MUCH! I WILL KEEP FIGHTING!

Vampire Doll
Guilt-na-Zan

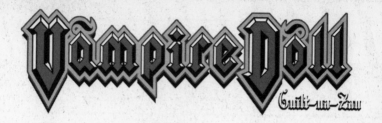

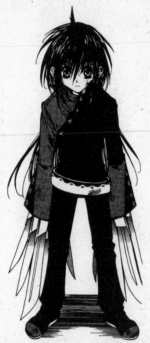

IN THE NEXT VOLUME!

THE WACKINESS CONTINUES IN VOLUME 3 AS OUR FAVORITE CAST OF FREAKS GETS INTO EVEN MORE TROUBLE. GUILT-NA-ZAN'S LIFE HAS NEVER BEEN EASY SINCE BEING PUT INTO THE BODY OF A FEMALE DOLL, BUT WHAT HAPPENS WHEN HE WAKES UP AND HE'S THE SIZE OF A MOUSE?! AND IF THAT WASN'T ENOUGH, HE THEN HAS TO BECOME A FASHION MODEL FOR SOME CRAZY STYLISTS? THE STORY THEN SHIFTS TO THE PAST TO REVEAL WHAT WENT ON BEFORE GUILT-NA-ZAN WAS SEALED AWAY FOR A HUNDRED YEARS. ALL THIS AND MUCH MORE IN THE NEXT VOLUME OF *VAMPIRE DOLL GUILT-NA-ZAN.*

TO BE CONTINUED IN *VAMPIRE DOLL GUILT-NA-ZAN* VOL. 3

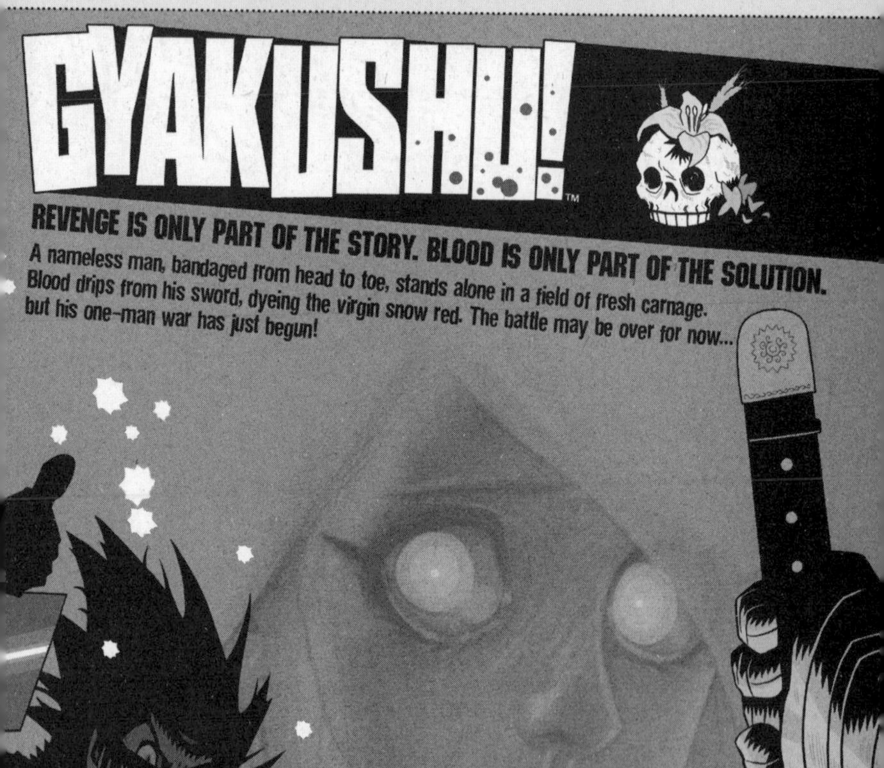
GYAKUSHU!™
REVENGE IS ONLY PART OF THE STORY. BLOOD IS ONLY PART OF THE SOLUTION.
A nameless man, bandaged from head to toe, stands alone in a field of fresh carnage. Blood drips from his sword, dyeing the virgin snow red. The battle may be over for now... but his one-man war has just begun!
A CLASSIC TALE OF REVENGE FROM DAN HIPP, THE CREATOR OF THE AMAZING JOY BUZZARDS.
ACTION
OT
OLDER TEEN AGE 16+
© Daniel Hipp and TOKYOPOP Inc.

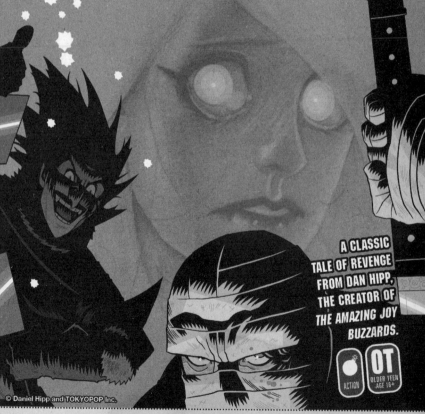

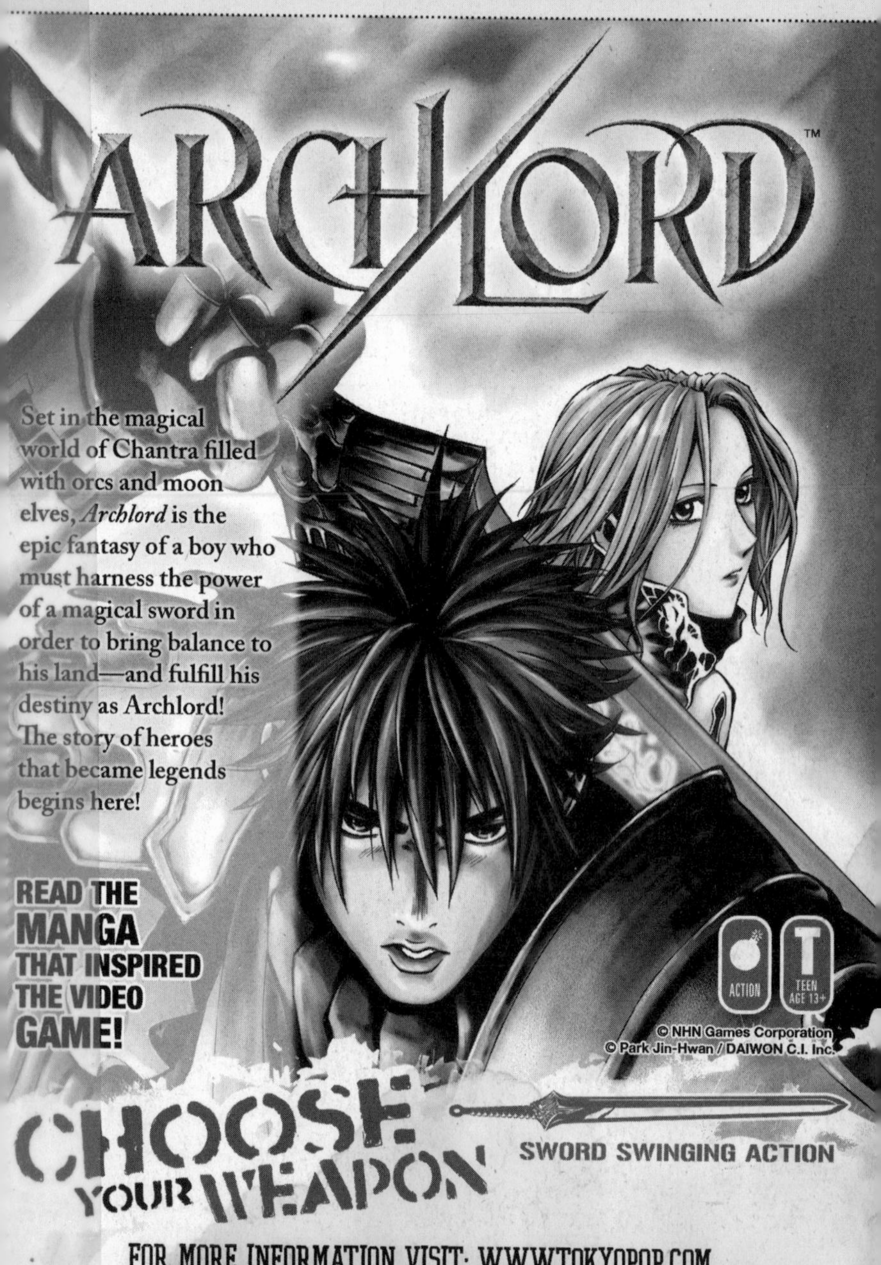
ARCHLORD™
Set in the magical world of Chantra filled with orcs and moon elves, *Archlord* is the epic fantasy of a boy who must harness the power of a magical sword in order to bring balance to his land—and fulfill his destiny as Archlord! The story of heroes that became legends begins here!
READ THE MANGA THAT INSPIRED THE VIDEO GAME!
ACTION
T TEEN AGE 13+
© NHN Games Corporation
© Park Jin-Hwan / DAIWON C.I. Inc.
CHOOSE YOUR WEAPON
SWORD SWINGING ACTION
FOR MORE INFORMATION VISIT: WWW.TOKYOPOP.COM